PRA

Bobby Ether and the Jade Academy

"The balanced blend of fantasy and action is superb, as is R. Scott Boyer's ability to juxtapose discovery, tension, and struggle. Even young adults who may have only light familiarity with either fantasy or thriller genres will find *Bobby Ether and the Jade Academy* fast-paced and thoroughly absorbing, making it a top pick for collections seeking genre-busting, action-packed adventure stories ala *Indiana Jones*."

—D. DONOVAN, SENIOR REVIEWER, MIDWEST BOOK REVIEW

"Author R. Scott Boyer merges science fiction with fantasy to fuel this wonderful story. There's doubt and belief. There's redemption and reward. But mostly there's a thrilling ride: *Bobby Ether and the Jade Academy* engages the mind while weaving a suspenseful, terrific story that delivers."

—INDIE READER ★★★★★

"A likable protagonist, engaging banter, and a fast-paced plot will appeal to teens."

—KIRKUS REVIEWS

"Tragedy, mystery, and suspense make this scientific coming-of-age story a fascinating read."

—CLARION REVIEW

*Bobby Ether and
the Jade Academy*

by R Scott Boyer

© Copyright 2018 R Scott Boyer

ISBN 978-1-63393-745-1

Published by

 köehlerbooks™

210 60th Street
Virginia Beach, VA 23451
800-435-4811
www.koehlerbooks.com

BOBBY ETHER AND THE JADE ACADEMY

R SCOTT BOYER

VIRGINIA BEACH
CAPE CHARLES

In loving memory of my big sister,
Michelle Boyer Dysktra
First editor
Toughest critic
Strongest Supporter
Mentor
Friend

You understood me better
than anyone else in the world.

Words can never describe how deeply you are loved
or how much you will be missed.

CHAPTER 1

The earthquake that woke Bobby Ether from his nightmare wasn't a typical Los Angeles tremor. Growing up in the suburbs of the San Fernando Valley, Bobby had experienced enough quakes to know most of them lasted only a few seconds— over by the time you realized they were happening. Not this one.

The entire room shook as Bobby sat upright in bed and rubbed his eyes. The windows rattled and the freestanding dresser in the corner bounced up and down. In a stupor, the long-legged sixteen-year-old stumbled out of bed and headed for his desk to climb underneath.

Nausea washed over him as the floor heaved. Still reliving the nightmare from moments before he awoke, Bobby scurried under his desk before the rumbling finally subsided. Climbing out slowly, he moved to the window, where a foot-long crack had appeared in the drywall below the sill.

It was almost midnight. The next-door neighbor's house was quiet and dark: no lights or alarms. The water in their backyard swimming pool stood placid.

What the heck?

Bobby brushed locks of wavy blond hair off his forehead, exposing beads of cold sweat. Racing downstairs, he turned on the television in the den and flipped through the channels, but there was no news about a quake. *It was only a dream,* he told himself. *The earthquake, the nightmare, none of it was real.*

The phone rang and Bobby jumped. Wiping his suddenly clammy hands on his pajamas, he headed across the dining room to the phone in the kitchen and snatched the receiver off the hook.

"Hello?" he said.

The female voice was cold and mechanical. "Is this Bobby Ether?"

"Who is this?"

"This is Saint Michelle's hospital. I'm calling from the emergency center."

Bobby felt the blood drain from his face.

"Hello, are you there?" asked the woman from the hospital.

Bobby's mouth had turned bone dry.

"We need you to come to the hospital right away," said the woman. "There's been an accident."

The phone slipped from Bobby's hand, nearly falling to the floor before he caught it and hauled it back up.

The voice on the other end was still speaking. "Sir? Are you still there?"

Bobby closed his eyes as tears pooled once again. In his mind, he saw the accident exactly as it had been in his nightmare. His parents were in his father's SUV, driving home from their Wednesday "date night" dinner and a movie. As they crossed the intersection at Chapel and La Grange, a truck on their right ran a red light and crashed into them.

"Was it a man with long hair?" asked Bobby. "In an old pickup?"

After a long pause, the woman said, "I'm afraid I can't discuss other patients' information."

It didn't matter. Bobby already knew the answer. The long-haired man had been drinking and didn't react in time to the changing light. His truck had barreled through the intersection and T-boned his father's Explorer just behind the passenger seat occupied by his mother.

The two vehicles had careened off in opposite directions. The pickup smashed through the window of a nearby delicatessen. The Explorer slid across oncoming traffic before slamming headfirst into a lamp post.

"You should check on the other driver," said Bobby flatly. "He's hurt pretty bad too."

"Sir, do you have someone who can bring you here?"

There was another long silence as Bobby shook his head.

"Sir, I can send someone to pick you up. Can you give me your address, please?"

Without responding, Bobby set the phone down and headed for his mom's Prius parked on the street. Grabbing her keys off of the console table, he flung open the front door and froze.

A woman stood in the doorway, arm extended to knock. Somewhere in her fifties, she looked like she could have been a supermodel in her younger years—tall and slender, with high cheekbones and piercing blue eyes. Dressed all in white, she wore an elegantly tailored dress suit with a golden silk scarf to match her hair.

Bobby took a step back and the woman stepped forward, towering over him in four-inch Prada heels. "Just who I was looking for," she exclaimed.

Bobby took another involuntary step back, opening space for the woman to cross the threshold. She did so, closing the door quickly behind her.

"Hello, Bobby."

Bobby retreated across the foyer to the base of the stairs.

"Who are you?" he asked. "Are you from the hospital?"

Even as he asked the question, Bobby knew the answer. He'd only just hung up with the hospital seconds ago. Besides, he hadn't given them his address.

The woman scanned the room, seemingly memorizing every detail of the small but tidy three-bedroom house. Bobby had never been ashamed of his home before, but something about this woman's gaze made him wish the house were nicer.

"Well, this place is . . . cozy," she said finally. "Not quite what I pictured for Jeremiah's family, but I suppose to each his own."

The mention of his grandfather caught Bobby by surprise. He relaxed his grip on the car keys and leaned against the banister, trying to act casual as he asked, "How do you know my grandfather?"

The woman's eyes narrowed for a split second, then she extended her arm. "My name is Cassandra," she said, offering her hand stiffly, like a soldier forced to salute. "Your grandfather and I go way back."

"But how do you—" began Bobby.

Before he finished, his stomach let loose a tremendous growl. Bobby's insides turned queasy and his knees buckled. The keys slipped from his hand and hit the hardwood floor with a clank. Cassandra caught Bobby under the arms and hoisted him back up before he followed the keys to the ground.

"Well, I can see I got here none too soon," she said with a heavy sigh. For an older woman, she was surprisingly strong. "Come on, let's get you to the kitchen."

Bobby lacked the strength to protest. Arms flopping at his sides, feet dragging, he let her escort him across the dining room to the narrow kitchen that ran down the left side of the house.

Depositing Bobby unceremoniously at the kitchen table, Cassandra rifled through the refrigerator. Bobby leaned over the tabletop, gripping his stomach as he fought to keep down his late-night snack of Hawaiian pizza and chicken wings.

Cassandra pulled something out of her pocket and stuffed it into the blender on the Formica countertop. Adding an assortment of vegetables and juice from the fridge, she ran the machine and poured the contents into a glass.

"Drink this," she said, shoving the cup into his hands.

Bobby took a deep breath and pulled himself upright.

"What's in it?"

"It'll help you recover from your *anima* event," said Cassandra.

Bobby sniffed and thrust the cup out to arm's length. It smelled like cat urine mixed with moldy cheese. "My what-a-what?"

Cassandra pushed the cup toward his face. "Drink!"

Something about her words echoed in his head like a siren's song. Before he knew it, he'd drained the contents. Cassandra leaned against the counter, watching him with a slight smile as he gagged from the aftertaste.

When he could speak, Bobby said, "How did you—"

"I'll explain later," said Cassandra. "Right now, we need to leave."

Still wobbly but feeling stronger by the second, Bobby rose. "Right now, I need to get to the hospital."

"I'm afraid that's not an option," said Cassandra. "It's the first place they'll look."

Bobby opened his mouth to protest. Then the doorbell rang.

"Just as I feared." Cassandra pushed Bobby toward the dining room. "Quickly, go pack a bag! I'll buy us some time, but you must hurry."

Bobby walked to the front window and peered through the blinds. Two men stood on the porch directly below the lamp. One was reed thin, with oily, slicked-back hair and pockmarked cheeks. The other was pudgy, with a receding hairline, heavy jowls, and cruel eyes that reminded Bobby of a hyena. On the curb behind them, men in black uniforms piled out of a line of black SUVs glimmering under the incandescent street lamps.

"What's with the rejects from *Saturday Night Fever*?" asked Bobby, noting the pastel suits, huge lapels, and bell-bottom pants of the two men on the porch.

Cassandra swept past Bobby and peeked between the slates. "Just my luck," she grumbled. "Bobby, get upstairs and get your things. I have a plan, but you must hurry."

Bobby drifted to the staircase and stopped with one hand on the banister.

Cassandra touched his arm. "Go on," she said. "I'll take care of this."

He searched her face for a long moment. Then he rushed upstairs and began to pack.

As Bobby hurriedly threw clothes into his bag, he heard the front door open and Cassandra's voice. It was one of the last things he expected.

"Hello, Simpkins. Hayward," she said. "What brings you by this evening?"

"Cassandra! What a surprise," the man said.

"That much is obvious from the blank look on your face," said Cassandra. "Be a dear and close your mouth, won't you, Hayward? I can feel my hair starting to frizz."

Cassandra stepped outside and closed the door behind her. Bobby set down his bag and moved to the top of the stairs. The voices were muffled, but through the transom window above the front door, he could make out the speakers' faces and piece together what they were saying.

"You had best watch your tone," said Hayward, the fat man with the cruel eyes.

"And explain what you're doing here," said Simpkins, the skinny one. "Do we have a situation?"

"Relax," said Cassandra. "The brass just thought it might be best for me to assist."

"What are you gonna do?" asked Hayward. "Read the kid a bedtime story?"

Cassandra's response sounded well-rehearsed, just like her answers to Bobby. "This kid has been off the grid until now. Which means you have no idea what he's capable of."

Hayward scoffed. "He's one lousy kid. I could handle this entire job by myself."

"We didn't receive any instructions about you assisting," said Simpkins. "I think it's best we handle this on our own."

"You felt the quake, right?" said Cassandra. "Are you sure you want to be on his bad side if he experiences another anima event?"

Bobby paused. There was that phrase again—*anima event*.

"We got the hospital report," said Hayward. "We know exactly what triggered him."

"But you don't know what else might—"

"Enough small talk," said Simpkins. "Where's the boy, Cassandra?"

"He's inside, but he's still pretty shaken up. The hospital called—he knows his dream was real."

"Then we should go in and comfort him," Hayward chuckled. The doorknob jiggled.

Cassandra held her ground. "Remember what happened with the Thompson kid?" she said coolly. "How was the recovery process? Not too painful, I hope."

"Kiss my—" said Hayward. Simpkins cut him off.

"Have it your way, Cassandra," said Simpkins. "Go back inside and get the kid. Hayward, get back to the truck and radio this in. Find out why we weren't informed that Miss Congeniality here was called in to assist."

Bobby didn't wait to hear anymore. Shoving the remaining clothes he'd pulled out into his bag, he cast a final glance around the room for anything else worth taking. He paused at an old photo on the corner of his desk. It was a picture of him, his parents, and his grandfather Jeremiah at the beach during one of Grandpa's rare visits. Bobby still remembered that day. Grandpa had been animated and intense that afternoon, warning Bobby about all sorts of things that made no sense—cautioning him to keep away from wild animals and to always carry a flashlight. Bizarre as he was, it had been nice to see the old man.

Bobby lifted the picture and the corner caught on something. Pulling harder, he exposed a tarnished silver necklace with a stone pendant shaped like a flower. He remembered it vaguely, a gift from Grandpa, given to him the day the photo was taken. Far too feminine for a teenage boy, it had sat on Bobby's desk for years, buried beneath piles of comic books and video games.

On impulse, Bobby stuffed both the picture and the pendant into his pocket and headed for the window. He had one foot over the windowsill when the door creaked open behind him.

"I hope you weren't planning on leaving without me," said Cassandra.

Bobby froze, half in, half out of the window. "You lied to me," he said. "You know those guys down there. And now you're going to turn me over to them."

"I didn't lie to you; I lied to *them* to buy us some time."

Bobby grimaced. "How do I know you aren't lying to me about lying to them?"

"Because I am going to help you escape."

Bobby swung his other leg out over the sill. "Thanks, but I've got that covered."

"Suit yourself," said Cassandra. "But you should know they'll see you from the curb." Bobby shot a quick glance outside. Six men, each wearing dark military garb, stood by the vans less than fifty feet away.

"Those are Core agents, sent to bring you in," said Cassandra. She retreated to the door. "I'm headed out the back. You can either come with me, or take your chances out the window."

Bobby balanced on the sill, staring into the distance. "What the heck is a *Core agent*? And what's an *anima event*?"

The men by the vans broke off into teams. Two of them headed down either side of the house. At least two more agents remained by the curb.

Cassandra disappeared down the steps. With a sigh, Bobby climbed back into his bedroom, grabbed his duffle bag, and hurried after her.

On tiptoes, they crept through the house to the back porch, located off the pantry, beyond the kitchen. Cassandra eased the door open with Bobby at her hip. The backyard was dark with no lights on except a single bulb by the garage entrance. Gravel crunched off to their left as the Core agents crept up the driveway.

"They're coming!" Bobby whispered to Cassandra. She held a finger to her lips and pointed through the darkness to the barely visible ivy-covered fence bordering the back alley.

From the front of the house, Simpkins shouted, "Hey, Cassandra! HQ has no info about an assist. Open up now or we're coming in." Bobby started across the lawn, but Cassandra grabbed his shoulder. A few seconds later, a loud clash of shattered hinges and splintered wood sounded as the front door was smashed in.

Cassandra threw open the back door. "Go now!" she yelled.

With his duffle bag bouncing on his shoulders, Bobby raced to the back fence. Encumbered as he was, he got there far ahead of Cassandra, who struggled with her high heels on the thick grass.

Bobby reached the back gate and stared in horror. A heavy chain wrapped around the latch, secured by a thick padlock. Behind him, light flickered in the gap between the garage and the corner of the house as the Core agents continued up the driveway. *No going back for the key.*

Bobby raced along the back fence, trampling through the vegetable garden until he found a spot not covered in ivy. A light flashed in his direction. A split second later, Simpkins shouted and broke into a sprint across the lawn.

"Stop! . . . Come back here!"

Bobby tossed his duffle bag over the fence and climbed. Meanwhile, Cassandra reached the fence and paused at the gate.

"What are you doing?" he yelled. "Climb!"

Instead, Cassandra grasped the hefty padlock in both hands as Bobby reached the top of the fence. Dropping to the ground on the far side, Bobby took a moment to gather his bag. When he straightened up, Cassandra stood next to him, the gate slightly ajar. She pushed the gate shut, replaced the chain, and clicked the padlock back into place.

Bobby froze. "Hey, that gate was locked! How did you—?"

Cassandra brushed his question aside with a wave. "No time for that. We need to leave, now!"

One house down, a white convertible Porsche sat in the middle of the alley. Cassandra slid into the driver's seat and started the engine. Behind them, the back fence rattled as their pursuers reached the wall and began to climb. Bobby threw his bag in the back of the Porsche and leapt over the door into his seat. Cassandra winced at the dark smudges his sneakers left on the leather upholstery. She revved the engine, sending up a deafening roar as two agents dropped into the alley.

The one in front pulled a pistol. "Stop!" he yelled.

Cassandra slammed the Porsche into gear, rocketing down the narrow backstreet at breakneck speed. There was a loud crack as a bullet lodged in the back bumper.

Cassandra tossed her middle finger in the air. "You'll pay for that!"

Bobby held his breath until they'd reached the end of the block and turned the corner. He leaned back in his seat and took a deep breath as the men disappeared behind him, ditched like a forgotten dream in the dawn of a new day.

CHAPTER 2

They'd traveled less than a mile before the reality of Bobby's situation set in.

"Start talking," he demanded. "Who were those guys back there?"

Cassandra kept both hands on the wheel, eyes straight ahead. "Calm down, Bobby. I promise I'll explain everything in due time."

Bobby's pulse quickened. "Don't tell me to calm down! I don't even know you. I definitely shouldn't be in a car with you. People are shooting at us. I need to get to the hospital to see my parents, but you keep telling me it's not safe.

"Oh, and let's not forget that I just caused an earthquake by dreaming that my parents were in an accident, which they were! I'm pretty sure I have the right to be upset. So, how about instead of telling me to calm down, you tell me what the heck is going on!"

Cassandra took a deep breath. "You're right. I am sure this is a lot to process, but I need you to trust me. Your grandfather knew something bad was going to happen and sent me to help you."

"Grandpa?" said Bobby. "I haven't seen Grandpa since I was a kid! You know what? This is crazy. Pull over. Let me out. I'll call an Uber to take me to the hospital."

Cassandra took her right hand off the wheel and placed it on his shoulder. "Bobby, listen to me. I want you to relax. Why don't you take a nap? I'm sure you'll feel much better once you've gotten some sleep."

Her hand was warm; the area where she touched his shoulder felt tingly. His heart slowed, taking with it all of his adrenaline. He yawned. The compulsion to sleep was suddenly overwhelming.

"I'm not sleepy," he lied.

"Then just lie back and close your eyes," she said. She brought her hand up to his neck. "Everything is going to be okay."

Bobby's head drooped to the side. "I don't need to sleep. I need to get to—"

—⟆⟆—

The steady purr of the engine must have caused Bobby to doze off. When Bobby awoke, the view was an unfamiliar landscape of glass-and-concrete industrial buildings. He wondered if Cassandra even knew where she was going. Probably not. As if in response to his thought, she punched buttons on the car's steering wheel. Program menus flashed onto the car's center console, followed by a phone list.

"Call Chief," said Cassandra.

The synthesized female voice of the car's onboard computer responded. "Dial Chief, is that correct?"

"Yes, yes, dial already," snapped Cassandra.

After a few rings, the line picked up. The gravelly voice on the other end sounded distant, the line full of static.

"Oh, thank goodness! . . . Chief, it's Cassandra."

"Cassandra? What is it?"

"I've got a bit of a situation."

"You've got the Ether kid, don't you?"

Cassandra flushed. "How on earth did you know that?"

"Never mind how I know," said Chief. "What are you doing?"

"We're in my car. We need a place to go."

"My gosh, Cassandra, do you have me on speaker?"

"Right, sorry." Cassandra reached into the center console and removed a small earpiece. With a quick flick, she turned the device on and affixed it to her ear.

"Okay, we're off speaker now," said Cassandra. "Chief, it's a long story. The bottom line is that right now we need a place to go. Isn't there any way you can come back?"

Cassandra's scowl cracked upward into a scheming smile. "Trust me, he's definitely worth it."

"Yeah, I remember the downtown entrance but—"

Chief interrupted.

Cassandra scowled before replying. "Fine, but just make sure you remember our deal!" She hung up abruptly and put the earpiece away.

Cassandra glanced at Bobby, who squeezed his eyes shut, pretending to still be asleep.

"For certain, someone is going to pay dearly for this," she said and placed a hand on Bobby's shoulder once again. He wasn't pretending moments later when his head rolled to the side and he began to snore.

—⟋⟍—

A change in the car's rhythm pulled Bobby from his induced slumber. He opened one eye to see the Porsche pull into the underground parking garage of a glass skyscraper. Descending three levels, Cassandra parked next to a bank of elevators, hopped out, and started walking.

Bobby bolted upright in his seat. "I need to get to the hospital! I need to see my parents!"

Cassandra turned, hands on her hips, and stared at him as if the subject bored her. "I spoke to someone at the hospital right before you woke up. Your parents are going to be fine. Now come on."

Bobby remained seated as relief and doubt battled within him. "You're certain?"

Cassandra walked to his door and placed a hand on his arm. "Everything is going to be alright, I promise."

Bobby felt a tremendous weight lift. "I want to see them," he said.

"We will, but right now I need to get you someplace safe. Now come on."

Bobby knew that, despite her reassurances, he shouldn't be going anywhere but to the hospital. And yet he found himself leaping from the car, grabbing his duffle bag, and following her to the elevators. As they drew close, Bobby angled toward the elevators, but Cassandra walked right past them.

In the far corner, an industrial air-conditioning unit rumbled like a snoring giant. Bobby followed Cassandra as she picked a path through the rattling machinery. After several turns, she stopped at a steel door tucked behind a series of massive air ducts. The door was perfectly smooth, with no knob or handle.

"How do we get in?"

Reaching behind the nearest duct, Cassandra flipped up a panel to reveal a luminescent keypad. Punching in a code, she stepped back as the door popped open with a whoosh of stale air. Beyond the entrance lay an elevator lobby with a caramel-colored marble floor and baroque walls trimmed in walnut. Bobby scratched his head.

Cassandra let slip a tiny smile as she led him into the room and over to the elevator. "Think that's confusing? Just wait 'til you see the rest," she said.

Punching the call button, she smirked. Bobby's mouth gaped as the doors slid open. On the other side sat a sphere on a rollercoaster-like metal track. An opening in the sphere revealed two chairs inside, each with shoulder straps and a harness.

"What kind of crazy ride is this?" said Bobby, following Cassandra as she strapped in.

"Think of it as a giant hamster ball," said Cassandra. "The outer shell is propelled along the track by magnetic impulses, while the inner chamber remains upright—more or less. Trust me; it's not my favorite form of transportation, but for where we're going, there's really no other option."

Fully secured, Cassandra punched a button on her armrest and the inner door slid shut, sealing them in. She punched another code and a button marked *EN* lit up on her console.

"You might want to hold onto something," she said, and jammed her thumb into the button.

Instantly, the sphere began to roll, quickening at a pace that made the Porsche Spyder's acceleration pale in comparison. The sphere briefly rose and then dropped precipitously, pressing Bobby into the shoulder straps of his harness.

"You're telling me that this thing goes up and down too?" he said, gripping his suddenly queasy stomach.

"And diagonal," said Cassandra, leaning back in her seat without the slightest sign of discomfort. When she saw Bobby's green face, she added, "Don't even think about it! There is no way I'm cleaning up after everything else I've had to deal with tonight."

"Everything *you've* had to deal with?"

Bobby tightened his grip on his handrails, losing track of both time and direction in his fight to hold onto his dinner. Finally, after what felt like an eternity, their ride slowed.

Bobby unbuckled himself and stood on wobbly legs. The outer shell opened to reveal a much larger baroque foyer, ten times as opulent as the one they'd just left. Renaissance-style marble statues and oil paintings adorned the perimeter, while gilded divans and overstuffed leather chairs sat on Persian rugs scattered throughout. At the far end, two massive oak doors were carved with the lifelike image of a golden eagle in flight.

Bobby let out an involuntary gasp. "Wow, this place is gorgeous."

Cassandra glanced around as if seeing the room for the first time. She tossed back her head and laughed—the first genuine show of humor he'd seen from her. "This is just the lobby."

Bobby stifled another gasp of surprise. "You mean there's more?"

Without reply, Cassandra headed across the room to a console embedded in the far wall where she submitted to a retina scan. Next, she placed her right hand on a luminescent scanner bed. The device lit up as it scanned her fingerprints before going dark once again.

"Identity confirmed," intoned a sexy female voice. "Welcome back, Cassandra. Please submit anima for final approval." A concealed compartment opened next to the touch screen. Out slid a glowing green orb the size of a grapefruit.

"There it is again—what is anima?" said Bobby. "And what is that thing?" He pointed to the glowing orb.

"Not now," said Cassandra and set her hand on the orb. Bobby fell silent as she closed her eyes in concentration. What happened next made Bobby's mouth fall open. Like wood smoldering until it catches fire, the orb beneath Cassandra's hand began to glow. Except that it wasn't the orb that glowed; it was Cassandra's hand. Light radiated directly from her skin onto the orb, which took up the glow like a wildfire until it burned so bright Bobby had to avert his eyes.

Bobby brought both hands up to cover his face. Cassandra took her hand off the orb. The light died instantly.

"Access granted."

"What the heck was that?" said Bobby, rubbing his eyes.

Offering no reply, Cassandra turned and headed toward the double oak doors. With a loud boom, the engraved eagle split open and the doors parted.

Cassandra placed a hand on his shoulder as she walked by. "Follow me," she said, and once again, Bobby complied without question.

The world beyond was so unexpected that Bobby lost a step from staring and had to hurry to catch up. Gone was the opulent decor of gilded furniture and elegant artwork, replaced by a beauty only Mother Nature could produce. A small grassy clearing lay just beyond the entrance, surrounded by a forest of majestic redwoods that soared hundreds of feet into the sky. Only, it wasn't the sky—not exactly. Between the branches of the uppermost canopy, Bobby spotted light reflected back from what appeared to be a domed ceiling.

"This is impossible," he stammered.

"I told you the sphere doesn't just go up and down."

"I know but—" Bobby rubbed his eyes again, this time in disbelief. "Where are we?"

"*Where* isn't important. It's the *what* that matters here."

"Okay, so *what* exactly is this place?"

"It's a self-contained, dense-energy ecosystem equipped with bio-conduits designed to channel the innate life energy of the indigenous flora and fauna contained within—"

"In English, please."

Cassandra sighed. "It a biodome used for anima work and training."

Bobby's head bobbed. "And exactly what are we doing here?"

"Hiding. This entire enclosure is insulated from ambient energy. Nothing gets in or out except as directed, which means they can't track us as long as we're in here."

Bobby had a million other questions. "Who runs this place? What's its purpose? Did they grow the forest inside the dome or place the dome over an existing forest?"

"Enough questions," said Cassandra. "It's time we got settled." She turned and headed deeper into the woods.

—⁓—

The path through the forest teemed with life. Squirrels chattered in the bushes while birds chirped in the trees. In the distance, a family of roe deer grazed in an oval-shaped meadow awash with yellow daisies. The deer moved from cluster to cluster, grazing on one succulent treat after another.

Throughout the forest, florescent green tubes with hexagonal heads poked up from the ground like geometric mushrooms.

Bobby slowed for a closer look. "Are these the conduits you were talking about?"

"Not now," said Cassandra without breaking stride. "There will be plenty of time to talk after I'm not walking through the forest in a thousand-dollar pair of Prada pumps."

The trees soon parted, revealing a broad hill with a slender game trail winding up the side. Bobby paused as they crested the rise. In the middle of a wide plateau sat the strangest structure he had ever seen.

At first glance, it appeared to be a glowing dome. As they got closer, Bobby realized it wasn't a dome, exactly, but a giant polyhedron made up of dozens of hexagonal panels. Brown and rough like tree bark, each panel was covered in a lattice of luminous green vines that gave the building its glow, weaving a net over the structure that pulsed like neon shrouded in fog.

Bobby stepped closer and discovered that the wood panels had no seams or cracks. In fact, the entire structure lacked bolts, screws, or nails.

"What is that thing?" Bobby asked in awe.

"We call it 'the Nexus,'" said Cassandra with a hint of reverence. "It was Chief's idea. But don't ask me how he did it. Even I don't know enough about energy work to create something like that."

"What does it do?"

"Remember those green boxes you asked me about? Those boxes collect the living energy generated throughout the forest. That energy is then transmitted through specially designed conduits to this central location. The Nexus acts as a focal point, making the energy inside its chamber infinitely more powerful than anything found in nature."

"Can we go inside?"

"No one is allowed inside without Chief's permission. Now come on, we need to get settled."

Still gawking, Bobby followed Cassandra around the bizarre building to a log cabin on the far side of the clearing. A single, open room, the inside of the cabin was warm and cozy, with solid oak furniture and a quilted rug by the stone hearth.

Setting his gym bag down, Bobby plopped onto the twin bed against the far wall. With drooping eyelids, he watched Cassandra go to the cupboard and withdraw a bowl of nuts and dried fruit. Not realizing how starved he felt until that moment, Bobby accepted the bowl and began shovelling the contents into his mouth.

Cassandra handed him a bottle of water to wash it down and went to the fireplace. "I'll leave you to rest in a while, but first I think we should talk."

The stack of logs burst into flames. Bobby leapt up in surprise, but Cassandra gave no notice as she sat on the rug by the now crackling fire. With a wave, she beckoned him.

"Tell me something, Bobby," she began. "What do you know of your aunt?"

Bobby frowned as he joined her on the rug. "I don't have an aunt. My mother only has one brother. He lives up in Vancouver with his family."

"I wasn't referring to your mother's side of the family," said Cassandra.

Bobby's frown deepened. "My father is an only child."

"Is that what he told you? Interesting—perhaps he even believes it. I doubt your grandfather has done much to set the record straight."

"Grandpa would never keep something like that a secret," Bobby protested.

"Sometimes people keep secrets for a reason."

Bobby's hand clenched. "Stop!" he yelled. "Whatever game you're playing, it isn't funny."

Cassandra didn't flinch, almost as if she'd been expecting his outburst. "Please relax, Bobby," she said in a calm voice. Bobby's fist opened involuntarily.

"You're right, this isn't a game," she said, her voice soft and soothing. "I can prove I am telling the truth, but only if you are willing to hear it."

He paused, then reached for a handful of dried cranberries. "I'm listening."

"It has to do with what you keep asking me about—anima. Every living creature on earth contains a form of energy that scientists have yet to fully understand. In humans, we call it our Chi, spirit, or soul. This *living energy* does more than just reside within us. It connects us with every other creature on the planet."

Bobby frowned but didn't interrupt. "Go on."

"Think of it like gravity," said Cassandra, "or the earth's magnetic field; it is invisible and yet it exists all around us. And, just like gravity or magnetism, this energy can be manipulated and controlled. We call it *anima* after the Latin word for 'breath of life.' A person who can tap into anima is called an *exso*, after the Latin *exsomnis,* for 'awake' or 'wakeful.' Such people can do things most others would consider impossible. That is how I was able to open the gate in your backyard, as well as convince you to accompany me despite your insistence on going to the hospital."

Bobby leapt to his feet, sending the contents of the bowl in his lap flying across the room. "I knew it! You've been controlling me this whole time, using magic to make me do what you want."

"Bobby, sit down and listen to me; there is no such thing as magic. There is only anima—life energy. Everything alive contains it. The key distinction is that you have the ability to control it while most others do not."

"You're talking about the earthquake—the one back at my house, when I had the nightmare about my parents in the car accident."

"Bobby, that was no earthquake. That was you losing control of your anima. Like all children, you are bonded closely to your parents. When that car hit them, you felt it and reacted instinctively, releasing a torrent of anima. Thankfully, it was powerful but localized, barely impacting the surrounding area."

Bobby thought back to the neighbor's pool and how there hadn't been so much as a ripple on the water. Still, this woman's explanation was too ridiculous to accept. Then again, *something* had definitely happened.

Bobby reclaimed his spot on the rug. "What happened was something else—a freak accident. If this anima stuff is real, scientists would have discovered it."

Cassandra sighed. "That's a long and complicated discussion. I think it would be best if we saved that for some other time."

Bobby folded his arms and scoffed. "You promised me answers, but all you've given me is a bunch of fairytales and pseudo-science."

Cassandra held his gaze. "Hold out your hand."

Bobby glowered at her but did as she requested. For a moment, nothing happened. Then the air began to hum. The fire flared, sending sparks precariously close to the rug. Bobby sat there stone-faced. He'd been to the Magic Castle with his parents. "I've seen amateurs do better tricks than that."

Then he felt a tingling in his gut. His eyes widened as the walnuts and cranberries he'd scattered moments before floated in midair. One by one, they flew back to the bowl, where they landed in a small pile.

Bobby remained speechless as Cassandra raised an eyebrow. "Maybe now you'll listen to the rest of what I have to say?"

Bobby swallowed hard and nodded.

"I believe you were asking about the exact nature of anima," said Cassandra. "What you need to know is that at its very base, everything in the universe is malleable. Cells, molecules, even atoms can be broken down into smaller and smaller particles. At the subatomic level, the smallest observable particle is called a *quark*. Are you with me so far?"

"I guess so. But what does this have to do with what you just did, or with my family, for that matter?"

"I'll get there. You see, studies have proven that matter at the lowest subatomic levels does not behave like the solid objects it constructs. Rather, smaller particles can be influenced by their surroundings. In this regard, it's much like the difference between water and ice. In its liquid form, water can change shape. Ice cannot—at least not without first being broken or thawed. Are you still with me?"

"I'm not an idiot," said Bobby. "I know the difference between water and ice."

"Okay, fine," said Cassandra, "but now imagine that ice is formed not by cooling water, but rather from shackling tiny pieces of water together so tightly that they eventually lose the ability to move. That is what it's like with quarks; they are malleable when they are loose but become rigid and restricted the more they are linked together. This, then, is the nature of the universe."

Bobby stared at the bowl in his hand as he tried to absorb what she'd just said. "I think I got it. The world is solid, right? But everything that's solid is actually made up of liquid, so to speak."

Cassandra nodded. "That's exactly right."

"But what about—"

"I think that's enough questions for now," interrupted Cassandra. "As I said, you need to get some rest. Plus, it's extremely late. We can talk more in the morning."

"You still haven't told me what any of this has to do with my family, or why those men came for me back at my house."

Cassandra shook her head. "Don't you see? Those men came for you because you possess the potential to manipulate anima at a *conscious* level. With training, you could learn to convert thought into reality, even when it bends the laws of physics."

Bobby sat, hands in his lap as he tried to put the pieces together. All he came up with was, "What about my aunt?"

Cassandra sighed. "Your aunt had the same ability. Which is why those same men that came for you today took her away when she was just a baby. It would appear that history truly has a funny way of repeating itself."

"Took her away? This is all making my head spin," Bobby said. "When can I see my parents? That's all I want."

"Get some sleep, Bobby. We'll discuss it in the morning."

CHAPTER 3

By the time Cassandra left him to settle in, Bobby's head buzzed with more questions than answers. He made a show of going to bed, visiting the outhouse by the cabin and yawning as many times as possible along the way and back.

Returning to the cabin, he turned off the lights and lay on the bed, still fully clothed. Sleep eluded him.

I need to get out of here if I'm ever going to see my parents, he thought.

Bobby stood and slid open the bedroom window. Retrieving his duffle bag, he shoved it through and lowered it by a strap onto the high grass below. Then he climbed out, grasping the sill to lower himself as quietly as possible.

Bobby listened for any sound of alarm, but the air remained quiet and peaceful. Tossing his bag over his shoulder, he headed for the tree line that skirted the plateau. He stuck to the shadows as he searched for the break in the brush that signaled the trailhead. After a few minutes, he spotted the path through the light mist. He was soon at the base of the hill and heading through the forest.

The woods seemed luminescent as Bobby moved through the brush. Surprised, he cast a glance up through the branches, half expecting a full moon. Instead his eyes met only darkness. *Strange*, he thought. *Where's the light coming from?*

Bobby reached the meadow where he'd seen the family of roe deer. The conduits with the beehive tops were all aglow, flooding the forest with the same pale light as the Nexus. Diffused by the fog, the glow made the entire forest look as though it were bathed in stardust.

Bobby half walked, half jogged the forest path, not stopping until the massive doors marking the lobby came into view. With trembling hands, he yanked open the right side and poked his head inside. No alarm sounded. *Thank goodness.*

Quickly, he crossed the marble expanse, sending up unnerving echoes in the vast hall. He rang the call button and paced nervously as he waited for the door to open. With a soft ping, the sphere tram arrived and he rushed inside. Strapping himself into the seat Cassandra had used, he closed the outer shell and pushed the large round button above the console to return him to the parking garage.

The button remained unlit, the sphere silent and dark. Beside his right hand sat a small green orb, similar to the one Cassandra had used to open the inner doors. He set his hand on the orb and thought about his parents and his urgent need to reach them. For a brief moment, his hand glowed, accompanied by a gentle warmth under his palm. Then the console lit up, this time displaying the letter *G*.

"Freedom, here I come," said Bobby, as he jammed his thumb into the button.

—⁂—

Bobby used his cell to hail Uber and arrived at St. Michelle's Hospital exactly forty-five minutes later. Going straight to the main reception, he gave his parents' names to the old lady behind the counter.

"They were in a car accident, but they're fine now," he told the receptionist. "They're probably in recovery or something."

The white-haired septuagenarian stared at her computer screen, then looked at him with a look of deep sympathy on her wrinkled face.

"What is it?" said Bobby, a sudden knot in his throat.

The old woman straightened her coke-bottle glasses. "According to the system, both of your parents are in ICU." She added a small cough by way of apology. "It says here they're in surgery."

"That can't be right. Cassandra told me—" The knot in Bobby's throat swelled until he could hardly breath. "Which way to the operating rooms?"

"I can call someone to escort you," said the woman. "If you'd just wait here a—"

Bobby turned to the nearest hallway. "Which way?" he shouted. "Tell me where my parents are!"

A pudgy security guard standing by the main entrance walked over and stopped in front of him. "Sir, I'm afraid I am going to have to ask you to calm down."

Bobby ignored him, instead scanning the three long hallways before him, narrowing his eyes as if he had X-ray vision. With a low rumble, the building shook. The security guard stumbled backwards, tripped on his untied shoes, and fell hard on his ample rear end. The reception desk rattled in place, the computer monitor flickering on and off.

The old receptionist shrank back in her seat. "Oh my," she said, placing a hand over her breast. "Was that an earthquake? We need to evacuate. Protocol dictates all non-essential—"

"Please," said Bobby, lowering his voice to a gentle tone. The tremor subsided slightly. "I need to find my parents. You said they're in critical condition."

The old lady's eyes refocused as if seeing him for the first time. She offered a slow, sympathetic nod. Lifting a feeble arm, she pointed down the wing to her left. "Through the double doors, take a left, then a right. It will be the third hallway on the right."

Bobby started running before the old lady finished. "But you're not allowed back there! You need to evacuate—"

With every step, Bobby's anxiety grew. The walls shook as he stumbled down the hallway. Pictures of smiling doctors and inspirational quotes rattled in their frames. The tiled floor heaved beneath his feet, forcing him to walk a jagged line.

He ignored the people fleeing in the opposite direction, rushing to exit the building. The double doors up ahead read *Authorized Personnel Only* in bold red letters. *Did I take a wrong turn? Is this the third hallway or the fourth?* Overhead, the glowing exit sign sputtered, sending out a burst of sparks before going dark.

Sirens wailed. Above every exit, red lights flashed, guiding the way to safety. Bobby ignored them and kept going. *Where is the operating room?*

He rounded a corner and came to a halt. Dead end. Some kind of observation room. He started to turn around and then froze. Two large flat screens sat against the far wall—live CC feeds for operating rooms located nearby. His father was on the screen on the left. His mother was on the screen on the right.

Surrounded by doctors, the lower portion of Nathan Ether's torso was exposed just below his ribcage. The flesh had been pulled back to reveal the red, pulpy jumble of internal organs beneath. With a sob, Bobby tore his gaze from his father's screen and looked at his mother.

Grace Ether was propped upright, her head tilted upward so Bobby could see her face. Her eyes were slightly ajar but unseeing. She appeared to be in a drug-induced stupor, awake but registering little if anything as the doctors worked on a huge gash on the side of her head and neck.

A nurse near the back of the room was handing instruments to the surgeon—forceps, needles, sutures. Blood spurted from the wound in his mother's neck.

Bobby cried out and sank to the carpet. "What are you doing? Heal her!" he yelled at the doctor on the screen.

The lights in the observation room flickered. The surgeon bending over his mother paused as the room shook. The doctors attending to his father stopped as well.

"Help them!" screamed Bobby. Frantic, he searched the room for a door or sign that would point the way to their actual location, but found nothing.

Then the scene on the televisions shifted. As Bobby watched in horror, two new figures entered the scene, one in each OR.

A man dressed in surgical scrubs and wearing a mask entered his father's room. All Bobby could tell about the man was that he was big and had dark skin. At first, Bobby thought he was just another doctor. But the surgeons already inside didn't react that way. One of them stepped in front of the new arrival to bar his path to the patient. The new arrival gripped the man's arm and the surgeon immediately yielded.

Meanwhile, a similar scene was playing out in his mother's operating room. A woman had arrived, also dressed in surgical scrubs and mask.

She looked familiar, but Bobby couldn't quite identify her. Then, one of the nurses grabbed her head and yanked off her surgical cap.

Cassandra's platinum blonde hair tumbled out and, with it, all of the air in Bobby's lungs. Cassandra grabbed the nurse, whose arms fell to her sides. The nurse left the OR, dropping from view.

The unauthorized man in the other room performed a similar feat. Every doctor or nurse who tried to stop him abruptly ceased their protests and exited the OR.

Bobby threw up his arms, yelling and screaming as both rooms emptied, doctors and nurses evacuating one at a time, taking with them all hope for his parents' survival.

The images on the screens waivered, the feeds cutting in and out.

Through a waterfall of tears, Bobby spotted a heart monitor beside his father's table. The machine was going nuts. The lights in his mother's OR went out, plunging her into darkness. All that remained was a flashing red light in the back of the room, pulsing in time to Cassandra's footsteps as she approached the prone figure of Grace Ether.

On his father's screen, the heart monitor traced a jagged path, the bright-green line bouncing up and down as it outlined Nathan's heartbeat. An alarm went off in the observation room: *Code Blue, Code Blue.*

Bobby picked up a nearby chair and flung it across the room. It slammed into the wall a few feet from the CC TVs, leaving a foot-long dent in the plaster. Both pictures were fuzzy now, constantly flickering in and out.

"Help! Someone help me!" Bobby cried. A split second later, a security guard appeared in the doorway.

"What are you doing here?" asked the burly guard. "You need to evacuate."

"My parents," said Bobby. That was all he could muster. "My parents . . ." he repeated.

The guard extended a hand. "I need you to come with me right now."

Bobby stepped toward the man and then stopped. There was something off about the guard's uniform. It didn't look the same as the security guard at reception. Bobby figured it out right as Simpkins and Hayward came around the corner.

"You're with them!" said Bobby.

With a sly smile, the burly guard lunged at him, snatching Bobby by his wrist. Spinning him around with a powerful yank, the guard pulled Bobby into a fierce bear hug. Now it was Hayward's turn. With a wicked grin that revealed thick gums and rotten, yellow teeth, the obese agent snatched Bobby by the hair and yanked his head back.

Simpkins came forth, raised a skeletal arm, and set two fingers in the center of Bobby's forehead.

"Nighty night," said Hayward.

Bobby closed his eyes and the darkness rushed in.

CHAPTER 4

Images fluttered across his consciousness like scenes from a play. He recognized what was going on around him but somehow was not a part of it. Driven to a private airport, he was put on a fancy jet—something that he knew should have excited him but didn't. He stared blankly out the window, seeing not the dark night but rather the image of that beat-up red pickup truck slamming into his parents' car over and over again.

When the plane landed, he took a ride, first by car, then train, then finally in the back of a wagon drawn by mules. Never once did he look around or ask where he was headed. It didn't matter. Nothing mattered.

Now he lay on his back with his eyes closed, trying to hold back tears. When he finally opened his eyes, he found himself in the middle of a huge mahogany four-post bed.

Bobby pushed himself up onto his elbows. Matching nightstands, an engraved armoire, and a long dresser adorned a room twice the size of his bedroom back home. To his left, a row of windows let in a cool breeze. The walls were stone, but the room looked more like the elegant suite of an expensive resort than a prison.

To his right, the armoire stood open, with the contents of his duffle bag inside. His jacket hung on a hook on the back of the door, the picture and pendant he'd grabbed protruding from the pocket. Clearly, these people had no interest in his possessions. His jacket looked cleaner than when he'd worn it. In fact, all his clothes appeared to have been cleaned and neatly folded. Among them, Bobby spotted the pants he'd had on when he ran away.

Throwing off his sheets, he discovered he was naked except for his underpants. He hastily checked himself for incisions or needle marks but found nothing out of the ordinary. With a sigh of relief, he lay back down, noticing a row of trays on the dresser across from him.

Hopping out of bed to investigate, he almost knocked over a large silver platter on the nightstand. The tray was laden with fresh fruits, yogurt, wheat toast, and a glass of fresh-squeezed orange juice. Next to the platter were additional pitchers filled with milk, tea, and coffee. At the dresser, he lifted the tray lids to reveal an assortment of entrées: pancakes, waffles, crepes, and hash browns.

Suddenly ravenous, Bobby attacked the meal with gusto, gorging on pancakes slathered with creamy butter, rich maple syrup, and mounds of fresh berries. He proceeded next to the waffles and then on to the crepes. He discovered another tray containing freshly baked biscuits and muffins.

An hour later, Bobby leaned back on the bed and let out an enormous belch, surveying the assortment of empty plates, bowls, and trays. He had just begun to drift into a blissfully memory-free food coma when a knock came at the door. He lay still, hoping whoever it was would go away. The knock came more insistently this time.

Bobby slid under the sheets and closed his eyes. A small boy with pale skin and a shaved head came in. He wore a blood-red robe and a severe expression, as if the burdens of life were too much to bear, even at his young age. A ferret as white as a ghost sat on his left shoulder.

The dour-faced boy stepped to the foot of the bed and said, "You will get dressed and follow me, please."

Bobby pretended to be asleep, making soft snoring noises. The boy waited a few seconds and then repeated his request. After the third attempt, he turned and headed for the doorway. "Perhaps Simpkins or Hayward can convince you."

Bobby leapt out of bed and raced to the armoire, where he dressed as quickly as possible. Thankfully, the strange boy walked slowly. He was barely halfway down the hall when Bobby caught up.

"So, where are we going?" asked Bobby.

The strange boy made no reply. Instead, he led Bobby through a twisting labyrinth of stone corridors. The ferret watched Bobby with a haunting grin. The boy, on the other hand, ignored him now that his charge was in tow, leaving Bobby to study his surroundings and ponder his fate.

Wherever they were, the structure was massive, with hallway after endless hallway leading in every direction. They passed small rooms that looked like classrooms and large rooms big enough to hold an entire school. Spread throughout were stairs of every shape and size, from grand staircases wider than most houses to spiral stairwells so narrow he doubted even the slender boy could use them.

"Would it have killed them to install a few elevators?" asked Bobby. The ferret hissed. The boy remained silent.

Eventually they reached an open terrace, affording Bobby his first look outside. What he saw made him dizzy. He stood amid an enormous monastery high atop a gray and treacherous mountain. Below, tile roofs in the traditional Chinese fashion sprawled across an expanse the size of a small city. *Is it possible I'm someplace in Asia?* The thought spun his head. The furthest from home he'd ever been was a two-week vacation in Cancun.

At the base of the monastery lay a huge courtyard with sculpted gardens and smaller courtyards off to either side. Beyond the courtyards rose a thirty-foot-high stone wall with a single gate.

A narrow dirt road snaked down the mountain to the lush valley below, disappearing into the folds of the terrain. In the vale sat a forest—a massive sea of green nestled inside the bowl of mountains like a verdant oyster in a granite bed. Bobby sighed deeply. Even if he knew where he was, there was nowhere to run, no sign of civilization beyond the monastery's walls, no way to return home.

The dour-faced boy hadn't stopped, forcing Bobby to run to catch up. There were more hallways, more stairs, all headed upward and deeper into the colossal fortress. After several minutes, his guide stopped in front of a large, ornate door.

The dour-faced boy stepped to the side and pointed. The message was clear: Bobby was to proceed alone.

—⟋⟍⟍—

Bobby opened the door and cautiously stepped inside. A huge office lay beyond. An elegant desk stood in front of a giant mural depicting a mountaintop monastery, its rooftops ablaze in sunlight. In the middle of the room, two overstuffed chairs faced a fireplace set into the left wall. A stack of logs sat unlit in the hearth, as cold and lifeless as the surrounding stone.

A slender woman with cadaverous skin and raven hair stood from behind the desk. She looked like a vulture, boasting high cheekbones, a beaked nose, and narrow eyes that seemed to bore into his soul as she crossed the room. She greeted him with a smile that felt completely out of place and yet somehow familiar.

"You must be Bobby. Please, have a seat."

Bobby remained standing. The woman appeared not to notice as she sat in the nearest overstuffed chair. "It's so nice to finally meet you. I have heard so much about you."

Again, Bobby gave no reply.

"Ah, yes, I can only imagine how upset you must be," continued the woman. "I promise I will answer all your questions in time. Now sit." Her voice cracked the air like a whip.

Bobby reluctantly complied, sinking deep into the chair's plush interior.

"My name is Ms. Grayson. You may call me 'Headmistress Grayson' or simply 'Headmistress.' And this," she said, gesturing to the space around her, "is the Jade Academy."

Bobby folded his arms. "So, Headmistress Grayson, why did you kidnap me?"

The headmistress sighed as though indulging a child. "In point of fact, Cassandra is the one who kidnapped you."

Bobby almost leapt out of his seat. "It was your men who abducted me from the hospital."

"Only for your protection. We had to make sure she couldn't grab you again. By the way, how did you manage to escape?"

Bobby frowned. "I didn't 'escape.' Not exactly."

The headmistress rubbed her chin. "So she wasn't holding you against your will?" Bobby shook his head, wondering why he was suddenly defending Cassandra when he knew full well she would never have allowed him to leave the Eagle's Nest had he asked.

"I see," said the headmistress. "Yet you ran away without her knowing. Which is precisely why we had to save you: it was only a matter of time before she tracked you down again."

"Save me?" asked Bobby incredulously. "You don't really expect me to believe that you were trying to save me after the way you broke into my house."

"Bobby, my men were sent to your home to bring you here; that's true. But they had no desire to kidnap you. In fact, we had hoped you would agree to come voluntarily."

"But I didn't come voluntarily, did I? Instead, you kidnapped me, just like you took my aunt!"

The headmistress paused, cocking her head. "Did you just say that we kidnapped your aunt?"

Bobby sat back in the chair, pleased that he knew something the headmistress apparently did not. "Cassandra said that when Dad's sister was just an infant, your people came and took her away."

Headmistress Grayson frowned. "I have reviewed your file extensively. There is nothing in it about an aunt."

"Yeah, well, you wouldn't exactly come right out and admit to kidnapping her if it were true, now would you?"

"I suppose that's true," replied Headmistress Grayson. "Unfortunately, it's a circular argument. I can't tell you that I'm not the bad guy because that's exactly what you think a bad guy would say. Tell me, Bobby, did Cassandra happen to tell you exactly who at the academy perpetrated this supposed abduction of your aunt?"

"No, but she didn't have to. I saw that goon squad that you have working for you. I'm sure it was one of them."

"An interesting conjecture. However, there is a flaw with your supposition. That 'goon squad' is a rather recent addition to our organization. If you do have an aunt, and if she was, in fact, abducted during infancy as Cassandra claims, then the act would have occurred many decades ago. Is that a fair assertion?"

Bobby thought about it for a moment and nodded.

"Very good," said the headmistress. "So we agree that those men could not have been responsible."

"I'm sure you had other people back then."

"Indeed, we did have people back then as well—people who helped bring *willing* children to the Jade Academy to learn. It was, however, a much smaller team back then."

"As if that makes a difference," said Bobby.

"Ah, but it does. It makes all the difference in the world. Bobby, do you know who was part of the team back then?"

"Let me guess. That big, fat guy, Hayward, and that creepy skeleton guy, Simpkins."

"An excellent guess, Bobby. In fact, those two have been in service to our organization far longer than you might expect. But there is someone else who worked here long ago, someone who was part of that team and would, therefore, have been involved in any so-called 'abductions.' Can you guess who that person is?"

Bobby flashed back to his house, when he was upstairs packing and listening to the conversation on the front porch. In an instant, he knew whom the headmistress meant.

"That's right, Bobby. I'm talking about Cassandra."

For several moments, Bobby sat, too stunned to move. Obviously, the headmistress might be lying, but somehow he knew she wasn't. Everything fit too well: Cassandra's sudden appearance at his home, her knowledge of the Jade Academy, her familiarity with Hayward and Simpkins.

When the headmistress spoke again, her voice was soft and gentle. "Try not to be upset, Bobby. You aren't the only person she's fooled."

"What do you mean?" he asked, curiosity creeping into his tone despite his best efforts.

"After Cassandra left us, she went freelance. We thought she'd moved on to recruiting for other programs, but it seems obvious now that she's involved in the exso black market."

"The what now?" asked Bobby.

"*Exsos*—awakened people like you with access to amazing abilities like what you did the other night."

"You're saying that she wanted to sell me?"

The headmistress folded her hands neatly in her lap. "You'd be surprised what some people will pay for a kid with your potential."

Bobby stood, tapping the top of his head as he paced the room. "I did hear her talking about a deal. She said someone was gonna pay."

Headmistress Grayson smiled and put a hand on Bobby's shoulder. "You see? We are not the ones you can't trust. She was going to sell you. She probably fabricated that whole story about your aunt to turn you against us and gain your trust."

Bobby leaned against the fireplace, his legs suddenly weak. "You're saying the whole story about me having an aunt is a lie? That she made it up just so I would run away with her?"

"It worked, didn't it? You didn't put up a struggle. I must say, it was a very clever ploy on her part."

Bobby slumped back into his seat. "I knew she wasn't telling me the whole truth, but I can't believe she was going to sell me like some kind of animal."

The headmistress gave him a sad look as if to say, "I told you so." A dark ember burned in his heart at the thought of what Cassandra had tried to do.

Long moments passed. Finally, Bobby said, "Tell me about this ability you say I possess. What exactly can I do with it?"

The headmistress grinned as though this were the question she'd been waiting for all along.

"Oh, and one more thing," said Bobby. "Where the heck is this place?"

Bobby's stomach felt like it was full of rocks as he tried to digest everything the headmistress told him. According to her, he was in Tibet, at a monastery founded by monks but now operated jointly by a secular group known as "Academics," who sought to help kids with special abilities such as him.

"I know it's a lot to take in," said Headmistress Grayson. "But after what you did the other night, and with Cassandra chasing you, it was imperative that we bring you here to keep you safe and help you learn to control your abilities."

"What about my parents? The house? My life back home?"

The headmistress sighed, a sound that sounded more annoyed than sympathetic. "Your parents are gone. What is there to return to—an empty house? Relatives in Toronto you hardly know? There is nothing worth going back to."

Bobby felt suddenly drained. It had been a long trip. Even after eating as much as he had, he still felt weak and tired. He sat motionless and numb except for the twitching of his left pinky finger.

Finally, he looked up. "I should at least go back for the funeral. My uncle and his family will want to know what happened."

The headmistress frowned. "It wouldn't be safe. Cassandra would find you, and I can't guarantee that my men would be able to protect you."

"I can't just run away."

The headmistress shook her head. "I'm sorry to do this, but there is something you need to know. The driver of the truck was a known associate of Cassandra's. It appears that the accident was not an accident at all. Cassandra had your parents murdered."

Bobby shook his head. "You're lying. Even if Cassandra wanted to kidnap me, she had no reason to murder my parents."

"Before she could sell you, she needed your abilities to manifest. The accident was designed to do that. Traumatic ordeals frequently result in anima events. Everything else was just an act, a charade to gain your trust so you wouldn't turn on her."

Bobby pulled his knees up to his chest and kept shaking his head. "It can't be."

From her desk, Headmistress Grayson retrieved a large manila envelope and handed it to Bobby. "I was hoping to spare you the discomfort of showing these to you, but I see now that you aren't going to accept what I tell you without proof. Go ahead; open it."

Wiping his eyes, Bobby removed a stack of photographs that turned his stomach to acid. The first photo showed his parents' car, badly damaged, with his parents still inside. Their bodies lay contorted. Bobby covered his face with a hand.

"I'm sorry," said the headmistress. "You don't need to look at that one if you don't want to, but you really should look at the others."

Hastily discarding the top photo, Bobby found an image of the truck that had caused the accident. Its front end was completely smashed. In the foreground, a gaunt man with long hair and tattoos all over his arms appeared dazed as he stepped out of the vehicle.

"Why are you showing these to me?" asked Bobby. "These don't prove anything."

"Keep going," said the headmistress.

Bobby flipped to a surveillance photo taken through a window into the living room of a dingy apartment. Inside, the tattooed driver could be seen in conversation with Cassandra.

"My men followed the driver home after he was released from the hospital," said the headmistress. Bobby stared at the photo, speechless. "As we suspected, he met up with Cassandra. Our assumption is that she was supposed to pay him for causing the accident."

"Your assumption?" said Bobby. "So you have no proof that she hired him? Maybe she was questioning him about what happened."

"Look at the next photo."

Bobby did as instructed and broke out in a cold sweat. The photo showed the tattooed man in a pool of blood on the living room floor, the hilt of a knife protruding from his back.

"Moments after Cassandra left the man's apartment, another man snuck in the back door and did that. It seems clear that she had it all arranged ahead of time."

"Why would Cassandra go to the man's house if she planned to have him killed?"

"We believe she went to ensure he hadn't said anything to the police that could lead back to her. As soon as she confirmed he hadn't talked, she had him killed to tie up loose ends."

"Did your men see the killer?" asked Bobby.

The headmistress gestured for him to go to the next photo.

Bobby flipped to the page and found a picture of a large Native American man with a weathered face and long, black hair. The man stood over the body of the driver, an intense look in his dark eyes.

"Tell me, Bobby, do you know that man?"

Bobby swallowed hard and shook his head, turning to the last photo—an image of Cassandra and the Native American man together.

"The killer was probably stationed at the back door with instructions to wait until she left. We tried to catch them both as soon as the murder happened, but they must have sensed us and gave us the slip."

Bobby was too stunned to reply.

The headmistress put a hand on his shoulder. "I hate to be so blunt, but you're all alone now. There is nothing for you back home, which leaves you with two choices. We can return you to your empty home, where Cassandra will likely come for you shortly after we leave, or you can stay here and train with our monks to master your abilities. Perhaps someday you'll even be able to get revenge for your parents' deaths."

Bobby had no reply. It was all so much to process.

"Take as much time as you need," said the headmistress. "Just tell Willy once you've made up your mind." The headmistress gestured toward the bald boy waiting in the hallway. "He'll take care of the rest."

With an imperceptible nod, Bobby walked to the door. Outside, the boy and his ferret waited silently to take him back to his room. The instant they arrived, Bobby shut the door, collapsed on the bed, pulled a pillow over his head, and burst into tears.

CHAPTER 5

Bobby stayed in his room the next several days, passing the time between crying and trying to sleep. Nighttime was the worst. Every time he closed his eyes he saw the accident, except now he knew it wasn't an accident. The specter of Cassandra's presence hovered over the scene, filling him with such rage that it jolted him upright whenever he came close to drifting off.

As for Willy and his ferret, the two remained outside the bedroom door around the clock. Silent as statues, they brought Bobby his meals and bused them away, untouched as often as not. On the morning of the fourth day, his eyes puffy and red from crying and lack of sleep, Bobby asked Willy to take him to the headmistress.

Wordlessly, Willy led him through the same passages he had traversed days before, ending at the large, carved door leading to Headmistress Grayson's office. Bobby pushed open the door to find her waiting, perched on the edge of her desk as though she had been expecting him.

"I've come to a decision," he said. "I want you to train me to use my skills. I want revenge on the people who murdered my parents. I want revenge on Cassandra."

—ɯ—

Almost instantly, Bobby's situation changed. As soon as they returned to his room, Willy and the ferret disappeared, replaced by a long-limbed, copper-haired girl named Lily. The chatty tween bubbled with excitement, talking all about the academy and how much Bobby was going to enjoy being there.

"Where are we going?" asked Bobby as Lily helped him pack up his possessions.

"You'll be with the rest of the kids now, in the student quarters."

Bobby fell silent, allowing Lily to carry on a largely one-sided conversation en route to the apprentice-level student section on the opposite wing of the monastery. As they walked, she explained that he would be joining the ranks of students studying at the Jade Academy, living in the school's dormitory, and eating in the dining hall with everyone else.

"So, when do I get started with classes?" asked Bobby.

"You'll start classes this afternoon after lunch, but your first anima session with Master Jong isn't until tomorrow morning," said Lily. "Right now, let's get your stuff put away and head to the dining hall. I don't know about you, but I'm starving."

—ɯ—

Bobby's new "quarters" fit the word perfectly. The space was a fraction of the room he'd been in. Gone was the massive four-post bed with matching furniture. The new room contained only a straw pallet, a small wooden table, and a mat in the corner for meditation.

"What's with the bathrobe?" said Bobby, lifting a black robe from the bed.

"Novice attire," said Lily, gesturing to her own, smoke-gray robe. "As you progress, the robes get lighter. It's supposed to represent our symbolic journey toward enlightenment. Then again, the masters can wear whatever they want, so I don't really see the point. Also, it's only for classes. You can wear whatever you want after hours."

"What does a red robe mean?" asked Bobby.

"You mean 'the Creep'?"

Bobby gave Lily a blank look.

"Right, sorry," said Lily. "I forgot you wouldn't know. That's what we call Willy, the kid that's been watching over you the last couple of days—the one that looks like he's been sucking on a lemon since the day he was born.

"His ferret is called *Siphon* by the way. Supposedly it's for *emotional support*—something to do with Willy's ability to sense other people's emotions. Nasty creature, that ferret. The only times I've ever seen it happy is when someone is upset. Anyway, we call Willy the 'Creep' because he gives everyone the willies." She giggled at her own joke and Bobby mustered a smile.

"What about the robe?" he said.

"Right, sorry. Red is supposed to symbolize service and self-sacrifice. It's basically so that people know he's working for the headmistress and is excused from classes. Although, personally, I think he just likes wearing those robes because it makes him look even creepier." She set his bag on the bed and headed for the door.

"Wait," said Bobby. "Where's the closet? I need someplace to put my clothes."

"The monks don't believe in personal possessions beyond the bare essentials. Store your things under your bed or on the table. Shared bathrooms are down the hall. Don't ask about the door. The monks don't believe in locks either."

Bobby shrugged at the Spartan amenities. He would gladly endure much worse if it meant getting his revenge on Cassandra.

After a quick tour of the residence area, Bobby followed Lily out of the dormitory wing and to the dining hall. The huge square room had a high, vaulted ceiling and marble floor, with dozens of round banquet tables spaced out like checkers on a chessboard. On each table lay dozens of bowls, plates, and carafes filled with food and drinks.

Lunch appeared to be just getting underway, with dozens of students dressed in various shades of gray, blue, and green filtering in from the side doors. The room quickly filled with the festive sound of kids talking and laughing as they grabbed seats and began to eat.

"What's with the other colors?" asked Bobby, pointing to an older boy in a bright-yellow robe.

"They denote the wearer's primary ability," said Lily. "All of us here are working to connect with the oneness of all things, but people study and excel in different ways. Some people are empathic, some merely intuitive. A few have telekinetic abilities. Most of the students here have a combination of minor abilities, though I did hear of a few rare students with clairvoyance."

As they talked, Bobby followed Lily to an open bench at the far end of the hall. Grabbing a bowl, Bobby discovered squash, zucchini, and spinach, as well as a variety of other vegetables he didn't recognize.

Discarding the bowl, Bobby grabbed another. The bowl held an assortment of beans: white, red, black, pinto, and black-eyed. Bobby frowned and grabbed another bowl. This one contained snow peas, green beans and asparagus. More bowls, more beans—garbanzo beans, lima beans, and lentils.

"What's up with all the vegan stuff?" asked Bobby. "Where's the real food?"

"If by 'real food' you mean the processed food you're used to eating, the answer is that we don't eat that stuff here. Everything we eat here is natural and organic."

"What about meat? Where are the hotdogs and hamburgers?"

"We don't eat meat," Lily said. "We have goats for cheese, butter, and milk, but there are no cows. Even if we did have them, the killing of animals causes trauma that taints the meat.

To consume a murdered animal is to take in the negative energy of the animal's death. We get our protein from legumes and other natural sources."

"So what am I supposed to eat? I can't eat all this veggie crap," Bobby said.

"Here, try this," said Lily, handing Bobby a bowl of mashed potatoes. Relieved to see something other than green, Bobby took a scoop, adding a chunk of sharp cheese and some stewed carrots to balance the plate.

"Hey, Lily. Who's your new friend?" Bobby looked up as a lanky boy with brown skin and short, twisted braids took a seat next to her. Perhaps eighteen or nineteen, he carried himself with the casual ease of an upperclassman close to graduating.

"Hey, Trevor," said Lily. "This is Bobby. He's going to be joining us in class and working with Master Jong for a while."

"Cool," said Trevor, shaking hands with Bobby. "So, what's your PS?"

"My what?"

"You know, your parental situation," said Trevor. "In case you haven't noticed, this isn't your normal boarding school. No going home for the holidays, or care packages filled with comic books and candy bars, if you know what I mean."

"I'd rather not talk about it," Bobby said through tight lips.

"That's cool," said Trevor with a shrug. "I was just curious. Usually the older kids that show up here have some pretty crazy stories."

"I said I don't want to talk about it," said Bobby.

Trevor raised his hands in surrender. "Sorry, man. It's just that, around here, almost everyone is either an orphan or sent by their parents to learn how to control their abilities before they burn the house down.

"Take us two, for example," he said, pointing at himself and Lily. "I was an orphan—in and out of five different foster homes before I was four years old. I kept making all the other kids cry just by touching 'em, or so they tell me, until the academics found me and brought me here to study."

Bobby turned to Lily. "What about you? What's your PS?"

Lily let out a small sigh, as if she'd told her story one too many times. "I was normal until I was ten. Then strange stuff started happening: light bulbs exploding, appliances turning on and off for no reason. My mother started looking for answers on the internet, and that's when the academics showed up. My parents were so relieved to have answers that they happily agreed to send me here to study."

"Do you see them often?"

"This place is too remote for visitors, but I send letters all the time," said Lily. "They miss me and can't wait to see me after I graduate."

She fell silent for a moment, lost in her thoughts. Twisting a tight braid between his fingers, Trevor said, "Hey, Bobby, which techniques are you and Master Jong gonna be working on?"

Bobby shrugged. "No idea. Guess I'll find out tomorrow."

The conversation ended as Trevor heaped a plate full of vegetables, piled on a mound of scalloped potatoes and topped it off with a thick layer of gooey white cheese. Bobby drank a glass of cranberry juice and peeled an orange.

A group of kids walked by, talking loudly amongst themselves. Bobby recognized Willy the Creep, now dressed in a dull, gray robe with Siphon poking out of his breast pocket. Willy walked beside a tall girl with high cheekbones and dirty-blonde hair. Everyone in the group, including Willy, seemed to flock around her except for a small, mousy boy with spiky hair who trailed a few yards behind.

"Who's that?" asked Bobby, gesturing to the blonde girl.

"Oh, that's Ashley," said Lily with a sour expression.

"What's her deal?" said Bobby. "Why are so many other kids following her?"

"They're following her because she's the headmistress's daughter, and the most talented student at the academy. Both of which she never lets anyone forget."

"Sounds adorable. What about the kid behind them?"

"Who, the young kid? That's Jinx, Ashley's little brother. Brilliant—knows more about anima than most of the instructors here," said Lily, "and he's only eleven."

"Just make sure you're not around if he ever tries to use his abilities," said Trevor. "He's another kid who has his nickname for a reason."

Ashley and her entourage headed straight for them. Lily let out a soft groan as the group came to a stop.

"So you're the new kid, huh?" said Ashley, hands on hips and head cocked to one side. "I heard you performed some big telekinesis stunt back home. Got any talent, or was it just luck?"

Bobby stared up at Ashley from his seat at the table. "Honestly, I have no idea."

Ashley shook her head in disgust. "Typical. Newbies like you never have a clue 'til they set something on fire. Still, an earthquake? That's impressive. Why don't you—"

"Why don't *you* leave him alone?" said Trevor.

Ashley flashed Trevor an icy glare. "Relax, I'm just trying to do the kid a favor. Something you obviously never appreciated."

"Appreciated? You mean like how you only liked me because of my talent?"

"You never did see the big picture, always too concerned with other people's feelings."

As the two of them traded barbs, Bobby ducked his head close to Lily. "What am I missing?"

"The two of them used to hang out," said Lily. "When he saw the way she treated other students with less talent, he bailed. She's hated him for it ever since."

"I see," said Bobby, turning back to the larger conversation.

"So what do you say, Bobby?" said Ashley. "Care to make something of yourself, or do you want to keep wasting your time with these losers?"

Bobby paused as if pondering the issue. "Sorry, Ashley. You

and your friends aren't really my type."

Ashley's eyes narrowed. "Your type? What exactly is your type, Bobby? Skilled? Talented? Naturally gifted?"

"Modest?" mumbled Lily.

"Humble?" said Bobby.

The dining hall fell deathly quiet. Siphon bobbed up and down on Willy's shoulder, chittering loudly. Nobody else moved. One of the boys at Ashley's side raised a hand to cover a laugh.

Finally, Ashley cleared her throat. "I'm going to cut you a break because you're new and don't know any better. In a week or two, when you're failing all your classes, come find me. I'll show you how winners do things around here. In the meantime, I suggest you learn some manners, or the next time you talk to me like that, you'll find out exactly why I'm the most talented student here since my mother."

Bobby waited until Ashley and the rest of her gang left before turning back to his new friends. "Wow, you were right," he said. "She really is a witch."

—◦◦◦—

Attending his first classes, Bobby was surprised to learn that a good portion of his instruction consisted of mundane topics, including math, science, and foreign languages. He even had a class in comparative religions scheduled for next semester.

Even more surprising was discovering that they used technology, and had science labs outfitted with state-of-the-art equipment. At dinner, Trevor told him that the monks still clung to the old ways, but the academics believed in using every means possible to accomplish their goal of understanding anima. And so they brought all sorts of technologies to the Jade Academy in order to aid them in their studies.

"How could a computer possibly help me learn to use my power?" Bobby asked Trevor. "It doesn't even have internet access."

"Beats me," said Trevor. "I usually just play solitaire when the instructor's not looking."

The more he saw, the more frustrated Bobby became. What use was there in learning algebra if his future lay in learning to wield the power within? He tried to focus during evening classes but nodded off several times, only to be jolted awake by nightmares of his parents' car accident.

That night, Bobby lay on his hard, lumpy pallet contemplating his future. In the morning he would start training with Master Jong and hopefully learn to control his special abilities. *I'll do whatever it takes to get revenge on Cassandra.*

Despite his new resolution, he stared at the stones on the ceiling for a long time before sleep finally found him.

CHAPTER 6

Bobby dressed quickly, eager to distance himself from his tiny bed and the visions that clung there. Despite his restless night, he felt awake and alert as he rushed to the dining hall to eat a quick meal of cheese blintzes and scrambled eggs before his session with Master Jong.

Shoveling the last of the eggs into his mouth, he washed them down with a glass of orange juice, sprang from the table, and raced for the courtyard. On the steps of the main entrance, he found a group of students setting up for yoga and asked them to point out Master Jong. A young girl with dimples and a long ponytail pointed to the far side of the clearing.

At first Bobby thought the girl was messing with him. The person in the distance looked like a child. As he drew closer, however, Bobby realized it was a monk after all. Probably less than five feet tall, the man sat with his legs crossed, eyes closed, and petite hands resting lightly in his lap. He wore a sky-blue robe trimmed with white lotus blossoms embroidered at the cuffs and collar. The baby-faced monk made no movement as Bobby approached.

"Excuse me. Are you Master Jong?"

The man gave no reply.

"I'm Bobby Ether. I'm here for my instruction."

Bobby sat beside the tiny monk.

"So, what are we working on?"

No response. *Maybe that girl was pointing to someone else.* Bobby glanced around, but there was no one else even remotely close. "Well, this is just great."

Bobby folded his legs and placed his hands in his lap in imitation of the monk's pose. He closed his eyes and tried to imagine what he was supposed to be learning. Nothing came to mind.

He sat there for two minutes. Five. Ten. Finally, he stood. "This is a complete waste of my time."

As he turned to go, the monk opened his eyes, revealing faded, blue-gray pupils. "Giving up so soon?"

"I wasn't . . . I'm not," stammered Bobby. "You were just sitting there. Heck, I wasn't sure I was even in the right place."

"But the young girl on the stairs told you where to go."

Bobby's mouth fell open. "How did you know that?"

Master Jong dismissed the question with a wave. "You knew the truth, and yet you chose to doubt it."

"I thought perhaps she was mistaken."

"Could you not sense the truth?"

"That would be a neat trick," said Bobby, finally starting to like the conversation. "Is that something you can teach me?"

"Truth is something everyone must learn for themselves."

"So that's a *no*, then," said Bobby with a frown.

"What is the truth, Bobby? Whether something is true or false, right or wrong, is often based on a person's point of view."

"I always thought right and wrong were things everyone knew instinctually," said Bobby.

Master Jong raised an eyebrow. "Tell me, Bobby, did you know that the academics possess scrolls of ancient wisdom? To my people, these texts are sacred. The academics allow us access but, in return, expect our assistance in training students and running the academy. Is it wrong for the academics to do this? Should my people complain that we are asked to serve, or be grateful that we are allowed access for a service many of us would gladly give anyway?"

Bobby threw up his hands. "I get it. Life is complicated. Now are we going to get to the lesson, or are you just going to badger me with questions?"

"Once again I see that you have much to learn. The lesson, my young student, has already begun."

—⋙—

An hour later, Bobby sat on the grass beside Master Jong, tasked with learning a meditation technique called "sitting in stillness." The goal was to count his breaths, starting over whenever stray thoughts entered his mind. So far, the furthest he'd gotten was four.

Perhaps sensing Bobby's unrest, Master Jong broke his lotus position to regard his student. "What is it that troubles you?"

Bobby frowned. "I still don't get why I have to learn all this breathing and meditation stuff. What does any of this have to do with me learning to access my powers?"

"That which some cultures call *chi* or *ki* is actually anima propelled by the movement of cerebrospinal fluid up and down your spine. Posture, breathing, and focus are what will gain you conscious control of this movement, which, in turn, generates the energy you need to perform the skills you seek to learn."

"I thought I was supposed to be getting power from nature. People keep talking to me about nature and the universal energy all around me."

"Ideally we get our energy from the environment," said Master Jong. "But in the absence of a natural source, it is essential to be able to generate your own. Otherwise, any power you use is drawn from your reserves."

"Is that why I felt sick to my stomach after the tremor?"

Master Jong nodded. "You drained yourself because you drew on energy you did not have to spare; similar to burning fat instead of carbohydrates, but far more dangerous."

Bobby's frown deepened. "Well, I still think this is a waste of time."

"And I think there is a deeper reason behind your discontent," said Master Jong. "Tell me, what is it you see when you close your eyes that troubles you so much?"

Bobby balked. "I have no idea what you're talking about."

"I can see the pain written on your face," said Master Jong gently. "I can help, but first you must trust me."

Bobby stared off into the distance. "It's the accident," he said finally. "I can't get it out of my head." Master Jong waited patiently for him to continue. "It's weird. I see the collision in my mind. I hear my parents scream as the truck slams into their car. But then I see them climb out unharmed. They're on the curb, safe, when the truck morphs into a giant grizzly bear and attacks. Their own car morphs into a white bear and tries to protect them, but it's smaller and badly injured from the accident. The grizzly defeats it easily, ripping its throat out before turning on my parents."

"Very interesting," said Master Jong. "And were there actual bears at the time of the incident?"

Bobby gave him a quizzical look. "On the streets of LA? Are you crazy?"

"My apologies," said the tiny monk. "I am unfamiliar with that particular locale. In any case, I find the presence of these animals most intriguing. Perhaps the significance goes beyond the actual memory itself."

Bobby perked up. "Like a vision? Some kind of power?"

"Doubtful," said Master Jong. "More likely, it is a message from your subconscious."

Bobby groaned and threw up his arms. "I don't care about my stupid subconscious. My parents didn't survive that accident, and they weren't mauled by a bear."

Master Jong frowned. "Regardless, I would like to consult with a colleague of mine from the West. In his culture, the bear can be a powerful spirit guide sent to help or warn someone in times of need. Perhaps my colleague can provide more insight into understanding your dream."

"Knock yourself out. Are we done here?" said Bobby, rising. "Because if you aren't going to teach me anything useful today, then I would just as soon leave."

"Words cannot be written on the pages of a book that is closed."

"Whatever that means," said Bobby, and he turned and walked away.

—⚏—

The following day broke sunny as Bobby joined Master Jong in the courtyard to continue their lessons. The tiny monk wore a shiny yellow robe with lavender trim that glittered in the warm morning light. They set to work quickly. If anything, Bobby's ability to concentrate was even worse than the day before.

Tired of getting stuck when meditating, Bobby opened his eyes and stretched his limbs. A group of monks sat on the other side of the clearing. None so much as twitched. *Show-offs*, thought Bobby.

A man in the back row had his hood pulled up. Bobby paused. A hooded monk wasn't strange, but this man had long raven hair cascading from beneath his cowl. Virtually all the monks were either bald, had buzz-cuts, or wore tight topknots. The man reached up and pulled back his hood, revealing a weathered, brown face with deep cracks like sunbaked clay.

Bobby rocked back. Even from a distance, there was no mistaking the man from the headmistress's photos—the one who murdered the driver of the car that killed his parents: Cassandra's assassin.

The man's eyes popped open, staring right at Bobby, locking their gazes. Then the assassin mouthed something, and, although he was over fifty feet away, Bobby heard the man's dry, gravelly voice as if it had spoken right in his ear.

"Cassandra sent me—"

Bobby sprang to his feet. He took a step toward the man but faltered. *No, I'm not ready yet.*

Apparently mistaking his actions for frustration, Master Jong stood. "I'm sorry you are having such a difficult time with today's lesson. Perhaps if we—"

"I can't do this yet. I'm not ready," repeated Bobby.

Master Jong appraised him coolly. "Perhaps it is best that we adjourn for today."

Bobby was halfway across the courtyard before Master Jong could say another word. Bobby would have his revenge against Cassandra—as well as any henchmen she might send after him. But he needed power first.

At the top of the stairs, Bobby slipped in with a group of students heading back from early morning yoga. Safely nestled in their midst, he turned and looked back at the group of monks meditating on the lawn. The big one with the earthen skin and raven hair was nowhere to be seen.

CHAPTER 7

Bobby pushed the rice pilaf on his plate around with his fork. The smell of the saffron turned his stomach. The taste was even worse: cardboard mixed with paste. Lunch was normally his favorite meal, but today he wouldn't have had an appetite even if the food were gourmet.

Days had quickly turned into weeks, and still he struggled with his studies. Despite every effort, his sessions with Master Jong continued to be an unmitigated disaster. Not only was he failing to achieve results, but the lack of progress left him increasingly disappointed. No, *disappointed* wasn't the right word. *Humiliated.* By now, the entire school knew that the new boy was a failure.

To make matters worse, he had caught several more glimpses of Cassandra's assassin. A few days earlier, he spotted the longhaired man among a pack of monks tending to the gardens. The day before, Bobby saw him during yoga lessons in the courtyard. Thankfully, Bobby was among other students both times. Averting his eyes, he'd stuck close to his peers.

These events put him in a foul mood that spilled over into the classroom. Just last period, he'd lashed out at a boy in his math class, insulting him when they couldn't agree on the proper way to solve a quadratic equation. Ultimately, Bobby had been proven wrong. He wanted to crawl into a hole after that. He wasn't just incompetent; he was a jerk to boot.

"Hey, Bobby," said Lily, sitting next to him in the dining hall. "How was class today?"

"Don't ask."

She set a hand on his shoulder. "Try not to be discouraged. A lot of people struggle at the beginning."

Bobby pushed the rice on his plate into a hill. Then he flipped the fork over and jammed the handle in to make a hole, creating a volcano. Lily looked on patiently. After a while, Bobby looked up.

"I'm a fraud," he said. "I can't do anything Master Jong asks me to do. I'm so embarrassed."

Lily gave him a warm smile. "I'm sure you'll get better. What exactly are you having trouble with?"

Bobby thought for a moment, not wanting to reveal the depths of his failure. "I guess my biggest problem is understanding the concepts Master Jong talks about. He talks about *chi*, and balancing, and cleansing my *chakras*. It makes it really tough to do what he asks when I don't know what the heck he's talking about."

"Well, that's perfectly understandable," said Lily. "Not everyone grew up at the academy. You could try the library in your free time. Maybe that would help?"

"I've already tried that," said Bobby. "Half the writing is more difficult to understand than my classes. The other half is written in foreign languages. There aren't even any pictures!"

"Well then, we could make a study group. Maybe there are things that I could help you with."

"I appreciate the offer, but I've already tried talking to Trevor. He knows how to do a bunch of the stuff I'm trying to learn but can't really explain *how* he does it. Let's face it; I'm just a loser." He smashed the volcano into a mangled mess of rice and vegetables.

Lily put a hand on his arm. "Maybe what you need is someone who knows more than Trevor or me."

"You mean someone like Master Jong? Gee, what a great idea."

"I mean someone you can talk to. Someone you aren't going to get frustrated, embarrassed, or intimidated by when you have questions."

"Forget it. Aside from you and Trevor, there isn't anyone who I'd be comfortable working with and isn't going to laugh at me whenever I fail."

Lily gently turned his shoulders so that he faced the table behind them. "I think you're wrong. In fact, I know just the right person."

—◊◊◊—

"Hey, Jinx. Mind if I join you?"

Ashley's spiky-haired little brother lifted his gaze from the book propped next to his soup bowl, took one look at Bobby, and dropped it again.

"Bobby Ether. Age: sixteen. Born and raised in Los Angeles. Duration of tenure at the Jade Academy: twenty-seven days. Acquired level of anima abilities: negligible. You're struggling in your studies and have come to take my sister up on her offer," he surmised bluntly. "Sorry, I don't know where she is."

A few rows down, Willy the Creep stared at them hard before turning back to his meal. Bobby lowered his head and said in a hushed tone, "I didn't come over here to talk to your sister. I came to talk to you."

Jinx paused with a spoon full of soup halfway to his mouth. "You want to talk to me about my sister," he said. It wasn't a question.

"No, Jinx. I want to talk to you—just you."

Jinx set down his fork, perplexed. "What is it?"

"I was hoping we could hang out. Maybe we could meet in the library later and study together?"

Jinx's eyes grew big at the mention of the library, then quickly faded. "Oh, I see. You want help with your homework."

"No, no," said Bobby quickly. "All my homework is done. Actually, I was hoping you could teach me a little about the esoteric arts and energy theory. You know, like extracurricular studies."

"Are you crazy? Know why I'm called Jinx? Everything I do backfires. I once tried to show someone how to levitate a book. Instead, it burst into flames. I really liked that book."

"Okay, I get it," said Bobby. "Still, maybe we could just hang out. I am sure I could learn stuff just by hanging with you."

Jinx opened his mouth to reply and shut it.

"What's going on here?" said a voice from behind Bobby. "Is this loser picking on you?"

Bobby turned to see Ashley, flanked by two upperclassmen.

"We were just having a friendly chat," said Bobby.

"I wasn't talking to you, *loser*," snapped Ashley. "I was talking to my brother." Jinx averted his eyes. "To think that I actually offered to help you. Good thing I didn't. Turns out I'm allergic to losers."

"I guess I deserve that," said Bobby, rising to leave.

But Ashley wasn't finished.

"Hey, boys, why don't you show this loser what we do to people who mess with my little brother?" The upperclassmen stepped up, eclipsing Bobby's field of vision.

Jinx shot up from the table and ducked between them.

"Bobby wasn't bothering me," he said, hands out wide. "Honest, he was just asking me for help with his homework, weren't you, Bobby?"

Bobby gulped. "Yeah, those quadratic equations are really kicking my butt."

Ashley smirked. "I heard about that. You really should make

more of an effort to fit in around here. Keep it up and even my little brother won't want to talk to you."

"Thanks for the advice," said Bobby. "I'll keep that in mind next time I want to make friends like yours."

Ashley's face twisted as she tried to decide if she'd been insulted. Finally she walked off. "Whatever. Just stay out of my way."

One of upperclassmen gave Bobby a sharp elbow in the ribs on the way past. "Go find someone else to help you with your stupid homework, or next time quadratic equations won't be the only thing kicking your butt."

—◊—

That night after evening sessions, Bobby went straight to the library. It took a while to locate Jinx, sitting alone at a desk tucked in the back of the library, far from the throng of other students in the main reading room. Stacks of books were piled so high that Bobby thought Jinx might end up buried alive if they fell.

"Hello, Jinx," said Bobby.

Jinx looked up from a tome on entomology. "Bobby Ether, age: sixteen—"

"How about you just call me Bobby, okay?"

Jinx set the book down. "I didn't think you would actually show up."

"I told you I wanted to hang out."

"Give it time. It'll pass."

"This looks like an interesting read," said Bobby, picking up one of the smaller books from the table. "*Path Notes of an American Ninja Master*, huh?" He flipped through the pages, looking for images of men in black, swinging swords and nunchucks. "Does it teach you how to become a ninja?" said Bobby. "That would be cool!"

"Actually, I am reading it in an effort to reconcile it with this other book," he said, picking up *Taking the Quantum Leap* by

Fred Alan Wolf. "I'm exploring how the Kundalini experience can be expressed by way of quantum physics. It's my theory that the meditation practices discussed in chapter five, which allow for the awaking of the hypothalamus and cerebellum, and also the conscious conduction of cerebral spinal fluid, actually involves the manipulation at the subatomic of—"

"Yeah, that sounds really exciting," said Bobby, setting the book back down. "But what do you do for fun?"

"That is fun. The part that talks about how Schrödinger's cat is both alive and dead at the same time is fascinating. Here, let me show you."

"That's okay," said Bobby. "I would rather save the surprise for class."

"This stuff isn't taught in any of the classes."

"Well, you're only eleven," Bobby reminded him. "I bet they get to it later on."

"I've already completed all the course classes up to and including the graduation exam. Most of my study now is either one-on-one with the professors or self-study."

Bobby gave a low whistle. "That's impressive. But don't you ever stop reading and play games or something?"

"The paradox of Schrödinger's cat is a type of game. You have to be able to visualize and hold in your mind the possibility that—"

"I mean a real game. You know, like checkers or backgammon."

"Children's games involving luck and chance hold no interest for me. As we both know, they are based almost entirely on probability, a field I have already studied at length."

"Well, then you simply haven't played the right games, or at least not with the right person. Come on," said Bobby, snatching a stack of books off the table. "It's time someone introduced you to your inner child."

"Hey, give that back," said Jinx, giving chase. "Where are you going?"

Bobby yelled back over his shoulder, "To have fun!"

Bobby zigged and zagged his way through the aisles. *Wow, this place is huge*, he thought as four more rows materialized before him. He glanced back to make sure Jinx saw him before picking a new path.

He made a few more turns and came to a halt. This section looked different. Wooden shelves were replaced by alcoves carved directly into the stone. Within the niches sat items of every shape and size. There were boxes, jars, and metal containers, along with an assortment of objects covered in sheets. He stepped over to the nearest wall, kicking up a cloud of dust as he lifted a heavy tarp to reveal a half dozen oil paintings and a statue of a horse standing on its hind legs. Bobby sneezed as he set the tarp back down.

A second later, Jinx appeared at his side, wheezing and out of breath. "Hey, no fair running off like that," said Jinx, smiling.

"Where are we?" asked Bobby.

Jinx swiveled his head as if seeing his surroundings for the first time. "The archives," he said, dropping his voice. "We're not supposed to be in here."

"Why? What is this place?"

"It's where they keep all the old stuff."

"What sort of stuff?"

"Everything from the school's history—old textbooks, study guides, research papers by old professors, photographs, even people's furniture and personal possessions."

"Why would anyone want to keep all that junk?"

"Knowledge is sacred. You never know when something from the past will be important to the future."

"And what's down there?" Bobby asked, pointing to the end of the hall where the ground sloped downward, disappearing into darkness.

"You don't really think that all the stuff from centuries of existence can fit on just one floor, do you? There are a bunch of lower sections, each one bigger than the last. Heaven only knows what's down there."

Bobby made a scary face, wriggling his fingers at his young friend. "Sounds *creeeepy.*"

"There are stories about the stuff in the lower levels—mummies and giant machines, top-secret experiments that were conducted by old headmasters. I've read essays that claim it's all a bunch of nonsense. Still, whenever someone goes missing from the academy, rumors always spread that they disappeared in the archives."

"This stuff looks harmless enough," said Bobby, trying in vain to pry the lid off one of the metal bins. Instead, his efforts sent up another billow of dust.

From the depths of his voluminous robes, Jinx pulled out an inhaler and took a puff.

"Hey, what's that for?"

"Asthma," said Jinx. "Had it ever since I was little."

"Why don't the monks heal you like they do everyone else around here?"

"Can't," said Jinx. "Something about my chi makes everything backfire. Almost died from them trying to heal me when I was young. This is one of the few medicines Mom allows in from the outside.

"Speaking of Mother, I was in here with her years ago. I found a really interesting treatise written by one of the professors from the sixteenth century about the typhus epidemic and how he believed that those who survived exposure developed a greater capability to control their anima. I'm sure I can find it again—"

"Maybe some other time," said Bobby, abandoning his efforts to open the box. "Come on. Let's head back to the common room."

Jinx led the way to the main reading room. As soon as Bobby had his bearings, he took over, steering them to a room where groups of students sat at round tables, talking and laughing.

"What's in here?" asked Jinx.

"Seriously? You've been at the academy your entire life and you don't know what's in this room? I've only been here a month and I know what's in here."

"All I know is that you're allowed to talk in here, which makes it too noisy to read."

Bobby frowned. "They're not just talking, Jinx. They're playing. This is the game room."

Jinx raised an eyebrow as Bobby led him to a small checkout counter in the back corner where a shriveled prune of a monk sat filing catalog cards using the Dewey Decimal System.

"Let's start simple," said Bobby, turning to the monk. "Checkers please."

Without a reply, the monk rose from the chair slowly, as if pulling up roots, and shambled over to the back cabinet. He shuffled back even slower, handed the boys the requested game, and resumed cataloging without so much as a glance at them.

Selecting a table off to the side, Bobby set up the board while Jinx read the instruction manual from cover to cover. *It's checkers!* Bobby wanted to say, but he kept his mouth shut as the younger boy finished examining the rulebook.

Bobby won the first game easily as Jinx moved his pieces seemingly at random. In the second game, Jinx developed a strategy and Bobby struggled to win. Jinx dominated the third game.

"King me!" said Jinx with a shy grin. "That's my fourth king this game."

"You're really good at this," said Bobby.

"It's simple, really. I just applied a basic algorithm such that whenever you angle your pieces in one direction I—"

"That's great. Let's play something else. Checkers is for babies anyway."

They packed up the game and Bobby swapped it for Risk. Once again, Bobby set up the game while Jinx read the instructions. The first game was a battle as Bobby's armies marched across Africa and eventually conquered Asia to secure victory. The second game was a blowout. Bobby's armies barely had control over Western Europe before Jinx had the rest of the world under his dominion.

"Another game?" asked Bobby, unperturbed by his losses.

"Sure," said Jinx. "But how about something a bit more challenging this time? Chess?"

Bobby smiled. The younger boy sat on the edge of his seat, bouncing up and down, his precious books forgotten on the floor.

"Oh, I get it. You think it's fun to pick on the big kid," teased Bobby.

"This was your idea," giggled Jinx.

They played chess, and this time, Jinx didn't lose at all. Instead, he systematically took every one of Bobby's pieces until Bobby was left with nothing but his king and a pawn.

"Why do I get the feeling that you've played this one before?" asked Bobby. Jinx grinned and took the pawn.

They played a few more matches, then switched to other board games. They'd just finished their third game of Battleship when the librarian announced, "The library will be closing in ten minutes."

"Not a moment too soon," said Jinx. "You were about to sink my cruiser."

"Yeah, well, this game is largely luck," said Bobby with a grin. "What time is it, anyway?"

"Almost midnight," said Jinx.

"Are you gonna get in trouble for being out this late?"

"I'm always here until closing, just usually in the back. One of the librarians is probably checking there now and wondering where I am," said Jinx with a chuckle. "He definitely won't think to look for me here."

"What about Ashley? Doesn't she come looking for you?"

"Ashley hangs out with her friends at night. She never comes to the library except to give me homework to do for her or one of the others."

"And your mom—I mean, the headmistress. Don't you ever spend time with her?"

"I see her sometimes, but not in public. Ever since we were old enough to start classes, she treats Ashley and me like all the other students. She checks in on us sometimes, but usually it's just to see how classes are going."

"I would give anything to have my mom here where I could see her and spend time with her," said Bobby with a distant gaze.

"Well, you can be part of my family now," said Jinx. "We can be brothers."

"Deal," said Bobby, and the two of them packed up and left the library, side by side.

———

At lunch the following day, Bobby told Lily and Trevor about his adventures with Jinx. Trevor's expression grew cloudy when he heard about the two boys hanging out together.

"Ashley isn't going to like you spending time with her little brother," he said.

"I'm not going to be bullied into who I can and can't be friends with," said Bobby. "Besides, Jinx is actually a pretty cool kid."

"Sure, but—"

Lily set a hand on Trevor's arm. "Tell us what happened in the archives," she told Bobby. "I hear that's where all the secrets are hidden."

"Honestly, I wouldn't be surprised if that's true," said Trevor. "This place has an amazing history." He explained that the Jade Academy was originally a Buddhist monastery. Back before the change, the monks lived in almost complete isolation.

"Part of the reason this site was selected was the jade in the tunnels below," said Trevor. "The type of jade in this mountain is extremely rare. By mining it, the monks were able to trade with the outside world for anything they wanted."

To increase its value, the monks taught themselves to carve the jade into jewelry, sculptures, and trinkets. Over time, they enhanced their artistry until their works became the stuff of legend.

The most coveted objects were puzzle boxes, which each contained a secret chamber. Upon selling a puzzle box, a monk opened the box, revealed the hidden space, and allowed the new owner to place an item within. In this way, the puzzle boxes became synonymous with secrets.

But that wasn't the only reason the puzzle boxes were so prized. Legend held that no one except a monk had ever opened a puzzle box without breaking it. Experiments of every kind failed to reveal how the devices worked. As a result, the legend of the puzzle boxes grew, and with it their prestige. At the height of production, wealthy kings and noblemen from all over the world paid huge sums for the fascinating novelties.

Ultimately, the attention garnered by the puzzle boxes proved to be too much. As more and more traders flocked to the sanctuary, the monks feared that production interfered with their religious mandates. In the end, the monks suspended production in order to protect their privacy.

After mining operations ceased, the rest of the world slowly forgot about the temple cloistered deep in the Himalayas. Within a few generations, only a handful of puzzle boxes remained. Lately, however, rumors had surfaced that puzzle boxes were reappearing on the market, causing speculation that someone inside the Jade Academy had revived the old craft.

"So, this whole place is based on this precious-jade industry?" asked Bobby, looking around and seeing the coarse walls of the dining hall in a whole new light.

"The stuff about the original trade is definitely true," said Trevor, "but the stuff about the puzzle boxes is mainly just myth and rumor. Either way, there is a far more important reason why this place has endured for so long."

"And what's that?" asked Bobby, leaning forward in anticipation.

"Jade is just a byproduct," said Trevor. "This place is a fount for the anima we work with and study."

"What do you mean?" asked Bobby, bewildered.

"Shortly after establishing the monastery, many of the monks noticed dramatic changes. They were able to meditate longer and deeper, becoming more connected to the oneness of all things while reaching higher levels of enlightenment and tranquility. More monks from this place experienced *kundalini*—or 'full enlightenment'—in a single generation than the rest of the world combined."

"That's amazing." Bobby leaned back in his chair, absorbing everything Trevor had said. "So, there's something inside the mountain that generates anima?"

Trevor nodded. "That's the theory."

"And the monks don't leave because they want to be close to the source, and because the academics hold their sacred texts, right?" asked Bobby. Trevor looked surprised, prompting Bobby to add, "Master Jong told me all about it during our first training session."

Trevor shrugged. "Supposedly it's no big deal. The monks don't seem to mind, and the academics never restrict access to the scrolls."

"But not everyone is okay with it," said Bobby.

"Yeah, that sounds an awful lot like oppression to me," said Lily. "Why would the academics need to keep the scrolls if there wasn't tension?"

Bobby rubbed his chin. "You're right, Lily. It doesn't make sense . . . unless there's something else going on besides a simple difference of opinion—something that the academics need to make sure the monks don't rebel against."

Bobby pondered the issue for days, never coming to a suitable conclusion.

CHAPTER 8

Divine Master Whimpley, spiritual leader of the Order of the Jade Temple, squirmed in the overstuffed chair like an ant under a magnifying glass. From across the desk, Headmistress Grayson took in every detail: the man's watery eyes, his weak chin, his narrow face pinched with anxiety, the way he wriggled in his seat whenever she gazed at him. *If only his wits were as sharp as his nose.*

Actually, she reminded herself, *he only appears dull witted.* Here was a man who had managed to get himself elected spiritual leader of his order despite being one of its least spiritual members. His guile, not his religious devotion, had earned him his position. This same guile made him perfect for her purposes.

She waited until the man's hands began to tremble. With an icy stare, she pushed the report across the table, directly under his offensive nose.

"Just so we're clear," she said, "you're telling me that after all the trouble I went through to acquire our newest student, we have nothing to show for it?"

"He's a clever kid. He's catching up on his studies very quickly given that he never learned most of our curriculum at his old school."

"I don't care how he's doing in algebra," snapped the headmistress. "You're telling me he has no aptitude whatsoever?"

The monk wrung his hands. "None that we can discern, Mistress. But perhaps you should talk to Master Jong. He is the one entrusted with the child's development, after all."

The headmistress steepled her hands. "I am aware of your decision to use Master Jong and must say I am concerned, given his reputation as a maverick."

"Of everyone in the order, he is by far the most gifted," said Whimpley. "I would teach the child myself except—"

"Except you're about as talented in the anima arts as you are sincerely devoted to your faith," interrupted the headmistress.

The monk shrank back as if slapped. "Forgive me, Headmistress Grayson; I know it is not my place to question, but is it possible that the boy doesn't belong here? We cannot train what is not there."

"You think the earthquake was a fluke?"

"Reports of the event could have been exaggerated."

The headmistress waved dismissively. "There is always residual energy, even in situations where eyewitness accounts are unreliable."

"What about the ledger?" asked the monk. "Perhaps his talents are simply more esoteric than what we are trying to cultivate."

The headmistress lifted a heavy, leather-bound ledger from her desk, examining its thick spine. "I've been over it a dozen times. Aside from revealing the boy's existence, there is nothing of value in it. We never sent the psychics to scan that area, that much is clear, but there is nothing in the ledger about the boy, or what his genealogy or abilities may be."

"What about the computer systems?"

"You mean the missing computer files that prompted me to search the hard copies in the first place?" snapped the headmistress. "Clearly someone sabotaged the data. Thankfully, the backup ledgers are all written in code. The would-be saboteur probably didn't even know the two were related."

"You were very wise to consult the old records."

"Those missing computer files were deleted for a reason. I intend to discover what that reason is," said the headmistress.

"Perhaps the reason will reveal itself in time."

"Master Whimpley," she said, her voice cracking like a whip, "I do not sit idly by and wait for time to reveal its secrets. Headmasters have been replaced for far less than failing to detect the presence of a talent such as what this boy appears to be capable of."

"But it wasn't your fault," said the monk. "If you hadn't noticed the missing files—"

"Don't worry; I intend to have Simpkins and Hayward perform a thorough investigation to figure out why the boy wasn't in our system."

The scrawny monk shuddered.

"Relax," said the headmistress. "You won't be working with Simpkins and Hayward. Heaven knows I have enough fiascos to deal with as it is. All that you need to worry about is producing results in our new pupil."

Whimpley let out a heavy sigh, but she couldn't tell whether it was from relief or fear. She couldn't have cared less either way. Looking the weasel-faced monk square in the eye, she said, "I am fully aware of the backroom dealings you used to gain your current position. I also know about the clandestine mining and carving operations. I even know that you hope to someday leverage that influence into a position within the Core."

She pressed on as Whimpley balked, dismissing his umbrage with a wave. "All of that is of no importance to me. What *is* important is that you know that I know and what it would mean if I made that information public. Failure is not an option, Whimpley. Unlock the boy's potential at any cost. Do I make myself clear?"

The monk swallowed hard, nodded, and leapt from his seat to the door.

No sooner did the door click shut behind Divine Master Whimpley than Headmistress Grayson withdrew a long-necked crystal decanter and matching shot glass from her desk drawer. Filling the glass, she tipped her head back and drained it.

Just a tonic to take the edge off, she thought as she poured a second shot.

More than a dozen reports lay scattered across her desk, all dealing with the Ether boy and the effort spent to obtain him. There were police reports, incident reports, reports dealing with the removal and destruction of physical evidence, reports detailing hypnosis procedures used to coerce witnesses . . . the list went on.

Next came the letter from her superiors. Penned by hand on thick stock, the elegant style did nothing to mask their displeasure with recent events. Her competency and judgment were being questioned, especially with the news that the boy had made no progress since his arrival.

Trying not to dwell on the negative, she forced herself to read on. According to the note, the off-site project run by her superiors had reached a critical stage. Ideally, they wanted blood samples from fully manifested specimens. Barring full manifestation, they would require the entire specimen for experimentation. It didn't take much to figure out that either case involved the Ether kid.

Setting the letter aside, the headmistress picked up the progress report from Master Jong. Three times she'd tried to read it from start to finish, and each time she had to stop, lest her anger overwhelm her. A soft knock on the door interrupted her thoughts. Quickly she replaced the decanter and snifter into her desk drawer. The door cracked open. She did not stand.

"Ah, Master Jong. Thank you for coming," she said. The tiny man stood in the doorway, making no move to enter the room.

"You asked to see me," said the monk.

"Please, come in." The headmistress emerged from behind her desk and moved to one of the overstuffed chairs. "Have a seat."

Master Jong crossed tentatively to the proffered chair and sat, his feet dangling over the edge like a kid in the principal's office. He folded his hands in his lap and waited.

"You mentioned in your note that you believe the Ether boy is blocked, is that correct?" she said.

Master Jong nodded. "Indeed, that is what I wrote in my report."

"And what do you attribute this to?"

"As I am sure you are aware, this type of blockage is usually the result of overstimulation. This is a fairly common condition for children from heavily industrialized societies where people are constantly bombarded with sensory overload from technological devices such as television, movies, video games, and the internet. The subconscious needed to access one's inner self cannot surface with so much interference."

"So you're saying that the boy can't connect with his subconscious because he watched too much TV growing up?"

"That is one factor, but not the only one. He is obviously upset about the death of his parents. He will not discuss it with me, but I have no doubt that their passing weighs heavily on him. He carries too much anger to focus."

"Strong emotion can be as much of a boon as an obstacle," said Headmistress Grayson. "Why not use his emotions to your advantage? After all, they fuel his purpose. Without them, he would not wish to study at all."

"What you ask can be done. Anger and grief may, in fact, be wielded as weapons. But that is not his only problem. Apart from being unable to connect with his energy, it appears to be shielded. Even if I could teach him to use his anger to connect to his power, it would do him no good."

"What do you mean?" asked the headmistress. "I am not aware of any of our other students suffering from this 'shielding' you describe."

"It is a very rare condition. I have only seen it once before, many years ago—a student named Jimmy Thompson. It turned out the boy had tremendous power but no desire to use it for fear of hurting others. As a result, his subconscious shielded itself so that even if he were able to sense it, it would be inert and worthless."

The headmistress arched an eyebrow. "So you are saying that the Ether boy may have tremendous power locked away within him?"

Master Jong shrugged. "There is no way to know for sure. The source of his power is hidden deep within, even from himself."

"But surely you are more skilled than he is. Why can you not sense it?" asked the headmistress.

"It is like trying to judge the brightness of a light that is hidden behind a curtain. The light could be bright, burning with the intensity of a thousand stars, or it might be as weak as the flickering flame of a waning candle. I can see light coming from around the edges, but there is no way to know for sure how bright the source is until the shield is removed."

"So, once the shield is down, the boy will manifest to his full potential?"

"Possibly, but not necessarily. The boy's shield is a product of his subconscious and, as such, serves its own purpose, one that we currently do not know. Much like a window, we may draw back the curtain and gaze upon the other side and yet not have access to what lies beyond."

The headmistress's jaw tightened. "You had better hope that is not the case. I just spoke with Divine Master Whimpley. He assures me you are the right person for this assignment, but I know all about your history of insubordination. You will do as instructed or suffer the consequences. Use whatever means necessary, including the boy's anger and pain over the loss of his parents, to accomplish your task."

Master Jong's expression betrayed nothing. "As you say."

"Good. Now, how do you intend to get the shield down?"

"I have a plan. You will have to trust my judgment on this matter."

"I have been extremely lenient with you and your fellow monks during my reign. I even allow unlimited access to your sacred texts," said Headmistress Grayson. "But know this; my patience has limits. If you fail me, I will see to it that all access to the scrolls is cut off, not just for you, but for all the other monks as well."

"The others would surely rebel if you restricted access to the scrolls. It is the basis of our entire order."

"Perhaps," said the headmistress. "Though I do not think all of the monks are as pious as you believe. In any case, see to it that you and your colleagues train the students properly, and I won't need to test my theory."

"You shall have your results. However, you would be wise to keep in mind that oldest of adages."

"And what might that be?"

Master Jong made a show of standing and walking calmly to the door. When he reached the threshold, he looked back over his shoulder.

"Be careful what you wish for," he said. Then he slipped out the door and was gone.

The headmistress waited until the door clicked. With trembling hands, she removed the decanter and poured another shot of her secret tonic, draining it in a single pull.

CHAPTER 9

Two months slipped by with little change. Bobby fell into a tedious but not unpleasant routine at his new home. During the day, he attended classes and studied with Master Jong. At night, he alternated between studying on his own, hanging out with Trevor and Lily, and spending time in the library with Jinx. Sometimes Trevor or Lily joined them in the library, but mostly it was just the two of them. They played games and told jokes, acting for all the world like normal children.

By the end of the third month, Bobby saw signs of improvement in his meditation sessions. He could focus more deeply and concentrate for longer periods of time. Master Jong noticed as well. One day during their session, the tiny monk asked Bobby about the change.

"Hanging out with my friends seems to help me cope with the death of my parents," said Bobby. "It still hurts, but not as bad, like a noise that fades into the background instead of ringing right in my ear."

Master Jong nodded as though he'd been awaiting this news. "It is time you worked on balancing your mind and raising your level of awareness." He began teaching Bobby about *vipassana* and *raja* yoga meditation.

"No matter what the issue is, a person can always sense what to do if they are in tune with their purpose," said Master Jong. "Learn to observe yourself, identify your true nature, and find your answers within."

After practicing for several hours, Bobby stood and stretched. "I can feel this barrier inside me. I sense power on the other side—I just can't touch it."

"I am aware of the barrier erected by your subconscious. As to its purpose—this is what I do not know. Tell me, Bobby, are you holding onto something besides sadness over your parents' passing? Anger or resentment, perhaps?"

Bobby thought about Cassandra and the assassin she'd sent. "Why do you ask?"

Master Jong studied him with piercing blue-gray eyes. "Strong emotions can often help a person connect with their inner spirit. But you must be careful. Feelings are often amplified in such a state and can easily become overwhelming—sometimes with terrible results."

Cassandra's conversation with Simpkins and Hayward the night of his abduction popped into Bobby's head.

"Is that what happened to that Thompson kid?" he asked, recalling the name Cassandra mentioned.

If Master Jong was surprised by the question, he didn't show it. "Jimmy Thompson had a great deal of bottled-up anger."

"But he used that anger to break through his shield, didn't he?"

"It is true. Jimmy's anger gave him strength, but at a horrible cost. All that rage corrupted his power, twisting his otherwise gentle demeanor. He was never the same person after that."

Bobby barely heard this last part. He had the answer he wanted. He could use his hatred for Cassandra to break down his shield. Once that was done, he would use the unleashed power to gain his revenge.

—⚭—

At the end of Bobby's fourth full month, the headmistress announced a field trip to the forest below. Autumn descended upon the mountainside, turning the air crisp and the ground soft. Clouds visited frequently, bringing heavy rains and casting the monastery in perpetual gloom. Soon, winter would arrive in earnest, blanketing the entire area in heavy snow. But before then, while the forest was moist but not yet white, some of the rarest plants in the region sprang to life. Uncommon molds and fungi took advantage of the soggy season, growing in the dark hollows and secret lairs of the forest. It was these plants, used for medicinal and energy-enhancing purposes, which the faculty wanted to collect.

A note went up in the dining hall stating that a select group of students would descend to the forest floor to gather the rare herbs blooming there. Bobby was surprised to find his name on the list, along with Lily, Trevor, and Jinx.

After breakfast the following morning, Bobby joined Trevor and Lily in the main courtyard where they huddled together against the chilly morning breeze.

"What's he doing here?" said Bobby, gesturing toward Simpkins, who stood at the head of the group.

"He's the academic assigned to oversee the trip," said Lily. "Though it doesn't seem right to call him an academic. I'm not even sure what he does around here."

"Maybe he travels backward in time," quipped Trevor. "Just look at that outfit."

Simpkins wore a lilac shirt and narrow, orange tie beneath a lavender suit with white lapels sticking out like condor wings. A pair of shiny black wingtips poked out beneath his bellbottom pants.

"He was wearing a crazy suit like that the first time I saw him," said Bobby. "Doesn't he have anything else?"

"Guess not," said Trevor. "Why else would you wear dress shoes on an expedition to the forest?"

They talked as the rest of the group assembled. Bobby was surprised to see Ashley accompanied by the twin boys he'd seen her with in the mess hall. Brown haired with thick arms and even thicker necks, the twins glared at anyone in their path as they cleared room for Ashley in the middle of the gathering.

"Who are those two?" he asked Trevor.

His lanky friend followed his gaze.

"You mean Scratch and Sniff?" said Trevor.

"Don't be mean!" said Lily. "Their real names are the Tex-Mex twins, or at least that's what they call themselves."

"Yeah, but everyone else calls them Scratch and Sniff," said Trevor. "On account that one can't keep his hands out of his pants, and the other can't keep his fingers out of his nose."

Lily gave Trevor a playful slap on the shoulder. "You're terrible! But, come to think of it, I'm pretty sure neither of them was on the list."

Trevor smiled at Lily and rubbed his shoulder in pretend pain. "Looks like someone can't leave home without her flunkies," he said, eyeing Ashley.

A few moments later, Willy and Siphon joined Ashley and her cohorts. Shortly after, Jinx showed up. Simpkins took roll call and headed toward the main gate. The giant doors swung open and a small boy in a forest-green cloak crossed the courtyard. As the figure drew near, Bobby recognized the intricate pattern of lotus blossoms embroidered on the cloak and realized it wasn't a boy at all.

"I seek permission to join your expedition," said Master Jong.

Simpkins's lips drew so tight they all but disappeared. "Your presence is not needed, monk."

"Nevertheless, I need supplies from the village beyond the forest. I see no reason why I should go alone when you are about to depart. I can offer my services with your endeavor once my business in the village is done."

"We have no need of your assistance," said Simpkins brusquely.

Master Jong remained unfazed. "Still, you are ready to depart, are you not? I shall accompany you to the forest floor. Unless, of course, you have some reason why my presence is unwelcome?"

Simpkins stood silently for several moments, his eyes intent upon the smaller man. Then, still without a word, he turned and headed toward the trail.

—⁓—

The road down the mountain was narrow and ancient. Carved hundreds of years ago by the monks who built the monastery, it was just wide enough to accommodate the mule-drawn wagons needed to bring up supplies. While that was apparently fine for the mules, the howling winds whipping through the high crags ensured that Bobby walked on the inside of the road, well away from the rocky edge.

They reached the valley floor a little before noon, stopping to rest at the edge of the forest. There, they ate a light lunch of bread and cheese prepared by the monks the day before. Master Jong then took his leave, continuing down the road to a village nestled at the neck of the valley on the other side of the woods. Simpkins seemed relieved by the monk's departure and yet, for some reason, kept glancing at the road long after Master Jong disappeared.

The students resumed their trek, plunging into the heart of the forest to a clearing where Simpkins had the group fan around him to hear his instructions.

"I have some illustrations of the plants we are looking for," he said, producing a handful of drawings from a satchel carried by one of the students. "Your goal is to locate and gather as many of these plants as you can. Given that it is the rainy season, your main focus should be the fungi. This one in particular," he said, holding up an artist's rendering of a spectral mushroom with a crimson cap and pale white stem, "should be your main focus. It is called *Transitivo paradoxa,* or the 'diffident ghost mushroom.' It is exceedingly rare, usually blooming for only a few weeks out of the year. The headmistress will be most pleased by anyone who finds some."

Several of the students looked eager to earn favor with the headmistress.

"Don't get excited," said Simpkins. "Most of you probably won't find anything at all. Honestly, I'm not even sure why the headmistress is doing this."

Simpkins explained that they would be divided up into groups of three. Their goal was to use their abilities to locate as many of the items on the list as possible.

"Don't bother looking with your eyes," Simpkins said. "You're not going to find any of these plants just lying around on the forest floor. I will be back in a few hours, after you've all completed your searches, and we will head back up the mountain."

"Wait, you're leaving us?" asked a dark-skinned chubby boy with big ears.

"I'm placing Ashley in charge. She's the most talented and has been doing this field trip since she was a toddler. She can divide you up into groups and answer any questions you have." With that, Simpkins disappeared into the forest.

A moment of stunned silence followed Simpkins's sudden departure. Then everyone began talking at once. Bobby glanced at Trevor and Lily, who looked just as confused as the rest.

"Quiet!" said Ashley, climbing on top of a nearby tree stump. "You all heard Professor Simpkins. I'm in charge. Now be quiet, and listen up."

"Just what Ashley needed," said Trevor under his breath, "an excuse to tell everyone what to do."

"We need to get started," said Ashley, looking down on them from the stump. "You will search in groups of three. But there's too many people for everyone to report to me, so we're going to split up into two teams. Half of you will report to me. The other half will report to . . ."

Ashley scanned the group.

What is she doing? thought Bobby. Simpkins hadn't told them to split up into teams.

Ashley's eyes settled in their direction.

"Trevor," she said with a smirk. "You'll handle the other half. Organize them and answer all of their stupid questions before you send them off. And remember, their screwups are your responsibility."

Ashley began calling out names. The Tex-Mex twins went on her team. Big surprise. Mex high-fived his brother with one hand while picking his nose with the other.

"So gross," said Lily under her breath.

In quick order, Ashley took all of the older and more talented students, leaving the younger, less gifted children for Trevor. Soon, all of the kids had been divided into groups of three— except for Bobby, who stood alone and humiliated.

"You last two will just have to group together, since there isn't a third person," said Ashley, reveling in Bobby's embarrassment. "So sorry," she said without a trace of sincerity.

Bobby looked around and saw no one else. A chill breeze blew through the clearing, carrying nervous tension and the smell of moist earth. Then, from the far side of the clearing, a small figure stepped forward. Bobby's heart broke in sympathy; it was Jinx. Bobby's young friend gave him a weak smile, and Bobby let out a breath he hadn't realized he'd been holding.

Ashley appeared not to have noticed. "That's all," she said. "Report to your team leader for search assignments. My group will be searching the north half of the forest. Trevor's group will head south."

The instant Ashley dismissed them, Lily rushed up to Bobby and Jinx and threw her arms around them.

"Oh my gosh, that was horrible," she said. "Are you guys okay?"

"I'm fine," said Jinx, pulling away. "Ashley knows that this assignment requires skill, not knowledge. It's to be expected that she left me for last."

Bobby shook his head in wonder that Ashley could be so cruel to her own brother as the rest of the team assembled around them. Trevor took out a map of the forest and assigned groups to specific locations. He had chosen Lily for his own team and added a boy named Jacob as well. The redhead seemed pleased by this selection, casting furtive glances at Lily as they prepared to depart.

Meanwhile, Bobby and Jinx were given a section far to the southeast, against the hillside. Trevor said it would give them lots of travel time to search, but Bobby couldn't help but wonder if Trevor shared Ashley's sentiment and wanted them out of the way.

Trevor gave every group a copy of the map and told them to report back in exactly three hours to regroup. "Make sure to stick together. And don't stray from your designated area. It's currently seven minutes till one. Be back here at four."

Jinx took the map from Bobby and sketched over it with a pencil. "I'm familiar with this particular section of the forest," said Jinx, gesturing to a line on the eastern edge of the map. "I suggest we form a grid pattern and conduct our search quadrant by quadrant."

Bobby shrugged. "You're in charge."

CHAPTER 10

Master Jong entered the village from the north, moving rapidly past the outlying farms with their verdant crops and thatch-roofed cottages. He passed the town square—a patch of dirt with a stone well in the middle—and hurried past the general store without a glance. Despite what he told Simpkins, he had not come here to trade.

On the far side of the village, Master Jong turned off the main road and headed toward a small cottage obscured by the gnarled oaks and sugar maples of the nearby forest. Climbing the rough-hewn steps, he tapped lightly on the cottage's heavy door and then, in his native tongue, called into the house.

"Hatou, are you there?"

The door soon opened to reveal an elderly man, his gentle face hidden behind a long gray beard. Formerly the head groundskeeper for the Jade Academy, he stooped from decades of tending plants in the harsh mountain terrain.

Hatou was one of the few staff members who was neither monk nor academic, and he had been given permission to retire to this village some years back, under the stipulation that he never discuss the academy or the nature of its work with anyone.

"It is good to see you, old friend," said Hatou.

"And I you," said Master Jong, stepping inside and closing the door behind him. They had been close friends long before the old gardener took his leave, making Hatou one of the few people Master Jong visited outside the monastery.

"Tell me, dear friend," said Master Jong, "has there been any word?"

Hatou shook his head. "It would appear your friend from the West has gone silent."

Master Jong also shook his head as he took a seat at the small worktable where Hatou ate most of his meals. "Most strange. He seemed quite eager to correspond about the scrolls when last he wrote."

"Perhaps he has simply been occupied with other matters," offered Hatou.

"Let us hope so," said Master Jong, removing his heavy outer robe. "His insights have been invaluable in the past. I hoped to rely on them once more."

"Would you like some food? Cheese or bread perhaps? I just baked a new loaf."

Despite the sweet fragrance of the honey-wheat bread cooling on the windowsill, Master Jong shook his head. "I fear that I haven't much time before I must depart," said the tiny monk. He removed his inner robe to reveal cloth swaddled around his waist like a cummerbund. Hatou helped Master Jong unravel the cloth, exposing a rectangular package pressed against the small of his back. Master Jong set the bundle on the table and unwrapped a thin stack of parchments.

"I see you are taking every precaution to keep the nature of your visit concealed," said Hatou.

"I do as I must," said Master Jong. "The consequences would be dire indeed if the headmistress found out I was making copies of the sacred scrolls."

"I understand why you must conceal your actions from the academics, but why not consult with your fellow monks? Surely they could be of more assistance to you than a withered old groundskeeper."

"Your assistance is invaluable, dear friend," said Master Jong, retying his robe. "Besides, Divine Master Whimpley refuses to sanction my mission to uncover the secret buried within the texts. As a matter of fact, he came to me just yesterday, insinuating ill consequences if I don't succeed with my newest student."

Hatou looked aghast. "Why would he do such a thing? Surely the salvation of your order lies in the scrolls."

"He claims religious grounds, but I believe it to be political. It has been foretold that discovering the secret means an end to the status quo. Undoubtedly, he fears for his own power. But I sense the hand of the headmistress more than his own."

"You believe he would betray one of his own to the academics?"

"The academics command our service because they have not given us a reason to rebel, but our coexistence has always been tense. As for the divine master—I cannot speak to his loyalty or the extent of his corruption, only that I prefer not to test either if it can be avoided."

"Then I will do everything in my power to aid you," said Hatou, moving to the far corner of the cottage where he pried up a loose floorboard to reveal a hidden compartment. Bending, he removed an ornately carved wooden box.

"Before we begin, I should tell you that I fear this may all be in vain," said Master Jong. Taking the box from Hatou, he opened it to reveal a stack of parchments similar to those he had just delivered. "I have already studied the new texts at great length and can find no hidden message. If the secret is somehow bound to the ancient scrolls themselves, then these transcripts are worthless."

"Then we will just have to pray that such is not the case," said Hatou.

"My time is short. Let us study them together," said Master Jong. "Perhaps your eyes will pick up something mine have not." The two men sat at the table, spread out the pages before them, and read.

For the next several hours the two friends studied in silence, poring over the transcripts for anything Master Jong might have previously missed.

"All I see are proverbs," said Hatou, setting down a scroll and replacing it with a cup of tea. "Almost everything is about patience, wisdom, and tolerance."

"You can skip all that," said Master Jong. "We are looking for something with tremendous power, something that will shift the balance between us and the academics. It must be some form of energy manipulation. No other secret would be so closely guarded."

They read on. Master Jong refused food or drink, choosing instead to spend every possible moment reading. Finally, Master Jong organized the pages, adding the new ones to the box, and returned it to its hiding place.

"If only the Westerner had provided us with his insights," he said, setting the floorboards back in place. "It would be tremendously helpful to at least have a suggestion about where to look."

"It is strange not to have heard from him," said Hatou. "Then again, everything about the man seems strange. What did you say his name means again in English?"

"It means *chief*," Master Jong said. "And he may be our only hope of finding the secret and liberating my people." The tiny monk emerged into the crisp autumn air and headed into the forest.

—m—

Behind the giant oak, Simpkins watched the door of the ramshackle cottage swing open and Master Jong step outside. The diminutive monk's head instantly swung in Simpkins's direction. Simpkins shrank back into the shadows. After a moment, the monk looked away and the rail-thin agent allowed himself to breathe. It wouldn't do for Jong to catch him spying—at least, not yet.

It had taken quite a bit of effort to follow the monk to the cottage. Normally reliant on his occult abilities to track, the nature of this prey forced Simpkins to improvise. The rainy season had left mud on the main trail. He hadn't really known what to look for, so he followed the freshest-looking tracks, which led him to this house at the edge of town.

Whatever the monk was up to inside, Simpkins intended to find out. He would send men back to investigate as soon as possible. For now, he needed to report to the headmistress. Stepping silently on the bed of damp leaves blanketing the ground, Simpkins slipped back into the forest and disappeared.

CHAPTER 11

The muddy ground sucked at their feet as Bobby and Jinx picked their way through the forest. With no path to follow, they had to scramble over fallen logs and around dense brush to maintain their heading. Both were tired when they got to their search site some twenty minutes later. Mopping his brow, Bobby sat on a mossy rock. Jinx collapsed next to him.

"This is difficult terrain," said Jinx between wheezes. "And we have to search this whole area, plus the base of the foothills themselves."

"What do you suggest?"

"You're bigger and more athletic than I am," said Jinx. "The logical course of action is for you to search the high quadrants along the hillside while I search the low ones in the forest proper."

"You want to split up? Trevor said to stick together."

"There's no way we can cover our whole area if we stay together. Besides, I'll only slow you down. Just stick to the areas I marked with a *B*. I already have my quadrants memorized," he said, handing the map back to Bobby. "We can meet back here every hour to check in with each other. It's the most efficient means to accomplish our task."

Bobby frowned as he took the map. He didn't like the idea of splitting up, but the plan made sense. By covering more ground, they improved their chances, and all Bobby cared about was showing the others that he and Jinx weren't worthless.

"I'll start over here," said Bobby, pointing to a section to the south. "I'll head to the far corner and work my way back toward you."

"And I'll start here and work my way down toward you," said Jinx. "I should be able to hear you up in the hills once we get close."

"All right," said Bobby, climbing to his feet. "Off I go."

"Oh, one last thing," said Jinx. "Be careful up there. Not only is the terrain treacherous when wet, but there are wild animals higher up in the hills. I've read up on all the predators and don't think they're anything to worry about. Just don't go up too high."

"Yes, Mommy," said Bobby with a grin as he took off walking.

—m—

The southeast corner of the valley was a jumble of splotchy granite boulders along a steep slope. Bobby stayed on the edge between rocks and trees, skirting his way southward until the hill turned east. Then he began to ascend.

Despite Simpkins's warning not to bother with a physical search, he couldn't help but study the ground. As he crossed the slope, he checked under outcroppings, peeking into every crack and crevice he found. He discovered lots of muddy holes and more than a few animal dens but nothing that matched anything on his list.

His back ached from bending and his legs burned from climbing. Still, he trudged on, becoming more and more halfhearted in his efforts as his energy waned. Soon it would be time to head back and rendezvous with Jinx.

Perching on a rock, he checked his watch. It had been forty minutes since he and Jinx split up. It would be quicker and easier to descend. That left him with ten more minutes to search. What he needed was a good vantage point—a place to sit and rest while surveying the area below.

Bobby climbed to the ledge of a massive boulder and took a seat. Beneath an azure sky, a living sea of emerald and russet glistened within a vast slate cradle. Due west, Bobby made out the faint outline of the village, with its farms and fields against the southern edge of the forest. On the northern slope, the Jade Academy sat like a granite jewel beneath a jagged, snowcapped crown.

Only one thing ruined the otherwise perfect vision. Far to the west, beyond the village, ivory clouds were rolling in, blanketing the area in dense fog. At their current speed, they would soon sweep across the forest and engulf the slope where he sat. Once that happened, he would have a tough time seeing where he was going, let alone spotting tiny fungi in dark hollows.

Bobby rose, stretched his sore limbs, and took one last look at the panorama. One swirling cloud looked like a crystal ball. Another puffy one reminded him of a mushroom. *If only I had a real crystal ball to tell me where some rare mushrooms are.* He thought about the rarest of the mushrooms—the one Simpkins had called "the diffident ghost" mushroom. *Man, I'd be a hero if I found one of those.*

A strange sensation gripped him: an awareness of something unseen that he nonetheless knew was there. He stood and the feeling changed. Every time he turned, his guts shifted. *It's like hot or cold*, he thought, turning in a slow circle to see which direction felt the strongest.

He ended up pointing uphill. From there, the sensation felt like someone pulling a rope attached to his navel. He didn't need Master Jong to figure out what it meant. A *Transitivo paradoxa* mushroom lay somewhere in the hillside above.

Bobby forgot all about his aching back and sore legs as he scrambled up the side of the mountain. Even his scheduled rendezvous with Jinx drifted away, forgotten as he reached a narrow ledge forming a trail against the slope. The advancing clouds now covered most of the forest. In fact, the vanguard had already reached the hillside, shrouding the path before him in the first tendrils of fog. He caught a brief glimpse of a ravine about a hundred yards away, and then it was gone. He took off running, eager to claim his prize.

It all happened so fast. One second he was racing through the fog toward the ravine. The next, the ground beneath his right foot gave way. With a sickening pop, his ankle twisted and his leg sank into a hole. He fell backward. Something hard struck the back of his head. A starburst of pain erupted at the base of his skull.

Bobby struggled to get his bearings through a haze of fog and tears. He lay flat on his back, staring up at the hillside. Movement on the opposite side of the gulch caught his eye, materializing into the silhouette of a man. A breeze swept in, and for a split second, Bobby got a clear view. There was no mistaking that dark, wavy hair. The assassin had found him.

Bobby stared in horror as the man picked his way across the ravine. Bobby tried desperately to rouse himself, but his limbs refused. The back of his head felt sticky and wet, all his strength draining away like water through a sieve.

The assassin dropped into the ravine and out of sight. Bobby stared at the mist and imagined how nice it would be to pull it around him tight like a blanket. He had one final thought of seeing his mother and father again, then he knew only oblivion.

—⟶—

Jinx's throat hurt. For the past ten minutes, he'd paced up and down the base of the foothills, yelling for Bobby. Not that it had done any good. The dense fog muffled the sound. *Heck,*

Bobby probably couldn't hear me if he was standing right on top of me. Clearly it was time to try something else.

Sticking his hands in front of him like a zombie, he took off walking. After a few steps, he adjusted his path, heading more to his right. He went a few more yards and turned again. He continued for several more minutes, constantly adjusting his heading to follow his senses. *Let instinct be my guide. Lead me to Bobby.*

He ended up at a rotten tree stump with a hollow base. As he approached, a badger emerged from the hollow. Rising on its hind legs, the badger growled and bared its teeth.

"Please don't eat me," said Jinx, stumbling back. "I'm a big fan of the University of Wisconsin. I hear they've got a great veterinary department." The angry badger retreated to its den, allowing Jinx to slump to the forest floor. *So much for trusting my intuition.*

Jinx sat, folded his legs, and closed his eyes. Perhaps he could create a telepathic link. He knew the technique in theory. All he needed was willpower and concentration.

It took several minutes, but finally he detected a nearby presence. Excitement spread through him like wildfire. *Bobby is close; I can feel it.* But something felt off. He sensed a primal rage. *His mind can't possibly be so primitive,* thought Jinx, *or so angry.*

In another moment, the presence formed fully in his mind.

"You've got to be kidding me," said Jinx, recognizing the rage coming from the badger he had encountered moments before. "Why do I get the feeling you and I aren't going to be friends?"

A second attempt put him in touch with something peaceful but wary. The creature's thoughts seemed focused on grass and leaves. *Probably a deer,* thought Jinx. A third attempt put him back in contact with the perturbed badger, at which point Jinx gave up rather than press his luck.

With his ideas nearly depleted, Jinx tried one last trick. Using what little energy he had to amplify his voice, he shouted again through the thick fog. With luck, the added power would carry his call far enough to reach Bobby. He knew imagery was crucial, and so he pictured his shouts slicing through the air like samurai swords.

When that failed to produce results, he switched to baseballs. His voice carried up into the air, over the outfield wall, and into the upper deck. Just for fun, he put his sister's face on one of the baseballs and watched it sail out of sight. "It's a grand slam!" said Jinx, throwing up his arms and dancing around in a circle. A moment later, he let his hands fall to his sides. Even if Bobby heard him, he wouldn't be able to respond.

Besides, it hadn't felt like it was working anyway. The ringing in his ear suggested that he'd only been amplifying the sound inside his head. *Better to quit while I'm ahead of the game*, thought Jinx, and giggled at his own pun.

Out of ideas, Jinx paced back and forth as he tried to think of what else to do. If he went for help and Bobby showed up, their earlier embarrassment would pale in comparison to the ridicule they'd both receive. On the other hand, he'd never be able to live with himself if Bobby lay somewhere injured while he stood around doing nothing. Making sure his shoes were double knotted, Jinx turned toward the heart of the forest and began to run.

―᙭―

Bobby awoke in a sea of confusion. The back of his head felt like an oil slick. He tried to push up onto his elbows and the slick caught fire, sending waves of agony hammering against the shore of his brain. A muffled noise came from his right. Bobby gritted his teeth, swung his upper body to the edge of the trail and looked down. Nothing.

With a grimace, he lay back on the ground and closed his eyes. *I'm losing it*, he told himself. *The assassin is not real. I hit my head so hard I'm seeing things that aren't real.* That's when he heard the voice.

"This will be easier if you do not struggle."

"Who's there?" said Bobby, trying to crane his neck.

"You are gravely injured," said the voice. "Do not try to move."

"Who are you?"

"There is no time to explain. Try to relax."

Rough hands gripped Bobby's head. The man leaned in close and long black hair brushed Bobby's cheek. *The assassin.* Bobby thrashed, kicking wildly with his left leg even as his right remained trapped in its subterranean prison.

"Be still," said the man sharply.

Bobby groped back over his head, trying to grab his assailant. He'd just managed to grab a fistful of hair when a powerful tingling sensation burst from the base of his skull.

Bobby screamed, releasing his grip as the tingling grew into a mind-numbing blizzard that left him gasping for air. He gnashed his teeth, the bitter taste of blood on his tongue. And then, slowly, he relaxed. His arms went limp, falling uselessly to his sides.

Everything grew hazy as pain invaded from all sides. He saw his parents sitting at home in their living room and knew he must be slipping away. His parents were dead, and he was about to join them. The images faded to shadow. Only the agony inside his skull remained. Then, right as everything turned pitch black, the pain abruptly ceased.

Bobby gasped. The assassin's hands were gone, taking with them the pain that had nearly consumed him. He twisted his neck, looking upside down to see what the assassin had planned for him next.

In place of the dark-haired killer, Bobby saw two familiar figures approaching—Trevor and Jinx. Bobby reached down and extracted his leg from the hole. Leaning heavily on his good leg, Bobby scrambled to his feet.

Flushed with a mix of exertion and concern, Jinx pulled out his inhaler and puffed. "Are you hurt?" he asked between deep breaths.

Bobby ignored the question as he peered over the ledge. "Did you see him?"

"See who?" asked Trevor.

"We've gotta get outta here," said Bobby, taking a tentative step only to pitch forward into Trevor's arms.

"Careful. I've got you," said Trevor, grabbing him around the waist.

"We need to run," said Bobby. "He could come back at any second."

"What are you talking about?" said Trevor.

"Is that from *you*?" said Jinx, pointing to the blood caked on Bobby's head.

"We don't have time for this!" said Bobby. He tried to take another step and failed. "He was about to finish me off when you guys showed up. We need to get out of here, now."

"Who are you talking about?" said Trevor, looking around. "There's no one here but us."

"The man who was sent to kill me," said Bobby. "We need to go now, before he comes back and kills us all."

"Dude, you hit your head wicked hard," said Trevor. "The only thing you need to do is sit down and let me take a look at your injuries."

"But—"

"Listen to me, Bobby, you've lost a lot of blood. You're clearly hallucinating. Besides, why would someone want to kill you?"

"But he was right there!"

"Jinx, back me up on this."

Jinx wasn't listening. He stood over the spot where Bobby had fallen, staring intently into the hole.

Trevor frowned. "Honestly, it doesn't matter. Either way, you're in no position to go anywhere. Now sit down so I can look at the back of your head."

Suddenly dizzy, Bobby allowed Trevor to help him over to a nearby boulder.

"Funny thing," said Trevor after a few moments of examining the area. "There's a lot of blood back here, but I don't see a wound."

"This is no time for jokes," said Bobby.

"I'm not joking. It must be there somewhere, but your hair is so matted with blood that I can't see your scalp. How do you feel?"

Bobby gently probed the back of his head. "I feel . . . okay!"

"Well, that's good. 'Cause you look like you should be dead."

"Gee, thanks."

"All I'm saying is there's a lot of blood. How long were you lying there, anyway?"

"I don't know. I think I blacked out for a while."

"Well, *that's* not a good sign, though it might explain a few things. Maybe it's a shallow wound that bled for a long time while you were unconscious."

"I don't think that's the case," said Jinx. The younger boy stood over the puddle of blood where Bobby laid moments before.

"What are you saying, Jinx?" asked Bobby.

"This blood is still warm," he said, sticking the tip of his finger into the puddle. "In this weather, it can't be more than a few minutes old."

"That doesn't make sense," said Trevor. "If all that blood spilled out just a few minutes ago, there's no way it would've stopped bleeding. You'd be dead first."

"You did say I looked like I was dead, didn't you?"

Trevor grimaced. "And you said this was no time for jokes."

"So, what do we do?"

"You're gonna have to let me look at that ankle and hope I can fix it," said Trevor. Bobby sat and lifted his leg. Jinx returned to studying the hole. After several minutes, Trevor stood. "It's definitely twisted, but I don't think it's broken."

"Well, that's fantastic. As long as it's not broken, I'll just skip down the mountain—not like it's already swelling to the size of a beach ball."

"Relax, Captain Sarcasm. I've taken classes on healing. I should be able to decrease most of the inflammation. We just need to make a splint before you put any weight on it."

Jinx took off for a nearby copse of cypress trees to scavenge wood for a splint while Trevor worked on Bobby's ankle. Five minutes later, Jinx came back with a long branch to use for a crutch and a couple of shorter ones for the split. Trevor selected the two straightest pieces, then slipped off his belt to bind the wood around Bobby's calf. Jinx volunteered one of his socks to tie the branches at his ankle and, together, they affixed the brace to Bobby's foot.

Bobby stood, testing his weight on the makeshift splint. "I'll probably still need some help on the hill, but I think I can walk."

"Then let's get going," said Trevor. But they didn't. Instead, a noise from the gorge brought them up short.

"What was that?" asked Bobby, struggling to turn around.

"Sounded like something coming up from the ravine," said Trevor.

Jinx grimaced. "Oh please, not the badger again!"

Trevor gave him a quizzical look. "I don't think that's a badger."

"Of course it is," said Jinx. "What else would it be?"

With a low growl, a Tibetan blue bear burst through the bushes and into the middle of the trail directly before them. A titanic mass of shaggy fur caked with mud, the bear rose onto its hind legs and roared, sending a thick rope of saliva swinging from the corner of its mouth.

Slowly, Bobby leaned over and picked up a rock. "Run," he said over his shoulder.

"Are you crazy?" said Trevor, eying the rock. "You won't even slow it down with that thing."

"The instant we turn our backs, it'll charge. I can at least buy you some time." The beast huffed and snorted as it advanced along the narrow ledge.

"No way," said Jinx, "I'm not leaving you."

"Then we're all going to die here," said Bobby.

He threw the rock, but the bear barely flinched. Bobby threw another as the bear approached undeterred.

"I don't think that's helping," said Trevor.

Bobby and the beast locked eyes and, for just a moment, it felt like the animal could see into his heart and spirit. Then the beast extended its front legs and lowered its head.

"What's it doing?" asked Trevor.

"It almost looks like it's bowing," said Jinx.

"What do you think it means?" asked Bobby, unable to break eye contact with the animal.

Jinx said, "I have no idea. I've never read about anything like this before."

"I don't care what it's doing, as long as it stays where it is," said Trevor. "Let's get the heck outta here before it changes its mind."

But Bobby didn't move. He stood transfixed as the bear took on a calm, almost docile expression—mouth open, tongue lolling lazily to one side. Trevor grabbed his arm and yanked Bobby around. "What's wrong with you? We gotta get outta here!"

Spell broken, Bobby limped backward. "I think it's gonna let us leave," he said as they gained distance under the beast's watchful gaze. Then the bear lowered its head and sniffed. It walked a few steps and took another sniff, then another.

Jinx figured it out first. "It's picked up the scent of your blood!"

The bear stuck its nose into the warm pool. Bobby's entire body went rigid as the bear sniffed around. *Please, please just forget about us and let us leave.*

When the bear looked up, its muzzle was covered in blood, and it was clear that something had changed. Froth foamed out of its mouth. Whatever brief connection they'd had was gone as the bear locked eyes with Bobby and licked its lips.

Bobby turned, hobbling as fast as he could on his injured leg. "For heaven's sake, run for your lives!"

With a mighty roar, the bear pinned its ears and charged. Trevor and Jinx both took off running. Bobby wasn't so lucky. One of the sticks binding his leg caught on a tree root, sending him sprawling to the ground.

Time seemed to slow as he tumbled to the dirt. Rolling onto his back, he saw the beast's eyes, now wild with rage. Its nostrils flared with the scent of his blood. Saliva boiled out over jagged yellow teeth.

Bobby threw up his arms and braced for impact.

Less than ten feet away, the bear broke stride, sliding to a halt so near that it left a bloody paw print less than a foot from his head. It roared again, and Bobby felt the hot sting of its rancid breath. Then the mighty beast turned and ran back the way it had come.

Bobby took a huge breath.

"What the heck was that?" said Jinx from behind him.

"Heck if I know," said Bobby. "That was the strangest thing I've ever seen—possibly the strangest thing *anyone* has ever seen. Where's Trevor?"

"Over here," called their friend. Bobby and Jinx walked to the ledge to find Trevor hanging by a tree root, his legs dangling over the precipice.

"What?" said Trevor as they hauled him back up. "I was gonna drop rather than let the bear get me." Jinx scowled, letting Trevor know what he thought of such a ridiculous idea. Trevor shrugged. "It seemed like a good idea at the time."

"It did seem rather hopeless," agreed Bobby. "If I didn't know any better, I'd say we just experienced a miracle."

"Based upon my knowledge of Tibetan blue bears and their aggressive behavior, I must concur," said Jinx. "I can think of no logical reason why this particular bear ceased its assault."

"It just turned and ran away for some reason," said Bobby.

"Let's go take a look," said Trevor.

"Are you insane?" said Jinx. "We just barely escaped being mauled, and now you want to go after it?"

"What can I say? The suspense is 'un-bear-able.'"

"You're horrible," said Jinx with a grimace.

Trevor put a finger to his lips. "Quiet. I think I hear something."

"I don't hear anything," said Jinx.

"I hear it," said Bobby. "It sounds like someone singing."

—⚏—

An icy wind whipped around the corner of the ravine, blowing hard in their faces as Bobby, Trevor, and Jinx reached the edge. The trail wrapped around and descended slowly and steadily into the gorge, like a stony road to hell. At the bottom lay a small clearing with a cave.

Bobby turned to Trevor. "Are you thinking what I'm thinking?"

"You mean that the cave in the distance is the bear's den, and we should go check it out?" asked Trevor.

Bobby had only been thinking one of those things and told him so. Trevor sloughed off his concern with a shrug. "Whoever is at that cave is in huge danger. We need to do something."

Jinx poked his head between them. "You mean like run down there and get ourselves killed along with them?"

"Okay, so we need a plan. Maybe we could distract the bear somehow." Trevor thought about it for a moment. "Maybe we could get close enough and then yell at the guy—"

"And draw the bear's attention back to us, when one of us is still limping and covered in blood. Brilliant! Why didn't I think of that?" said Jinx.

"Well, we can't just stand here and do nothing," said Trevor. "Sounds like someone is down there. We need to at least take a closer look."

They hurried down the ravine toward the cave, trying to make as little noise as possible. As they got closer, Bobby hesitated.

"It's not exactly singing," he said. "It sounds almost like chanting."

They found a boulder shaped like an elephant and scrambled up the protruding rump to a perch behind the left ear. In front of the den, three dark spots that could only be bear cubs paced back and forth, yipping frantically at a fourth splotch sitting in front of the cave.

"That explains it," said Jinx. "The bear we saw must be the mother."

"And she's racing back to protect her cubs from whoever that is," said Trevor, pointing at the fourth splotch.

"The cubs were probably sleeping inside the den when she came to investigate," said Bobby.

They hopped off the boulder and headed closer, stopping a dozen yards away to crouch behind some bushes.

By that time, the mother bear had reached the clearing. She stood near the cave, swiping at the air and thrashing her head as if haunted by the music.

The boys stared at the man in a forest-green outfit sitting in front of the cave—his diminutive size; his smooth, bald head; the sweet, pure tone of his voice.

"Holy crap, that's Master Jong!" Jinx said.

"I can see that," said Trevor. "But what is he doing here?"

Calm and as cool as the breeze swirling around him, Master Jong sat chanting as the mother bear's three cubs paced by the cave mouth behind him.

On the opposite side of the clearing, the mother bear rose on her hind legs and roared her displeasure. Swiping at the air with paws the size of catcher's mitts, the bear dropped onto all fours and stomped.

Master Jong remained seated, arms and legs folded, chanting

as the enormous beast drew steadily closer. With less than ten yards between them, the mother bear pinned her ears back and charged.

Instantly, Master Jong changed the cadence of his melody. He hit a high note and the bear yowled in rage. Less than a foot away, the bear veered to the side and slammed into the hillside.

Master Jong's melody reverted to its normal cadence as the mother bear regained her legs. She roared and charged again, but, once again, Master Jong changed his tone, causing the mother bear to howl and abort her attack. The bear charged three more times, with Master Jong thwarting every effort.

Finally exhausted, the mother bear collapsed a few yards away. Tongue hanging out, she lay there, huffing and snorting, staring back and forth between Master Jong and her cubs.

In time, the mother bear straightened up and walked a few steps closer. For a long time, she stood there, watching the tiny monk. Then the bear mimicked the bizarre gesture she had made toward Bobby—extending her front paws and lowering her head. Instantly, the cubs ran over to meet their mother. With a final huff, the mother bear gathered up her cubs and trotted off down the far side of the ravine.

"What the heck just happened?" said Trevor, stepping out from the bushes. Bobby and Jinx said nothing as the mother bear and her cubs descended into the gorge, where they quickly disappeared amid the bramble.

Bears gone, the boys approached Master Jong. No sooner did they reach him than Master Jong opened his eyes and stood.

"Hello, boys," said Master Jong with just the slightest hint of a smile. "What brings you here?"

CHAPTER 12

"Where is he?" said Ashley to no one in particular. The students around her looked down at their feet or off into the woods. A few from Trevor's team mumbled apologies, but no one spoke up loud enough to draw attention.

"I swear that if no one can tell me where my brother is by the time Professor Simpkins shows up, I am going to make all of your lives miserable."

A chubby girl with a mole on her left cheek turned visibly pale.

Ashley lifted an eyebrow. "Isn't there a single one of you trained well enough to sense anything?"

The short, stocky boy named Jacob said, "What about you? I thought you were a superstar."

Tex and Mex both went for the boy, but Ashley waved them off. "Are you questioning me?" she said, holding up the satchel full of herbs she'd found during their search. "Did any of you losers even find anything? You're worse than useless. Now, instead of basking in my triumph when Professor Simpkins shows up, I have to explain why people are missing 'cause you're all too stupid to follow simple instructions."

She scanned the group of shamed faces until she found the skinny girl with the pale skin and knobby knees. "You, what's your name again?"

The girl's tone was surprisingly confident. "I'm Lily. Lily Green."

"Right, whatever," said Ashley. "Just tell me again what happened."

"Like I said before, I was searching with Trevor and Jacob when Jinx came running up. He didn't say much—just that Bobby was missing and that they needed to go find him."

"Bobby Ether? I don't care about that loser," said Ashley. "Tell me about my brother."

"Well," said Lily, "he was flushed and out of breath but didn't look injured or hurt, if that's what you mean. I mean, he looked red—redder than usual—"

"Shut up," snapped Ashley. "You said he went with Trevor. Why couldn't Trevor go by himself?"

"I don't know. Honest," said Lily. "All I know is that Jinx wanted his help to search the 'upper quadrants.' Whatever that means."

"That's complete nonsense," snapped Ashley. "Jinx would be completely useless in a search for a missing person."

"Trevor wasn't about to tell him he couldn't come. After all, they're—"

Ashley cut her off. "Trevor will pay for dragging my brother into this fiasco. How long does it take to find one bumbling idiot, anyway?"

Hands trembling, Lily sat on a nearby stump and stared into her lap. Jacob placed a hand on her shoulder.

"So you have no idea where they went?" said Ashley, glaring at her as if to somehow force the answer she wanted out of Lily.

Lily shook her head. "A bunch of us already looked where Bobby and Jinx were assigned to search but didn't find anything. I figured that since Simpkins put you in charge, you would know."

Ashley slapped Lily across the cheek. "Don't ever question me," she said, towering over the smaller girl. "Now shut up while I decide what to do."

—m—

Bobby stared in disbelief as Master Jong stood and brushed himself off. Beside him, Trevor's mouth flapped open and closed as he tried to compose himself. "What the heck just happened?" he finally stammered.

Jinx was the only one who didn't look surprised. "You spoke to the bear, didn't you?" he said in awe.

"I wouldn't exactly say 'spoke to,'" said Master Jong.

Jinx bounced up and down, tugging on the monk's sleeve. "You *gotta* show me how you did it. You gotta, gotta, gotta."

Bobby placed a hand on Jinx's shoulder. "Let me see if I've got this straight," he said to Master Jong. "You just talked to that bear and convinced it not to maul us to death?"

Master Jong shook his head. "Not at all. I simply made her aware of my presence. Maternal instinct took care of the rest."

"And what about just now, when the bear tried to tear you to pieces?"

Master Jong shrugged innocently. "What can I say? I have a way with animals."

"Wait one minute," said Jinx, scratching his chin. "How did you even know we were in trouble?"

"Dude, who cares?" said Trevor. "That was wicked cool. I can't believe we almost got mauled by a bear!"

"That brings up an important point," said Master Jong. "The bears are going to want their den back before long."

"Wait, how *did* you know we were up here?" said Bobby.

Master Jong's eyes wandered to the cave. "I would have thought it was obvious."

Between the bear and the assassin, Bobby had almost completely forgotten why he was here. He rubbed his head.

"I was sitting down below, taking a break, when I sensed something up the side of the mountain . . . wait a second, do you mean to tell me there's something inside the bears' den?"

Jinx eyed the cave suspiciously. "You know, it's possible you were just sensing the bears. I actually have a funny story about a badger—"

"I don't think that's the case," said Master Jong. "I sense something up here as well."

"So what is it?" said Trevor.

Master Jong smiled and headed into the cave. "Let's go find out."

The boys followed Master Jong. Inside was pitch black. Jinx produced a halogen lamp from his backpack.

"What?" he said to his friends' surprised looks. "The monks may not use technology, but the academics do. I borrowed this from Mom's collection. It never hurts to be prepared."

Trevor tousled Jinx's hair as he took the light from him, brandishing it high overhead. "Dude, you're pretty cool for a nerd."

The cave was chilly, with the dank smell of mildew and animal. Once they passed the narrow mouth, the cave broadened, exposing an oblong chamber over a dozen yards deep with animal bones littered throughout. Thankfully, none of the bones appeared large enough to be human.

Toward the rear by the left wall, Bobby saw a low, shallow depression lined with matted fur. "I guess that's where they sleep," said Jinx.

"Give me a waterbed any day of the week," said Trevor, panning the light to reveal the rest of the cave. The left wall was smooth and straight, running behind the bear's sleeping area before joining the heap of granite rubble that formed the back wall. Near the back on the right side, a vertical crack roughly the width of a small person stabbed into the mountain. The crevice seemed to swallow the light as Trevor passed the lamp to Master Jong, who thrust it into the crack to expose a narrow passage.

"So what's so special?" asked Jinx. "This looks like a normal cave to me."

"There is nothing normal about that smell," said Trevor, waving a hand in front of his face. His arm smacked Master Jong, and the torch lamp went sailing, crashing to the floor. Instantly, the cave turned dark.

"Remain calm," said Master Jong. "Tell me, Jinx, did you bring a flashlight as well, something with a focused beam, perchance?"

"And you guys teased me for coming prepared," said Jinx, opening his backpack again.

"No wonder you get winded so easily," quipped Trevor. "You're running around with a hardware store strapped to your back."

Jinx made a face his friend couldn't see and handed the flashlight to Master Jong.

"Thank you, young sir," said the monk, adjusting the beam. Even with the powerful flashlight, Bobby didn't see anything special, just damp rock walls and piles of refuse stacked at the front of the passage like a makeshift latrine.

And then he felt it—that odd tugging sensation he'd experienced while resting on the slope, except now it felt ten times stronger. Something significant lay hidden in the silent depths of the crevice, calling to him with a strange yet powerful allure.

"So, umm, what are we looking at?" asked Jinx, poking his head between Trevor and Bobby to get a better look.

"Nothing at the moment," said Master Jong. "It would appear that our prize lies beyond the light's reach."

Jinx's expression turned fretful. "You're saying someone has to go in there?"

"I'll do it!" said Trevor. "That place looks wicked cool."

"I think Bobby should be the one to do it," said Jinx. "He's the one that led us up here."

"Indeed," said Master Jong.

"My ankle is still sore," said Bobby. "Maybe Jinx should go. He's the smallest."

"No, thanks," said Jinx, eying the dark void. "I, umm . . . I'm still tired from running up the mountain."

"Bobby will be the one to go," said Master Jong with finality. "The space is narrow. Lean on the sides to support your ankle if you need to."

"Alright, hand me the light," said Bobby, suddenly flushed with excitement. Whatever had drawn him up here was in that crevice. He crept forward, probing the walls with his hands as he stepped gingerly over the refuse pile guarding the entrance. On the other side, a trail of animal remains and bits of mottled fur formed a path. *Like disgusting, decaying breadcrumbs*, thought Bobby as he picked his way through the mess.

After a dozen or so paces, the passage hooked sharply to the right. *That's why we couldn't see anything*, thought Bobby, turning to survey the bend. The fissure proved narrow but not long, running only a few feet before opening up again into a small chamber. Bobby turned sideways and squeezed into the slender space.

It took three sidesteps, leading with his good foot, to slide through. He waved the light around, examining his new surroundings. The path extended for only a few more feet. He let the flashlight drop to his waist in disappointment. *Dead end*.

He turned around to make his way back out, and that's when he saw it. In a niche by his feet lay a pile of refuse and bones similar to the one at the entrance. He bent down for a closer look and almost dropped the flashlight. On the crest of the mound, gleaming like a ruby crown upon a beggar's brow, sat a giant colony of diffident ghost mushrooms.

—✹—

The last rays of the sun hung golden on the mountain crest as Master Jong and the boys made ready to head down off the hillside. Trevor and Jinx took turns extracting the mushrooms from the refuse mound. When they were done, a pile of fungi the size of a cantaloupe rested on the floor of the cave. Against his protests, they used Jinx's handkerchief to wrap up their prize.

"Hey, that's for my allergies," he whimpered.

"Just do what everyone else does and use your sleeve," said Trevor, placing the precious cargo in his backpack. "I'd put some in your bag, but there's no room, what with the refrigerator and microwave and all."

Meanwhile, Master Jong examined Bobby's ankle at the cave's entrance. He declared Trevor's work quite excellent, adding only a pungent salve he produced from beneath his thick forest robe, saying that it would speed the recovery process.

Finally ready to depart, Jinx found another sturdy branch for Bobby to use as a crutch and they headed out. The going was slow, with Bobby leaning heavily on Trevor as they maneuvered down the loose gravel. Once they reached the forest floor, Bobby walked on his own and they moved much quicker.

The sky grew dark as they hurried through the forest. Master Jong led the way, using Jinx's small and now-dying flashlight. Between the approaching night and the cloud cover, it was soon difficult to see more than a few feet in front of them.

Trevor checked his watch. "The others should have headed back up the mountain by now."

"Maybe they waited," said Bobby. "I'll bet Ashley probably still has people out looking for us."

Trevor shot him a dubious glance. "Are we talking about the same Ashley?"

A few minutes later they found the clearing, dark and empty except for an army of footprints.

"Let's go, boys," said Master Jong, not bothering to slow down. "It's a long walk back to the monastery."

CHAPTER 13

Bobby flexed his ankle, testing for pain as he headed to breakfast the next morning. Between the remedies applied by Trevor and Master Jong on the hill and the healing provided by the monks after he got back, he felt almost injury free. Sitting next to Trevor, he barely managed to ladle himself a bowl of oatmeal before other students bombarded him with questions about his encounter and discovery.

Jacob, the redheaded lowerclassman assigned to Trevor's team, burst through the crowd like an angry bull. "Where were you guys? I almost got pummeled by Ashley's goons because of you two."

Trevor turned away and shoveled a forkful of strawberry waffle into his mouth.

"What are you talking about?" asked Bobby.

"After you went missing yesterday, Ashley got up in Lily's face," said Jacob, "asking her where you guys went and why you weren't back yet."

Trevor spun back around, his elbow sending his plate of eggs and waffle sailing across the floor. "Ashley went after Lily?"

"You heard me," said Jacob. "She started yelling at Lily, saying that she was with you when Jinx showed up, so she should've known where you guys went. Lily just kept repeating over and over again that she didn't know anything, until it got physical."

Trevor's tone was deadly calm. "Did Ashley hurt her?"

"Ashley got pissed, gave Lily a slap. That's when I stepped in. Next thing I know, Ashley's apes were all up in my face."

Trevor came halfway out of his seat. "Did Ashley hurt her?" he repeated slowly.

"Why do you care so much?" asked Jacob. "She your girlfriend or something?"

Trevor sank back down. "I don't . . . I just don't like bullies."

"Wow," said Jacob with a sardonic laugh. "I'm just fine by the way. Thanks for asking."

Trevor rose. "You know something, Jacob?"

Jacob raised his fists. "What's that, Trevor?"

Bobby jumped between them as students gathered around, anticipating a fight. He turned to Jacob as the circle grew. "So you stood up to Ashley and her friends. That was cool of you. And you almost got in a fight—but didn't. You're fine. Lily's fine. No harm done."

"No thanks to you two," said Jacob, still scowling at Trevor. "Simpkins showed up right then and ordered everyone to head back."

Trevor scowled. "You mean to tell me that you guys were going to look for us, and Simpkins made you stop?"

"Something like that. Ashley wanted to look for Jinx, but Simpkins insisted we head back up the mountain." Jacob unclenched his fists and let his hands drop. "Now that you mention it, the whole thing was pretty weird. We told him you guys were still missing, but he didn't seem to care. He wasn't even mad at Ashley or anything."

"So, Lily's okay then?" asked Trevor.

"I told you, she's fine!" Jacob yelled at him.

Trevor seemed to relax after that. Reclaiming his seat, he fixed himself another plate of eggs. The crowd slowly dispersed to disappointed mumbles and speculation about who would have won.

When the onlookers were gone, Jacob leaned in close. "So, tell me, what exactly did happen to you guys last night?"

Embellishing the story for anyone still in earshot, Trevor recounted a tale that Bobby hardly recognized. When he got to the part about the pack of ravenous bears, Bobby gave a polite cough. "Excuse me. I'm going to be late for morning sessions." As quickly as he could, Bobby bussed his half-eaten tray and left the dining hall.

—◊—

"Hey, Bobby, wait up." Jinx ran up to Bobby, huffing and winded. "Why are you in such a hurry?"

"Sorry, Jinx, I can't talk now. I'm late for class."

"School doesn't start for another twenty minutes, and I know your schedule; your first class is right around the corner."

"Just leave me alone," said Bobby.

"I saw the crowd back there. Are you upset that Trevor is hogging all the glory?"

Bobby kept walking, letting his longer legs outpace his smaller friend.

"So, what is it?" said Jinx, jogging to keep up. "You don't like being the hero?"

"Hero?" said Bobby, pulling up short. "Is that how you think I look to everyone?"

"Well, you're the one that discovered the mushrooms. I am sure that's how it will look when Trevor gets there."

Bobby started walking again. "Yeah, right. I had to be rescued by you and Trevor, and we all know it." He started walking again, heading nowhere in particular.

"Bobby, if you hadn't hurt yourself, you would have run

straight into that bear's den. Good ankle or not, the bear would have killed you for sure."

"Wow, so you're saying it's a good thing I injured my ankle?"

"What I'm saying is that the hole did far more to save your life than Trevor or me."

Bobby wanted to say, *If you guys hadn't come along, the assassin would have killed me.* Instead, he shrugged. "You guys saved my life, not that stupid hole."

"Have it your way, but it sure seems to me that whoever dug that hole saved your life."

Bobby pulled up again, midstride. "What do you mean *whoever*?"

"That's what I wanted to talk to you about. While Trevor was patching up your ankle, I got a good look at that hole. Turns out, it wasn't some random pothole from the rain. There were score marks on the sides from some kind of shovel or trowel."

Bobby was dumbfounded. "You're saying that someone dug that hole on purpose?"

"Not only that, I found a broken mat of twigs at the bottom—clearly woven together to sit on top."

"What are you saying?" asked Bobby.

Jinx lowered his voice conspiratorially. "I'm saying that you stepping on that hole was no accident. It was a trap."

—◊◊◊—

The attention at breakfast was nothing compared to the treatment Bobby got once word of his discovery spread. Welcome or not, he'd somehow gone from being the awkward and inept new kid to an unsolicited celebrity. Kids in class gave him high fives. People he didn't know cheered him as he walked by. Even his instructors treated him differently.

As Bobby sat to begin his meditation session with Master

Jong that afternoon, the wiry monk waved him off. The monk wore a rich, rust-brown robe that matched the dusky mountaintops around them. He sprang to his feet, beckoning Bobby to follow.

"Your accomplishment yesterday was impressive," he said, heading for the main entrance. "You demonstrated that you are ready for the next stage in your training."

Bobby stared at him, confused. "Master?"

"You demonstrated the ability to follow your instincts and connect with the anima around you. You should be quite proud."

"But I almost got myself killed. I had no idea what I was doing racing up that mountain, or that I was about to walk into a bear cave."

"That is because you tapped into your energy at only a subconscious level. Just like the earthquake back home, you performed an amazing task. You simply lacked control."

"So, how do I learn control?" asked Bobby.

"We must wear down the walls of your subconscious," said Master Jong. "Only when you can consciously touch the *presence* can you learn to control it."

Bobby tried to hide his disappointment as Master Jong went on to remind him that his barrier had always been, and continued to be, an impregnable wall. The goal of their meditation sessions had been to teach him mental discipline— not to destroy the barrier, but simply to peek behind it.

"We have achieved the first step in the process," said Master Jong. "Your inner barrier is now translucent, metaphorically speaking. That is what allowed you to sense the presence of the mushrooms and follow your instincts to the source. Which means that it is now time to bring down the barrier completely."

"So, what now? Some new form of meditation?" said Bobby, disappointed but not surprised.

Master Jong shook his head. "This calls for a completely different technique."

"What's that?" asked Bobby. He felt a hint of excitement at the idea of learning something new.

"Physical exertion," said Master Jong.

"You have something specific in mind?"

"Indeed I do," said Master Jong. "It's not exactly basketball, but don't worry. The lesson should still work out well with the message I have been given by the headmistress."

Bobby scowled. "And what message is that?"

"The headmistress has instructed me to inform you that by leaving your assigned search area and ascending the hillside, you violated several of the school's rules. As such, you are to be given an official reprimand and assigned punishment."

"Punishment?" Bobby balked. "What the heck? I thought everyone was ecstatic that we found all those mushrooms. So why am I in trouble?"

"I'm sorry, Bobby. There is nothing I can do to change the assignment, even if I wanted to."

Bobby stopped following the tiny monk. "What do you mean 'even if you wanted to'? You're happy that I'm being punished?"

"Like I said, it works out perfectly in this situation," said Master Jong. "Yet another example of how everything happens for a reason."

Bobby put his hands on his hips. "Yeah? And how's that exactly?"

The monk's expression betrayed nothing. "The punishment assigned by the headmistress is for you to work in the mines."

CHAPTER 14

In the still of the night, there was no one to interrupt Headmistress Grayson in her office. On her desk lay the pile of *Transitivo paradoxa* mushrooms, delivered to her by Master Jong. The faintest frown touched the corners of her mouth. According to Simpkins, the troublesome monk was up to something, but that was an issue for another time.

Next to the pile of fibrous mushrooms stood her crystal decanter, empty except for the dregs of her last elixir. *Not even enough for a sip.* Some would have called the new boy's discovery coincidence, but she knew better. She was meant to have this precious treasure, just as she was meant to rule.

Swiveling in her chair, she reached along the bottom edge of the mural behind her desk for the hidden catch. In one fluid motion, the picture ascended, disappearing into the ceiling to reveal a chemistry lab recessed into a secret alcove. Beakers, flasks, and apparatus of all different shapes and sizes filled the space. Bunsen burners hooked up to a portable propane tank in one corner. In the other corner sat over a dozen rows of glass vials filled with chemicals and compounds, all neatly labeled in tiny, spidery script.

She pushed a button on the alcove wall and soft music streamed into the room through hidden speakers: "Ride of the Valkyries" by Richard Wagner. She smiled; the theme was not without significance. She had delivered fallen heroes up to Valhalla on more than one occasion and would no doubt do so again before her days as headmistress were over.

She hummed as she set one of the mushrooms into the mortar—an exquisitely carved jade bowl shaped like a man's palms cupped together—and ground it up with a pestle shaped like a woman's arm, her delicate hand curled into a tight fist.

Her mind wandered as she worked, back to her days as a student, like the first time she partook in a foraging expedition as a youth. To be certain, her discovery was much smaller than this one. Nevertheless, the impact on her life had been enormous. *Even back then, circumstances always worked out to my advantage.*

When she discovered a small colony of tiny fungi growing under a rotted tree stump, a little voice inside her head told her to keep some. Trusting her instincts, she secreted away a few mushrooms before turning the rest of the colony over to the headmaster. Her discovery earned her the envy of her fellow students as well as many of her teachers, but that was not what changed her life. In fact, her short-lived celebrity was nothing compared to what came after.

She smiled as "Ride of the Valkyries" segued into "Flight of the Bumblebee" by Korsakov—another piece with a fitting theme. When she was a student, the academics had no idea that this innocuous little fungus with its scarlet cap and ghostly white stalk had any real use except for making a mild incense. *Worker bees without the slightest clue as to the amazing mushroom's true potential.*

Even with her exceptional intuition, she spent weeks uncovering the truth. First, she studied all the existing data in the library on the rare mushroom's biology and chemical composition. Its red cap was poisonous if not prepared properly.

Not only that, but experimenting with the fungus was hazardous. Even after the poison was leeched out, the remaining extract was volatile.

Next, she consulted with the monks, whose lore was often not shared with the academics. From the eldest among them, she heard tales about efforts to derive a serum from the stalk as well as the cap. Some claimed the combination of the two granted the imbiber tremendous power. Others argued the dangerous concoction had no positive effect at all but only the hallucinogenic illusion of power. They all agreed on one thing— digesting the mushroom consistently over time led to psychosis, neurosis, and, in some cases, even death.

Undeterred, the future headmistress experimented with recreating the serum described by the monks. It was impossible to use the school's laboratories during normal hours without prying eyes, so she snuck in late at night when no one else was around.

The first step was to create an extract. That part wasn't difficult. Notes from previous experiments offered clues about this process. Finding a way to control the volatility and neutralize the poison was another matter entirely. It took many months and almost all of her supply of the precious fungus to finally derive an extract that appeared to be safe. From there, it was a short journey to find the proper balancing agents to create a drinkable concoction.

After that, the trick was testing it. At first she tried her mixtures on rabbits and squirrels in the gardens. She was forced to stop, however, when several turned up dead and another turned rabid and attacked the gardeners. She tried a tiny portion of the tincture on herself and became ill for days.

Eventually, she settled for slipping her concoctions into other students' meals and studying the effects from afar. She felt no remorse when several of her unwitting test subjects fell violently ill. A young boy even went crazy, screaming that he saw ghosts of monks from generations past stalking the halls. He disappeared from the academy shortly after that and was never seen or heard from again. Still, she learned a little from each test and improved future products as a result. Real progress was achieved. That's what mattered.

Then came the fateful day when she slipped her newest tonic into the drink of a young student and, instead of becoming violently ill, the girl became magnificently gifted. That day in class, the girl performed feats she had struggled with for years. She fell into a deep trance in which she touched the void, sensing the universal Being. Afterward, she could read people's thoughts and sense their emotions. When the future headmistress heard about this, she made sure to avoid the girl until the effects wore off.

Two days later, the girl was back to her normal, inept self. The future headmistress, however, was changed forever. She'd discovered a powerful, energy-enhancing drug. Knowing that the Jade Academy prized ability above all else, she took full advantage, using the elixir whenever she had important tests to take or feats to perform. In only a few short months, she went from an average student to the head of her class.

By the time she graduated, she was regarded as one of the most gifted students to ever pass through the academy. She took a staff position to stay close to the source of her success and bask in her accolades. Becoming headmistress was inevitable—fate delivering what she deserved. Now she was the queen bee and all the bumblebees worked for her.

But for how long? The most recent message from her superiors was quite clear. While her talent was not in question, her skill as a leader was. Recent graduates had failed to satisfy her masters' requirements. If she couldn't produce new candidates for their experiments soon, her future would be in serious jeopardy.

She debated her options. Blood samples would no longer suffice. They wanted the complete subject for their experiments. One of the upperclassmen, perhaps—Trevor Williams, or one of the twins.

But the headmistress had always been one to think big and act bigger. Delivering a modestly competent student might mollify her superiors for now, but not for long. What she needed was someone with talent so powerful that her methods would not be questioned ever again.

She could give them Ashley, of course. Her daughter met all the requirements and then some. But the headmistress had other plans—plans that did not involve her daughter being used as a guinea pig. That left only one option, one possible way to emerge truly triumphant from her current predicament—the Ether kid.

The results from the blood work when he'd been brought in unconscious confirmed that he had the potential to be extraordinary. Now, if only he would manifest it, so she could hand him over and claim her reward.

—m—

Just before dawn, the headmistress set down the Erlenmeyer flask and raised two fingers to each temple. The long night spent measuring ingredients, boiling solutions, filtering byproducts, and distilling results made her head feel like a balloon ready to pop. Now, in the last few hours, other symptoms started to appear—the shaking, the chills, the uncontrollable hunger for the cure that now, thankfully, lay just moments away.

The instant it was ready, the headmistress took a long swig straight from the flask, then another. With the fire in her veins quenched, she transferred the rest of the flask's contents into the crystal decanter. She placed the unused mushrooms in an airtight container that she put into a tiny refrigerator in the back of the alcove. Then she sat back to admire her work.

Some would call the brew ugly, a sickly green, but she knew better. It was the color of energy, the color of power, the color of control. Now, thanks to Bobby Ether and the favors of fortune, she was guaranteed control for a long time to come.

CHAPTER 15

The east wing of the Jade Academy was a deserted jumble of dead ends and broken stairwells, forcing Bobby to constantly backtrack. After what felt like hours, he found the thick iron doors marking the entrance to the jade mines.

On the other side, the polished walls of the monastery gave way to raw earth. The air grew heavy and dry as Bobby followed the tunnel into a large cavern from which six shafts branched off in various directions. Around each opening, thick wood frames held up the ceiling.

A familiar fat figure stood alone in the center of the room, next to a propane-powered generator for the lights. Bobby slowed as Hayward's pudgy face came into view.

"Ah, Bobby Ether. So nice of you to join us," said Hayward, smiling to reveal tiny crooked teeth with a large gap in the front.

Bobby stared at the wall behind Hayward rather than look the man in the face. "What is it I have to do?" he said brusquely.

"The first thing you need to do is fix that attitude," said Hayward.

"Why? Do I get in trouble if I refuse to smile? Smiling isn't for everyone, ya know."

Hayward raised a hand and Bobby's throat constricted, choking off his windpipe.

"What's the matter?" asked Hayward as Bobby struggled to breathe. "No more smartass comments? After what you did to that hospital, I thought maybe you were a fighter. Looks like I was wrong."

Bobby put his hands to his throat, gasping for breath. Hayward watched him for another moment before turning away. "Such a waste," he said, waving dismissively. The pressure on Bobby's throat vanished. He dropped to his hands and knees, gulping air.

"Grab a wheelbarrow and one of the pickaxes from the container over here," said Hayward as if nothing had happened. "Then come back here and I'll assign you a spot to work."

When Bobby could talk again, he said, "What did you just do to me?"

"What, that? Just a little lesson in respect," said Hayward. "Now, let's see, I could send you off someplace at random. With luck, you'd get lost, stumble into the Spine of the World, and disappear forever. Then again, the headmistress might object. Too much paperwork. Not that you have any parents to notify."

Bobby stepped toward Hayward, fists clenched. Then he stopped, took a deep breath, and relaxed his hands.

Hayward watched, amused. "So, you can learn after all," he said, giving Bobby another gap-toothed smile. "Good for you."

"Just tell me what I have to do," said Bobby, panting as he regained control.

"Hmm, I know. We'll put you down the west tunnel," said Hayward. "Normally, I'd refrain from putting you close to other students for fear that you'd enjoy the company, but, in this case, I don't think that'll be a problem."

"So, I'm just smashing the walls and stuff, looking for jade?" asked Bobby.

Hayward burst into laughter, his blubbery jowls bouncing up and down. "Looking for jade? Oh my, no, that might make it fun. You'll be working in a section of the mines that's been bone dry for decades. The whole point is to work knowing that it serves no purpose."

Bobby grabbed a pickax and tossed it into a cart. Heading in the designated direction, he passed below several support beams before arriving at an intersection. Unsure which path to take, he listened down each tunnel but heard no sign of other students. Determined to do anything but return to Hayward, he picked a direction at random and continued walking.

After a few minutes, he heard voices. Following the sound, he peeked around a corner to discover Tex and Mex hammering away at a small quarry while Ashley sat on a wheelbarrow watching them work. Tex swung his ax with one hand and scratched his rear with the other. All three had their backs to Bobby as they worked and chatted. Bobby turned around to tiptoe back the way he'd come.

"Well, speak of the devil," said Ashley, spinning around as a rock crunched under Bobby's foot. "Hey, boys, look who decided to join the party."

"Oh, hey," said Bobby. "What are you guys doing here?" *What a stupid thing to say!*

"What do you think we're doing here, mister?" said Tex in a thick Southern drawl. "We're here because of you."

It took Bobby a moment to make sense of the comment. "You mean you got in trouble for picking a fight with Lily and Jacob after I went missing."

"That little punk had it coming," said Mex, the slightly taller and darker of the twins. "He tried to be a hero. He wasn't so heroic with my fist in his face."

"So what's the deal, Ashley?" asked Bobby. "Mommy dearest wouldn't give you a free pass for picking on kids half your size?"

Ashley remained seated on the wheelbarrow with a look of utter disdain. "That little brat was babbling like a baby. I had to do something to get her to make sense."

"She didn't know anything and you know it," said Bobby. "You're the one who was being a witch, picking on her like that."

Tex stepped toward Bobby, hefting the ax over his shoulder with one hand while scratching his butt with the other. "What did you say, mister?"

"You got a death wish or something?" asked Mex.

Bobby held his ground. "Maybe I'm just tired of people picking on my friends."

"Is that so?" said Mex, sticking a finger up his nose. "Well, how about we pick on you instead?"

"Hey, Sniff! You really shouldn't pick at all," said someone behind them. "Or haven't you learned that lesson yet?"

Bobby wheeled around to find Jacob standing behind him.

Mex gave the stocky redhead one glance and burst into laughter. "Look, guys, it's the little hero again."

"Oh, I'm *so* scared," said Tex.

"You should be," said Jacob, without a hint of sarcasm. "It's a lot easier to pick on someone when the odds are stacked in your favor."

Tex stopped scratching long enough to do a slow count on his fingers. "It's three against two," he said finally. "I'd say that's fair enough."

"Guess again," said a new voice behind Jacob. Bobby looked over Jacob's shoulder to see Trevor and Lily running up.

"Nice timing," whispered Bobby as all three friends came to stand next to him.

Trevor gave him a roguish grin. "Apparently, it's my lot in life to keep you from getting yourself killed."

"So, what's it gonna be?" Jacob asked Ashley. "Wanna see who ends up with a fist in their face this time?"

Ashley stared at them, clearly weighing her options. Her eyes locked on Lily. "I know that little blabbermouth will just tell on us again."

Lily twisted an imaginary lock in her mouth and threw away the key. "Not a word."

Ashley's expression soured. "As much as I'd enjoy making you all cry, embarrassing you isn't worth more of this horrendous digging. This place stinks worse than Trevor's dorm room."

Jacob looked ready to press the issue, but Lily grabbed his arm. "Come on, guys. I can't believe I'm saying this, but she's right; it's not worth it. Let's go find someplace else to dig and leave these jerks to themselves. Maybe they can find an earthworm to pick on."

— �m —

The gang spent over half an hour wandering the tunnels, looking for a suitable dig site. They finally settled on a cul-de-sac where part of the wall was cracked and crumbling.

"This stinks," complained Jacob. He slammed his ax into the unyielding stone. "I didn't sign up for this."

"Neither did I," said Trevor, "but you don't hear me complaining."

"That reminds me," said Bobby. "What *are* you doing here? Lily and Jacob are here because of the fight, but you were with me. You can't possibly be in trouble for rescuing me."

Trevor just shrugged. Jacob faked a loud cough. "Lily," he said under his breath. Trevor ducked his head, but even with his dark skin and the dim light, he was clearly blushing.

"I see you two have patched up your differences," said Bobby.

"Trevor is still annoying," grumbled Jacob. "But those jerks back there are even worse. I can't wait for the day they get theirs."

Trevor clapped him on the back. "You're a real charmer, you know that, Jacob?"

The two of them continued a steady stream of banter as they worked. Bobby edged down the tunnel, closer to Lily, who was waiting to break up large rocks into smaller chunks.

"Hey, Lily, mind if I ask you a question?" asked Bobby. "What's up with the wood frames all over the place?"

Lily set down her ax. "Supposedly the same abundance of anima that drew the monks here also makes the mountain unstable. Because of all the excavation over the centuries, the mines are the worst. That's why they built all those support frames—to keep the tunnels from collapsing. It doesn't always work, though. There was a cave-in in the northern passages just last week. A bunch of monks are over there right now, working to repair the damage."

"And do these tunnels have anything to do with 'the Spine of the World'?"

Lily brushed a lock of dirty copper hair out of her sweaty face. "Why do you ask?"

"Hayward made some comment about it. I was just wondering if there's a story."

"More like a myth," said Lily.

"I'd love to hear it."

"Honestly, I don't know anything but gossip," said Lily.

"And we all know how you *hate* gossip." Bobby tried to keep a straight face as Lily gave him her best angry scowl. Then they broke into laughter.

—ₘ—

According to legend, the Spine of the World was a secret passage that ran from the base of the mountain to the summit, like a backbone. Countless rumors existed about what lay inside the hidden tunnel. The story Lily told Bobby was simply the most recent.

A few decades back, a survey team of academics went missing while attempting to map the labyrinth of crisscrossing tunnels that had been dug, mined, and then abandoned over the centuries. A week after their disappearance, the leader of the team was found in the valley below, delirious from hunger and dehydration, and yet surprisingly coherent about what had transpired.

While surveying some outlying passages, the team encountered an arched doorway they were convinced hadn't been there before. Curious, they investigated and discovered a small chamber with three doors covered in ancient runes. They found their return route sealed and, reluctant to split up, picked a passage at random and continued onward.

The path they followed ascended to a grand library filled with scrolls and books beyond imagination. The team immediately set to studying the ancient texts, losing themselves in the library's vast collection. But the library held no food or water. And so, after a few hours, the leader decided to head back to the central chamber. Two of the men reluctantly agreed, but the others refused, claiming that they dared not waste even a single moment apart from such precious knowledge. With no other choice, the three academics left their colleagues behind with promises to send back a team with supplies as soon as they found an exit.

The three comrades backtracked to the central chamber where they chose between the remaining two doors. This time, the door led to an immense room piled high with treasure—gold and silver, diamonds and rubies, sapphires and emeralds, and a rainbow of other gems. Just like the library, however, the room contained no food, water, or alternative exit.

Once again, the leader ordered his men to depart, but both men refused, claiming that the priceless treasure was too valuable to be left unguarded. For nearly two days, the leader tried persuading his comrades to leave. Only when he became too hungry and thirsty to risk waiting any longer did he abandon his foolhardy friends.

Bobby took a break from digging, setting down his ax to give Lily his complete attention. "So what happened? How did he find a way out?"

"According to the man's story, the third passage led to an exit at the base of the mountain. From there, he wandered out into the countryside, where a search party found him a few days later, starving and near death."

"And what about the others?"

Lily shook her head. "Search parties combed both the mines and the base of the mountain, but no one ever found the arched doorway, the exit, or the other men in the party."

"Maybe he imagined it," said Bobby. "You did say he was delirious when they found him."

"That's true," said Lily, "but that doesn't explain what happened to the other men or how he turned up in the valley after he and his team disappeared in the mines."

"Maybe you have the story wrong. Like you said, it happened a long time ago."

"Or there is another possibility," said Lily. "Maybe everything the man said was true and the doorway simply disappeared."

Bobby laughed. "Rooms filled with books and treasure are one thing, but disappearing doorways? Come on. How many times since being here have I heard that there is no such thing as magic?"

"That's true," said Lily. "But we have also learned that certain unexplained phenomena do exist."

Bobby scoffed. "So, you're saying it's possible that an entire tunnel system just vanished?"

Lily shrugged. "If there is one thing I've learned since coming here, it's that, with enough power, almost anything is possible. The laws of the universe can be bent, if not broken, and the monastery was built on this remote mountain for a reason. It's rumored that the Spine of the World is a fount of energy, a deep reservoir of anima. Who's to know what's possible with that much power?"

Bobby was about to resume his protest when he heard someone approaching.

"Hello, children," said Hayward. "I hope I am not interrupting your social time."

"We're just working," said Bobby.

"Yeah, we're almost done," said Lily.

"Very interesting," said Hayward. "I see two partially filled carts, which is fine, except that, since you are working together, you obviously need to fill twice as much." Bobby's and Lily's mouths fell open as Hayward's lips parted in the barest hint of a smile.

"But we haven't been working together, not really," said Lily. "Most of this was done separately."

"It's my fault, really," said Hayward. "I forgot that there are students down here that are actually willing to talk to Mr. Ether."

"We'll be quiet," said Lily quickly.

"I am sure you will. As a matter of fact, I am certain of it. Mr. Ether, gather your things. You are being relocated."

"But that's not fair," said Bobby. "You left Ashley and the twins to work together."

"The conduct of the other students is none of your concern. Now dump out your wheelbarrow and go find another place to work, or you will be joining me here again tomorrow."

Bobby overturned his cart right at Hayward's feet.

"Careful, Mr. Ether."

Bobby picked up his ax and flung it into the now-empty cart. Without looking at Lily or Hayward, he pushed his cart back down the tunnel.

—◊◊◊—

It took Bobby forever to find another suitable spot. He was forced to backtrack all the way to the first intersection of the western wing. Of the four tunnels, one led back to the main entrance, another led toward Ashley and her goons, and he'd come from the third, which left one option.

An overturned cart with a flat tire lay perpendicular across the path, but whether to bar the entrance or simply abandoned, Bobby couldn't say. Too upset to care, he skirted it and kept walking.

The tunnel was noticeably different than the others—cool and damp with thick patches of pale lichen. The squeak of his cart's lone wheel echoed softly as he followed the path to an old abandoned quarry. A narrow side passage was blocked with sawhorses and a rusted yellow sign that read, *Danger: Unstable Area. Do Not Enter.*

Dropping his wheelbarrow, Bobby gathered the collection of rocks and small boulders scattered on the ground. *No harm in profiting from someone else's work.* Once done, he raised his ax and started on the closest niche. He thought about Master Jong and his comments about manual labor as he worked. *This is supposed to wear down the barrier in my subconscious? Yeah, right. The only thing wearing down is my patience.*

Yet he couldn't help but succumb to the mind-numbing rhythm of the work—lift, swing, pry, lift, swing, pry. The more he worked, the less he felt. Even the pain of his parents' deaths seemed to fade as he hammered away at the wall.

In time, his arms turned to rubber, each swing weaker than the last. He set the ax down and leaned against the wall. That's when he felt it.

Bobby placed both palms on the hard stone. He hadn't imagined it; the wall felt warm and alive, like the heaving side of a living animal. He shifted his hands along the wall. Something pulsed beneath the surface—an earthen telltale heart. He stopped at a spot at shoulder height, about four feet left of his original position. Whatever it was, it lay here, just a few inches below the surface. Bobby picked up his ax and assaulted the wall with renewed fervor, hollowing the area around his prize.

Flipping the ax over, he tapped gently on a chunk in the middle with the butt of the handle. The mass broke loose easily, the wall eager to deliver its gift. Tossing the ax away, he scooped up the lump in both hands, breaking off the outer layers of dirt until all that was left was a smooth, pale stone, winking at him in the dim light.

It took a moment for his discovery to sink in. In his hand sat a piece of the precious jade from which the legend of the Jade Academy had been born.

—⟋⟍—

None of Bobby's friends so much as glanced at him at dinner. In fact, barely anyone spoke. Instead, heads sagged and conversation dragged as they propped their elbows on the table to keep from falling over, exhausted from their day in the mines.

Lily sat next to Trevor, her head resting on his shoulder. Jacob glowered at Trevor whenever Lily wasn't looking, but there was no weight to it. Even Trevor and Jacob's bickering sounded tired.

"Pass the salt," said Trevor.

"Get it yourself," said Jacob.

"Wow, what are you, six?"

"I know you are, but what am I?"

Lily scowled, but Bobby couldn't help but smile at their juvenile banter. Thankfully, no one asked him about his time spent working alone, and he was happy not to bring it up. The piece of jade sat in his pocket, a black hole sucking in all of his thoughts and attention. He'd share it with his friends, but first he wanted to examine it alone and figure out why he'd been drawn to it.

Bobby said his goodbyes, bused his plate, and headed to his room. Even more than answers, what he needed was a long, hot shower and sleep.

—⟋⟍—

Bobby tossed and turned on his bed. The tiny pallet felt like a block of ice. The blanket covering him was a sheet of fire. Not for the first time, he thought of his plush, queen-size bed back home—a home he would probably never see again.

Bobby slugged his pillow and rolled over, trying to find a comfortable position on the lumpy bed of straw. The corner of the pillow rewarded him with a poke in the ear. The pallet jabbed him in the ribs. Bobby threw off the blanket and sat up. The small round clock on the table showed 2:13. The bags under his eyes felt like anchors as he stood, donned a jacket, and shuffled to the window.

As he passed the table, he scooped up the small chunk of jade. Holding it up to the light, he studied the walnut-sized rock, noticing how the moonlight penetrated the outer layers to give the stone a glossy luster. The slender length looked translucent, almost glowing in the gray shadows. He stared at it, admiring its beauty even as he struggled to focus his eyes.

Turning away from the window, he spotted a pile of long-forgotten "suggested reading material," given to him by Jinx, on the far corner of the desk. Beneath a gigantic tome on flora and fauna native to northwestern Tibet rested the picture of his family he'd grabbed the day he fled his home with Cassandra.

Bobby picked up the photo, looking at himself as a young boy alongside the smiling faces of his mother, father, and grandfather. He tucked the photo into his jacket pocket and was about to head back to bed when something else caught his eye. Back behind the books, like a coiled snake, lay the silver necklace with the lotus pendant his grandfather gave him.

Bobby gingerly drew out the medallion, feeling its cool, reassuring presence in his palm. The translucent sheen suggested secrets buried just below the surface. He held up the stone from the mines and compared the two side by side. And, just like that, he understood.

Before he crawled back into bed, Bobby took the family photo and tucked it into the breast pocket of his jacket. His head was still full of questions, but he also had two very important answers. He now knew why he'd been drawn to the stone in the wall. He also knew what he needed to do next.

CHAPTER 16

Midmorning light drifted through the autumn trees as Master Jong strolled along the forest trail. Birds chirped merrily in the treetops, accompanied by the rustle of animals foraging in the underbrush. A fat brown squirrel with a tail as long as the monk's arm broke onto the road. Sitting back on its haunches, it chittered indignation at being disturbed before scampering back into the bushes.

Master Jong couldn't help but smile. It was a beautiful day. The forest was a kaleidoscope of greens and browns formed by sugar maples blended with oak and cedar. The colors touched him, moving him with their beauty. It was a perfect scene of forest tranquility. And yet something felt wrong.

He walked on, content to let whatever had triggered his subconscious float to the surface on its own accord. It wasn't until he neared the outskirts of the village that he grew concerned. Something about the forest's song was off. *The notes are the same as usual, but the tune is different*, he thought. A disturbance like that could only mean one thing—someone else was in the forest.

Master Jong ducked behind a mighty oak and sat among the gnarled roots. Crossing his legs, he aligned his posture so his back was straight with his head and shoulders positioned directly over his hips. *It's always important to remember the basics*, he reminded himself as he took several slow, deep breaths. *In through the nose, out through the mouth . . .*

He anchored his energy, sending his chi down to wrap around the core of the earth and up to meet the heavens. Then he took that energy and wrapped it around himself in a shield—invisible armor to protect him against harmful backlash.

Satisfied that he was thoroughly grounded, Master Jong stretched out his senses and probed the surrounding area. The presence of the forest's living creatures lit up his mind like a thousand tiny torches. A majestic buck grazed with a young fawn in a nearby meadow. A family of beavers was busy building a dam in the creek. A badger with an angry aura nestled deep in its den. Master Jong let his mind linger over each animal for just a moment before moving on to the next. *No sign of the transgressor.*

He directed his attention toward the outskirts of the village. A handful of local farmers worked in the fields—all perfectly normal. The townsfolk appeared undisturbed. He continued searching for several minutes but discovered nothing out of place. *You're a tricky one; I'll give you that.* There were only a handful of people at the academy—in the entire world, for that matter—who had the skill to evade him in this manner.

He paused as he contemplated inducing a trance state to gain higher levels of awareness. Doing so would undoubtedly reveal the identity of his tail. It would also take a great deal of time—time he did not have.

If only Chief would respond to my letters, thought Master Jong. It had been over two weeks since the monk last checked in with Hatou, but instinct told him his old friend had nothing new to report. Now, a growing sense of desperation tugged at him as he struggled to remain optimistic.

Master Jong reached back to touch the oilcloth bundle pressed against his spine—copies of a new section of the sacred text that he had laboriously memorized and transferred to parchment one page at a time. Satisfied that they were tightly secured and outwardly undetectable, he dropped his hand.

What to do, what to do? The village lay just down the road, and Hatou's cottage just beyond that. Master Jong stood, staring into the distance as if he could see the answer in the wind. Finally, he left the mighty oak and plunged toward the heart of the forest, away from Hatou's. If there was one thing Master Jong had learned in all his years as a master, it was to never ignore his instincts.

—◊◊—

The viewing room for the ancient scrolls sat at the very top of the monastery. With its secluded location, open terrace, and panoramic view of the valley below, the earthen chamber provided an ideal setting to stir the soul and inspire the imagination. Only the two academics stationed by the door encroached on the otherwise perfect tranquility.

Master Jong paid heed to neither the guards nor the landscape as he crossed over to the protective alcove housing the sacred texts. Carefully extracting six pages, he took a seat on a cushion by the low table upon which the scrolls could be comfortably viewed.

He methodically studied each page, creating a mental image down to the coloration and grain pattern of the thick papyrus. When he was done, he went back over each page to compare the actual text with the image in his head.

Finally satisfied that he had every detail thoroughly committed to memory, Master Jong stacked the pages and prepared to depart. As he stood, something brushed his aura—a taint on the energy around him, the faintest hint of something rancid in the otherwise pure mountain air.

The guards watched as Master Jong casually sat back down and pretended to read once again. In fact, he reached out with his senses to probe the surrounding area. Just as he suspected, someone sat in one of the contemplation rooms directly below.

Master Jong extended his thoughts and probed the man's aura. He instantly encountered a crimson aura full of anger and hostility. *Definitely not the unreadable man who followed me in the woods*, thought Master Jong. He probed deeper, sensing a cruel and sadistic nature.

Having felt more than enough to identify the headmistress's lackey Hayward, Master Jong began to withdraw. But Hayward's energy clung to him, latching onto his as he tried to pull away. He tried again, gagging and choking now as the oily stench invaded his nose and throat.

With the guards watching curiously, Master Jong finally managed to sever the link, feeling instantly weaker as he surrendered the energy used to make the connection. *An effective defense*, he thought as he regained his strength. Despite a vile persona, Hayward clearly commanded tremendous power— which left Master Jong with the question of what to do next. With Hayward watching him, going back to his bedchamber to transcribe the pages was out of the question, as was going to the village. What he needed was a new place to work, one where no one would think to look.

In time, an idea took root. Forcing himself not to rush, he spent another half hour pretending to pore over the scrolls. Then he stood, returned the scrolls to the alcove, smiled at the guards, and left.

CHAPTER 17

Bobby went to the library immediately after dinner. He found Jinx at his usual desk in the back. Jinx put his pen down and closed his book as Bobby approached.

"I'm glad to see you're feeling better," said Jinx.

"The monks worked on my ankle after we got back," said Bobby. "I was up and walking around the next day, good as new."

"And your head?"

"They looked at that, too, but couldn't find anything wrong. They said all that blood must have come from someplace else."

Jinx gave him a deep frown. "I heard about what happened in the mines. My sister can be a real b—"

Bobby waved him off. "Don't worry about it. Like they always say around here, 'Everything happens for a reason.'"

Jinx looked puzzled. "You think there was a reason you got in trouble? I mean, *besides* the reason you got in trouble."

Bobby placed the chunk of jade from his pocket on the desk, alongside the amulet.

Jinx picked up the amulet. "What's this?"

"It was a gift from my grandfather when I was a little boy," said Bobby. "I found the rock yesterday, while digging in the mines."

Jinx studied the two items side by side. His eyes grew wide. "Both have virtually no visible signs of spotting or mottling," said Jinx. "And the pigmentation and level of translucence in the two stones are almost identical."

Bobby grinned widely.

"But that means—"

"Yup."

"But the academy hasn't traded in jade in over two centuries. Even if they did, it's virtually impossible that your grandfather bought it. The cost would have been astronomical."

"Yup," said Bobby.

Jinx scowled at him. "Well, since you seem to have figured out so much already, why don't you clue me in?"

Bobby beamed at him. "I thought you'd never ask."

It took almost no time for Jinx to catch on. Before Bobby was halfway through his explanation, his clever friend had beaten him to the punch. "So you think that your grandfather must have been at the academy at some point?"

"It makes sense, right?" said Bobby. "What are the odds that he found the amulet? Or that he bought it? That means he had to have been here. He probably got it from one of the monks."

"Well, if he was a student," said Jinx, "there would be a record of it."

"That's exactly what I'm counting on," said Bobby.

"So you want to search for evidence of your grandfather?"

Bobby nodded. "And I know just the place to start. Actually, you're the one who told me about it."

"Wait a minute. You're not talking about the archives, are you? Do you have any idea how massive that place is?"

Bobby shrugged. "You told me it's big."

"I don't think you understand. There are at least five sublevels to the archives, maybe more from before they started keeping charts. Each sublevel is at least as large as the academy itself. It could take years for us to find something in all that mess. And that's assuming there's even something to find."

Bobby frowned, but just for a second. "I'm sure something will turn up. I seem to have a knack for finding things."

"That may be true," said Jinx, "but the archives are like catacombs. There are dead ends and unmarked sections all over the place. Even if you're somehow able to sense which direction to go, you could still easily end up way off target."

"What if we got the others to help out?"

Jinx shook his head. "It wouldn't matter. Whether together or alone, even the most gifted individuals would have a tough time finding anything in all of the stuff. It's just too big."

"What's this about searching for something?"

Both boys turned to see Ashley standing beside the stacks, for once unaccompanied by the Tex-Mex twins.

"Hey, Ash. What are you doing here?" stammered Jinx. "You don't normally come to the library. Did you come to give me your homework?"

"Actually, I came to apologize."

Jinx couldn't have looked more surprised if she'd told him his hair was on fire. "You what?"

Ashley put her hands on her hips and gave her brother a stern look. "You heard me. I came to apologize for leaving you alone on a team with him," she said, jerking a thumb at Bobby. "But now I come to find you hanging out with him, like you two are best friends."

"You mean that Mom heard about what you did and told you to apologize."

Ashley glared at her little brother, her face a deep crimson. "Technically, the words she used were 'poor judgment' and 'preserving viable resources.'"

"Yeah, well, I don't want your apology."

"Good, because you're not getting one now," snapped Ashley. "The fact that you're sitting here with this loser makes it obvious that you're the one with poor judgment."

Bobby shot to his feet. "Now wait just a minute."

Jinx broke in before he went any further. "I think we are done here. Don't you, Ashley?"

"You're darn right we're done. I'm also done looking out for you, little brother. From now on, if you want to hang out with loser trash like this, you're on your own."

Without waiting for a reply, Ashley turned and walked away. When she reached the end of the book stacks, she turned back around.

"Oh, and one more thing, boys, I don't know what kind of search you two have planned, but you'd better watch your backs. The next time either of you crosses the line, I promise you'll get everything coming to you and much, much more."

—–ᴠᴠ–—

Jacob put his feet on the desk and folded his arms. "So. What's the big secret?"

"Yeah," said Trevor. "Why are we hiding in the back of the library like a bunch of nerds?" Lily elbowed him in the ribs.

"Sorry, Jinx. No offense," mumbled Trevor.

"You're here because I need your help," said Bobby.

"If it involves any more digging, count me out," said Jacob. "I've still got dirt in places I didn't even know existed."

"Gross," said Lily as Jacob shot her a sly grin.

"This is serious," said Jinx. "Bobby and I have a theory, and if we're right, there could be huge implications."

Bobby filled his friends in on his discussion with Jinx the night before and how they'd surmised that Bobby's grandfather must have been at the academy.

"That's great," said Jacob. "But I don't see how it matters. I mean, even if your grandpa was here at some point, he's obviously long gone."

Bobby turned to Trevor. "Do you remember telling me how the monks used to make puzzle boxes out of the jade?"

"Sure, but what does that have to do with—"

"Oh!" Jacob dropped his feet and sat up straight. "You think the pendant is a puzzle box!"

"It makes sense," said Bobby. "It can't be an accident he gave me something that special. Maybe it contains a message."

"There's just one problem with that scenario—" said Jacob.

"Even if the amulet is a puzzle box," said Trevor, "no one knows how to open them."

Jacob shot daggers at Trevor. "Thanks for stealing my thunder, jerk."

"Anytime," said Trevor with a self-satisfied grin.

Lily set a hand on Trevor's thigh to settle him down. "So, what's the goal if we can't get it open?"

"Maybe you could ask Master Jong?" said Trevor.

Jacob scoffed. "I heard that it's been so long since they made puzzle boxes that the monks nowadays don't know how to open them."

"You've got it wrong, as usual," Trevor rebuked him. "The monks know how the boxes open. They're just sworn to secrecy."

"Either way, Master Jong probably won't be of any help," sighed Lily. "Sorry, Bobby. We can still ask him if you want."

"That's okay. I want to keep this just between us for now. At least until I know what's inside."

"Well, maybe we can figure it out on our own," said Jacob. "Let me take a look."

Bobby pulled out the amulet, now off of its chain. He handed it to Jacob, but Trevor snatched it first.

"Gimme that," said Jacob, grabbing for it. Trevor deflected with an elbow.

"Relax, munchkin," said Trevor. "You don't know what to look for anyway."

Jacob shot him a glare full of daggers. "Like you do."

"All right, boys," said Lily, reaching for the trinket. She cupped her hands around Trevor's and gently pried the amulet free. Trevor seemed to hold on longer than necessary.

She offered the pendant to Jinx, who waved her off.

"I've already studied it at length," he said. "Despite a most thorough investigation, I can find no moving parts or points of ingress."

Lily shrugged, took a chair, and studied it herself.

"Maybe we need a microscope?" suggested Jacob. "There's some in the science lab."

"Puzzle boxes have been around for centuries, dummy. Which means they don't require modern tools," said Trevor. "Besides, they've been opened in public before, right in front of people."

Jacob scooted closer to Lily, trying to look over her shoulder.

"Hey, man," said Trevor. "Give the lady some space."

"Oh, right. *Now* you remember your manners."

"Both of you, simmer down!" said Lily. She handed the amulet to Jacob, who seized it in both hands like a championship trophy.

The rest of the group watched as he bombarded the amulet with an assortment of tactics—holding it to his ear, shaking it, tapping it lightly with his knuckles, even spitting on it. Trevor sprang up when Jacob pried at it with the tip of a penknife.

"Hey, man, be careful with that."

"It's alright," said Bobby. "I did that myself. I don't think there is anything inside—at least not anything that you can pry open."

Finally, Jacob handed the pendant back to Bobby. "Sorry, man. I really wish I could help."

"That's okay. I have another idea."

When he was done explaining his plan, he leaned back and studied his friends' faces. Trevor looked excited. Jacob seemed incredulous. Jinx already knew the idea. That left Lily.

"Let me see if I've got this straight," she said. "You want to search the entire archives for some small piece of proof that your grandfather was here, in the hopes that it will help you open the pendant, which we don't even know for sure is a puzzle box?"

"Well, when you put it like that . . ."

Lily frowned. "I want to support you, Bobby, honestly, I do, but don't you think that plan is just a little far-fetched?"

Jacob jumped up. "Thank goodness someone here has some sense. So we're done, right?" he said, starting for the door. "'Cause I think they're still serving dessert in the dining hall."

Lily's glare froze him in his tracks. "I didn't say we shouldn't help; I just said it sounds like a lot."

"Jacob, what are you even doing here if you don't want to help?" said Trevor.

Jacob shrugged. "I was hoping this was about getting revenge on Ashley and her goons. I still haven't paid them back for what happened in the forest."

"Well, apparently it's not," snapped Trevor. "So either sit down and shut up, or leave."

"Alright, alright," said Jacob, throwing up his hands in surrender. "No need to get all bossy. So, what are we looking for anyway?"

"Well, that's kind of the problem," said Bobby.

Now it was Trevor's turn to be put off. "You're telling me you don't even know what we're after?"

Bobby glanced sheepishly at Jinx. "Well, not exactly."

"I can't believe I'm saying this," said Trevor, "but if that's the case, then I'm with Jacob. Don't get me wrong; it would be cool to run around in the archives, but it would be pointless without a clue as to what we're after."

"Actually, Jinx has an idea that should help with that," said Bobby.

"That's great," said Lily, cheerfully. "What is it?"

Jinx took center stage. "Have you guys ever heard of the Chronenberg Technique?" he asked. Bobby didn't have a clue, and from the look of it, neither did Jacob or Lily.

"He's talking about Franz Chronenberg's technique for relational and directional approximation," said Trevor with a self-satisfied smile. "Don't worry about it, Jacob. I'm sure you'll learn about it one day when you're bigger."

"I know what it is," bristled Jacob. "It helps point you in the direction of something when you don't know where or what it is. But I don't see how it helps. We've already established that there are a bunch of levels to the archives and hundreds, perhaps thousands, of passages down there. The Chronenberg Technique won't do anything but point to a dead end, or the floor, or straight into a row of shelves."

"You haven't heard the whole idea," said Bobby.

"Well then, let's hear it. I'm sure I've missed dessert by now, but there's a poker game in Mikey Blanchert's room at eight. That chump had to do my homework twice last week."

Jinx spread out a series of maps on the table. "As you can see, the archives are massive, expanded countless times over the centuries. Plus there are multiple levels, some of which aren't even on here . . ."

Jinx paused as Trevor held up his hand. "You're kind of making Jacob's point. If the archives are that big, then how is the Chronenberg Technique possibly going to help? Like he said, the reading could point us straight into a stone wall."

"Ah, but we aren't going to use just *one* reading. If we split up and go to different spots along the perimeter, we can combine results to triangulate the approximate location of the item we're looking for."

"Won't that still be extremely vague?" said Lily.

"Sure it will. But after we have our initial survey, we can move in closer and do it again. Each time we do, I can cross-reference the results and get a better idea of where to look. It shouldn't take more than three or four divinations to narrow the field down to a section that is searchable by foot."

"I must say," said Lily, "that sounds like a brilliant idea to me."

"Count me in," said Trevor. "Nothing I like more than mixing a chance to use my skills with dark and dirty places."

Bobby slapped Jinx on the back. "Good job, buddy. I knew you could do it."

"We haven't done anything yet," said Jacob. "We still gotta go and actually find this thing. For all we know, there isn't even anything to find."

Bobby refused to be deflated. "Don't worry, Jacob; we'll make a believer out of you yet."

CHAPTER 18

Headmistress Grayson ignored Ashley while she finished the paperwork on her desk. Taking her time, she carefully read the requisition request before signing it. Only then did she lean back in her high-back leather chair and appraise her daughter.

Ashley sat straight, hands folded in her lap, eyes darting around the room.

"Do you know why I asked to see you, Ashley?"

"Is this about what happened in the mines? I swear I had nothing to do with it."

"I wasn't aware that anything happened in the mines that required my attention. Is there something you wish to share with me?"

"No, of course not," she said hurriedly. "I just meant that I served my punishment."

"Hayward informed me that you and your friends completed your service. I consider the matter closed. Unless, of course, you have something to add?"

Ashley shook her head.

"That's interesting," said the headmistress. "Because I understand that the other students I assigned to punishment were there as well. Did you happen to see them while you were working?"

Ashley mulled over the question for a moment. "I suppose we saw them, but we kept to ourselves as ordered."

"And one of these people was Bobby Ether, was it not?"

Ashley hesitated. "I believe I recall him being there."

"And what can you tell me about him?"

"I don't know him well, but from what I know, I would say that Bobby is . . . difficult."

"I understand that some of the students are calling him a prodigy for his discovery the other day. What do you make of that?"

"You want my honest opinion?"

The headmistress waved her on.

"I think he's an obnoxious jerk," blurted Ashley. "He's no prodigy. He's a complete idiot. He got himself lost during the field trip and had to be rescued. He and his entire group of friends are nothing but trouble."

"And yet he made a remarkable discovery."

"He didn't find those mushrooms; he was tracking a bear. Heck, he probably would have been eaten if the others hadn't come along."

"So, you think the discovery was luck?"

Ashley shook her head. "I know better than to believe in luck. I'm just saying that it was Master Jong who made it happen, not that loser, Bobby."

"What about his overall talent; do you think he is gifted?"

"Definitely not," said Ashley. "I don't even know what he's doing here."

"I see," said the headmistress. "Thank you for your input, Ashley. That will be all."

Ashley remained in her seat, unmoving.

The headmistress looked up from her desk. "Did you have something more to add?"

"I just thought you would want to know. It's about Jinx, he's—"

"Ashley," interrupted the headmistress. "What have I told you before?"

"Sorry, I mean *Theodore*. He's been hanging out with those kids—Bobby and his friends."

The headmistress leaned back in her chair. "Go on."

"Like I said, Bobby Ether is a loser. And so are his friends."

"You said only that you believe Bobby has no talent. In which case, I don't see a problem with him spending time with Theodore. Perhaps he will learn something."

"But they don't listen to anyone—"

"You mean they don't listen to you," said the headmistress. Ashley began to protest, but the headmistress silenced her with a look. "You know, Ashley, there are many things that I would like to share with you, mother to daughter, as it were." As she spoke, her hand drifted toward the drawer containing the elixir.

Ashley looked on expectantly. The headmistress locked eyes with her daughter and slowly withdrew her hand. "But clearly you are still too immature to appreciate such knowledge."

"Mother, I swear I'm—"

The headmistress's voice cracked like a whip. "You will address me by my proper title as headmistress of the Jade Academy."

Ashley blushed. "Of course. My apologies. It's just that I know I am ready to learn more than the same boring lessons the monks have been teaching me since I was a child. I'm ready to learn what *you* have to teach me."

"If you are truly ready, then prove it."

"Anything," said Ashley reverently.

"Good," said the headmistress. "Then I have a task for you—one which I think you will be both delighted and perfectly suited to perform. I want you to provoke Bobby Ether. Get him to manifest his abilities. A physical altercation will not suffice. Understood?"

Ashley frowned. "What do you suggest?"

"I will leave that up to you. I have only two requirements. First, whatever happens cannot be public like the scene in the forest. Such an incident would require me to take action. Second, no harm is to come to your brother or the boy under any circumstance. At least, not yet. Is that clear?"

"Perfectly."

"Good. Now leave me. I have work to do."

—⚏—

The report sat untouched on the headmistress's desk. There was no point in reviewing it again when the contents were already committed to memory. The only question that remained was how to proceed.

A soft knock on the door brought her to attention. She looked up as the door cracked open. It was young Willy, dressed in the crimson robes of service.

"Simpkins is here, as you requested," said the boy.

"Show him in," she replied. The headmistress's top lieutenant entered the room and took a chair across from her.

"Your latest report mentions a visit by Master Jong to one of the local villagers, a retired old gardener," she said. "Tell me, why would you make mention of this particular incident in your report?"

"I believe the circumstances were suspicious, Headmistress. He insisted upon accompanying us during our recent field trip but departed in quite a hurry once we reached the forest."

"Did you sense anything unusual?"

"No, headmistress," said Simpkins, "not at first. But I was curious."

"So, you followed him to the gardener's cottage. And what were you able to discover?"

"That's the interesting part," said Simpkins. "Despite my efforts, I was unable to detect anything at all."

"Explain yourself," said the headmistress.

"It appears that he shielded the entire house from intrusion. If he were merely going to visit with a friend, why go to such measures?"

The headmistress leaned back thoughtfully. "Go on."

"Well, that made me suspicious," said Simpkins, "so I assigned Hayward to follow Jong while I went to speak with Whimpley, per your earlier request. Incidentally, he is prepared to apply pressure on Jong to push the Ether boy, should you deem it necessary."

"Very good," said the headmistress, picking up the report and flipping the page. "And while you were speaking with Whimpley, Master Jong visited the viewing room for the sacred scrolls?"

"Yes, and once again, he seemed wary of being observed. He even slipped out past Hayward undetected."

"That does seem unusual," said the headmistress. "Viewing the sacred texts is an open privilege for the monks. There is no reason for him to be concerned about being observed. Unless . . ."

"What is it, Headmistress? Do you know what it means?"

"I am not certain, but I intend to find out. Have Hayward coordinate continued observation of Jong. In the meantime, I want you to take Willy and go back to the village. See if you can put the boy's talents to good use. Interrogate the old gardener and discover what he knows."

"As you command," said Simpkins. "Anything in particular you want me to inquire about?"

"I have a few ideas," said the headmistress.

—⁂—

The weather was cold and windy as Simpkins climbed the steps to the tiny cottage and knocked on the door. After a moment, the door cracked open to reveal a wizened old man, bent and wrinkled like a raisin.

"Can I help you?" asked the old man.

"Are you Hatou, former groundskeeper at the Jade Academy?"

"Yes, yes. That's me."

"I'm a friend of Master Jong," said Simpkins. "May I come in?"

"What's that you say? You're a friend of Jong's?" said the man, angling his head to hear better.

"That's right," said Simpkins, speaking louder.

The door opened a tad wider. "Is it about . . . you know?"

"I think it's best if we speak inside, don't you?" said Simpkins.

"Of course," said Hatou, opening the door and stepping aside. "Please, come in. I'm just surprised. Jong always said he didn't want others involved."

Simpkins crossed the threshold into the tiny, single-room cottage.

"I haven't seen Jong in quite some time," said Hatou, still squinting. "Is everything okay?"

"He told me to tell you that he will not be able to come anymore. He asked that you share with me everything that the two of you have been working on."

The old gardener paused. "What did you say your name was?"

"It's rather urgent," said Simpkins. "He wants to finish very soon and feels that I can help."

Hatou stepped closer to Simpkins. "I don't see too well these days. Too many hours spent working in the bright sun ruined my eyes. Do I know you?"

"As I said, I was sent by Master Jong."

"I knew a man once back when I worked at the academy who wore clothes like yours," said Hatou. "Very fashionable back then. Times changed, but the man's wardrobe never did." The old man waved a hand in dismissal. "But that was over thirty years ago."

"That was . . . my father," said Simpkins. "I grew up at the academy. Now, about the project."

"There was something else about that man," said Hatou, taking a big sniff. "His breath always smelt like peppermint."

Simpkins slowly placed himself before the front door. "I really wish you hadn't done that."

"I think you should leave now," said Hatou. "Please go, and don't ever return."

"I'm sorry you feel that way," said Simpkins, reaching for the doorknob.

"Yes, well, I'm sorry I can't help you, but thank you for leaving."

"Oh, I'm not going anywhere," said Simpkins, opening the door. On the doorstep, Willy the Creep stood dressed in red robes with his hood up and Siphon on his shoulder. Hatou took an involuntary step back as the boy pulled back his hood to reveal dead eyes and the impassive expression he wore at all times.

"You are hiding something, and I need to know what it is," said Simpkins casually.

"Please, I have no idea what you are talking about," said Hatou, backpedaling away from Willy and his albino ferret. "Who is this boy? What do you want from me?"

"Please, old-timer, the time for charades is over. Tell me what I want to know and things will go easier for you."

"Please," begged Hatou. "There is nothing here to find; I swear it."

"We shall see," said Simpkins, closing the door behind Willy. Not long afterward, the screaming began.

CHAPTER 19

It took nearly a week for Bobby and his friends to coordinate a time to venture into the archives. They met in a cul-de-sac of shelves in the back of the library, away from prying eyes, to review their plan. Everyone gathered around as Jinx unrolled the maps he'd procured.

"I've identified six high-value locations to use to triangulate a position for the item," said Jinx. "Each location is identified on both the horizontal and vertical maps, making it extremely likely that those areas are still there and haven't been walled off or blocked. Also, each area lies along the outer section of the archives, so they should be easily accessible and yield a reading that points inward."

"You said there are six locations," said Lily. "But there are only five of us."

"I know," said Jinx. "I don't believe it's necessary for us to get readings from every location in order to get our initial heading. Technically, we only need three readings to triangulate."

"That means we can group up," said Jacob. "I'll go with Lily. Jinx can go with Bobby."

Trevor's face boiled with anger. "I'm not going alone. I'll go with Lily. You can go by yourself."

"What makes you guys think I want to go with either one of you?" said Lily. "Maybe I want to go with Jinx. I think it will be fun for us to spend some time together."

Jinx blushed.

"Fine," said Jacob. "You go with the pipsqueak. I'll go with Bobby. Sorry, Trev, guess that means you're all alone—again." Trevor shot him an angry glare but held his tongue.

"Then it's settled," said Lily, turning to Jinx. "Show us where to go."

—◊◊◊—

After taking a map and lanterns supplied by Jinx, Bobby and Jacob plotted the easiest path to their destination and set off. They didn't make it out of the library, however, before they got their first unwelcome surprise. Ashley and Willy stepped into the hallway at the end of the aisle. Siphon perched on Willy's shoulder.

"Where do you two think you're going?" said Ashley.

"None of your business," said Bobby, brushing past her. Jacob feinted at Willy as he went by, prompting Siphon to stand on its hind legs and let out an ear-piercing screech.

"Man, you're creepy," said Jacob. Willy just looked at him, stone-faced.

"You better watch your back," Ashley called after them.

Bobby pulled up short. "What's that supposed to mean?"

"I know you guys are up to something," said Ashley. "But you better be careful. There's no telling what might happen without my little brother around to shield you from harm."

Bobby waved dismissively. "I'm not scared of you, and we hang out with your brother because he's our friend, not because we need protection."

"Yeah," said Jacob. "Not like you and those goons you call friends. We actually like each other—most of the time."

"We'll see about you not needing protection," said Ashley. She and Willy turned to leave and Bobby could have sworn he saw a smile on Willy's face, mirrored by Siphon's bizarre grin.

———※———

For the next hour, Bobby and Jacob navigated the halls of the academy en route to the archives. Unlike the entrance by the library, the passage Jinx designated for their task lay deep in the unused western wing of the monastery.

"Do you think she's following us?" asked Bobby.

Jacob shrugged. "I doubt she'd have bothered with that lame attempt to scare us if she planned to stalk us. Even she's not that stupid."

Bobby nodded, feeling more at ease. "So, what can you tell me about the Chronenberg Technique? It sounds pretty amazing to be able to find something just by meditating."

"Not much to it, really," said Jacob. "The goal is to hold the idea of what you're looking for in your mind. As long as you're thinking about it, you're sending signals out into the universe that will guide you to it, and it to you. Like Jinx said, given that we don't know exactly what we're looking for and because the archives are so big, the best we can probably hope for is an approximate direction, but you never know."

They stopped before a giant oak door with a heavy padlock. Jacob wiped away a thick layer of dust and examined the lock. "You wanna do the honors, or shall I?"

"What? Oh, right," said Bobby. "Why don't you go ahead and take this one."

"I figured you'd say that," said Jacob, bending down to scoop up a stone set there to serve as a doorstop. Two quick strikes and the lock was broken and discarded on the floor.

"You just smashed it!" Bobby said.

Jacob laughed. "You think too much. Besides, sometimes it feels good to do things the old-fashioned way."

Prying the door open on rusty hinges, the boys discovered a short hallway with a long stairwell at the end. Heavy dust motes floated in the air as they ventured into the pitch black with their lanterns held high. Both boys paused when they reached the bottom of the stairs. An engraving on the wall read *Sublevel Five*.

"What is this place?" said Jacob. "This isn't on the map."

"The stairs we took must lead directly to the lower levels. Jinx did say this place was massive."

Before them stood a vast open space filled with an assortment of vehicles. An ancient Roman chariot with swords and shields leaning against the side sat directly in their path. Beside it stood a stagecoach from the Wild West.

"What is all this stuff?" said Bobby, his voice echoing in the cavernous hall.

"I learned in class that the academics have always sought to understand the strength of powerful cultures. They must have recreated these things from books and interactions with the outside world," said Jacob.

"But why would they do that?"

"My guess is they wanted to understand, and perhaps even exploit, the power of these devices. They must have been purchased using jade, then brought up the mountain piece by piece and reassembled here to study."

"It's like an underground Bermuda Triangle," said Bobby, unable to mask his awe.

"For sure. According to Jinx's map, this isn't even close to where we're supposed to be."

"Should we go back?" asked Bobby.

"Naw. Let's just find a good spot and take the reading from here. As long as we can show Jinx where we took it from, it should be fine. Besides, I want to check this stuff out," said Jacob with an edge of excitement. "Don't you?"

Bobby was eager to explore the bizarre museum. Behind the chariot, they found rows of wooden dummies, each equipped with a round fur cap, leather tunic, and leggings made of animal skin. A javelin and iron sword leaned against each base. After that came a Viking longship with three square sails and oars sticking out the sides, followed by a classic steam-powered locomotive, complete with two boxcars and a caboose.

"This place is a total mess," said Jacob, stopping in front of a freestanding bookcase heaped with thick metal binders. Each volume had large block-letter print on the spine in a language Bobby didn't recognize.

"I wonder what these are," said Bobby, eying the strange lettering.

Jacob pulled one down and flipped through it. "It appears to be records of old laboratory experiments. Scientific research stuff."

"How can you tell?" asked Bobby.

"I recognize some of the symbols on these charts. They're used in my biology class."

"What do they mean?" said Bobby.

Jacob studied the book in silence for a minute. "Hmm, that's interesting," he said at last.

"What is it?"

"Unless I'm mistaken, this left column is a list of gene sequences. I don't recognize all the stuff to the right, but it appears to all be some kind of code, possibly some kind of mapping or pattern."

"What's so interesting about that?" said Bobby.

"Look at the heading above the chart." Jacob turned the book so Bobby could see. "I can't be certain, but I think that's someone's name and personal information—date of birth, height, weight, etcetera."

"I still don't see what's so odd about it," said Bobby. "We don't really focus on science a lot around here, but people do study it, right?"

"Yeah, but take a look at the date on the binder and the birthday of the person on the chart. If I'm right, the person listed here was only fifteen years old when these tests were done."

It took a moment for comprehension to set in. "You think it was a student at the academy?"

Jacob flipped the page. "This one is thirteen . . . ten . . . twelve," he said, turning page after page. "And that's not the only thing that's odd."

"There's more?" Bobby leaned in, as if the words would translate themselves if he got close enough.

"Judging from the date on this binder, these tests were done almost fifty years ago."

"What's so interesting about that?" asked Bobby.

"Nothing," said Jacob, "except that the most advanced scientific research laboratories in the world didn't start studying DNA until the early 1980s."

"You're saying that these are lab results of experiments that took place thirty years before the world knew about this stuff?"

"Not just *any* experiments. If my hunch is right, these are genetic tests run on kids here at the academy."

"You must be misinterpreting it," Bobby said. "There aren't even any labs here. Where would they do all the tests?"

Jacob closed the book. "You're probably right. I don't understand the language, after all. Who knows, those symbols could be used for lots of different stuff."

He'd just slipped the binder back into place when a hollow noise carried through the stillness.

"What was that?" said Bobby, cocking his head as the noise echoed in the vast hall.

"Sounded like footsteps from over there," said Jacob, pointing into the darkness. "I'll bet it's Ashley and her goons trying to scare us again. What do you say we go find them and put an end to this crap once and for all?"

"I don't know if that's such a good idea."

But Jacob was already off and running, his lantern swinging wildly. Bobby sighed and rushed after him, dodging past an old Sherman tank and a gigantic B-29 bomber with a painting of a long-legged woman reclining over the name *Velva Jean*.

Ahead of him, Jacob stopped.

"I lost them," he said, breathing heavily from his short sprint. They stood in a small gap between vehicles where someone had set up a table covered with parchments, a bottle of ink, and a set of quills.

"This place just keeps getting weirder and weirder," said Bobby, lifting a sheaf off the table. "Why would someone leave this stuff just lying out like this?"

Jacob glanced at the text, only half focused as he strained to pick up sounds of their antagonists. "Well, no one comes down here, but you're right; that is strange," he said, coming over for a closer look. "These look like the ancient scrolls the monks study—except they can't be. Those are up in the viewing room under guard."

Footsteps echoed to their right. "There!" said Jacob, spinning toward the noise. This time Bobby was right on his heels. Up ahead was a hallway, bookcases lining one side and shelves stacked with glass jars on the other. They ran down the aisle and heard a crash. A row of shelves had fallen. Broken jars littered the floor, oozing a liquid that dissolved everything it touched.

Bobby tried to step over the glass and goo by climbing over the fallen bookcase, but he lost his footing in the debris and stepped on a shard of glass. Bobby screamed and rolled into another shelf already on the verge of collapse. With a loud crash, the shelf toppled over, trapping him beneath it.

"Bobby, where are you? Are you hurt?" Jacob called.

"I'm all right," said Bobby with a groan. "Just hurt my foot."

"Hold on, I'll get you out." Bobby saw the glow of Jacob's lantern as his friend probed for a way to reach him.

"Is there a way to lift it so I can crawl out?"

Jacob grunted with exertion. "It's too heavy. Maybe if you push from inside while I lift?"

"Forget it. I don't want this whole thing coming down on top of me. Go get the others. Maybe you guys can lift it off of me together."

Jacob stubbornly pried at a few more places, but all it bought was a shower of dirt on Bobby's head. "All right," he said. "Hang tight, buddy. I'll be back as quickly as possible." The light from Jacob's lantern faded and then he was gone.

Suddenly alone in the silent darkness, Bobby soon noticed the pain. His left heel throbbed. He probed the bottom of his shoe and discovered a shard of glass sticking through the sole.

Gently, he pried it out, gritting his teeth as the glass slid from his flesh. The tips of his fingers burned, suggesting that the shard was coated with the acid that had eroded the ground. Worse yet, the pain seemed to be spreading. He closed his eyes, trying to blink back the fire igniting in his ankle and lower calf.

Bobby pulled out the penlight he'd brought as a backup. Slowly rolling up his pant leg, Bobby exposed yellow flesh covered with black boils that seemed to grow bigger as he watched. He touched one and yanked his hand back as electric pain lanced up his leg.

Clearly, he needed treatment. In the absence of a monk, he'd have to settle for taking his mind off the pain. With no other option, he stowed his light, closed his eyes, and meditated.

—⚓—

Alone in the dark, cramped space under the collapsed bookshelf, Bobby visualized the invisible barrier at the core of his being. Gently, he ran a metaphysical hand across the tiny dents on its surface—mementos from past tantrums spent pounding away at the impregnable citadel.

He walked around the barrier. Aside from the dents, the structure was perfectly smooth, with no doors, windows, or other means by which to breach its perimeter. He was reminded briefly of the Nexus, the strange hexagonal structure he'd seen inside the Eagle's Nest during his time with Cassandra. He wondered absently if his subconscious had erected this barrier in facsimile of that edifice. *How fitting that an image given to me by Cassandra would be at the center of my problems.*

The instant he thought of Cassandra, the scene shifted. He was looking down at his old bedroom back in San Fernando seeing a version of himself. He watched himself open the bedroom closet and rummage around before tossing a duffle bag on the bed, and instantly Bobby knew what he was witnessing. It was the night it all started—the night of the accident. This was the moment everything changed.

His other self hurried around the room, collecting items and throwing them in the bag. He remembered the conversation on the front porch and suddenly the words were there, filling the otherwise silent scene. He listened to Cassandra lying to Simpkins and Hayward and his anger rose. Instantly, the scene wavered. Bobby pushed the conversation aside and concentrated on the boy in the room. The image snapped back into focus as the conversation downstairs disappeared.

His other self was almost done now, the duffle bag nearly full. He took one more quick spin around the room, looking for anything he might have forgotten or missed. He stopped at the old wooden desk. There, exactly as he remembered, was the jade amulet from his grandfather. Past-Bobby picked it up.

I'm supposed to figure out something about the amulet, he thought. The scene grew shadowy and dark. *Okay, so that's not it.* He broadened his attention and the image refocused. *There must be something else.* He took another look around and spotted the photo of him and his family.

With perfect clarity, Bobby knew what his subconscious was trying to tell him. A split second later, he let the scene dissolve and opened his eyes.

—ᵴᵴᵴ—

Extracting his penlight once again, Bobby inspected his leg. His injury looked even worse. The skin was ashen, with sickly black boils running all the way up his thigh. No doubt the infection would soon spread to his torso. No telling what would happen after that.

I've gotta do something fast, thought Bobby, reaching into his jacket pocket. There, right where he'd left it, was the photograph of his family at the beach. On the right, his mother had her arms around him, heaps of golden locks framing her beautiful freckled face. His father stood on the left, a broad hand resting proudly on Bobby's shoulder. Behind them stood his grandfather, arms outstretched in a gigantic hug that encompassed them all as he gazed into the camera with that warm smile Bobby remembered so well.

On impulse, Bobby flipped the picture over. In the upper left corner was a faded inscription. *To Bobby: May you always find love at the center of your life. Love, Grandpa.*

He flipped it over and stared at the photo again as tears welled.

Like a levee in a flood, the reservoir of pain and anger over his parents' death broke wide open. He clutched the picture tight to his chest as he sobbed. The answer to accessing his power had been with him all along, carried right next to his heart.

He pulled a few deep breaths to regain his focus. His upper thigh burned. *I don't have much time*, he thought, hurriedly stowing his penlight and closing his eyes to meditate once again, drifting back into a metaphysical state to face his subconscious wall.

This time, he knew exactly what to do. Holding tight to images of his family, he placed a hand on the cold wall. His hand melted into the structure, sinking into the invisible barrier up to his wrist. Tentative at first, he pushed his arm forward, staring in amazement as his arm slipped easily into the translucent structure. He took a small step and felt his body merge into the wall with no more resistance than wading into a swimming pool.

Now fully immersed inside the barrier, Bobby pushed toward the core. Heavy mist rose around him, disorienting him, but he held tightly to the euphoric images of his family until a passage appeared through the haze. In moments, he emerged into a small clearing.

Before him lay an elegant Japanese rock garden. Ancient bonsai trees nestled among intricate arrangements of polished stones atop manicured sands of white, black, and gray. Sandalwood walkways offered scenic strolls alongside a crystal-blue stream that branched off into small pools where gentle eddies caressed pads of green lilies. In the center of it all, a single, iridescent flower sat on a marble dais.

He recognized the lotus blossom from his medallion. That had to be his final destination. Careful not to disturb the delicate arrangements, Bobby approached the dais.

A gentle breeze swept over him, carrying the tangy sweet fragrance of jasmine and pine. He could not imagine a more tranquil setting. Everything about the garden spoke of comfort and peace. But that was only natural, given that the entire landscape had been created by his imagination.

Reaching the dais, Bobby stopped to admire the perfectly formed crystalline petals of the incandescent lotus blossom. Ever so gently, he reached out and cupped the base of the delicate flower. The instant his fingers touched the stem, everything turned white as a wave of pure anima washed over him. He let go of the scene and opened his eyes to the real world as power flooded through him.

—〰—

With his penlight off, Bobby should have been in absolute darkness when he withdrew from his meditative state. Instead, he saw everything clear as day. He looked for the light source and flinched as his leg throbbed in protest at the slight movement.

That's when he realized that the glow came from the leg itself.

The leg, previously ashen with infection, now glowed an angry red with bright spots where the boils had been. He stared at the offending lesions, wishing they would heal, and watched in fascination as the aura around his leg changed. In seconds, the ruddy hue faded, replaced by a dull yellow.

The amber tone grew brighter and brighter until he was forced to avert his eyes. When he looked back, the glow was gone, taking with it all signs of infection—the boils, the blistering skin, even the puncture wound on the ball of his foot had completely disappeared. He flexed his leg and discovered no pain.

"Well, that's a neat trick," he said, lifting his gaze to the rubble. "Let's see what else I can do."

Gently, he touched the broken bookcase above his head. It felt warm from the weight atop it. He tried another piece, this one a splintered beam by his waist. He snatched his hand back from the scalding heat. Clearly the post was extremely weak and ready to break at any moment——but it also gave him an idea.

Focusing on the beam as he had his leg, he pictured healing the wood and stared in amazement as the cracks knit together. When it was done, the beam was crooked but cool to the touch. More importantly, he could now shift the broken plank beneath it without trouble.

He searched for more weak spots, channeling energy into anything weight-bearing until he could shift the objects beneath. Soon a small hole materialized through the debris. Three more pieces and he had a passage wide enough to crawl through.

Dropping to his belly, he'd just begun his journey to freedom when he heard a noise. There, just beyond the wreckage, was the silhouette of a hulking figure with long, black hair. *The assassin, come to finish the job!*

Bobby lunged forward as the remains of the bookcase crashed down at his heels. A second later, he was on his feet, ready to face his would-be murderer. However, the silhouette and the intruder who'd made it were gone. Instead, a tiny speck of light illuminated the tunnel ahead.

The pinprick grew larger until it materialized into a lantern held by Jacob, followed closely by Trevor, Lily, and Jinx. The three ran to greet their disheveled friend.

Lily threw open her arms and gave him a big hug. "Jacob said you were trapped under there. When we heard it collapse just now, I thought maybe—"

"Speaking of which," said Jacob, "how exactly did you get out? I searched that whole pile from top to bottom. I couldn't move anything."

Bobby shrugged. "Just lucky, I guess. I felt it starting to come down around me, so I got aggressive and forced my way out. Guess it held together just long enough for me to get clear."

"We should probably get you to the monks to get checked out," said Lily. "We can tell them you slipped on some steps or something—heaven knows there are enough of them around here."

"I'm fine," said Bobby hastily. "But you're right; we should definitely go."

"What about your foot?" said Jacob. "You said you hurt it when the bookcase came down."

"False alarm," said Bobby. "See?" He hopped up and down as he made for the exit. "Now come on, let's get outta here."

"Hey, what's this?" said Jinx, picking up a book. "It looks like a yearbook of some kind. Maybe it's a clue."

"Great," said Bobby. "Take it with you and let's go."

"Bobby's right," said Trevor. "We can talk more back at the library."

—⟨〰⟩—

It didn't take them long to make their way back. They'd just reached the exit with the chariot and stagecoach leading back to the academy proper when Hayward stepped out of the shadows.

He wore a broad grin on his pudgy face as he said, "Ah, more rats scurrying out of the maze."

Behind Hayward, Bobby spotted Ashley with her head bent low, looking dejected. Next to her were Willy and the twins, as well as several other boys. Bobby and his friends stood silently, knowing they were busted.

At first Hayward seemed only interested in giving them detention again—this time for being in the restricted archives. But then he asked if they had seen anyone else in the archives. One of the monks, perhaps?

Bobby barely paid attention as the other kids gave their answers, giving a curt "no" when it was his turn. Clearly unsatisfied with their answers but lacking proof, Hayward let them go, saying that they would hear soon about their detention assignments.

The instant he was dismissed, Bobby headed straight for his room. He knew his friends were still worried and wanted to talk, but he couldn't be bothered, not now. He had something very important to do and, if he was right, very little time left to do it.

CHAPTER 20

The instant he got to his room, Bobby shoved a towel under the door, drew the window shades, and scooped his grandfather's amulet off the nightstand. *Please let the power still be there.*

As he'd hoped, the amulet glowed with a pale white light similar to his injured leg back in the archives. He ran his fingertips over the surface, trying to sense the amulet as he had the planks and beams in the rubble. As always, it felt cool to the touch.

Bobby set the amulet down and paced the room. No telling how much longer his newfound abilities would last. *The surface feels normal.* Suddenly, a thought occurred to him. Bobby snatched up the pendant once again. Focusing on the light emanating from it, he willed it to change. The light pooled together into small clumps.

With little scooping motions, Bobby gathered the light, bundling it into a tiny ball. Then he stretched it out into a slender pole, like a toothpick. Next, he pictured a murky pond at the center of the amulet. When he had the image firmly in place, he built a point on the end of the pole, forming a miniature spear. Then, with all his mental strength, he thrust the spear of light down into the dark waters.

The inside of the amulet lit up with a flash. For a brief moment, Bobby saw words and images etched on the wall of the pendant's inner chamber. And there was something else—a pillar in the middle of the chamber. At the bottom of the pillar, a small hole disappeared into the floor.

The scene dimmed, fading as the energy he'd gathered dissipated. Quickly, Bobby gathered the remaining light and thrust it into the hole. An instant later, the image in his head went black, but not before the amulet came apart in his hands with an audible click.

He spread the pieces out on his pillow. There were over a dozen pieces to what had once been the single lotus-blossom pendant. Most of them were shaped like the flower's petals. He set those pieces aside and focused on the base housing the pistil.

Clearly this was the central pillar he'd seen inside the amulet's secret chamber. At the base, he could just make out the tiny hole where he'd thrust the energy to open the locket. Bobby checked all around the pillar but found nothing further of interest.

Setting the base aside, he shifted his attention to the petals. Most held nothing of interest. He moved those pieces back to the box. A few had markings at their bases. He set those in a separate pile. By the time he was done, he had five pieces, each containing fragments of words and images at the bottom that he recognized from his vision of the secret chamber.

He laid the five pieces out in front of him, playing with different configurations. His hands trembled when he realized that the contours of the lower halves fit into one another. Placing three facing up and two facing down, he quickly arranged the petals so they fit together. Assembled, they formed a tableau upon which words and images took shape.

Bobby threw up his hands in exasperation, almost knocking the shoebox off the bed. There could be no doubt that the pieces were assembled correctly, and yet what lay before him made no more sense than before.

He stared at the puzzle for hours, trying to figure out what it meant. As the sun rose, he put the pieces back in the shoebox and shoved it under his bed. Only one thing was clear—whatever the answer was, he needed help to find it.

—◆—

Bobby slept through most of the morning, arising just in time for breakfast. He'd just begun to eat when Willy presented him with a note from the headmistress that he was to meet in the courtyard after classes for detention. So, following an

English class spent in a futile attempt to write haiku, he trudged to the main steps, where he found the other students already assembled.

A chill wind numbed the tips of his ears and nose. He huddled close to his friends as Ashley and her gang formed a tight group a short distance away. Only Jinx stood alone, trying not to look at anyone. Ashley said something to the others and a chorus of laughs went up. They all turned to look at Bobby. Tex said something in response and they all laughed again.

"What's so funny?" snapped Trevor.

"We were just wondering what Bobby looked like trapped under that bookcase," said Ashley. "I bet he cried like a little baby."

"I'll give you something to cry about," said Jacob with clenched fists.

But Hayward was there before he could act, freezing everyone in place with a venomous glare. "Follow me," said the balding fat man, crossing the courtyard. Bobby and the others had no choice but to fall in behind him.

Hayward took them around the eastern perimeter of the monastery, stopping at the far edge where the wind tore down the mountainside with gale force. Below them, the terrain sloped in a series of carved terraces. Each terrace was lined with neat rows of plants.

"The gardens?" said Mex. "What the heck are we going to do here—plant tulips?"

Hayward let out a deep belly laugh. "I assure you, it won't be anything nearly as pleasant."

"But we are gardening, right?" asked Lily. Lowering her voice, she said, "I love gardening."

"Of course you do," said Jacob. "Along with knitting and sewing, I'll bet."

"And you wonder why no one likes you, Jacob," said Trevor.

"Actually," said Hayward, raising his voice to be heard over the wind, "the monks tend to the gardens. Your presence there would only hinder their efforts."

"So, what are we doing here?" Jacob asked.

"I thought it would be obvious," said Hayward, looking at a plot of barren land. "Your job is to convert that open space into a workable field for planting more crops."

"But that's solid bedrock!" said one of the boys with Ashley.

Hayward turned slowly to face him. "Do you have a point, Stanley?"

The boy lowered his head and Hayward continued.

"On the far side of the garden you will find spades, shovels, trowels, and pickaxes, which were salvaged from the mines. These gardens have not been expanded in nearly two hundred years. I think it's about time we changed that."

People grumbled until Hayward held up his hand for silence. "Unlike your assignments in the mines, you will work on this for however long it takes, so I suggest you get started. Use whatever means you desire; just make sure it's focused on the rock. The headmistress has been quite clear that additional altercations will not be tolerated."

He turned to leave and then stopped. "Oh, and one more thing. Given recent events, the headmistress has decided that supervision is in order. Monks will be along shortly to work in the garden nearby and monitor your progress. I recommend that they find you all hard at work when they arrive."

—⟨⟨⟨—

It didn't take long for Bobby and his friends to discover why Hayward considered their new task at least as unpleasant as their work in the mines. Not only was the earth just as hard, but the wind assaulted them relentlessly across the open field. In less than ten minutes, Bobby's hands were so numb that he barely felt the shovel in his hands.

R SCOTT BOYER 183

Monks showed up to inspect the work. When Bobby asked them about breaks, they replied, "To rest is to give in to inner weakness." Bobby shrugged and continued laboring alongside Trevor, Jacob, and Lily.

They alternated tasks. First Bobby and Jacob used axes to break the earth while Trevor and Lily used shovels and trowels to smash the upturned rock into workable soil. Then they switched.

Progress was agonizingly slow. After three hours, they'd created a plot just two yards across and not even a foot deep. Bobby wiped sweat from his eyes as he bent over to remove dirt from a hole so Trevor could strike the bedrock below. As he leaned over, Bobby lost his balance and pitched forward.

"Dude, I can't dig the hole with you laying in it," said Trevor.

With an audible growl, Bobby's stomach flipped and he heaved the remains of his lunch onto the broken soil.

Lily threw down her spade and rushed to his side. "Bobby, what's the matter?"

Bobby grabbed his midsection and retched again. Everyone stopped and stared at the commotion. Even Ashley looked over, though she pretended not to care.

From the nearby garden, one of the monks came over and leaned over Bobby. "Let me take a look at you."

Bobby crawled into a sitting position and wiped the sting from his eyes. The monk had rosy cheeks and a bulbous nose like a clown. The monk put his hands on Bobby's neck and Bobby flinched, flashing back to the assassin on the hillside.

"Relax. I'm just trying to help."

The monk shifted a hand to Bobby's forehead. Instantly, warm, soothing energy washed over him. He closed his eyes and let his whole body go limp. By then, Jinx had arrived, pushing his way through the quickly gathering crowd until he was at Bobby's side.

"What happened?" he said.

"We don't know," said Lily. "We were digging and he just collapsed."

"Probably too wimpy to handle the work," said one of the boys in the crowd.

"Who said that?" said Lily, spinning toward the group of onlookers gawking at the site of Bobby Ether making a spectacle yet again.

In the distance, Mex stood next to Ashley, pretending not to watch with his back turned and a finger up his nose. It hadn't been his voice. When no one spoke up, Lily returned her attention to Bobby.

"Coward," she said loud enough to be heard by all.

Trevor dipped his head close to hers. "You know, it *is* possible he overexerted himself. The altitude, digging in the mines the other day . . . most of us know how to control our anima."

"Or maybe he's just a wimp," said another boy to a chorus of laughs.

"All right, that's it," said Jacob, rising.

The monk stood too. "This boy has used tremendous energy recently without replenishing himself."

"I told you, he's a wimp." This time no one laughed.

"The depletion is not from digging," said the monk. "The anima missing from this boy is a hundred times greater than what is being used here today." Murmurs rippled through the crowd.

"What do we do?" asked Lily.

"The balance must be restored. Go to the garden. Find the small plant with spiky leaves and bright yellow flowers. Make sure you get the whole plant when you pull it up."

Trevor took off for the garden. "Hey, wait for me," said Jinx, grabbing a trowel. "I know which plant he's talking about."

From somewhere, a jacket was produced and placed beneath Bobby's head. People headed back to their plots to resume work. In moments, Trevor and Jinx were back. Jinx handed the monk a small gray tuber. "You only want the root, right?"

"Yes, but how did you know that?"

"Solis Viridis, 'the Blooming Sun.' I've read about it in class. It has an intense concentration of energy in the roots. Used for healing and medicinal purposes. Pungent odor, tastes incredibly bitter."

"He'll have to make do," said the monk, ripping off a small piece of the tuber and placing it in Bobby's mouth. "Chew this slowly so that you absorb as much as possible." Bobby's eyes flew open as the taste hit his tongue. He clenched his stomach and tried to roll to the side, but the monk restrained him.

"Do not spit it out. You must eat it all to regain your strength." Bobby made a sour face and swallowed as the monk handed him another piece.

"It tastes like the veggie shake Cassandra gave me in my kitchen," said Bobby.

"This herb is very rare," said the monk. "I doubt you have tasted it before."

"Who's Cassandra?" asked Lily from over the monk's shoulder.

"What?" said Bobby. "I don't know. I must be delirious."

After several minutes, Bobby sat up and took the root from the monk. "I can do it by myself now."

"Remember, you must eat it all," said the monk. "Once you are done, it will still take several hours for you to regain your strength." The monk turned and walked back to the garden, where he picked up a hoe and worked the soil once again.

"I'm sorry, guys," Bobby said to his friends as he eased off to the side of the work area.

Jacob gave Bobby a hearty slap on the back. "No worries, buddy. You can do double the work tomorrow."

"Right after you explain what's really going on," said Lily.

Bobby stared into his hands. "What are you talking about?"

Lily set hands to hips and glared at him. "You know perfectly well what I am talking about, Bobby Ether. First, a massive bookcase and shelves fall on you; then you escape from under a pile of rubble. Then a monk says you've exerted vast amounts of energy. Next, you recognize the root he gives you to chew on. And then you mention some lady named 'Cassandra' and claim you're 'delirious.' Give me a break."

One look at her face and Bobby knew he couldn't lie. "Alright, I'll tell you guys everything; I promise. But not here."

"Fine," said Lily. "Tonight at our spot in the library after dinner."

Bobby swallowed hard. "Fine. Tonight after dinner, I'll tell you all what's really going on."

—⫘—

The way Lily crossed her arms and glared at him told Bobby how hurt she felt, but it was Trevor who spoke the words. "I can't believe you got it open and didn't tell us. Not cool, man."

"I heard you the first twelve times," replied Bobby. "And I said I'm sorry."

"Heck, I can't believe you got it open, period," said Jacob.

The four of them were gathered in the back of the library. The amulet lay spread on the table with the five keys pieces aligned to reveal the code. Despite everyone's best efforts, no one could figure out what it meant.

"Hi, guys," said Jinx, walking into the room.

Jacob looked up and frowned. "Who invited him?"

"Jinx is my friend," said Bobby. "He deserves to know the truth as much as anyone."

"In case you haven't noticed, his sister has it out for us," said Jacob. "Not to mention she's the reason we were breaking rocks in the freezing cold all day. We never would have been caught if she hadn't followed us down there."

"What Ashley does is not his fault," said Bobby. "Besides, I trust him." Trevor and Lily voiced their agreement.

"Well, aren't we one big, happy family," said Jacob, gesturing for Jinx to sit.

"Thanks, guys," said Jinx. He carried the yearbook he'd

discovered on the archive floor after the shelf collapsed. He handed the book to Bobby and saw what was on the table. "Is that what I think it is?"

"Yeah, Boy Wonder here got the pendant open and didn't bother to tell anyone," said Jacob.

"I was planning on telling you guys."

"So get to it," said Lily. "And start at the beginning. I know there's more to it than just the amulet."

"All right, take a seat and get comfortable," said Bobby, flipping through the yearbook as he spoke. "This could take a while."

He told them about the night he met Cassandra and how she helped him after he got sick. He told them how he fled the Core agents with her but then ran away, resulting in his encounter at the hospital. Everyone gasped when he recounted witnessing his parents' deaths, followed by his capture by Hayward and Simpkins. Silently, Lily came over and put her arms around him.

Jinx scratched his head. "I'm sorry for your loss, but I don't get what any of that has to do with your grandfather or the amulet."

"Honestly, I wasn't sure there was a connection myself, at least not until now." Bobby placed the yearbook on the table and spun it around for the others to see. "I asked you to bring this book because if there is one thing I've learned since arriving here, it's that there is no such thing as coincidence. This yearbook covers the time period my grandfather would have been here if he was a student."

The others stood and gathered closer. "What did you find?" asked Trevor. "Is it a picture of your grandfather?"

"Better than that," said Bobby, pointing to a picture of two teenage girls and a boy. "That's my grandfather in the middle. The girl on the left is my grandmother. I'd recognize those dimples anywhere. Now look at the girl with the pale blonde hair on the other side. That's Cassandra."

The room fell silent.

Finally, Lily said, "But that's great, right? That means you have a family friend looking out for you on the outside. I bet she'd be willing to take you in after you graduate from the academy."

"I would rather die than live with that woman," said Bobby. They sat back down as he explained about the photos the headmistress had showed him. He told them about Cassandra's involvement with the driver in the car accident that killed his parents, and the assassin who later murdered the driver.

"She had your parents murdered?" said Jinx. "That's horrible!"

"There's more," said Bobby. And he told them about how he'd seen the assassin, disguised as a monk, during his first training session with Master Jong, and how the man had whispered Cassandra's name in his mind. He went on to explain how that same man attacked him and tried to kill him on the mountainside by the bear cave.

"That explains why the hole looked manmade!" said Jinx. "He must have dug it and covered it up as a trap!"

"Exactly," said Bobby. "Plus, I think he tried to bring the bookcase down on top of me when I was about to escape."

"Are you sure? I thought you said you saw Willy near the wreckage in the archives."

"I thought I did, but I also saw the assassin right before you guys showed up."

Lily's face turned ashen. "My gosh, Bobby, why didn't you say something?"

"I didn't want to scare you. Besides, I needed to get out of there and back to my room as quickly as possible to open the pendant."

"Okay, so your grandparents' old friend killed your parents and is trying to kill you," said Jinx. "I *still* don't understand what that has to do with the pendant or how you got it open."

"That's a whole other story. Truth is that I *was* injured and completely trapped under that bookcase."

"So how did you manage to get out?" said Lily.

"I'm still not exactly sure. Somehow I tapped into my chi and used anima to heal myself and then dig my way out."

Trevor sat up straight. "Dude, that is wicked cool! I don't think even Master Jong or the headmistress could do something like that."

"Hardly. Once I got back to my bedroom, I used the last of the anima to get the amulet open. I've tried a dozen times since then to tap into my core again, but I always hit this barrier. It's like a wall. I can't get past it."

"Well, that explains why you were so exhausted today at the garden," said Lily. "You must be completely depleted."

"It also explains why you can't access it again," said Jinx. "You probably need to recuperate in order to restore your energy."

"So, what's next?" asked Trevor.

"I guess the next thing to do is figure out what this code means," said Bobby, gesturing toward the amulet. "Hopefully whatever message Grandpa left will help us figure this whole thing out."

"I think I may be able to help with that," said Jinx.

"You figured out what it says?" said Bobby, staring at his young friend in disbelief.

"Of course," said Jinx with a smile.

"Wait. Don't tell me," said Bobby. "I want another chance to see if I can figure it out."

"Be my guest," said Jinx, stepping back from the table so the others could move in for a better look at the tableau.

"I don't get it," said Jacob. "What is 'With-below'? And what's with those strange-colored gems?"

"Maybe there's a piece missing," suggested Trevor.

"Do you want that hint now?" said Jinx, a look of smug satisfaction on his face.

"Yes," said Jacob.

"No," said Bobby. Then, after a long pause: "Okay, fine, give us a hint. But make it a small one."

Jinx smiled wryly. "Remember where you are."

"What kind of hint is that?" snapped Jacob. "We're in the library. Fat lot of good that does us."

"Think bigger," said Jinx.

"The academy?" said Trevor.

"Bigger."

"We're in a remote region of Tibet, right?" said Bobby, genuinely confused.

"That's it," said Lily with excitement. "We're in Tibet!"

Trevor's brow knitted together. "How does that help?"

"We've been trying to read it the way a Westerner would read it, but here in Tibet, they read things using a different system."

"Exactly," said Jinx. "In traditional Chinese, reading is done from top to bottom and from right to left, not left to right."

"So, we reorganize the words," said Jacob. "'Below-across-up-inside-with-beneath-with.' Yeah, wow, that cleared everything right up. Thanks for the help, genius."

"But you've missed something."

"You mean all the little gems? What are we supposed to do, buy a vowel?"

"Wait, I think I get it," said Bobby. "Those gems aren't for decoration; they're part of the puzzle."

"Bravo," said Jinx. "You have to combine the images with the words in the proper sequence in order to understand the riddle."

"Okay, so let me see if I have this correct," said Trevor. "The puzzle basically says, 'Below something brownish-gray, across something green, up another gray-brown thing, into something black with something dark gray, within some black lightning bolt thingy, beneath something red with white'? Is that it?"

"Basically, yes."

"And that's where we will find whatever it is we're looking for?" said Jacob.

"I presume so, yes."

"And you know where it refers to?"

"Unfortunately, no. I deciphered the code, but I have no idea where it refers to."

"Sounds like we're back to square one," said Jacob. "I'm off to Mikey's room to play poker. Let me know when you guys figure it out."

CHAPTER 21

That night, Bobby dreamed that he searched for the object hidden by his grandfather. In his dream, he went down into the archives where he discovered shelves filled with ancient texts. He read book after book, but none of them contained what he looked for, so he left the archives and continued his search.

He went to the mines, where he found the fabled Spine of the World and followed it into the heart of the mountain. He emerged in a giant throne room full of gold, jewels, and priceless treasure. Carefully, he examined each gem, artifact, and relic, and yet none of them was the item he sought.

From there he went to the courtyard below the monastery. Following the path to the gardens, he descended through the terraced fields to the barren plot where he and his friends had labored during the day. He continued past the windswept rock until he stood upon the side of the mountain, overlooking the valley below. He took it all in, studying every detail of the terrain. And then he saw it—the place where his grandfather's secret lay. The place that held the answers to all of his questions.

—⁓—

After morning sessions the following day, Bobby and the others returned to the gardens for their detention. With barely a quarter of the barren field converted into suitable soil, no one looked happy except Hayward, who whistled merrily as he escorted the group to the work site. He disappeared soon after but was quickly replaced by a group of monks working the gardens nearby. Bobby recognized one of them as the monk who helped him the day before.

"Hey, guys, when's our next field trip?"

"Winter is almost here, so probably not for a couple of months," said Trevor. "Why?"

"Cover for me for a second, will you? I want to go talk to that monk from yesterday."

Jacob didn't bother to look up from digging. "Don't be too long, sunshine, or I'll start to think you don't love me anymore."

Bobby ignored him and approached the monk, who rose from tending a zucchini plant.

"I didn't thank you properly yesterday for helping me," said Bobby, extending his hand. "My name is Bobby Ether."

The man replied with a slight bow. "I am called Yemoni."

"I really appreciate all your help yesterday," said Bobby. "But there is something I don't understand. How did you know what was wrong with me?"

"Reading a person's energy is no more difficult than reading a plant's or an animal's."

"What do you mean?"

"Come," said Yemoni. "Look at this plant I am tending. Place your hands on its stem." Bobby did as instructed. "Now, relax. Allow your senses to merge with the plant. Do not feel it just with your fingers. Feel it with your whole being. Allow your senses to penetrate it, to become one with the plant until you can sense what it feels."

"What do you mean? It's a plant; it doesn't feel anything."

"All living creatures, whether plant or animal, have feelings. This plant knows whether it is healthy or sick, whether it is cold or hot, in sunlight or shade. Can you not sense it?"

Bobby closed his eyes and focused on the zucchini. "I . . . I think I can. It feels. . . happy!"

"Yes. I watered this plant just before you arrived. Its roots are now swollen with nutrients that it will carry to its leaves and the vegetable it grows for us. And now it basks in the midafternoon sun, soaking up the energy that will help it grow big and strong."

"Is it possible for inorganic things to have feelings too? Like rocks or gems?"

"Inorganic matter may hold energy, and that energy may even be imbued with feelings or emotions. In this way, an object may feel alive and even have a sense of personality. But the energy does not originate there. It is only from living creatures that such power comes."

"Thank you, Master Yemoni," said Bobby. He gave a small bow and turned to leave. "Oh, I have one other question, if you don't mind."

"What is it, child?"

"Have you seen Master Jong lately? I have had a different instructor lately and was just curious whether he'll be back soon."

"I have not seen my dear friend Jong for some time. I assume that whatever he is doing is very important to take him away from his teaching. Is that all?"

"Yes, Master. Thank you for your time."

"Go in peace, child."

Several nights later, Bobby met with Jinx in the library to study. They sat across from one another, studying in silence until Bobby set aside his book. Jinx looked up from a heavy volume on ancient Egyptian pharaohs. "Something on your mind?"

"I was just wondering, are students ever allowed outside the monastery?"

"Only on field trips or on assignment after they graduate."

"What about with special permission?"

"Only my mom has the power to do that."

"Do you think it would be possible to get it without telling her what it's for?"

Jinx's brow furrowed. "What's going on, Bobby? Why are you asking about getting out of the academy?"

"What if I told you that I solved the riddle? That I knew where my grandfather hid whatever it is he wants me to find?"

"I'd say that's great. But if it's outside the academy, I'd also say that you're never going to find it, at least not until next spring when we have another field trip."

"What about the supply carts?"

"Are you insane? Do you know what they did to the last student that tried to sneak out?"

"You mean, what your mother did," said Bobby. Jinx looked wounded.

"I'm sorry," said Bobby. "That was uncalled for."

"No, it's fine. My mother has to make difficult choices sometimes. Like not giving Ashley and me special treatment. I think that's why Ashley is so mean sometimes. She's just trying to prove herself."

"I hope you're right. In any case, I know that you are not like her. You're a good person, Theodore Grayson, age eleven."

"Oh, shut up," Jinx laughed. "Now tell me the solution to the puzzle. Maybe together we can figure out a way to get you to it."

That night, Bobby and his friends hatched a plan.

"I'm going to stow away in the back of one of those wagons right before they leave for the village. I should be able to hop out when they get down to the forest. Then I can find my grandfather's secret. After that, I can sneak back onto the wagons when they're heading back."

"That won't leave you much time," said Trevor. "It won't take the caravan long to exchange the tanks at the village."

"Well then, let's hope I don't need that long."

"And what if someone notices you're gone?" said Lily.

"I am counting on you guys to cover for me. If anyone asks, tell them I'm sick. If they check my room, tell them I went to the nurse."

"And what if they check with the nurse?"

"They won't. But if they do . . . I'm not sure."

Jinx came up with a solution. "I can steal some stationery from my mom's office and forge a letter saying you're with her," he said. "No one will dare question that."

"You sure you can pull that off?" said Jacob. "It sounds like a big job for such a little pipsqueak."

"My sister has done it for years. I even know where she keeps the key she stole to Mom's office."

"What about you, Bobby?" said Trevor. "Are you sure you know where you're going?"

Lily put her hands on her hips as Bobby nodded. "And you aren't going to tell us, are you?"

"It's safer for everyone if you don't know. The academics would find a way to get it out of you if anything went wrong."

"What if something happens to you?"

Bobby shrugged. "That's a risk I'm willing to take."

Lily wrapped her arms around his neck. "Please be careful."

Bobby winked. "Careful is my middle name."

"I've seen your file," said Jinx. "Your middle name is Alexander."

CHAPTER 22

Late afternoon shadows lay across the forest as Master Jong made his way to Hatou's house. Stepping from the dense underbrush into the open, he gasped as the house came into view. The tiny structure lay in ruins, the exterior burnt to a husk.

Dashing to the front, he faltered as he reached the doorstep. The front window had only jagged shards around the edges, the missing pane smashed and scattered on the ground outside. The thick oak door was charred black and the bottom hinge had ripped off, leaving the heavy plank to sag.

Gingerly, Master Jong stepped over the broken porch steps and into the house where the damage was even worse. The table where Hatou had worked and taken his meals lay smashed to pieces like so much kindling. The pallet where he slept was ripped apart, the frame bent virtually beyond recognition. The stove had been dismantled, its pieces scattered. Everywhere he looked, there were holes—holes in the walls, ceiling, and floor.

Master Jong called out to his friend but got no reply. He had come to tell Hatou about being followed and to warn him that it would be unwise to continue his visits—that he had arranged to study the scrolls in the archives instead. All that fled his mind now.

In two strides, he crossed to the corner with the secret compartment. The boards were ripped up, exposing the space below like an open wound. Master Jong sank to the floor and closed his eyes as the world around him spun. The box containing the copies of the scrolls was gone.

For a long time, he lay on the ground, his head in his hands, lost to despair and regret. *How could I have been so stupid?* Clearly the academics knew what he was up to. Searching for the answer to free Master Jong's people had cost Hatou his home and quite possibly his life as well.

For the first time since he'd begun his crusade, Master Jong wished he'd left it alone instead of trying to do what he felt was right. At least then none of this would have happened.

Then he heard the words of one of his students in his head. "It's better to do the right thing, regardless of the consequences, than to allow an evil to persist."

Just like that, Master Jong understood the secret of the scrolls. Truth be told, it wasn't a secret at all. Regaining his composure, Master Jong stood and left the cottage. In moments, he was on the forest trail back to the academy.

—⟋⟍—

Jinx pushed open the door and stepped into his mother's office. "Mom, are you in here?" When no reply came, he stepped inside, closed the door behind him, and tiptoed to the gigantic mahogany desk. As usual, everything was in perfect order, with papers stacked in neat piles. "Cleanliness is next to godliness," or so the headmistress always said.

Tiptoeing around the desk, Jinx opened the second drawer. His hand was halfway into the drawer before he realized that the compartment that normally housed the stationery was empty. *Oh crap.* She must have run out. Or maybe she moved it.

He opened the bottom drawer and scanned the contents:

official-looking rubber stamps, a stapler, and a few other miscellaneous items, but no stationery. The top drawer held rows of pens, paper clips, and rubber bands. Quickly, he maneuvered behind the massive leather chair to the drawers on the other side. He pulled on the bottom drawer, but it refused to budge.

Giving silent thanks for all the years spent in this office as a young child, Jinx tipped back the large, freestanding quartz crystal on the corner of the desk and scooped up the gold key beneath it. Lowering the crystal back into place, he inserted the key and opened the drawer.

Within a deep cushion of black velvet lay a beautiful crystal decanter and matching shot glass. Pulling the stopper from the decanter, Jinx raised the bottle to his nose and sniffed. The odor was unlike anything he recognized, heady and strong with a hint of something musky and dank. He wrinkled his nose. There was something foul about the concoction he couldn't quite place.

Forcing himself back to the task at hand, Jinx carefully replaced the decanter, closed the drawer, and opened the one above it. This one contained a stack of papers, all of which had writing on them. Curious, he glanced at the one on top and paused when the heading caught his attention. He scanned the report. "What the heck is this?"

"I was about to ask you the same thing."

Jinx sprang up from behind the desk. Simpkins stood on the other side, staring down at him. Somehow the man had slipped into the room without making a sound.

"It's okay, my mom sent me to—"

"Save it," said Simpkins. "I much prefer that you tell your lies directly to the headmistress. Now come on. I was just on my way to find her."

CHAPTER 23

It was five thirty and the sun was just rising. The monks would be performing their morning oblations before eating a sparse meal and setting about their daily chores. When finished, they would drive a caravan of wagons filled with empty propane tanks into the small nearby village. There, they would swap their empty containers for full ones and return to the monastery.

Checking that no one was around, Bobby climbed into the back of the last covered wagon. He quickly stowed his backpack containing a flashlight, water bottle, and snacks he'd snagged from the dining hall the night before. Then he settled down among the empty propane tanks to wait.

It didn't take long. Less than five minutes later, monks arrived to hitch the mules. Bobby held his breath as a monk walked past the canvas tarp concealing him. *Will they check inside the wagons before departing? Maybe I should get out now and find another way.* He rose to a crouch, uncertain.

Then he heard a loud groan as the main gate swung open. Seconds later, his wagon lurched forward, heading for the rocky path that led to the forest floor. *Too late to turn back now*, thought Bobby. In roughly two hours he would reach the bottom of the mountain. *Then the real journey begins.*

—〰—

From his spot at the back of the caravan, Bobby watched the wagons below wind around the final bend of the mountain pass and disappear into the verdant folds of the forest. Balancing on the tailgate, he waited until his wagon reached the last turn, then jumped down and dashed for the tree line. Ducking behind a speckled elm, he stopped to listen. The caravan kept rolling, oblivious to his departure. *Stage one complete. Now for stage two.*

Turning toward the heart of the forest, Bobby cinched up his backpack and took off running. Mist hung heavily in the air as he pressed through the thicket. He skirted a small pond that had been a meadow during his previous visit, and gave wide berth to a hollow tree trunk with a bad vibe.

In time he emerged at the base of the hills he had searched with Jinx in the southeast corner of the woods. Finding a suitable path, he picked his way up the hillside to the ledge. Following it to the end, he paused at the hole where he'd injured himself. The rainy season had eroded the edges, transforming the once-sinister trap into a murky mud puddle. *You can't miss it this time.* He gave the sinkhole one last look and headed for the ravine.

Reaching the corner, he crept down the gorge until he was only a stone's throw from the cave entrance. Then, ducking behind a blackberry briar, he removed his backpack and sat down. Crossing his legs, he closed his eyes and began to meditate. In moments, he stood before his inner core. Remembering his prior success, he conjured up images of his family and probed the barrier.

His hand sank a few inches into the invisible wall, but no further. In fact, the harder he pushed, the more resistance he encountered. After several more attempts, he reluctantly retreated from his meditative state and opened his eyes. *Looks like I'll have to do this the hard way.*

Tiptoeing forward, Bobby reached the mouth of the cave and paused. No sound came from within. *Perhaps the bears are out foraging?* Heart pounding, Bobby opened his backpack and took out his flashlight. Clicking it on, he followed the right wall into the cave.

Wading into the darkness, Bobby pictured the riddle from the puzzle box as he mentally recited the clues that had led him here: *Below the mountain, across the forest, up the hill, inside the cave with the black bears, within the crevice . . .* Whatever his grandfather had left for him was inside that crevice.

Unable to resist, Bobby turned the light toward the far corner. Huddled together on the ground lay three small, black mounds and one big mound. The flashlight almost slipped from his hand as the big mound rose a few inches before settling back down. *Oh my gosh,* Bobby screamed inside his head, *they're hibernating!*

Hands suddenly shaky, Bobby swiveled the light back to the wall and dashed into the crevice. With trembling legs, he listened for signs that the bears had woken but heard nothing but deathly silence.

Careful not to disturb anything, Bobby worked his way into the fissure. The musky smell of bears mingled with the putrid odor of refuse. At the tight spot where the passage hooked to the right, he squeezed through the narrow gap and took a deep breath as the main chamber disappeared behind him.

Bobby fought to keep from gagging on the malodorous stench. Pulling his jacket up to cover his nose, he widened the beam of his flashlight to reveal the contents of the crevice's final cavity. There on the ground, only a few feet away, sat the pile of bones and excrement from which Bobby and his friends had extracted the *Transitivo paradoxa* mushroom. He was surprised to see that a lone toadstool had regrown on top of the mound.

He went over the end of the riddle once again: *Within the crevice . . . below the red-capped mushroom with the white stalk . . .* This was it. His grandfather's secret lay hidden beneath this mound. He still couldn't believe it. He had been so close before and had no idea.

Gently, Bobby pried up the new toadstool and put it in his backpack. *No sense it letting it go to waste.* Then he rolled up his sleeves and sank a hand down into the muck. At first he felt nothing but dirt and slime. He pushed deeper and encountered something solid. *A bone?* No, the object had a sharp edge. *Something metal—a box perhaps?*

He dug with his fingers until he got his hand around it and pulled. The box shifted slightly but did not come free. Bobby took a deep breath through his jacket, sank his other hand into the muck, grabbed the other side of the container, and yanked.

The box came loose easier than he'd expected, sending him tumbling backward to land with a heavy thud. Bobby froze as the sound reverberated off the cavern walls. When the other room remained quiet, Bobby slowly picked himself up and examined the box. Long and narrow and made of stainless steel, it reminded him of a security deposit box. With trembling hands, Bobby unbuckled the latch and lifted the lid to gaze upon a faded blue book with the word *Diary* printed across the cover.

Bobby wiped his hands on his pants seven times. Gingerly, he ran a finger over the lettering. So, this was what his grandfather had gone to such great lengths to place into his hands.

He opened the cover and an envelope fell out, fluttering to his feet. Retrieving it, Bobby discovered a handwritten note, still perfectly preserved after all the years in the box.

Slowly, he unfolded the note and read.

Dear Bobby,

By this stage, there are undoubtedly many things you have discovered about who you are and the special abilities you possess. There are also many things you still need to learn. The gift comes to people in different ways, and, while it can be used for many purposes, only a few have the power of clairvoyance. I am one of those people.

From the moment I first laid eyes on you as a newborn child, I knew you were special. With that knowledge came the additional certainty that you would someday end up at the academy. Bobby, beware of the Jade Academy! I do not know all that there is to know, but I do know that the academy is not what it appears. Perhaps you can discover its secrets where I could not. I know only that I had to warn you.

Years ago, I had a vision of you in the cave where you now stand. Using that knowledge, I crafted the message inside the pendant that guided you to this place. And now I give to you my diary. In it is all my history with the Jade Academy, as well as my suspicions about the evil that resides within. I pray that you can solve the mystery, for I have one last prediction. There are forces within the academy that seek to control you, and if they cannot control you, they will seek to destroy you instead. You must hurry, for I sense that time works against you.

May fortune guide you, my beautiful grandson.

With All My Love,

Grandpa

Bobby wiped tears from his eyes as he gently placed the note and the diary into his backpack, double-checking to make sure both were secure before heading back toward the main cave.

Keeping the light on the ground, he crept along the crevice until he reached the main chamber and then, unable to resist, flicked the flashlight toward the far wall. Just as before, the silhouettes of the three cubs rose and fell in a steady rhythm. Not willing to risk a peek at the mother bear, Bobby turned and tiptoed toward the cave entrance.

A sudden movement near the mouth of the cave caught his eye. Bobby flung himself to the ground as the assassin rushed at him from out of the dark. Flat on the ground, Bobby rolled to the side and kicked. The man stumbled over his prostrate legs but did not fall down. Bobby scrambled to his feet, ready to face his attacker.

But the assassin did not come at him again. Instead, the man picked up a thick tree branch from the cave floor and turned to the back wall. Bobby did a double take, trying to make sense of the man's actions. That's when he heard the growl.

The bear came from the shadows like a demon ascending from the gates of hell, her face contorted, her amber eyes ablaze with maternal wrath as they locked onto the assassin. She lunged, swiping a massive forepaw at his head, but the assassin danced back out of reach. The bear lunged again, snapping and clawing at the man's face. The assassin stepped to the side, deftly deflecting the barrage with a few lightning-fast flicks of the tree branch.

Bobby wasted no time. Jumping to his feet, he raced to the mouth of cave. He heard a roar followed by a solid thunk as the assassin repelled another attack.

"Bobby, wait! You don't understand—"

Whatever else the man had to say was lost as the bear renewed its assault. Bobby paused. With the man's attention focused on the bear, now would be the perfect time to strike him down. Then again, doing so would leave Bobby alone with the enraged beast.

Bobby hesitated for only a moment before turning toward the forest. "I know Cassandra sent you," he yelled at the would-be assassin. "I only wish she were here to get eaten as well."

Behind him, the sounds of the struggle between man and beast continued as Bobby took off.

—m—

Bobby never slowed down as he raced across the forest. Several times he thought he heard noises behind him. Each time, he pushed himself to greater speeds. When he reached the pond, he leapt over it, drenching his feet in freezing water as he landed in the shallows on the far shore. He pushed on, charging through brambles and leaping over fallen logs in his haste to get back to the trail before the caravan.

He arrived not a moment too soon. Already the first of the wagons were leaving the forest, heading back up the mountain. He reached the last wagon right as it hit the bend. The wagon struck a pothole and Bobby seized his opportunity. Dashing from the forest cover, he grasped the bouncing tailgate and hoisted himself up into the flatbed where he held his breath and waited.

When the wagon began the steep climb up the hill without incident, Bobby relaxed his shoulders and settled in among the now-full propane tanks. Opening his backpack, he removed his flashlight and the diary. He made himself comfortable and flipped the book open.

From the picture in the yearbook, Bobby already knew that his grandfather Jeremiah had been a student at the Jade Academy along with Cassandra and his grandmother Melody. What he hadn't known was that Jeremiah and Melody had been in love since childhood and planned to wed after graduation.

Unfortunately, the academy did not allow for student relationships. Marriages in those days were all arranged. Fearing what the academics would do if they found out, the lovers kept their feelings a secret, telling no one except for their best friend, Cassandra.

From his entries, it was clear that Jeremiah tried not to worry about the situation. He was the most talented student of his time, a protégé with the gift of clairvoyance. Melody was talented in her own right, gifted with exceptional empathic abilities. Certainly the two of them would be chosen to wed.

And then came the fateful day when the headmaster announced that Jeremiah was to take a bride from within the ranks of the female students. Jeremiah's heart swelled with excitement. At last, he would be paired with Melody and be able to display his love openly.

Except, the marriage announcement did not go as expected. The headmaster selected someone else to be Jeremiah's wife— Cassandra.

The diary became almost impossible to follow after that, with pages torn out and the remaining writing nearly illegible. At some point, Jeremiah went to Cassandra and begged her to decline the arrangement—together they would make the headmaster pick someone else.

Cassandra was outraged that Jeremiah would ask such a thing. To her, rejecting the arrangement meant rejecting her sworn duty. It would shame her for the rest of her life. Besides, she didn't want to reject it. And that's when the truth came out. Cassandra, his longtime friend, was also in love with him.

At first, Jeremiah was dumbstruck. For years she'd been the sole confidant of the love between him and Melody. She knew that they dreamed of the day they could be together, and yet Cassandra had secretly prayed for a very different outcome. Now the moment had arrived. The headmaster picked her over Melody, delivering to Cassandra the prize she most desired.

According to the diary, a horrible fight ensued. Jeremiah didn't love Cassandra. He loved Melody. Why couldn't she let them be happy? Cassandra had her own opinion—would it really be so bad to marry your best friend? In time, he would get over his love for Melody. He and Cassandra would find their own happiness—perhaps even a love of their own someday.

Jeremiah refused to listen. Feeling hurt and betrayed, he vowed never to marry Cassandra. Instead, he snuck into Melody's quarters late one night. Together, they sought to flee the academy. But the monastery's walls were well protected. Spotted trying to slip through the main gate, the two young lovers ran back inside.

The young couple ran through the halls, desperately searching for a means to escape the monastery and the academics chasing them. Whether by luck or destiny, they ended up at the jade mines, where they fled deep into the tunnels until they were lost. Exhausted and with their pursuers closing in, Jeremiah and Melody did the only thing they could think to do. They prayed for a miracle.

That's when Jeremiah opened his eyes and discovered a bright, shining door where before there had been only darkness. "Bathed in love for one another and at our moment of greatest need, a door appeared where before there had been none." That was how Bobby's grandfather described discovering the Spine of the World.

Following the path beyond the glowing door, the lovers came to a circular room with three identical doors. Unable to decipher the writing above the archways, they picked a path at random, traveling deep into the heart of the mountain to emerge into an enormous room filled with diamonds, emeralds, and sapphires stacked upon heaps of gold. And yet the room contained no exit, forcing the couple to leave the priceless treasure and backtrack to the circular room.

Choosing between the remaining two doors, the lovers ascended to a room high up near the peak of the mountain. There they discovered a grand library the likes of which they'd never imagined. Ancient scrolls and books lay everywhere, and yet, like the treasure room, the room contained no exit. The lovers backtracked to the circular room once again, this time proceeding down the third and final tunnel.

Bobby's grandfather didn't provide details about the third passage, saying only that it led to an exit somewhere at the base of the mountain. From there, the couple journeyed out of the region and eventually to the United States.

Two years after getting married, the couple had their first child, Bobby's father, Nathaniel. In the diary, Jeremiah described knowing right away that their son was normal, lacking the special gift that both parents possessed. Instead of being disappointed, Jeremiah was elated by the knowledge that their son would have a chance at a normal life.

For a few years, the small family lived in bliss. Grandpa made few entries during that time. Most of his notes were about special events—birthdays, vacations, and trips to the zoo. Bobby flipped through those pages quickly. As much as he wanted to read the whole thing, he was running out of time before the caravan arrived back at the academy.

He read carefully when Grandpa described the birth of their second child, a baby girl. Bobby set the book down for a moment as he tried to reconcile the information in front of him with what Cassandra had told him the day they met. It was true. He did have an aunt. *But why haven't I heard of her before, and where is she now?* Bobby had only to turn the page to discover the answer.

Within hours of the child's birth, Grandpa had a vision. The infant would grow up to have tremendous power. Afraid of being discovered now more than ever, the couple sold their house in Maine and moved to Indiana.

They'd been living in Eagledale, just outside Indianapolis, for only two months when everything came unraveled. Bobby could almost picture the scene as he read what happened.

Chapter 24

The night was cold and rainy. Melody was home sick with their son, Nate. Jeremiah had the newborn with him as he ran to the drugstore to get medicine for his ailing wife and child. Pushing the baby's stroller, he went to the back aisle toward the pharmacy. As he stood comparing cough suppressants, he heard a voice from behind.

"Hello, Jeremiah," said Simpkins. The bottle of cough syrup slipped from Jeremiah's grasp and shattered on the floor.

"Please don't run," said Hayward from the other end of the row. "It's always annoying when people try to run. It's not as if anyone ever gets away."

Jeremiah's gaze shifted from Hayward to the pool of blood-red liquid spreading across the white tiles at his feet. "Whatever you do to me, please don't hurt my baby."

"Hurt your baby?" said Simpkins indignantly. "Of course not. We intend to take excellent care of this little bundle of joy."

Hayward gave a low laugh. "Quite the little homing beacon, that one," he said. "At first we thought it was you and Melody in here. But don't worry, we'll have her soon enough."

"You stay away from my wife. We're not going back with you. You hear me? Never."

Hayward smiled broadly. "I rather hoped you'd say that."

He stepped toward Jeremiah but Simpkins waved him off. "Relax, Hayward. We don't need to cause a scene. He won't try anything stupid—not with his baby here. Isn't that right, Jeremiah?"

Jeremiah didn't respond; instead, he shifted his stance toward Hayward to keep a better eye on him. An instant later he felt a tiny prick, like a bee sting, at the base of his neck.

Jeremiah had no idea what happened next. One minute he was standing in the aisle with the two agents. The next, he woke up in a van parked outside, with straps around his wrists and ankles. Hayward sat on his right by the door. Simpkins sat across from him, holding the baby at arm's length like an alien lifeform. It was the person next to Simpkins, however, that held Jeremiah's attention.

"Cassandra?" he said, unable to mask his shock.

"Another surprise? Wonderful!" said Hayward, clapping with delight. "Yes, indeed, the whole gang is here. Everyone except that precious peach of yours, Melody."

Jeremiah ignored him, his eyes locked on Cassandra. "What are you doing here?"

Hayward arched a brow. "You don't know? Cassandra came to work for us after graduation. She's now an apprentice—quite promising, really. In fact, she's the reason we found you. Tell him, Cass."

Jeremiah searched Cassandra's face for an explanation, but she turned to stare out the window.

"Fine," said Hayward, "If she won't brag, I will—"

"Enough," said Simpkins. "There is no need to torture him, Hayward. Simply put, Jeremiah, it seems that you and your wife formed a very special bond with your love for one another. From all your time spent together, Cassandra can sense that connection. That's how we tracked you."

"I must say, the scent is quite intoxicating," said Hayward, with a sniff. "I can't wait to see how wonderful your wife smells in the flesh."

Judging from the description in his diary, Jeremiah seemed quite pleased with what happened next. Leaning back against his seat, he pulled his knees up to his chest and thrust his feet at Hayward. The blow caught Hayward squarely in the face. Holding the baby in one hand, Simpkins leaned over and restrained Jeremiah with the other, but the damage was done.

"You broke my nose!" said Hayward, cupping his face. "I'm going to kill you."

This time it was Hayward who needed a restraining hand. "Go to the other van and get yourself cleaned up," said Simpkins. "After that, go inside and get some ice for your nose. And get some diapers and baby formula as well."

"But—"

"Don't argue with me, Hayward. Go. Now."

With one last glare at Jeremiah, Hayward opened the van's sliding door and stepped out into the night. "This isn't over," he said, slamming the door behind him.

Simpkins returned his attention to Jeremiah. "In a moment, you and I are going to have a little chat about the whereabouts of that lovely wife of yours. But first, I need to have my hands free. Cassandra, watch over our guest while I take the child to the other van."

"Why don't you just have me hold her?" asked Cassandra.

"Because I don't want it in here. All these things do is eat, poop, and cry."

"What about our orders?"

"I'll radio in our situation while I'm over there and see if they have any new instructions. Just sit tight. I'll be back in a minute."

Simpkins handed the baby to Cassandra as he climbed out of the van. For a moment, she cradled the infant as it cooed in her arms. Then Simpkins took the child back and made for the other vehicle.

Alone in the van with Cassandra, Jeremiah gazed deep into the face of his former best friend. "How could you do this to me?"

Cassandra offered no reply as she stared out the window once again.

Jeremiah shook his head sadly. "I can't believe you betrayed your best friends and you're not even going to tell me why."

Cassandra spun around to face him. "You think I betrayed you? What about how you betrayed me? You left me at the academy with no husband and no friends. I was humiliated in front of everyone for failing my assignment. I'm lucky they didn't kick me out after what you did."

"*Failing your assignment*? What are you talking about?"

"You were supposed to love me! All those years I tried to get you to see that it was me you were truly meant to be with, but you never noticed. You only had eyes for Melody. So don't blame me for your mess. We could have been happy together. You'd have learned to love me."

Jeremiah swallowed hard. "Cassandra, look at me. I know it hurts for you to hear this, but I have my happiness. I am sorry that it isn't with you, but think about my baby girl. If you truly love me, if you were ever truly my friend, don't do this."

Cassandra looked down at her arms as if remembering the beautiful baby girl she'd held just moments before. Then she waved a hand as if to wipe away the memory. "It's done. There is nothing I can do now."

"That's not true. It's not too late. Loosen these straps. Help me escape. We can make it look like I overpowered you. I could reach Melody and together we can run away."

"Weren't you listening? The connection between the two of you is too strong. Now that they know what to look for, the others will be able to find you no matter where you go."

"I'll deal with that later. What matters now is that when Simpkins gets back, he's going to force me to tell him where Melody and my son are. Please, Cass, we were your best friends once. You've gotta stop this."

Cassandra turned back to him with tears in her eyes. "You promise to disappear? You'd never be able to see Melody again or they'd be able to find you."

"Maybe we'll find a way to stay together. Maybe we won't. At least we'll be free."

"Then we haven't much time. They can never suspect that I helped you escape."

Moments later, Jeremiah threw open the van's sliding door and slipped out into the dimly lit parking lot. Behind him, Cassandra lay crumpled on the floor, tied up but otherwise unharmed. Sneaking over to the van containing Simpkins and his daughter, Jeremiah pressed his face against the rear window. An agent sat with his daughter on his lap in the middle row. Two other agents sat with them, one on either side. Three more sat up front, and two sat in the back.

Simpkins sat in the driver's seat, talking on the van's two-way radio. Jeremiah's heart sank. There were so many of them. Still, he had to try. Perhaps if he created some kind of a diversion.

Then the door to the grocery store opened and Hayward stepped out, an ice pack held to his face with one hand, a grocery bag filled with diapers in the other.

"Hey, why is the van door open?" he said, dropping the bag and reaching for his radio. A second later, the doors to the van popped open and Simpkins and three men jumped out. Jeremiah did a quick calculation. That left five men still inside.

"What is going on out here?" said Simpkins.

"Why are you asking me?" growled Hayward. "I'm the one who's been inside the store, remember? I just walked out and found the door open."

Without another word, the partners raced to the van. Jeremiah heard noises as the agents untied Cassandra.

"What happened?"

"I'm not sure," said Cassandra in a weak voice. "He must have overpowered me and then taken off. He is probably long gone by now."

"Hayward, secure the baby," said Simpkins. "I want half the men in there with her. Everyone else spread out and find Jeremiah."

Jeremiah had heard enough. Simpkins and Hayward were no fools. He wouldn't get within five feet of his daughter without being captured again. He gave the van one last mournful look and took off. Keeping his head low, he ducked from one parked car to another until he was a safe distance away. Then he ran.

In the distance, Simpkins called for additional backup and gave orders to search the area. By the time the backup arrived, Jeremiah had already escaped.

—✺—

All was quiet outside the small, two-bedroom house as Jeremiah came in the back door and made straight for the master bedroom. Melody lay on the bed with her eyes closed, a damp cloth pressed to her forehead. On the floor nearby, their young son played quietly with a set of Legos.

Jeremiah opened the closet, pulled out their suitcases, and began packing. "Melody, honey, you've got to get up."

"What's going on?" she said, removing the cold compress from her eyes. She took one glance at Jeremiah and sat up straight. "What happened? Where's Victoria?"

Jeremiah couldn't bear to look at her. "I'll explain everything," he said, grabbing another suitcase from under the bed and stuffing clothes into it. "Right now we need to get out of here."

"Jeremiah Ether, you have until the count of three to tell me where our daughter is."

Jeremiah stopped and looked at his wife. Silently he took in her bright green eyes, her luxurious golden locks and dimpled cheeks. Even flushed with a fever, she looked like an angel.

"They found us. I'm so sorry, honey. There was nothing I could do. I tried, but—" Softly, he began to weep.

"Jeremiah, what do you mean 'they found us'?"

Quickly, he explained how Simpkins and Hayward had cornered him in the market. He told her that he managed to escape but left out the part about Cassandra.

"So they have our daughter?"

"And they will have us too, including our son, if we don't hurry."

That was enough to get her moving. Within minutes, they'd shoved all the suitcases and unpacked boxes from their last move into their bulky SUV. Melody started to climb into the passenger seat, but Jeremiah stopped her.

"I can't go with you," he said.

"What are you talking about? Of course you can."

"Listen to me very carefully; being close to you is how they were able to track us in the first place. As long as we are together, they will always be able to find us."

Melody's mouth fell open but no words came out. Finally, she managed to say, "Are you sure? How can you be certain?"

Jeremiah gently cupped her beautiful face. "I'm certain. Oh, how I wish I wasn't." His angel smiled sadly as a tear rolled down her cheek.

"I will find a way to get word to you, wherever you go; I promise," he said. "For now, you must save yourself and our son."

"How will you know where I am?"

"Go to California. Remember the place we always talked about seeing when we were kids? I will leave word for you there."

"But what about you? Where will you go?"

"I'll be fine. Take this," he said, pressing something into her hands. She opened her palms to reveal several large rubies and a stack of gold coins.

"What is this?" said Melody.

"I took them from the treasure room in the Spine of the World. Don't worry; I've kept a few for myself." From his pocket he pulled out a jade pendant shaped like a lotus blossom and showed it to her. "I planned to give this to you as an anniversary present someday. I'm going to keep that promise. I swear it."

"But you can't leave me. I need you," said Melody.

"We will always be together in our hearts, my love. Besides, someone has to look after our son while I try to get our daughter back."

—∽∽—

Bobby looked up from the diary to find that the caravan was almost back at the academy. He hurriedly scanned the remaining pages. After Melody left with their son, Grandpa hid nearby and waited. In time, the agents from the Core arrived. With great skill, Jeremiah isolated and captured one of them, knocking him out and dragging him off without being discovered. Jeremiah questioned the man in secret, discovering that Hayward and several agents had already been dispatched back to the Core to deliver his daughter.

Jeremiah tracked the men who'd abducted his newborn as they traveled across the country toward China. Twice he lured an agent away from the rest of the team. Both times he took his revenge. The second time, the other agents almost caught him, and he barely managed to escape. After that, the agents stayed together at all times. Try as he might, Jeremiah never got an opening that didn't amount to suicide.

Hayward eventually reunited with Simpkins and a half-dozen more agents. They took Jeremiah's daughter and left the country. Without a disguise and fake passport to prevent discovery, Jeremiah was forced to abandon the chase.

He doubled back and traveled to California, where he got word to his wife. In time, she settled down in a small town near the ocean to raise their son. The two of them moved every few years, always making sure to leave word for Jeremiah so he'd know where they'd gone. Jeremiah moved constantly as well but always stayed nearby. Once a year, every year following the abduction of his daughter, he returned to Tibet to search for a way to rescue her.

Disguised as a local, Jeremiah searched the region below the monastery, searching for the entrance to the Spine of the World. He canvassed the base of the mountain for weeks at a time, looking for the passage from which he and Melody had fled. Despite over a decade of pilgrimages, he never found so much as a single sign of the secret entrance. It was as if the doorway had disappeared without a trace.

As the years slipped by, Jeremiah's trips to the mountain grew fewer and further between. His son grew up and married, all while Jeremiah watched from a distance. Jeremiah never discovered what became of his daughter.

Then came the fateful day when Bobby was born. Jeremiah arranged with Melody a time when she would not be around so that he could drop by and see his new grandson. The instant he held the infant, he knew Bobby was special. That was the moment Jeremiah began his plans to ensure that what happened to his daughter would never happen to his grandson.

CHAPTER 25

The courtyard echoed with the clatter of men and beasts as the last of the caravan pulled into the academy. Monks unhitched mules and led them away while others offloaded the propane tanks. From his hiding spot in the last wagon, Bobby crawled to the tailgate. He was about to jump down and make his escape when a voice rang out over the cacophony.

"Bobby Ether, we know you are here. Come out now and show yourself."

Bobby froze. It was the headmistress. Carefully, he lifted the canvas flap and peeked out. Headmistress Grayson stood atop the steps overlooking the courtyard. Jinx stood at her side, his head hung low. *Well, that explains it.*

Crawling to the front of the flatbed, Bobby tucked the diary between the wood frame and the canvas cover so that the tension held it in place.

The headmistress called out again, more insistently this time. "Come now, Mr. Ether. There is no point in pretending. I know you're in there; I can feel your presence."

Checking to make sure the diary was secure, Bobby threw his backpack over his shoulder and climbed out of the wagon.

Hayward and Simpkins walked up on either side. Hayward grabbed his arm. Bobby yanked it free. Hayward reached for him again, but the headmistress waved him off. "You're going to cooperate, aren't you, Bobby? After all, it's not as if you have a choice."

Bobby held her gaze. "I'm not afraid of you."

Hayward leaned over and whispered in his ear, "Oh, but you should be." Then he grabbed Bobby's elbow and, this time, the headmistress said nothing. Placing a guiding hand on Jinx's shoulder, she turned and headed into the monastery.

—⚬—

Sandwiched between Hayward and Simpkins, Bobby half walked and was half dragged to the headmistress's office. At the door, Headmistress Grayson released Jinx and turned to the entourage.

"You two wait with my son out here," she said to the agents. "I will speak with Bobby in private."

"But, Headmistress, what about the boy's—" began Simpkins.

"That will be all," she said curtly.

Jinx gave Bobby a woeful look as Bobby followed Headmistress Grayson into her office. "I'm so sorry," he whispered.

"It's okay," said Bobby. "Everything works out as it's supposed to."

"Wise words," said the headmistress, closing the door behind him and gesturing for Bobby to take a seat. "Where did you learn such insight?"

Bobby unslung his backpack and sat. "Just something I picked up from Master Jong. He always says that things happen for a reason, even if we don't understand it at the time."

"Ah, Master Jong. Someone else I need to deal with shortly. Clearly the student takes after the teacher. Or perhaps it is the other way around. Did Master Jong put you up to leaving the academy?"

Bobby paused. "I haven't seen Master Jong in days. I assumed he was on some sort of assignment for you."

"In a manner of speaking, that is true. Though I doubt he realizes it. Tell me something, Bobby; why did you sneak out of the academy?"

Bobby's gazed at his backpack. "I wanted to see if I could find more of those mushrooms we looked for."

The headmistress raised an eyebrow. "Interesting. And did you manage to find any?"

"I had a tough time, but I did manage to find one."

"Let me see it," demanded the headmistress.

Bobby opened his backpack and removed the small toadstool he'd collected.

"Bring it to me."

Bobby placed the tiny toadstool on the headmistress's desk. She studied the mushroom before leaning back in her chair. "Perhaps you can explain, Bobby, what made you want to search for this mushroom so badly that you snuck out of the academy, in direct violation of our rules?"

"I don't know. I guess I figured there is something special about them."

"And do you have any idea what that special thing is?"

"No."

"Do you have anything else in the backpack you want to share with me?"

"No, ma'am."

"Give it to me."

Bobby handed the headmistress his backpack and stepped back, watching as she opened all the pouches, inspecting the remains of its contents. Finally, she closed the bag and handed it back to him.

"This is not at all what I expected," she said. "Normally, your actions would call for severe consequences, but your motives intrigue me. You show incredible insight and ambition, not unlike another young person who once attended school here."

Bobby sighed with relief. "Does this mean I'm not going to be expelled?"

"A good question. For the moment, I will allow you to remain. You are to return to your quarters and stay there while I decide what to do." As she spoke, she fondled a piece of paper on the desk in front of her.

"Thank you, Headmistress." Bobby stood and was halfway to the door when a loud knock forestalled his exit.

"Enter," said the headmistress.

Willy the Creep pushed open the door and stepped into the room. Siphon sat on his shoulder, perched atop the folded cowl of his blood-red robe. In his hands, Willy held Jeremiah's diary. Bobby's heart thundered inside his rib cage as Willy ignored him and walked past. The ferret, on the other hand, pulled its cheeks back in what could only be described as a hideous smile.

"What is this?" asked the headmistress.

"We found it in the last wagon, stuck between the canvas and the front of the flatbed."

The headmistress came around the desk and took Jeremiah's journal from the boy. "Well, what have we here?"

—⚇—

The hallway appeared deserted, but still Master Jong remained in the shadows. He peeked into the adjacent hall one last time and then hurried into the open. He was almost to the end when Lily, Trevor, and Jacob rounded the corner.

"Master Jong! It's great to see you," said Lily.

"Hello, children," said the monk with a weak smile.

"Man, where have you been?" said Trevor.

"It's like you've been hiding under a rock, or been beaten up with one," said Jacob, appraising the disheveled monk.

Master Jong straightened his robes. "I have been attending to matters of great importance."

"Really? What have you been up to?"

"For your own good, Jacob, I think it's best that we do not discuss such matters."

Lily's eyes grew wide. "Really top secret, huh?"

Master Jong bowed. "It is good to see you all, but I'm afraid I'm in a bit of a hurry," he said, sidestepping the students. "We can talk more when I see you again."

Lily seemed unfazed. "Well, welcome back. We missed you," she said, waving goodbye.

Master Jong stopped. "I need a favor before you go."

"What's up, Master J?" said Trevor.

"I am just now returning and haven't had a chance to settle in yet. If you don't mind, please don't mention my return to anyone else."

"You want to take a nice hot shower and eat a good meal before everyone starts bugging you," said Lily, winking. "We get it."

"Precisely," said Master Jong, his smile faint. With that, he turned and disappeared.

—⁓—

Ashley stepped back behind the statue before the troublemakers had a chance to spot her. All her time spent trailing them had finally paid off. The conversation seemed innocuous enough, but the monk's behavior was odd, not to mention his request that the kids not reveal his return to the academy.

Something very strange was going on. If the monk didn't want people to know that he had returned, then it probably meant that someone should know. Perhaps there was even a way to get Lily, Jacob, and Trevor in trouble as well. Ashley waited until the others were gone before emerging from her hiding spot. Calculating the quickest route to her mother's chambers, she hurried off to share the news.

It was strange to see people standing outside her mother's office. The hall was barren of furniture specifically to discourage people from waiting. Yet, as Ashley drew close, she found Simpkins pacing back and forth across the narrow hallway, his face a solemn mask. Hayward stood nearby with a hand on Jinx's shoulder and a secret smile on his lips. Cowering beneath the big man's grip, her brother looked grim, as if ready to bolt while at the same time determined to stay.

Ashley had no time for her brother's issues. She marched straight up to Simpkins and said, "I need to see my mother right away."

"No one is allowed inside at the moment," said Simpkins, stopping in front of the door and folding his arms across his slender chest.

"Is she with someone?"

"She's with Bobby," said Jinx meekly.

Ashley couldn't help but grin. "Well now, normally I wouldn't want to interrupt, but she's going to want to hear what I have to say."

"Tell me," said Simpkins.

"I demand that you let me in to see my mother this instant," she said in her most commanding tone.

Hayward shrugged. "I say let her go in. It's her own funeral."

"Not unless I know what this is about," said Simpkins. Ashley tried to walk around him. Simpkins slid over and barred her path.

"It's about Master Jong. I saw him in the hallway. He didn't seem to want anyone to know he was here."

"You saw him here at the academy?" asked Hayward. "Where was he? What direction was he headed?"

Ashley told him what she knew. The instant she finished, Hayward started down the hall. "I'm going after him."

"Stop," said Simpkins. "You will do no such thing."

Hayward jerked back like a dog on a leash. "What are you talking about? We need to catch Jong before he ruins everything."

"I need you to wait out here and keep an eye on these two while I inform the headmistress. You can go after Jong once I return."

"No way. I'm not going to sit here and babysit these brats while Jong gets away."

Simpkins gave him a level stare. "That wasn't a request."

Hayward said something under his breath.

"What was that?" said Simpkins.

"I said, I hope you are *quick*. We don't want that little bastard getting away."

—ᴍ—

Bobby gripped the armrests of his chair like the bars of a prison. Across from him, the headmistress sat in silence, reading his grandfather's diary. For over an hour, she'd turned page after page without offering him so much as a glance. Finally, she put down the book and looked up.

"So, this is why you snuck out of the academy." Bobby made no reply. "It's an interesting read. According to this, your grandfather not only predicted your enrollment here but also created the means by which to get this journal to you years before your actual arrival.

"I can see why my predecessor pursued him to such lengths. Clearly, Jeremiah is immensely talented. As for the rest of the story—"

"It's not a story," said Bobby. "It's the truth."

"Perhaps," said the headmistress. "But all of these alleged events happened before my time. Thus, I cannot speak to the validity of what Jeremiah claims happened here."

"So, you think he made it all up?"

The headmistress shrugged. "The matter is irrelevant. It is your knowledge of these alleged events which concerns me."

"You mean like how Simpkins and Hayward kidnapped my aunt and tried to do the same to my grandmother and grandfather under the instruction of the people that run this place? The only thing I don't understand is their ages. Grandpa is in his sixties. That means that Simpkins and Hayward should be at least in their seventies or eighties by now."

"A wonderful observation," said the headmistress. "Actually, there is no reason why that part of the story can't be true."

"What are you talking about?"

The headmistress studied him for several moments, as if trying to decide his fate. "Given this new turn of events, I suppose the decision has been made. Ergo, there is no harm in satisfying your curiosity."

Bobby folded his arms and waited.

"I understand you took a little tour of the archives not too long ago," said the headmistress. "You're a clever boy. I'm surprised you haven't figured it out by now."

Bobby's eyes widened. "Those ledgers that Jacob and I saw—they really were about DNA sequences, weren't they? I bet even that caustic goop that dissolved the shelves is somehow related. It's all material for experimentation in genetic manipulation."

"Very good, Bobby. But your picture is incomplete. Our mission here is not simply to nurture special abilities in people, but to literally *create* future generations of humans with anima capabilities."

"Are you telling me that Simpkins and Hayward are *clones*?"

"Not clones, exactly. That is too restrictive and simplistic of a description. What we do goes far beyond mere cloning. We combine selective breeding with genetic modification to produce the greatest potential for human evolution. The current Simpkins and Hayward are the third generation of their kind, which I inherited from my predecessor. Ironically, despite all the modifications we have made, there are some errant traits that persist. Take, for example, their inclination toward attire native to their original era."

Bobby's mouth fell open. "You're telling me that those hideous suits from the seventies are part of some crazy genetic predisposition?"

The headmistress shrugged. "Some things are still a mystery, even to us. In any case, Simpkins and Hayward serve their purpose. I must admit, however, that the project is getting rather long in the tooth. Which brings me to the matter at hand: your lack of progress over the past several months suggests to me that you simply aren't suitable for the 'personal evolution' project we pursue here. Furthermore, considering your record of persistent disobedience, coupled with the contents of this journal, I find it highly unlikely that we will be able to rely on your continued cooperation."

"You got that right."

The headmistress lifted the paper in front of her. "On the other hand, your DNA profile suggests that you might be particularly useful in advancing our exsos program by providing a new model from which to build."

"My DNA? Oh, heck no. You're not going to use me for some crazy experiment."

The headmistress withdrew a decanter from her desk and poured the ugly green liquid into a shot glass. She shivered slightly as she drank it down, then turned back to him. "As I said before, I can tell you all of this now because I have already decided how we shall proceed, and there is nothing you can do about it."

"I beg to differ," said Bobby, rising. "I'm getting outta here."

"You will stay in your seat!" Her words lashed out like a whip, wrapping around his brain. Against his will, Bobby sank back into his chair.

"You will relax and make no further attempt to resist," she said. Bobby's body went flaccid. He still wanted to fight but found that he no longer had the energy.

She gave him a cold smile. "That's a good boy."

Bobby shivered. Something about the way the corners of her mouth curled up made him pause. The effect was completely different, but the shape was almost the same.

"It's you," he said in a hushed tone. "You're the little girl in the diary—the one who was abducted and brought to the academy.

You're my aunt."

She locked eyes with him and the smile widened.

Bobby stared back at her. "And you already knew."

The headmistress picked up the journal and walked to the unlit fireplace, where the logs suddenly burst into flames. In seconds, a blazing fire roared in the hearth.

The headmistress turned back to Bobby. "I have been aware that you and I are related for some time now. Unfortunately, due to an apparent oversight in our systems, I was unaware that the connection extended to Jeremiah and Melody. Of course, none of that makes any difference. As I am sure you can see from the way I treat Ashley and Jinx, there is no room for nepotism in this organization."

"You mean I get no special treatment because I'm your nephew."

"Exactly."

"But doesn't it mean anything to you? I know how to get word to Grandpa back home. We could leave here together. I could take you to meet your father."

The headmistress paused, but only for a second. "The identities of my biological mother and father are irrelevant. I realized long ago that if my parents wanted me, they would have found a way to keep me."

"But you read the diary, Grandpa tried desperately to get you back."

"As I said before, Jeremiah is obviously a very talented and resourceful man. If he truly wanted to rescue me, he would have found a way."

"So that's it, then? You don't care at all that we're family?"

"I do not blame you for Jeremiah's shortcomings, but I have a responsibility as headmistress and to the people that actually took care of me as a child. They are my true family."

"What about Jinx and Ashley? They're family too."

"I am sure Jinx will be upset by your disappearance, but he's young. He'll get over it. I think it's safe to say that Ashley will not mourn your disappearance at all, especially since neither of them will ever know about their relation."

"What do you mean 'my disappearance'?"

"I have another assignment for you—one which requires facilities not available at this site."

"You're talking about using me for those crazy experiments that made Simpkins and Hayward."

She gave him an icy smile. "You catch on quickly."

"What do you plan to do?"

"First, I intend to get rid of this," the headmistress said, and tossed the diary into the fire.

"Are you crazy?" protested Bobby, raising half out of his seat as the book hit the burning logs and began to crisp.

"You have the willpower to resist me. Impressive. Now sit down!" The command pressed him back into his chair with physical force.

"You can't do this," he said, struggling to get up again. "Why would you destroy your own father's journal with all those precious memories?"

The headmistress turned to the door where Simpkins had poked his head in. "What are you doing in here?" she snapped. "I specifically said that I was not to be disturbed."

"My apologies, Headmistress," said Simpkins. "It's just that . . ."

With the headmistress distracted, the weight holding Bobby eased. Grinding his teeth, he pushed against the remaining pressure until it broke. Hitting the floor softly, he rolled over to see if Simpkins or the headmistress had noticed. They were still talking.

Down on all fours, Bobby scrambled to the fireplace. The book had tumbled off the stack of burning logs and lay on the perimeter of the blaze, the corners just beginning to smoke.

Quickly, Bobby grabbed a wrought-iron poker. Jamming it into the hearth, he slapped at the journal like a hockey puck. The book caromed off the firebox wall and slid across the stone floor to rest under a nearby chair.

Replacing the poker, Bobby checked again to see if he'd been observed. He dashed back to his chair and retook his seat right as the headmistress turned around.

"It's a shame we won't be able to finish our little discussion, but an urgent matter requires my attention. Simpkins will see to it that you are taken care of."

She opened the door and stopped at the threshold. "Where is Hayward?"

"He's supposed to be out there, watching Ashley and Jinx."

"Well, he's not. My son and my daughter are here alone."

"I can't believe it," said Simpkins. "He must have run off after Jong by himself, after I expressly told him not to."

The headmistress looked ready to burst. "I will deal with his insubordination later," she said. "For the moment, I will take Ashley with me. Bring Jinx in here with you. Keep an eye on him till I get back. I will deal with the Ether boy when I return."

"Yes, Headmistress," said Simpkins, signaling Jinx to come into the room. Jinx entered with his head down and shoulders slumped. His head lifted slightly when he saw Bobby.

"Are you okay?" whispered Jinx.

"No talking," said Simpkins, gesturing toward the fireplace. "Have a seat over there." Jinx sighed as he crossed the room and sat in the chair with the journal hidden beneath it.

The headmistress seemed satisfied. "I'll be back as soon as I can. Keep them under control until I return." She gave Bobby one last look and then she was gone.

—⟋⟍—

Master Jong silently cursed himself as he slipped out of the monk's common room and into the hallway. He should have realized the monks' living quarters would be deserted in the middle of the afternoon. At this hour, his fellow monks would be tending to their daily tasks: working in the gardens, cooking in the kitchen, teaching classes, or off in private contemplation. His best bet to find a large group without being spotted by the academics was the gardens. Unfortunately, that meant backtracking all the way to the lower levels and across the open courtyard.

Taking back routes as much as possible, he worked his way to the main entrance. He stopped short as he passed along an outer terrace. The yard below was covered with academics. *They must know I'm back.*

Voices down the hall gave him just enough warning to duck into an alcove as a group of academics appeared from around a corner. The men raced past, clearly in a hurry. *They must be blocking off the exits. Once that's done, they'll begin searching the interior.*

Thinking about the interior gave him an idea. There was one other place besides the gardens where a large number of his cohorts had been working recently. It would be guarded, of course, but perhaps he could find another monk and have them spread the word.

He changed course, moving back into the bowels of the monastery. He had no idea if his new plan would succeed, but it at least gave him a fighting chance.

CHAPTER 26

A deep sense of déjà vu crept over Bobby as he sat in the headmistress's office and stared at Simpkins. *Things did not go well the last time I was here.* His left leg quivered ever so slightly. The headmistress would be back soon to deal with him; that's what she'd said. Next to him, Jinx looked equally distraught, wringing his hands as he stared into his lap.

Bobby cleared his throat. "By the way, Jinx, I found it."

"That's terrific," exclaimed Jinx. "What is it?"

"I said, no talking," said Simpkins.

"I found it *down there*," said Bobby, gesturing downward with his head. His friend looked genuinely confused. So did Simpkins.

"That's great," said Jinx. "But what is it?"

"It's a journal. It proves that this place is involved in all sorts of immoral stuff: kidnapping, genetic experiments—"

"All right, that's it!" roared Simpkins.

But Bobby would not be silenced. "You're in it too, Simpkins. The journal talks all about how you led the search to hunt down and capture my grandparents when all they wanted was to be left in peace."

At the mention of Bobby's grandfather, something dark flashed across Simpkins's face. As quickly as it came, the look disappeared, replaced by perfect composure once again. "Not another word out of either of you."

"Or what?" snapped Bobby. "The headmistress already threatened to send me to your other facility. Why don't you just tell me the truth? Tell me what's really going on around here."

"Did she now?" said Simpkins. "Interesting. If she's planning to send you off, then your physical condition is of little concern."

"You wouldn't dare hurt me. She told you to look after me until she got back."

"True, but I'm sure she won't mind a few bumps and bruises. Not after I tell her how you tried to escape."

Simpkins stepped toward him and Bobby cringed. There was something missing in the man's dark eyes. His soul looked faded, like a photocopy repeated beyond recognition. While Hayward reveled in dark emotions, Simpkins had detached himself from emotion altogether, leaving him cold, empty, and utterly insane.

Bobby leapt out of his chair, dashed over to the fireplace, and grabbed the poker. "Don't make me use this," he said, brandishing it like a sword.

"Come now, boy," said Simpkins with a grin full of yellow, rotten teeth. "You shouldn't play with sticks."

Bobby swiped at the air. "Stay back. I swear I'll hurt you!"

Still grinning, Simpkins took another step forward so that he was only a few feet away. Gritting his teeth, Bobby pulled the poker back and swung with all his strength. It never made contact. With lightning speed, Simpkins's hand shot out and snatched Bobby's wrist. With his other hand, he pried the poker from Bobby and flung it across the room. Then he lifted Bobby by the wrist, forcing Bobby to stand on his tiptoes to keep his shoulder from dislocating.

"Now, where were we?" said Simpkins, close enough now that Bobby choked on the sickly stench of his breath, normally masked by peppermint gum.

"Get away from me," said Bobby, shoving the man in the chest with his free hand. He might as well have been pushing a brick wall.

"Bobby, do you know what makes me so good at my job?" asked Simpkins. "It's my ability to control my emotions. It's one of the things that separate Hayward and me. He lacks discipline. Not me. I follow every instruction down to the letter. As a result, I always accomplish my goal. Which is why your escape the night we first met was particularly irksome."

"I'm so sorry that I ruined your day," said Bobby.

"Yes, well, no harm done. I did, of course, catch you later that night at the hospital."

"Cassandra was right about you; you really are a creep."

"Ah, yes, Cassandra. I look forward to catching up with her as well. Which brings me back to my point—my ability to follow directions. Headmistress Grayson said to keep you here and under control. It certainly looks to me like you are attempting to get out of control."

"Let go of me and I'll show you *out of control*," said Bobby, trying to wriggle free of the man's iron grasp.

"Clearly, the situation requires me to neutralize your aggression," said Simpkins. "Before I do, however, keep in mind that this outcome is entirely your fault."

"I've got a request for you; get bent, you piece of crap!"

Simpkins drew his free hand back by his head and made a fist. "Some kids never learn." Bobby's stomach roiled as energy coalesced in Simpkins's palm, building until the air hummed with electricity.

The madness in Simpkins's eyes grew. He opened his hand and Bobby saw energy rippling along the surface of his palm. "I do believe I am going to enjoy this," he said with maniacal laughter.

Bobby stared into the face of insanity and waited for Simpkins to unleash his terrible power upon him. Then, inexplicably, the iron grip holding his arm relaxed. Bobby wrested his arm free as

Simpkins's smug grin was replaced by a look of disbelief. Then his eyes glazed, his knees buckled, and he slumped to the ground.

Jinx stood on the desk behind him, the quartz crystal ornament from the headmistress's desk gripped firmly in both hands. A corner of the base was chipped.

Bobby stared at him. "Did you just—"

Jinx dropped the crystal, a look of abject horror on his face. "Oh my gosh, I didn't mean to hit him that hard. Is he—?"

"He's fine," said Bobby, noting the rise and fall of the man's chest. "Much better than I would have been if you hadn't done what you did. Come on; we gotta get outta here."

"Wait. Is it true?"

"Is what true?" said Bobby, already halfway to the door.

Jinx grabbed the diary off the desk and waved it at him. "I found this under my chair while you and Simpkins were arguing. I didn't think hitting him with it would have quite the same effect as the crystal."

"I've always said you're a genius."

"Is this really what I think it is?"

"Yes," said Bobby, walking back and taking the book from his friend. "It's my grandfather's diary. Everything I told Simpkins is true. This place is evil."

"I believe you," said Jinx. "I skimmed it briefly before things got heated." The boy blushed. "Sorry I didn't catch your 'down there' hint earlier. It was a little obtuse."

"Yes, well, I was improvising."

"So, is the rest of it true as well? You know, about you and . . ."

Bobby put a hand on Jinx's shoulder. "It's true. We aren't just friends. We're cousins."

The boys set off down the hall, with Bobby racing ahead while Jinx huffed and wheezed in an effort to keep up.

"Where are we going?" said Jinx in between gasps.

"You know, you don't have to come with me," said Bobby.

"This isn't your fight."

Jinx stopped in his tracks. "You're kidding, right? Let's review for a minute. First, I just found out that we're cousins. Second, I just discovered that this place, my mother's job, and everything I've ever known about the Jade Academy is a lie. Third, I just knocked out my mother's top lieutenant. Did I mention that quartz crystal was her favorite? I think you're stuck with me for the time being."

"She's your mother. She'll forgive you."

"Have you met my mother?" asked Jinx. "Besides, what kind of friend would I be if I didn't help you out in a jam?"

Bobby put an arm around Jinx. "You really are the best friend anyone could ever hope for."

"Not just friend—cousin," said Jinx, grinning.

"That too," said Bobby with a laugh.

"So," said Jinx, "do you have a plan?"

"Working on it."

"You know this way leads to the mines, right? There's no exit from the academy that way."

"One step at a time, buddy."

At the final turn before the mines, Bobby poked his head around the corner. Three academics guarded the thick iron doors at the end of the hall.

"They must be on the lookout for Master Jong," said Jinx. "Apparently you aren't the only one who thought this might be a good place to hide."

Bobby put his hands on his head. "Just give me a second. There's gotta be another way. What about the main gate?"

"If they've got three people stationed down here, then the courtyard is going to have ten times as many. There's no way we're slipping out that way."

"Good point," said Bobby. "Unfortunately, that doesn't leave us many options."

Jinx ticked fingers off on one hand. "By my calculations, I'd say that leaves us exactly zero options."

"There is always another way," Bobby said, and took off back the way they had come.

"Hey, wait for me," said Jinx, running after him.

After running for a good ten minutes, the two boys stood at the back of the library. In front of them loomed the archives.

"*This* is your big idea?" asked Jinx.

"I told you, I have a plan."

"Are we part of that plan?" said a voice behind them.

Bobby spun around to see Lily, Trevor, and Jacob come running up.

"My gosh, it's good to see you guys," said Bobby. "But how did you find us?"

Trevor shrugged. "We figured your disappearance had something to do with all the teachers running around, so we decided to come to our meeting place and see if we could find you."

"An interesting conjecture," said Jinx. "Your hypothesis was sound; indeed we—"

"Don't know anything about what's going on," said Bobby quickly.

Jacob gave them a quizzical look. "All right then, don't tell us. But I'm guessing whatever's going on, we shouldn't be standing around here."

Before Bobby could reply, shouts echoed from across the library. "You're probably right," said Bobby. "It's definitely best if we're not spotted."

"You can explain on the way," said Trevor, heading for the archives.

"Wait, what about light?" said Lily. "It's pitch black in there."

Everyone exchanged troubled looks until Jinx spoke up. "I

stashed the equipment from our last trip just inside the door, in case we needed it again."

"Everything happens for a reason," intoned Trevor.

"Maybe," said Bobby, patting his cousin on the back, "but being a genius who obsesses about being prepared doesn't hurt either. Now come on; let's get the heck outta here."

—⋙—

As they trekked through the archives, Bobby told his friends all about the diary and its contents. Everyone had questions, including Jinx, who'd only skimmed the journal back at the headmistress's office.

"You guys are actually cousins?" said Jacob.

"Dude, that's heavy," said Trevor, rubbing his head as if to help absorb the information.

Lily hugged them both. "That's incredible. Congratulations."

They worked their way down to the lower levels, passing through halls filled with artifacts out of ancient history as Bobby recounted the events in the headmistress's office.

"Now *that* guy I knew was a jackhole," said Jacob when Bobby told them about Simpkins's assault. "I just wish I could have been there to see Jinx whack him with that crystal."

Moments later, they arrived at the entrance to sublevel five, with its Roman chariot and Western stagecoach. In the faint lantern light, Trevor all but disappeared, while Jacob's pale skin made him look like a ghost.

"It's so dry and dusty," said Jinx, pulling out his inhaler and taking a drag.

"And spooky," said Lily, scooting closer to Trevor, who put his arm around her. Jacob glowered at them but said nothing. They crept forward, cautious of the dark, with Bobby in the lead. As they approached the stagecoach, something skittered just outside the nimbus of his lantern.

"What was that?" said Jinx, pointing into the darkness.

"Probably just a rat," said Trevor.

"Ouch! That rat just bit me!" exclaimed Jacob, reaching down to rub his ankle. Another skitter echoed off to the left this time. Lily swung her flashlight. From between the long spokes of the stagecoach's wheel, two amber eyes stared at them. Lily stepped closer. The creature stood on its hind legs and hissed.

"That's one pale rat," said Jacob.

The creature dashed off into the darkness. Lily gasped. "Since when do rats have furry tails?"

"I've got a better question," said Trevor, looking not at the rodent but at the chariot. "Since when does that chariot have soldiers?"

Sure enough, nearly a dozen figures stood on and around the ancient vehicle. Lily peered closer. "Wait, is one of them picking his nose?" She jumped back as the figures moved, pouring out of the darkness and heading straight for them.

"It's about time you guys showed up," said Ashley, stepping into the light. Behind her were the twins, along with a gang of upperclassmen. Willy the Creep stood in the shadows nearby. Dressed in red laced with black, the bald boy lowered his arm. Siphon leapt onto his shoulder, its beady amber eyes laughing at Bobby and his friends.

"Well, that explains the rat," said Jacob.

"What's the matter, Bobby?" said Ashley. "Aren't you glad to see me, *cousin*?"

"What are you doing down here, Ashley?" Jinx asked his sister. "And how do you know about us being cousins?"

Ashley's eyes flashed with anger. "You have the nerve to ask me what *I'm* doing down here? What are *you* doing down here, little brother?"

"It's a long story," said Jinx.

"You mean like how you knocked out Professor Simpkins and ran away with this delinquent?" asked Ashley, gesturing to Bobby. "That's right. I know all about your little jailbreak. Once Simpkins woke up, he tracked down Mom and I and gave us a full report. She knows all about your treachery, and so do I."

She paused for dramatic effect. "Honestly, little brother, I didn't think you had it in you."

"It's not that simple," said Jinx.

"Save it," snapped Ashley. "The time for talking is over."

"So, you're here to fight?"

"Mom went after Jong. She sent Simpkins to track down Hayward. That left me to deal with you losers. For the record, she gave me permission to bring you back by any means I deem necessary. Right now, I think a major butt-kicking is very, very necessary."

"Beating up my friends won't change my mind," said Bobby. "I'm never going back."

Surprise registered on Lily's face. "Is that what you were doing when we found you in the library? Running away?"

"Let me explain," began Bobby.

"Actually, let me," said Ashley. "You see, some people just don't have what it takes to face their fears. Bobby couldn't face Simpkins, just like he can't face me now. His 'big plan' was to hide down here like a coward and try to slip past the guards after things died down."

"That's not true," said Bobby.

"How else did I know you'd be down here?" asked Ashley.

"I don't know, but that's not why I'm here."

"That's actually a good point," Trevor said to Ashley. "Even if you knew he was headed down here, how did you know where to look? There are dozens of entrances to the archives."

"Ah, Trevor, I'm so glad to see you still appreciate my genius." Trevor rolled his eyes as she went on. "Last time I was down here, I saw bottles of ink and parchments. It only took a glance to realize someone was making copies of the ancient scriptures. I didn't report it then, because I wanted to catch the forger myself before turning him into Mother. Now, it's obvious that it was that ingrate Jong. Once I realized that, I figured you had to be working with him as well. So I brought my boys down here to wait until someone showed up to dispose of the evidence.

Whether it was you or Jong, either way I end up a hero."

Trevor smirked. "Still all about you, eh, Ashley?"

"Naturally."

"Don't do this," said Jinx.

"It's done, little brother. It's about time you and your friends learned your place—under my heel."

CHAPTER 27

In the depths of the archives, lit only by the flickering lanterns, friend and foe squared off. Ashley barked an order and her gang rushed at Bobby and his friends. Tex and two others went after Trevor. Mex and another upperclassman came for Jacob and Bobby.

"You don't have to do this," Trevor told Tex as he easily ducked the hefty twin's opening salvo. "You can make your own decisions instead of always doing what Ashley tells you."

"Shut your mouth," growled Tex. "Ashley was right to ditch you. You're stupid if you think you'll ever get anywhere with these losers."

Jacob shoved Bobby out of the way as Mex swung a ham-sized fist at Bobby's head. Jacob ducked another blow, casually landing an uppercut to the twin's kidney. "You gotta be kidding me," he said. "All your studies at the academy, and that's the best you can do?"

Mex glowered and launched another furious attack. Jacob dodged easily.

"How do you do that?" asked Bobby, struggling to stay clear of the two boys trying to box him in.

"You've got to feel the flow," said Jacob. "Read your opponent's energy to know what they're going to do before they do it."

Bobby watched in amazement as the movements of his stocky friend took on a fluid, almost graceful quality. Throwing quick jabs and fierce kicks, he took out the boys surrounding Bobby in a matter of seconds. Sneaking up from behind, Tex swung at the back of Jacob's head. Jacob spun at the last second. Ducking, he slipped inside Mex's guard and delivered a vicious knee to the groin.

"That's for 'hide-n-seek' in the archives," said Jacob as the heavy brute fell and rolled onto his back, groaning and holding himself. "Scratch *that*."

"I'm pretty sure that's Sniff," said Bobby.

"Whatever."

Next to them, long-limbed Trevor deftly deflected every blow while countering with skillful strikes. Back to back, he and Jacob made a formidable pair, giving far more than they got and still managing to keep Bobby from harm. But the onslaught of opponents seemed never ending. Worse yet, the ones that went down seemed to recover almost instantly—already Mex was standing and rejoining the fray.

"It's like they're on drugs," said Trevor. "Every time I knock one down, they bounce right back up."

"There!" said Bobby, spotting Willy the Creep by the stagecoach with faint yellow tendrils flowing out from him to the rest of the gang.

"I think the Creep is somehow feeding them energy," Bobby yelled to his friends.

"You mind?" asked Jacob, dodging another punch from Tex. "I'm a little busy at the moment."

"I'm on it," said Bobby, heading toward Willy. He was almost there when the Creep turned to him, his eyes penetrating Bobby's soul. All of the sadness and anger Bobby had conquered while trapped under the bookshelf flooded back. He fell to his knees, screaming as he envisioned the accident that killed his parents, weeping uncontrollably as they lay dying in the hospital. An instant later, his blood boiled as Cassandra and the assassin left the operating room, laughing as they made their escape.

Bobby snapped back to the present and looked up to see Willy's attention redirected at Trevor, who had knocked down all of the boys around him and was making his way over.

"Watch your back," said Trevor, offering Bobby a hand. "Focus on happy thoughts or that freak will get inside your dome."

Bobby nodded as he regained his feet. "Thanks for the tip."

Willy turned away, his attention on the boys Trevor and Jacob had knocked down. Trevor confronted them while Bobby scooped up the lantern and ducked behind the chariot. Shuttering the light, he looped around the stagecoach, coming up behind Willy. Bobby opened the shutter to reveal a sliver of light until he saw Willy's feet just ahead. Bobby took a soft step forward, then another. He was almost in arm's reach . . .

Sudden movement caught his eye. Something small and white streaked across the top of the wagon. Bobby flung his arms up as Siphon launched itself at his face. Bobby's lantern struck the ferret in midair, shattering the glass and spraying kerosene everywhere. The animal burst into flames before it hit the side of the wagon. It fell to the ground not as a ferret but as a hissing, snarling ball of fire.

Willy spun around at the commotion. When he saw his pet with its fur ablaze, skin already blackening, he rushed forward to save it. But the animal was too close to the wagon. Doused with kerosene, the wooden stagecoach went up like a matchbox. The sudden blaze sent both Willy and Bobby stumbling back from the heat.

With the wagon aflame, the entire area lit up clear as day. Bobby saw Jacob and Trevor surrounded by upperclassmen. Close by, Lily faced Ashley, both of them surrounded by an intense aura that matched the angry red of the fire. Jinx stood between them with his back to Lily as he tried to keep his sister at bay.

And then Willy let out an ear-piercing scream. Abruptly, everyone stopped and turned. The Creep lay on the ground, mimicking the writhing of his dying pet—movements that grew fainter and fainter by the second.

"Pain," he cried. "Pain!"

Only Ashley seemed untouched by the horrific scene. With everyone focused on Willy, she calmly stepped around her little brother and, thrusting out her hands, let loose a burst of crimson energy that slammed into Lily's chest, sending the smaller girl sprawling to the floor.

Trevor's eyes went wide as he caught the tail end of Ashley's treachery. Almost dismissively, he dispatched any opponent in his way and dashed across the room to kneel at Lily's side. Ashley's aura went dark after her outburst. She retreated quickly, joining her companions as they gathered around Willy's prone figure.

Bobby and Jacob rushed over to Lily. Trevor cradled her head in his hands. Jinx placed a hand on her neck. "She's unconscious," he said, "but her breathing is steady."

"What does that mean?" asked Trevor, tears streaming down his cheeks. "Is she okay?"

"Most likely it's some form of psychic shock. She should be fine just as soon as her mind catches up with her body."

"I don't know what I would do if something happened to her," said Trevor. "When I was with Ashley and her gang, I couldn't hang out with anyone else or Ashley would get mad. But then I met Lily, and, well, I started to have feelings for her. I tell people that I split with Ashley because of how she acts, but the truth is that it was really about Lily. I think I love her."

"Now there's a real shock," said Jacob. "If only she had the slightest idea."

Trevor wiped at his eyes. "You think she already knows?" The look on his face made clear that the thought both thrilled and horrified him at the same time.

"Of course I know," said a tiny voice. Everyone looked down to see Lily, eyes open, smiling weakly.

Trevor lifted her head and brushed the hair out of her face. "If you knew, why didn't you say something?" he asked, almost pleading.

"And ruin all the fun?" said Lily with a feeble laugh. "I figured you'd tell me when you were ready. I must say, you picked a heck of a time."

Gingerly, Trevor cupped her face. "In that case, I suppose it's a heck of a time for this as well," he said. With that, he leaned over and kissed her firmly on the lips.

The moment was short-lived. Driven mad by Siphon's death, Willy snatched a spear from the Roman chariot. With a terrible wail, he lowered the tip and rushed at Bobby, who knelt with his back to Willy, still focused on his friends.

Leaping to his feet, Jacob knocked Bobby out of the way as Willy charged through. Willy wheeled back around and pulled the spear back to jab. Instead, the butt caught Jinx in the temple. Jinx slumped to the ground with a sigh as blood streamed down his forehead.

Willy stood dumbstruck, the spear held limply in his hand. Jacob wrenched the haft out of his grip and Willy stepped back, throwing his hands up. For a moment, it looked like the fight was over. Then Ashley started yelling again. On her command, Tex and his companions rushed at Bobby and his friends once more.

Trevor dragged Jinx to his feet. "You okay, little buddy?" he said, trying to inspect Jinx's head in the flicker of the smoldering stagecoach.

"What happened?" said Jinx, wincing as Trevor gingerly probed his temple.

"Probably a concussion," said Jacob, holding their attackers at bay with the newly acquired spear.

"Get Jinx out of this mess," said Lily. "No one wants to see him get hurt."

"But what about you guys?" said Bobby. "I'm not going to just leave you."

"We'll be fine," said Trevor. "Besides, it's you they're really after."

"Yeah, never better," said Jacob, jabbing at Tex as the brute tried to duck inside his guard. "Don't worry; I'm not going to stab anyone—unless they deserve it."

Bobby looked at his friends one last time and then put his arm around Jinx's waist. "Come on, buddy. Let's get you out of here."

As they ventured further into the archive's vast interior, Ashley's voice drifted through the darkness. "Don't worry, boys; I'll see you again sooner or later."

—⚊⚊—

Deep in the bowels of sublevel five, Bobby and Jinx stumbled past a shadowy menagerie of vehicles and machines. Behind them, noises from the fight dimmed until there was nothing left but silence. When Jinx could go no farther, they rested on the pontoon of a DHC-3 Otter seaplane.

Bobby pulled out his penlight and bent over Jinx. "Let's take a look at your forehead."

"It's fine," said Jinx, grimacing as he removed his hand.

Bobby examined the wound. "It's stopped bleeding, but you should keep pressure on it for a while."

"Maybe I should try to heal myself," said Jinx, raising a hand to his temple. "I've read extensive studies on—"

Bobby snatched his hand away. "Maybe next time."

Jinx nodded. "So, where are we?"

"Hopefully we're close to the east wall," said Bobby, panning the light around their surroundings.

"Why, you got a plan?"

"Same one I had before Ashley and her goons showed up."

"You still haven't told me what it is."

"I'll explain as soon as I find what I'm looking for. Wait here while I have a look." Bobby disappeared into the dark.

He returned a few minutes later. Taking Jinx's hand, he led his little cousin past a red 1964 Volkswagen Deluxe Microbus painted with sunflowers and rainbows, then down the side of a Russian ironclad frigate. He stopped in front of a World War II–era Sherman tank.

"I saw this during my trip down here with Jacob. It's absolutely perfect."

Jinx's mouth fell open. "What, exactly, do you mean by 'perfect'?"

Bobby smiled and scrambled up the side. "Come on; help me get the hatch open." Together, they pried open the iron lid and climbed inside. The inner chamber of the tank was tight and cramped. Jinx sat in the rear while Bobby slid into the driver's seat and pushed buttons.

"Do you know what you're doing?" said Jinx, eying the instrument panels.

Bobby shrugged. "I figured you'd be able to help."

"Sorry, but no one told me when I woke up this morning that I'd be asked to operate an M4 US Medium Sherman tank."

Bobby shrugged again. "I'm sure we'll figure it out."

"I'm not so sure," he said as Bobby flipped more switches. "You know, I really doubt this thing even has fuel. It's probably just a mock—" The rest of the sentence died on his lips as the engine roared to life.

Bobby pumped his fist and grabbed the steering wheel. "Now we're talking!"

"Do you even know how to drive?" asked Jinx, shouted over the sudden roar of the monstrous engine.

"I once had a birthday party at a go-kart track."

Jinx threw up his hands as the tank lurched forward. "I hope you at least managed to stay on the track."

Bobby gave him his most innocent smile. "Most of the time."

Bobby maneuvered the tank into the narrow space between the other vehicles. Once aligned, he paused for a moment, giving Jinx just enough time to buckle up before starting forward again.

The tank shuddered and shook as it rumbled down the aisle, bouncing the boys and rattling their teeth. After a few moments, the east wall came into view. Bobby brought the tank to a halt. He cut the engine and climbed into the back.

"Help me aim the cannon," said Bobby.

"Help you do *what*?"

Bobby ignored the question as he slid into the gunner's chair. As soon as he was settled, he began pushing buttons.

"Hold on just one second," said Jinx. "Turning on the engine was one thing. You can't just go pushing buttons on the artillery controls!"

"You're right. I should use my instincts," said Bobby. "After all, Master Jong always says that a person can sense what to do if they're in tune with their purpose." Bobby closed his eyes and let his hands hover over the instrument panel.

Jinx sighed. "I'm going to look for an instruction manual."

For several minutes, the two boys worked in silence. Jinx searched the tank while Bobby sat in the gunner's seat, eyes closed, hands suspended inches above the controls. Finally, as if in a trance, Bobby opened his eyes, flipped a series of levers, and pulled the trigger. A hollow click echoed in the narrow chamber.

Bobby rubbed his chin. "That should have worked."

Jinx looked at the indicators on the controls and then down at a book in his lap. "Hmm," he said, rubbing his head.

"Well," said Bobby, "what do the instructions say?"

Jinx continued to study the book for another minute before looking back at the controls. "They say we're out of ammo, or, more accurately, that we probably never had any ammunition in the first place. I told you this is a mock-up."

"Oh well," said Bobby. "Then I guess we'll just have to do this the hard way."

Hopping out of the gunner's chair, Bobby climbed back up to the driver's seat.

"What are you going to do?" asked Jinx with a touch of panic in his voice.

"Don't worry, buddy. Just sit down and buckle up," said Bobby. "This could get bumpy."

—⚬—

Giant dust clouds billowed around the tank as it rumbled toward the east wall of sublevel five. With just over twenty yards to go, Bobby stomped on the gas pedal. The bulky machine rattled violently and lurched forward, covering the final distance in a miasma of speed and noise.

"Hold on, buddy," yelled Bobby over the roar.

Jinx screamed and covered his face as the massive vehicle slammed into the archive wall. The impact rippled through the cabin, tossing their heads back as the tank climbed up the wall briefly before settling back down.

Bobby rubbed his neck as he backed the tank up and cut the power. Hopping out of the driver's seat, he grabbed a flashlight and opened the hatch. Dust from the collision made it impossible to see, so he jumped down and approached the damaged wall. He scanned the area closely for a moment and then headed back to the tank.

When he got back in the driver's seat, Jinx was fuming. "You mind telling me what the heck is going on?"

Bobby started the engine and threw the massive vehicle into reverse before replying. "We have to do it again."

The second impact was much softer than the first, as if the stone understood the futility of resistance. After the dust settled, Bobby backed the tank up and got out to inspect the damage again. Jinx followed, peering over Bobby's shoulder as they waded into the dark indent, now over three feet deep.

"I knew it," said Bobby, shining his flashlight into the deepest recesses.

Jinx maneuvered around Bobby so he could see. "What is that?"

"It's a hole."

Jinx gave him a flat look. "I know it's a hole. What's inside the hole?"

"That's what I'm saying; it's a hole."

It took a moment for Jinx to catch on. "You mean there's an opening?"

Bobby kicked at the crumbled wall. After a few violent thrusts, a big section fell away, revealing an inky void. "Not just an opening—a way out."

CHAPTER 28

From the moment Bobby climbed through the hole, every-thing looked wrong. He should have been in a tunnel. The walls should have been dirt and rock. Instead, they winked back at him with a metallic sheen.

"Where are we?" asked Bobby.

"What are you asking me for?" snapped Jinx. "Given that it was your idea to slam the tank into the wall in the first place, I assumed you at least knew what was on the other side."

"I did . . . I mean, I thought I did," said Bobby. "From studying those maps of the archives you gave us earlier, I thought we were up against the western part of the mines. The plan was to smash into one of the lower tunnels, not whatever this is."

"Shield your eyes," said Jinx. "I think I found a light switch."

Bobby blinked as a bank of fluorescent bulbs buzzed to life overhead. "What is all this stuff?" he said, taking in row after row of tables stacked with binders and computer equipment.

"It looks like a laboratory of some kind."

"Wait a second. I recognize those," said Bobby, pulling down a brown leather binder from a nearby shelf. "Jacob and I saw a bunch of folders just like this during our trip to perform our Chronenberg reading."

"It's some kind of cipher," said Jinx, examining the contents.

Bobby told him Jacob's theory about genetic experimentation. "I think he's correct," said Jinx. "These records definitely deal with DNA sequencing."

"Is that what these computers are for?"

Jinx shrugged and examined one of the folders. "I don't spend a lot of time on computers. My abilities don't play well with electronics. Still, I recognize some of these medical terms from science journals. I can tell you one thing: what they're doing here is state of the art."

"So what is all this stuff?"

"Give me a sec," said Jinx. Bobby waited patiently as Jinx continued reading.

"From what I can tell, they're testing each subject for twenty-seven markers they call *omega genes*. Apparently, they're extremely rare recessive genes with eighteen inherited from the female X chromosome and the other nine inherited from the male Y."

"For what purpose?" asked Bobby. "I mean, why look for people with those genes?"

"I'm not sure. There appears to be something else, too—something they call an *alpha gene,* which is only inherited from males. There's a whole other report just for that," said Jinx, flipping pages. "Most of the subjects in this binder have only two or three of the omega genes, almost all of which appear to be dormant. I don't see anyone that has the alpha gene."

"Can you tell what the genes do?"

"It's impossible to know for sure without completely deciphering the code, but if I had to guess, I'd say they're responsible for the special abilities demonstrated by people here at the Jade Academy. Perhaps these genes are what allow some people to manipulate energy with relative ease while others struggle no matter how much training they receive."

"All right, put the binder back," said Bobby. "We should get outta here before someone finds us." Jinx set down the journal and moved to a nearby computer terminal.

"What are you doing?" said Bobby. "I thought you and computers didn't mix."

"I should be fine as long as we're quick and don't try any of that meld-mind-with-machine stuff they had us doing in class. Why anyone would want to give a computer subliminal messages is beyond me." Jinx paused as a new window appeared on the monitor.

"What is it?" asked Bobby, leaning over his cousin's shoulder.

"Remember how I said most subjects had only a few of the omega genes, almost all of which were dormant?" Bobby nodded. "Well, I did a search command for subjects whose genes were active. Look at the dates of those tests, and then look at the subjects' current status."

It took a moment for Bobby to see what Jinx was talking about. "Each of those students graduated and left the academy right after their genes became active."

"Exactly," said Jinx. "It's like the academy trained them just for that purpose—to switch their special genes from dormant to active, like a farm, waiting for the livestock to grow big enough to sell."

"Or send to the slaughterhouse."

Jinx paused, his hands still on the keyboard. "What makes you say that?"

"Something just doesn't feel right—this lab hidden down here in the mines, the tests for active gene sequences, the sudden graduations. How many people even know about all this stuff?"

"Gimme a sec," said Jinx. "Now that's interesting. According to the user list, only my mother, Simpkins and Hayward have access to this lab."

"So, how did you gain access?"

Jinx gave him a sly smile. "It's possible I noted a password or two when I was snooping around Mom's office looking for stationery."

"Way to go, buddy," said Bobby, patting him on the back. "Can you see where the students were sent after graduation?"

Jinx pushed a few more buttons. "That can't be right."

"What is it?" said Bobby.

"According to this, every single student who graduated was sent to either a facility in the Ukraine or some location in Guatemala."

"You're telling me that not a single student went home to their family or left to travel the world after they graduated?"

"It doesn't look like they had a choice," said Jinx. "According to this, the students were all evaluated prior to graduation and selected for one location or the other."

"I'll bet that's what the headmistress meant when she said I would be sent off to further their projects," said Bobby. "I wonder which location she meant. Somehow I doubt either is a vacation destination."

"But that means that students were sent off to be used as guinea pigs for these experiments. Wow, there are dozens of them in this one journal alone."

"I'm assuming there are no records of what goes on at either location?" asked Bobby.

Jinx shook his head. "These records only track the test results up to their graduation. There's no information on the other facilities."

Bobby frowned at this news. "Can you at least pull up the records for a specific person?"

"I think so. Why?"

"Search for Jimmy Thompson if you can. I want to see something."

Jinx punched in commands. "Hey, where do I know that name from?"

"Master Jong mentioned him to me once," said Bobby. "He said Jimmy was shielded just like me, but then something happened. I'm curious what it says in his records."

"That's right; I remember now," said Jinx, pulling the results up on the screen. "Help me look for journal number 924-R. I'll tell you what I know while we search. They used to call him *Slab* on account of his size. Supposedly, he had dull wits and no skill of any kind save one—complete immunity from other peoples' abilities."

"I can image how unsettling that would be for a school full of psychics and empathies," said Bobby as they scanned the shelves for the ledger.

According to Jinx, Jimmy was nearly six and a half feet tall and barely spoke a word to anyone. He particularly frustrated Hayward, who was unable to twist the boy's emotions. Hayward compensated by abusing Jimmy every chance he got, using any excuse to give him detention and calling him Slab to make him feel like a useless hunk of meat.

One day during a field trip, Jimmy found a rabbit with a broken leg. He wanted desperately to keep it, asking if he could bring it to the healers at the academy to mend. As leader of the expedition, it was Hayward's decision. Taking the hare from Jimmy, Hayward held it up and snapped the poor animal's neck.

"What happened after that is unclear," said Jinx. "Supposedly some kind of psionic blast killed all the plant life in the surrounding area. The release created the clearing we use for our field trips. Over half the kids there ended up in the nursing ward."

"What about Hayward?" asked Bobby, remembering Cassandra's comment on the front porch the night he ran away. "Was he injured?"

"Right after it happened, people said that Hayward was dead. But then he showed up a few days later. Funny thing," said Jinx, rubbing his chin. "That part of the story doesn't seem quite so impossible anymore."

"And what about Jimmy?" asked Bobby. "Any idea what happened to him?"

"That's the real kicker," said Jinx. "Jimmy graduated two days later. I guess we now know where he went."

Bobby found binder 924-R and handed it to Jinx, who flipped a few pages and stopped. "Here it is," he said, studying the page. "According to this, Jimmy only had two genetic markers. Hardly a *viable asset*, as Mother would say."

"Are you sure?"

"Of course I'm sure," said Jinx. "There was absolutely nothing special about this kid's—" He stopped.

"What is it?" said Bobby.

"I take it back," said Jinx. "This kid was special—very special. Jimmy Thompson tested positive for the presence of the alpha gene."

"Who else can you look up?" said Bobby, pulling up a chair next to Jinx. "Can we access your records?"

"Me?" said Jinx, balking. "I don't know if that's such a good idea."

"Come on, Jinx, aren't you curious?"

A timid look crept over Jinx's face as he typed. "Journal number 708-L," he said.

This time finding the correct binder went much faster. "Well, that explains a lot," said Jinx, flipping through the pages until he came to the right section.

"What is it?" asked Bobby.

"I have quite a few of the genetic markers, but apparently the sequencing is all wrong."

"Does that mean your abilities will never properly manifest?"

"Hard to say. From what I know about genetics, it's more like a hose that is kinked in various places. It's always possible to straighten out the kinks, but as long as the flow is blocked, nothing is going to come out right."

"All right, well, we should probably get going."

"Wait," said Jinx. "What about you? Don't you want to know what it says in your file?"

"Not particularly."

"Why not?"

"I don't know," confessed Bobby. "I guess I just don't want to be defined by my genetics. I am who I am, regardless of what some test says about me."

"Well, would you mind if I take a look?" said Jinx. "After the way Simpkins was talking, I'm curious to know what the big deal is all about."

"Oh, all right. But don't tell me if it's bad. I don't wanna know if I have terminal cancer or something," quipped Bobby.

Jinx repeated the procedure, searching first on the computer and then locating the corresponding ledger from the nearby shelves. He studied the pages in silence for several minutes while Bobby paced impatiently nearby. "You done yet?"

"Almost," said Jinx. "You sure you don't want to know? It's really interesting."

Bobby shook his head. "Come on, let's get outta here." Grudgingly, Jinx replaced the book and followed Bobby to the stainless steel door at the far end of the lab.

"Well, I have perfect recall," said Jinx. "Let me know if you ever change your mind."

Without responding, Bobby yanked open the door to reveal a closed-off section of the mines. Rock camouflage on the other side of the door blended perfectly with the surrounding tunnel. At the far end stood a barricade with a familiar sign that read *Danger: Unstable Area. Do Not Enter.*

The two cousins slipped into the hall, making their way toward the barricade. Neither of them noticed the small flashing red light beside the door as it slid closed behind them.

"I know this place," said Bobby. "We're at the abandoned quarry where I discovered the jade piece."

"Now, isn't that a coincidence," said Jinx. "I wouldn't be surprised if you were sensing the archives through the stone without even realizing it when you dug up that stone."

Bobby shrugged as he studied the walls around them.

"All right, cousin," said Jinx, "you're the one with the master plan; where do we go now?"

Bobby gave him a sheepish grin. "Now comes the hard part."

Jinx looked ready to throw a fit. "You mean slamming into a wall with a tank wasn't the hard part? What do we have to do now? Magically teleport out of here?"

"No, but you're not too far off. Now we have to find the Spine of the World."

—— ⟆⟆⟆ ——

For more than an hour, Bobby and Jinx wandered through the western mine shafts, searching every nook and corner they came across. Finally, Jinx set down his lantern and sat in the dirt.

"What are we doing?" he asked.

"You're right. It's obviously not in this section of the mines. We need to head over to the main chamber and try one of the other trunk lines."

"I don't mean about searching this section. I mean about searching, period. The Spine of the World is a myth."

"You read my—I mean *our* grandfather's diary. That's how he and Grandma escaped from this place, and that's how we're going to get out."

"Bobby, the monks know every square inch of this place. If there really was a hidden tunnel, especially one that leads to the kinds of treasures your grandfather described, don't you figure they'd have found it?"

"So you think Grandpa made it up?"

"I didn't say that. I'm just saying that if it is down here, why hasn't anyone ever found it?"

"Maybe they didn't know how to search," said Bobby.

"And you do?"

Bobby set down his backpack. "Ever since I was brought here, people have been telling me to trust my instincts. That's all I'm doing. It's down here, Jinx. I can feel it in my gut."

260 BOBBY ETHER AND THE JADE ACADEMY

With a long look at his cousin, Jinx stood and dusted himself off. "That's good enough for me."

The main chamber appeared deserted as the two boys crept from their location in the west mine shafts. Then a guard passed in front of the mouth of the tunnel, casting a long shadow in their direction. Bobby pressed himself against the wall with Jinx tucked behind him. The man paused for a few seconds, then moved on, only to be replaced by another guard less than a minute later.

The boys retreated back around the corner. Jinx sank to the ground. "We're never going to get past those guards without being spotted."

"Something will come up," said Bobby. "Just stay positive."

"And what if that *something* is us getting caught?" asked Jinx. "There's no telling what they'll do if they find out we've been inside that lab."

One of the bare bulbs in the tunnel flickered. Bobby shot up. "I've got an idea," he said. "Keep that lantern shuttered and follow me."

Jinx followed as Bobby headed back the way they'd come. "What do you know about portable generators?" he said over his shoulder.

"They're not exactly rocket science," said Jinx.

"I suppose you'd know," said Bobby with a grin for his genius cousin. "What about propane tanks?"

"Even simpler. Why do you ask?"

"I saw one in a side tunnel a little ways back. Was thinking maybe we could create a diversion."

Jinx almost dropped his lantern. "First you drive a tank into a wall. Now you want to create an explosion?"

Bobby chuckled. "I told you something would come up. I didn't say you'd like it."

It took Jinx a few seconds of studying the generator to come to a conclusion. "Simple enough," he said. "We can disconnect the propane tank, open the valve and—"

"That's great," said Bobby. "Is there any way to delay the blast?"

Jinx scratched his head. "I guess we can leave the lantern here. If we space them far enough apart, it should take a few minutes before the tank ignites."

"But that will leave us without light," said Bobby.

"I told you I could make it work. I didn't say you'd like it," said Jinx.

"Touché, Mr. Smarty-Pants," said Bobby. "All right, try to give us about a minute. We need to get back to one of those other side tunnels before it blows."

A few minutes later, everything was set. Bobby disconnected the tank from the generator and broke the gas valve. Instantly the air filled with the acrid smell of propane. Covering his mouth, Bobby rushed to the tunnel entrance, where Jinx set the lantern down and opened the shutter.

In almost complete darkness, the boys made their way back to the main chamber. A few yards before the final side passage, a guard stepped into the mouth of the tunnel. His long, spidery shadow stopped just inches from where the boys stood.

Bobby and Jinx pressed against the wall and held their breath as the man held up a lantern. "Who's there?" he said, staring into the darkness.

Jinx tugged on Bobby's sleeve. "We gotta move," he whispered. "We can't be here when that tank blows."

Finally, the patrolman lowered his lantern and turned away. "Stupid rats," he muttered and disappeared out of sight. The boys dashed into the side passage, ducking behind a broken wheelbarrow right as the explosion rocked the cavern. Voices rang out, followed by hurried footsteps as the academics patrolling the main chamber raced to investigate.

"Get ready to run," said Bobby, rising into a crouch. Jinx took out his inhaler and took a puff as two guards ran by, followed moments later by four more. "Now's our chance to get across the main chamber."

The boys sprinted out of the side tunnel as a mild tremor shook the walls. "I think we may have destroyed the support beams," said Jinx, huffing to keep up.

"No time to worry about that now," said Bobby, reaching the end of the tunnel. Exactly as planned, the large cavern was vacant. The boys ran across to the north passage. It wasn't until they were almost there that they spotted Hayward.

—∽—

Bobby slid to a stop as Hayward stepped into the mouth of the north tunnel, barring passage with his gelatinous bulk.

"Get out of my way, *Professor*," said Bobby.

"Oh, I don't think so," said the obese agent. "I was expecting Jong, but you two will do almost as well. I suppose it was your idea to break into the lab?" He fixed his eyes on Bobby.

"I have no idea what you're talking about," said Bobby.

"Don't play coy with me," growled Hayward. "I don't know how you got in without tripping the alarm, but the security system lit up like Christmas the instant you left."

Bobby dropped the pretense with a shrug. "What's the matter? Afraid people will find out about your sick little experiments?"

"I couldn't care less who knows about the experiments," said Hayward. "As far as I'm concerned, the whole world should know that we're going to change the face of humanity. Unfortunately for you, it's not my call."

"So, you just expect us to come along quietly and pretend like we don't know anything?"

"On the contrary, I'm rather hoping you'll put up a struggle. Little Theodore here is less than useless. Oh, the shame his mother must feel. As for you, Mr. Ether, let's just say that the more you fight, the more fun it will be . . . for me."

"Tell me something, Hayward," said Bobby. "How does it feels to be a clone—a mere copy of a real person?"

Hayward's massive belly shook with laughter. "You really

have been snooping where you don't belong. But you have it all wrong. To call Simpkins and me clones is to suggest that a stealth bomber is a copy of the *Spirit of St. Louis*. We share the same basic design but have been changed virtually beyond recognition. We are not less than human; we are more, so much more. We represent the future, the evolution of humankind into what our species is meant to be."

"You're a perverted distortion of Mother Nature."

Hayward waved a hand dismissively. "Perspective, nothing more. In any case, being me has certain advantages. Take, for instance, the memory retention. Decades ago, the original me helped ruin your traitorous grandfather's dream of living happily with that tramp wife of his. And now, I get to destroy the life of his son's only child."

Red spots swam before Bobby's eyes. Chest heaving and nostrils flared, Bobby clenched his hands into tight fists. Hayward laughed as if amused by the antics of an infant. "Why are you holding back?" he taunted. "I can see the anger on your face. Give in. Use it to fuel your power. Not that it ever did your grandfather any good."

That did it. Bobby lunged, swinging wildly at Hayward in an effort to wipe the smirk off his arrogant, fat face. A second later, a strange odor assailed Bobby's nostrils, coating his nose and throat with noxious fumes. Bobby fell to his knees, pressing his hands to his throat as he struggled to breathe.

"Stop! You're killing him," yelled Jinx.

"He'll wish I had by the time I'm done," said Hayward, making a fist. Spasms racked Bobby's body, sending him writhing to the floor as black spots swam before his eyes. He tried to draw breath and tasted only bitterness as his entire world reduced to a mere pinprick of light. And then, within that tiny speck of hope, a distant voice spoke to him. *Don't give up, Bobby. You must fight it.*

Bobby clung to the voice. *He's too strong*, he called back.

You must control your anger. His only power is that which you give him.

Bobby gritted his teeth and tried to focus on something positive. Beside him, Jinx kicked Hayward feebly in the shins. The sight of his little cousin gave Bobby strength. Slowly, he braced his arms and raised his head. Hayward's eyes went wide.

That's it, said the voice. *Fight it. He cannot control your energy unless you let him.* Inch by inch, Bobby rose, first to his knees and then to his feet. Hayward almost tripped as he staggered back.

"I'm not afraid of you," said Bobby, gasping to catch his breath. "Now get outta my head!" The poisonous stench surrounding him disappeared. Bobby choked down lungfuls of air while Hayward sagged to the ground.

Bobby took Jinx's arm and led him away. "We're leaving now," he said to Hayward. "We're leaving, and there's nothing you can do to stop us."

CHAPTER 29

The doors to the academy swung open with a boom that echoed like thunder in the vast chamber. Bobby and Jinx froze as Simpkins stormed across the room with the wizened leader of the monks, Divine Master Whimpley, trailing at his heels like a dog on a leash. The doors swung shut behind them.

"What is going on here?" said Simpkins.

"Nothing I can't handle," said Hayward, struggling upright.

"This wouldn't have happened if you'd stayed at your post," said Simpkins. "You can't just go running off every time something pisses you off."

Hayward shook his head. "I grow tired of service with nothing in it for us."

"Completing our tasks, accomplishing the goals set forth by the Core—that is what's in it for us."

"This whole project is a waste of our time. The headmistress alone commands my respect. These silly monks have no power. Just look at their leader," Hayward said, gesturing at Whimpley. "He's worse than a dog begging for table scraps. At least a dog knows who its master is."

"The kids are what matter," said Simpkins.

"The *kids*?" said Hayward, spitting out the word like an insult. "Ha! The kids are the worst part of this stupid assignment. The whole lot of them can't light a candle without a barrel of lighter fluid and a blowtorch. Tell me, why do we continue with this charade? I say we send the entire lot of them off to be used for experiments and be done with it."

"Wait just one minute," said Bobby.

Simpkins raised his arm. "Quiet," he snapped. "You will not speak unless given permission."

Bobby found himself unable to utter a sound as the partners argued. Remembering the voice in his head, Bobby cleared his mind and tried to speak again without success.

Simpkins turned and appraised him coolly. "Unlike my partner, you will find that I do not require your anima in order to wield my own. Be thankful that Jong is still on the loose. Otherwise," he said, turning a lingering gaze on Jinx, "I might be tempted to indulge in a little retribution of my own."

Turning back to Hayward, he said, "We are done here, agreed?"

Hayward nodded slowly. "But if the headmistress decides she doesn't need the boy, I get to pick up where I left off."

Simpkins nodded. "Follow me."

Bobby tried to tell him where to stick it, but his lips wouldn't work. In fact, his entire body seemed out of his control. *What do I do? I can't move*, thought Bobby. But the voice in his head was gone.

Simpkins headed toward the door and Bobby followed. Without wanting to, he fell in next to Whimpley and Hayward, who put one hand on Bobby's shoulder and the other on Jinx. "This is going to be fun," he said and gave Bobby's shoulder a tight squeeze.

They reached the exit, and Simpkins brought the small company to a halt while Hayward went to open the doors. Hayward had barely extended his hand, however, before the gigantic iron doors swung open once again.

Bobby would have cheered if he'd been able. On the other side of the door was a small band of monks led by Master Jong.

"Well now, what have we here?" growled Hayward.

"My fellow monks have come to bear witness," said Master Jong.

Simpkins studied the monk's childlike face. "Whatever game you're playing, it won't work. Surrender now and we'll go easy on you."

No one moved, but several of the monks exchanged nervous glances, especially at Whimpley, who cowered behind Simpkins.

"You heard my partner," said Hayward, making shooing gestures with his hands. "Go back to tending your stupid herb gardens, or whatever it is you people do."

Another dozen monks emerged from the north tunnels. Bobby recognized Yemoni from the gardens. The funny-looking monk hurried over to Master Jong.

"I'm sorry we're late," he said. "Per your request, I gathered as many of our brothers as I could find."

Master Jong turned to his fellow monks. "For generations now, the academics have held us in thrall, allowing us access to the sacred scrolls in exchange for our service. As many of you know, I have dedicated my life's work to discovering the legendary secret of the texts in the hopes that the secret will free us from these shackles.

"I tell you now that I have discovered the secret, and the power of the secret has released me—I am a slave no more. I will share the secret with you now and invite you, my brothers, to join me in the peace found only in true freedom."

Simpkins nudged Whimpley. The monk sniveled and cleared his throat in a halfhearted attempt to get everyone's attention. No one noticed. Simpkins leaned over and whispered in his ear. "Remember, the headmistress knows all about your personal agenda. If you want to remain in power through the end of the day, I suggest you get out there and put a stop to this."

Grudgingly, Whimpley elbowed his way past the others until he stood before Master Jong. "This so-called secret is a lie," he declared. "There is no written record to suggest that it is anything more than a fable told to acolytes to encourage them in their studies."

Several of the monks voiced their agreement. A few even moved to stand beside Whimpley in support of his words.

"The secret is real," protested Master Jong, "And I can prove it."

"You speak blasphemy," said the elder guru. "Whatever it is you think you have discovered, it has not been sanctioned by the Order. I forbid you to speak of it until the validity of your claim can be verified."

"You mean, until the headmistress can bury the truth so she can keep control of you and her other puppets within the order," said Yemoni.

Hayward smirked, his power growing by the second as the two groups of monks squared off against one another.

"I am the exalted leader of the Order of the Jade Temple," bristled Whimpley. "You will show me the respect I deserve or I will see to it that all of you are expelled from the Order."

"I care not what happens to me," said Master Jong. "I have come to speak the truth and will do so to any who would hear it."

Whimpley started to reply but the other monks drowned him out. "Tell us, brother," one of them said. "I want to hear the secret of the ancient texts." Several others murmured their agreement.

"I forbid it!" shouted Whimpley. But the monks with Jong and Yemoni paid their leader no heed, instead clamoring for Jong to speak.

"As you all know," said Master Jong, "the ancient scrolls speak of virtue. They speak of beauty, of honesty, of truth. They speak of knowing one's self and, in doing so, knowing the inherent difference between right and wrong. For over thirty years, I read those words, all the while looking for some deeper, hidden message."

The room was silent now, save for the soft voice of Master Jong. Even Hayward and Simpkins remained silent, gauging the response in the room.

"The reason I searched all these years and never found it," said Master Jong, "is because the secret is not in the text."

"Brother, I do not understand. If it's not in the text, then where is it?" asked Yemoni.

Master Jong raised his voice so that it echoed off the walls. "In order to reach enlightenment, body and soul must be in harmony. Your beliefs and your actions must be as one. You cannot simply read the texts; you must live them. The secret is to live by the code, regardless of the consequences. And that, my brothers, is where we have failed."

All the monks began talking at once. Those who stood alongside Divine Master Whimpley denounced Master Jong's words, decrying him as a blasphemer and calling for his expulsion from the order. But Master Jong was not done.

"Knowing what is right and choosing to do otherwise is the worst betrayal of all, a betrayal of the soul. For many years, we have allowed ourselves to be manipulated—to be used by the academics for their own selfish reasons."

"But you have always been steadfast in your pursuit of the secret," said one of the monks.

"And yet I have been unworthy until now," said Master Jong. "'Always do what you know is right.' That is the real secret. I ask you, brothers, is it right for these men to hold us hostage, a lifetime of service in exchange for access to texts which are rightfully ours? Is it right for us to stand by as child after child is brought to this once-sacred place to serve the will of a system we all know to be corrupt and yet do nothing to oppose? The secret is simple, brothers. We shame ourselves with our inaction."

"You're wrong," said Simpkins. "These kids are misfits, orphans abandoned by their own families. If not for the

headmistress and the academy, they would have no place to go."
Bobby's blood boiled at Simpkins's words. *Lies, all lies.* As the
rage within him grew, the bonds holding him loosened.

Still unable to move but able to speak, Bobby shouted, "The
headmistress is using us! We found the lab down in the archives.
Students who manifest abilities don't 'graduate,' they're sent off
for experimentation."

Master Jong pointed at Hayward and Simpkins. "See the
truth for yourselves, brothers! Grayson is the first headmaster
completely raised by the academics from infancy. Her actions
and agenda are a symptom of their corruption: a thirst for power
without moral restraint. Even now, the headmistress's lapdogs
attempt to control these boys against their will."

Several of the monks standing with Whimpley inched away
from Hayward and Simpkins.

Master Jong turned to Simpkins. "Release the boys. Your
reign here is over."

Simpkins glanced around. There were seven men with him
and over twice as many with Master Jong. With an impassive
stare, Simpkins dropped his arm. Like being jolted awake,
Bobby regained control of his limbs. He grabbed Jinx and raced
over to Master Jong.

"The academy is no longer safe for you," said Master Jong.
"You must go, before it is too late."

As he spoke, several patrols sent to investigate the explosion
returned to the main chamber. Having gathered reinforcements
along the way, over two dozen academics poured into the main
chamber, joining Simpkins and Hayward.

Simpkins ordered the new arrivals to fan out, encircling
Master Jong and his men. "We'll be taking the boys back now,"
he said.

Master Jong didn't move. Hayward rubbed his hands
together. "I knew this was gonna be fun!"

Turning to Jinx, Master Jong said, "You should go and find the headmistress. As much as I can no longer tolerate her actions, she is your mother and will keep you safe."

Jinx shook his head. "I am not leaving Bobby."

"I cannot guarantee your safety," said Master Jong. "Either of you."

"It's okay," said Bobby. "I know what to do."

Master Jong stared at him closely, the monk's pale blue-gray eyes penetrating deep inside. "You are very special, Bobby Ether," he said with a bow. "Go. Find what you seek."

A mild tremor shook the cave. "We must have damaged the support beams when we rigged that propane tank," said Bobby. "Come on, we gotta go quickly." He led Jinx to the far tunnel. Simpkins and Hayward made to intercept, but a group of monks blocked their path.

"Out of my way, you bathrobe-wearing, bald-headed sissies," said Hayward. The corpulent agent took another step toward the boys. Immediately, an old monk with a gnarled cane moved to match him.

"What are you going to do, old man, chant me to death?" asked Hayward. "You know exactly what'll happen if you try to use any of that spiritual crap on me."

"One does not poke a poisonous toad with his finger," said the old monk. "One uses a stick instead." Quick as a whip, the old monk flicked his cane and cracked Hayward over the head.

A red welt instantly appeared on Hayward's forehead. "Why you little—" he said, and sank to the ground.

"Bobby," said Master Jong, "I think it would be best for you to depart now."

"Right," said Bobby. "Oh, and thanks, by the way, for the advice earlier with Hayward."

Master Jong gave him a quizzical look. "What do you mean?"

"The voice in my head—"

"I'm sorry, Bobby, I have no idea what you're talking about."

For a moment, the two stared at one another in confusion. Then Bobby grabbed Jinx and headed down the north tunnel. The sounds of fighting broke out behind them. For a moment, Bobby thought about going back. Then a massive earthquake shook the mountain. The ceiling behind them crashed down, blocking their retreat.

"My gosh," said Jinx. "Our explosion must have destabilized the area that caved in last week. And we're headed straight for it."

Bobby grabbed Jinx's arm and dragged him on. "Nothing we can do about it now."

"What's the plan?" asked Jinx.

Bobby shrugged. "Simple, really: find the Spine of the World before this whole place comes down around us."

CHAPTER 30

The northern section of the mines was a rabbit's warren of tunnels and shafts. Despite the labyrinth, Bobby barely hesitated, pausing for only a moment at each intersection before choosing a new path. Tremors shook the mountain as the boys worked their way deeper into the mines. Several times they encountered passages blocked by cave-ins. Each time, Bobby found another route.

Finally, after what felt like hours, Bobby stopped and placed a hand on the wall. "It's close," he said.

Jinx looked at the surrounding bedrock. "I don't see anything."

"I can feel it. I just can't tell exactly where."

"If it's here, then why can't we see it?" said Jinx.

"I don't know, but I've got a theory," said Bobby. "Remember those books with the holographic pictures? You know, the ones where you have to let your eyes relax and go out of focus to see the images?"

Jinx looked thoroughly confused. "Actually—no, I don't."

"Right, sorry," said Bobby. "I forgot you were too busy reading the encyclopedia to do that sort of thing."

BOBBY ETHER AND THE JADE ACADEMY

Jinx stuck out his tongue.

"But seriously," said Bobby, "Master Jong once explained to me that people can see auras if they train their eyes properly, like seeing those holograms."

"So you want to train your eyes, in two minutes, to see the Spine of the World?"

"You got any better ideas?"

When Jinx didn't reply, Bobby sat, folded his legs, and closed his eyes. In moments, he stood outside the invisible barrier surrounding his core. Thinking only of his need to escape, he reached out and touched the transparent shield, watching in fascination as his hand passed right through. *I guess I really have learned a thing or two.*

Pushing deeper, Bobby walked through the surrounding fog until he arrived at the sculptured rock garden. Not sure what to look for, he wandered over to the crystal brook meandering through the pristine garden. On a whim, he picked up a rock and tossed it into a tiny whirlpool. The rock instantly disappeared beneath the swirling eddy. Curious, Bobby reached out and altered the flow upstream. The surface of the water calmed, allowing him a clear view of the rocks on the bottom.

—⚬—

Bobby opened his eyes and looked at Jinx. "I know what to do. I know how to see the Spine of the World."

"How?" asked Jinx.

"Just take my hand," said Bobby. "We won't have much time."

Jinx gripped his hand and they waited together. Within seconds, a tremor rippled through the passage, making a nearby support beam groan with pressure. Fifty yards ahead, Bobby spotted an arched doorway covered with runes. It winked in and out of existence several times before reverting back to solid rock.

"There!" said Bobby, pointing to the spot. "When the earthquake hit, that portion of the wall shifted."

"But how can that be?" said Jinx. "There's nothing there now."

"I think it's the tremors," said Bobby. "I'm not sure exactly how, but they are upstream from the energy of the door. The power unleashed by the quakes somehow disturbs the flow of whatever masks the entrance. We're going to have to time it when the next blast hits."

They stood side by side, silently waiting. Long moments ticked by. Then a voice called out from behind them. "Oh, thank goodness you are all right."

Bobby and Jinx turned to discover the headmistress standing at the other end of the tunnel. "Headmistress?" said Jinx, surprised.

Bobby's aunt looked haggard, with her raven hair a mess and deep lines etched on her pallid face.

"Jinx, it's me. It's your mother."

"Did you just call me 'Jinx'? You never call me that."

"I've been worried sick about you, Son. When I heard that you ran away, I sensed where you were and came to get you."

"But I thought you were off searching for Master Jong," said Jinx.

"I left the others to handle Jong. You are my only son. I wanted to make sure you were safe."

Jinx wrung his hands nervously. "I'm fine, Mom."

"Thank goodness. Now come on. I don't want to force you against your will, but we need to leave now. These tunnels are unsafe. You too, Bobby."

Jinx hesitated for a moment. "I'm sorry, Mom; I can't."

A harsh tone crept into the headmistress's voice. "What do you mean 'you can't'?"

"Bobby told me all about the diary and what happened with our grandparents. I can't stay here any longer. The two of us are leaving."

The headmistress fixed Bobby with an angry glare. "This is all your fault. You will pay for what you've done." Removing a large green vial from her pocket, she threw her head back and guzzled the contents. "I will not allow you to leave," she said to Jinx. "You are my only son. I command you to stay."

"And what happens to Bobby?" said Jinx.

The headmistress paused, her eyes suddenly glazed. "He will be punished, of course. Examples must be made of all who defy me. But you are my son. I will not allow anything to destroy my family."

"He's your nephew," said Jinx. "He's family, too."

"Ashley was right. He's a meddlesome brat who has done nothing but cause problems since the moment he arrived. Now come away before I lose my temper."

Jinx stared at her as if seeing her for the first time. "You may be my mother, but I see now that we've never truly been a family. The only thing you care about is power." Bobby put a hand on his shoulder, but Jinx shrugged it off. "Even as a student, I never truly fit in. Despite my intellect, I was never able to excel in ways that matter at the Jade Academy—in ways that matter to you. Let's face it; if I hadn't been your child, I wouldn't have even been allowed here."

"I know I haven't always shown it, but I do care for you, Jinx," she said, reaching out to him. "I . . . I love you."

Jinx faltered and took a step back. "I'm sorry, Mom," he said finally. "I love you too, but I can't stay. If there is one thing I have learned in all of this, it's that you should always do what you know is right. Leaving this place is the right thing to do."

Rage contorted the headmistress's face.

"I will not allow it!" she bellowed.

Reaching into her pocket, she withdrew another vial and drank it. Bobby shielded his eyes as she began to glow a sickly green. The intensity grew until he could no longer look at her.

"I will destroy this place before I let you leave," she said.

"You don't want to do this," said Bobby. "Please just let us go."

"No one defies me," she said. Electricity sparked all around her.

"I'm sorry," whispered Jinx.

If the headmistress heard, she made no reply. She staggered toward them. "I am in charge," she yelled. "I command all the energy of the universe, and I command you to stay."

"Mom, you've got to stop," said Jinx. "You're going to cause another cave-in."

In fact, it was already too late. The air surrounding the headmistress ignited in a brilliant array of emerald light and crimson heat. With a loud crack, a support beam shattered into pieces. The boys were thrown to the ground as the earth ruptured.

Dirt and rock poured into the tunnel, forming a raging storm of living earth around the headmistress. Her high-pitched scream erupted like a siren's wail above the din of the tempest.

Bobby scrambled to his knees and grabbed Jinx's arm. In the wake of the explosion, the narrow doorway at the end of the tunnel had opened up again. "We've gotta go," he said.

"No! I need to save her," said Jinx, trying to pry his arm loose. Bobby looked where the headmistress had been standing. An endless stream of earth poured into the void as if the entire mountain sought to collapse on that one spot. Even the headmistress's screams had died away.

"I'm sorry," said Bobby, wrapping his arms around Jinx as his cousin tried desperately to run to his mother's aid. "And I'm sorry for this, too."

Lifting Jinx, Bobby dashed for the open doorway. With Jinx cradled in his arms, he dove through right as a massive boulder crashed down behind them.

The other side of the door was like a whole other world. Instantly the tremors stopped. Bobby barely felt the earth move or heard the collapsing tunnel, as if their new location was insulated somehow.

Jinx brushed tears from his eyes as Bobby helped him up. He looked shell-shocked.

"I'm so sorry," said Bobby. "I know what it's like to lose a mother."

Jinx nodded in appreciation as he took in their new surroundings. Eventually, he spoke. "How is this even possible?" He stared at smooth granite walls covered in ancient glyphs. "It defies all the laws of physics."

"Master Jong once told me that if enough energy is focused at a single location, the very essence of the universe can shift. Reality itself can be changed. Apparently that's what makes miracles."

"Well then, I'd call this tunnel a miracle," said Jinx. Another tremor shook the corridor, much milder than the ones back in the mines but still strong enough to shake the stone around them.

"Looks like this miracle isn't going to last forever," said Bobby. "We'd better get moving."

A short distance down the hall, the boys discovered an octagonal chamber with ornate carvings and arched doorways on every other side. "We know what's back that way," said Bobby, hooking a thumb over his shoulder. "That leaves us three choices."

"With the tremors getting worse, I don't think we have time to explore them one at a time."

"Can you read any of the inscriptions?" asked Bobby.

Jinx examined the thick stone pillar running up the side of the closest door. "It appears to be an ancient cuneiform of some kind. I'd say roughly seventeenth century BC. I'm not versed well enough to say for sure, and I'm not sure I can decipher it."

"Just try," said Bobby. "I guarantee you'll do better than I would."

Jinx smiled weakly. "Alright, give me a few minutes and let me see what I can come up with."

Bobby sat while Jinx studied the glyphs, comparing the different doorways and making notes. While he worked, another quake shook the chamber, showering dirt on their heads.

"No hurry or anything," said Bobby.

"All right," said Jinx, rising from the base of the last pillar. "I'm not going to garner anything further without reference materials back at the library."

"So, what do they say?"

"They appear to be some sort of warning; stuff about needing to be of pure intent and clear of purpose—stuff like that."

"What about the inscriptions at the top?"

"Well, that's the interesting part. Unless I am totally misinterpreting them, they all say basically the same thing."

"And what's that?"

"Well, there's no exact translation in English, but I suppose the closest approximation for this archway would be, 'Beyond this door lies that which you need.'"

"That's perfect. We need a way out," said Bobby, heading for the opening.

Jinx laid a hand on his arm. "Hold on just one second. Before we go running off, ask yourself something: How can the door possibly know what we need?"

"How can a passage appear out of solid rock? And why isn't it shaking in here like the tunnels in the mines? Some things you just need to accept on faith and move on."

"Good point. But I still think we should consider the rest of the doors. Like I said, they are all very similar. This arch over here, for example, says, *Beyond this door lies that which you want.*"

Bobby stopped and scratched his head. "Well that's just lame. We need a way out, but we obviously also want a way out. What about the last one?"

"The best interpretation for the last one is, *Beyond this door lies that which you seek.*"

"Let me see if I have this straight," said Bobby. "The three doors are what we need, what we want, and what we seek?"

"That appears to be the case, yes."

"Great!" said Bobby, rubbing his temples with both hands. "Maybe we should just pick at random."

"Wait a minute," said Jinx. "Didn't Grandpa talk about the different passages in his diary?"

"That's right!" said Bobby. "Maybe there are clues about which passage to take." He dropped to the floor, pulled out the diary, and flipped through pages.

"Here," said Bobby, pointing at the text. "It says that the grand library was located at the top of the mountain."

"All of these passages appear to go straight," said Jinx. "Maybe we should go down one for a while and see if it heads upward?" Another tremor rocked the chamber, this one much stronger than the last.

"I think you were right before—we don't have time for exploring," said Bobby, sliding the book over so they could share as Jinx sat next to him.

"What's this here?" said Jinx, pointing to the page. "It says the room containing the treasure was located deep in the heart of the mountain."

"How does that help? All of the passages go straight for as far as we can see."

"I know, but don't you think it's strange that, of the three passages, one goes up, one goes down and the third goes straight into the heart?"

"Actually, no, I don't think that's strange at all," said Bobby. "If they all went to the same place, now *that* would be strange."

"Think about it, Bobby; this place is called the Spine of the World."

Bobby shot to his feet. "That's it, Jinx; you're a genius! Each of the tunnels leads to a corresponding body part. The library is at the head. The treasure room is at the heart. And the way out is at the base of the spine, which would be the sacrum or the pelvis."

"What I don't understand," said Jinx, "is how they correspond to the inscriptions above each door."

Bobby scratched his head. "Aren't internal organs often associated with various emotions?"

"In the Chinese culture the liver and gall bladder are often associated with anger or rage," said Jinx. "The stomach is often associated with greed and disappointment——and hunger, of course."

"So what about our three clues: want, need, and seek?"

"Let me think," said Jinx, pacing the tiny chamber. "Those are all pretty generic terms. Nothing would seem to correspond directly. I mean, *need* could be hunger, but it could also be love, or happiness, or just a good night's sleep."

Bobby continued to flip through the diary for additional clues. "So maybe they aren't that specific. We just need a general direction. Something about each one that corresponds to the right organ: brain, heart and sacrum."

"Well, the heart is often considered the source of desire, love and happiness, stuff like that. So that could be *want*," said Jinx.

"I don't know if that's right. I mean, the sacrum is the basically the same as the pelvis, where the genitals are, right? That seems like a pretty strong argument for *want* to me."

"Okay then, let's skip that one for the moment. What about *need*?"

"I think I've got that one," said Bobby. "*Need* doesn't have the emotion of *want*. It's logical and analytical. There is only one place where logic is used, and that's in our heads."

"If you're right, then this tunnel," said Jinx, walking to the far-right passage, "leads to the grand library."

"Which also means it goes up to the top of the mountain," said Bobby.

A strange look crept over Jinx as he caressed the glyphs on the archway. "We should go," he said. "Just imagine all the knowledge contained in those books."

Bobby grabbed Jinx's arm and snatched him back as his cousin started across the threshold. "Jinx, you read the diary; there is no exit up there. If these tunnels collapse, we could be trapped up there forever."

Jinx shook his head as if waking from a dream. "You're right. I'm not sure what I was thinking."

"I think it's the warning you mentioned," said Bobby. "We can only pursue our true purpose. I have a feeling something bad will happen if we try to exploit the other passages, knowing where they lead."

"Well, we've figured out *need* and disagree on *want*," said Jinx. "What about *seek*?"

"Let's compare the two that are left. *Seek* seems deeper, more soul-based than *want*,'" said Bobby. "It makes sense for someone to talk about seeking what their heart desires."

"If *seek* refers to the heart," said Jinx, "then this passage leads to the treasure room. I'm not sure that treasure is really what most people seek in their lives."

"Maybe not, but for most people the freedom to pursue their dreams requires money. Remember, you have to be pure of intent in order to access these tunnels. Maybe the treasure simply gives people the means to go after what they truly seek in life. After all, it's not as if there could be a room full of true love, contentment, or peace on earth."

Jinx moving to the middle door. "Then this passage leads straight into the heart of the mountain."

"And to a room filled with gold and precious gems," said Bobby, setting a hand on the doorframe. "Imagine what we could do with all of that wealth. We could live like kings once we got out of here."

"Bobby, you said yourself that straying down the wrong path could be disastrous."

"We would only take a few items. We could be in and out in minutes."

Jinx ducked in front of his older cousin and spread his feet. "Not going to happen."

Bobby towered over him. "Get out of my way."

"I have a better idea," said Jinx. He stomped on Bobby's foot. Bobby winced and stumbled back. Jinx leapt on him, knocking both of them to the ground.

"What the heck?" said Bobby, struggling to get up with Jinx still wrapped around him.

"I'm not letting go until you come to your senses," said Jinx.

"I'm all right, Jinx, honest," said Bobby, prying himself loose of his little cousin's grasp. "I'm not sure what came over me." For the second time since entering the tunnel, the boys stood and dusted themselves off.

"So, what do you think?" said Bobby. "Will this door lead us to the base of the mountain and the secret exit?"

A violent tremor rocked the chamber, creating a long crack in the ceiling. "I think we're out of time," said Jinx. "We ruled out one passage, so even if your logic is wrong, we've still got a fifty-fifty chance."

Bobby took Jinx's hand. "Okay then, on three, we rush through the door together. I just hope we solved the riddle correctly."

Jinx looked nervous. "I just hope I got the translations correct."

CHAPTER 31

The boys had gone less than a dozen yards when a stone block slid from the ceiling, blocking their exit.

"Hopefully that won't be a problem," said Jinx.

"It won't," Bobby said confidently. "We're on the right path. I can feel it."

A hundred yards farther on, they came to a massive marble staircase that spiraled down, shrinking with each revolution until it disappeared into the unseen depths below.

"Watch your step," Bobby said as they descended. "It's really slippery."

"Probably from the cold," said Jinx, shivering. "It must have dropped ten degrees since we entered the Spine."

"At least," said Bobby, pulling his jacket tight. "There must be a storm outside."

"I'd almost forgotten that it's nearly winter," said Jinx. "When the snow comes, this entire mountain turns into a giant block of ice."

"I promise we'll find someplace warm once we're safe. For now, we need to hurry. I don't even want to think about what would happen if a quake hit with us on this stairwell."

As if on cue, a rumble echoed high overhead, followed by the clatter of stone on stone. Bobby shoved Jinx against the wall as a chunk of broken handrail smashed into the steps above them.

The boys exchanged glances and took off down the stairs as fast as their legs would carry them. The rest of their flight turned into a blur, with the two of them leaping over missing steps and scrambling over broken rails in their haste to avoid falling debris. The instant they hit the landing, they heard a loud crack. High above, a huge chunk of marble crashed down, obliterating the steps below as it tumbled through open space. The boys sprinted across the foyer to a hallway at the far end as tons of granite and marble smashed to the ground, sending shards of broken stone flying in every direction.

When the air was still, Jinx climbed out from behind an overturned statue and dusted himself off. They were in a small antechamber between the crumbled staircase and the door to the outside world.

"I can't believe we made it," said Jinx.

Bobby put a hand on his shoulder and looked Jinx in the eye. "I never could have made it without you."

Jinx blushed. "I guess I'm not such bad luck after all."

"Definitely not," said Bobby. "But the name *Jinx* stays. Theodore sounds like an old person. Now, come on. Let's get out of here before something else tries to fall on us."

A stone slab blocked their way, covered with ancient runes. "Is there anything else that could possibly go wrong?" asked Jinx. There could be no doubt that the stone marked the exit, and yet it had no door handle or other means by which to be opened. "I mean, seriously, what are the odds of finding a secret passage, picking the right tunnel, and still not being able to get out?"

"Perhaps we're better off in here than we are out there," said Bobby, running a hand over the icy cold surface of the door.

"In case you haven't noticed, we aren't exactly prepared for this. We have no water, no food, and only the clothes on our backs. Plus, both our flashlights are about to die. Even if there's a blizzard out there, we can at least find water and some wood for a fire."

"Alright, so we need to open the door. I get it," said Bobby. "But we've searched every inch of this place and haven't found anything. So what do you want to do?"

"We keep searching."

"This is crazy," said Bobby, sitting in the frozen dirt. "I never expected that we'd have problems getting *out*. I mean, it's a secret passage, right? The whole point is that it's difficult to find, not leave."

"You know, something is bugging me about that," said Jinx. "You see all these inscriptions? They're just like the ones back in the room of doors."

"So what?" said Bobby.

"So why warn us again when they already told us all about the 'pure of intent' stuff back there?"

"That's it!" said Bobby jumping to his feet. "I know what to do."

"What is it?" said Jinx

Bobby rushed to the door and placed both hands on the cold surface. "Yes, that's it," he said. "I can feel the stone."

"Tell me something I don't already know."

"That's not what I meant," said Bobby. "The stone is alive. I can sense its awareness, almost as if it's waiting."

"Waiting?" said Jinx. "Waiting for what?"

"I think we have to prove ourselves." Closing his eyes, Bobby focused on the Zen garden at his core. *Peace begins with me*, he meditated. *Peace begins with me.* With a heavy groan, the massive door swung out, revealing a narrow crack of daylight before grinding to a halt.

"I wonder why it stopped," said Bobby, covering his face as a blast of icy wind ripped through the narrow breach.

"It's probably blocked by a snowbank," said Jinx. "All the better, actually—we can take a look without having to face the full force of the storm."

"I'll go," said Bobby.

"Let me," said Jinx. "I can fit through the door easier." He slipped through the crack and disappeared. He was back almost instantly, the blood drained from his face—but not from the cold.

"What is it?" said Bobby.

"It's storming pretty bad," said Jinx. "But there's something else. Bobby . . . there's a man sitting out there in the snow."

"Yeah, right. You really need to work on your jokes, buddy. I know you're trying to lighten up, but you're never gonna trick anyone with a cheesy story like that."

"I'm not joking, Bobby. Come see for yourself."

Bobby squeezed through the opening and took a peek. He quickly squeezed back inside, grabbed Jinx by the arm, and dragged him away from the door.

"Hey, what the—" said Jinx.

Bobby slammed a hand down over Jinx's mouth. "That's him," hissed Bobby.

Jinx peeled Bobby's hand off. "Him who?"

"The assassin—the man who tried to kill me outside the bear cave, and then in the archives when the bookcase collapsed, and then again inside the bear cave when I went to retrieve Grandpa's diary."

Jinx turned as pale as the snow outside. "What do we do? He's just sitting out there, right in front of the entrance."

"I don't know," said Bobby, pressing against the wall. "Do you think he saw us?"

"You mean, after the thunderous sound of the door opening?"

Bobby frowned. "When I looked out, he had his eyes closed, like he was sleeping or something."

"He must be meditating," said Jinx. "People who know how can regulate their body temperature so that they stay warm even in extreme conditions."

"Well, if he is meditating, then I know exactly what to do," said Bobby. With a sidelong glance at the door, he walked back to the broken staircase. Sifting through the rubble, he found a bowling-ball-sized chunk with a jagged edge. He returned to the entrance with the rock cupped under his arm. "Wait here, and stay out of sight," he said.

"What are you going to do?" said Jinx.

"What I have dreamt about doing for a long time."

—◊◊◊—

Wind and ice assaulted Bobby as he trudged out into the freezing cold. The assassin sat in the open, twenty feet from the secret entrance, with snowdrift piled up to his knees. He wore a thick brown coat with the hood down despite the storm. His long black hair swirled around his face. Bobby was halfway to the man before he realized Jinx was following him.

"Go back," hissed Bobby.

His younger cousin just stared at him, wide-eyed. "What are you going to do with that rock?"

"I'm doing what has to be done. Now go back," said Bobby.

Jinx hesitated, looking anguished.

"Go back, now!"

Finally, Jinx dropped his shoulders and trudged back to the doorway. Bobby turned back to the assassin. Not for the first time, he wondered why the man was sitting there, completely defenseless, in the middle of a snowstorm. Walking up behind him, Bobby shifted the rock so the jagged edge pointed down. Then he lifted the rock high above the man's head.

"Bobby, stop!"

Snow billowed around the approaching woman dressed in white; she all but disappeared against the frozen backdrop. Bobby shielded his face with his forearm, squinting as the woman drew closer.

"Cassandra! I should have known you would show up."

"Bobby, put the rock down."

"It's too late," said Bobby, repositioning his grip. "I don't know what's wrong with your assassin, but I don't care. You murdered my family and sent this man to kill me. Well, he failed, and now I am going to kill him instead."

Cassandra's face flushed. "That man in front of you isn't an assassin," she said. "He's been trying to save you."

Bobby snickered. "You really expect me to believe your lies again, after what you did?"

"Bobby, I don't know what it is you think I did, but I'm telling you the truth. I was trying to help you when I first met you, and I'm still trying to help."

"You tried to help me?" laughed Bobby. "You murdered my parents! Tell me, Cassandra, exactly how is that *helping*?"

Cassandra raised both hands to her freezing face. "I would never do something like that."

"Liar!" yelled Bobby. "I saw you at the hospital. I saw you go into the operating room and make all the doctors leave. Are you going to lie to my face and tell me it didn't happen?"

Cassandra staggered as a blast of wind tore into her. "It's true, I went to the hospital after I left you at the Eagle's Nest, but I went there to help your parents. I was in the room, channeling anima into your mother, when the earthquakes started. Once the power went out, the surgeons were of no use, so I compelled the staff to get to safety. But my companion and I stayed behind to help save your parents."

"Liar!" screamed Bobby. "My parents are dead because of you!"

Cassandra lowered her voice until it was barely more than a whisper on the wind. "Is that what they told you? That your parents are dead? Bobby, your parents were in the hospital for a long time, but they are both at home now, very much alive and on the mend."

The rock sagged in Bobby's arms as he struggled to make sense of Cassandra's words. The assassin remained still and silent as if in a trance. Bobby shook his head and lifted the stone again.

"More lies!" he said. "The headmistress showed me photos of the accident. I saw how you met with the driver and had your assassin plunge a knife into his back after you left."

Cassandra cursed under her breath. "I knew I felt someone watching us . . . Yes, Bobby, it's true; I went to meet the driver from the accident, but only after your father woke up and asked me to check on him. Your father is a good man, Bobby."

"So, you didn't kill him either?" Bobby said sarcastically.

"I didn't kill anyone, and neither did my companion. I spoke to the driver and gave him some money to help with his medical bills because he didn't have any insurance. I was out on the street, about to leave, when I heard a loud noise. My companion went back to check on him and found the man dead."

Cassandra sighed. "Don't you see, Bobby? The people who abducted you and brought you here must have orchestrated the whole thing. They murdered that man and framed me to motivate you to stay here."

Bobby scowled. "Then why has this man been sneaking around the monastery, setting traps for me, and trying to get me killed?"

"Bobby, this man was sent here to rescue you. He says you refused to listen, so he's been trying to protect you instead."

"Oh really? Then why did he dig that trap on the hillside that nearly killed me?"

"He did that to save you!" said Cassandra. "To keep you from running into a cave full of bears."

Bobby couldn't believe his ears. "He didn't save me! He tortured me. He was going to kill me until my friends arrived and he ran away."

Cassandra shook her head. "You have it all wrong. He set that trap to incapacitate you so you wouldn't disturb the bears. You weren't supposed to hit your head. When you did, he had to heal you so you wouldn't bleed out."

"What about in the archives, when the bookcase almost collapsed on top of me? I saw him on the other side."

"He was there watching you, but so was a girl and a young boy with a pet. My companion said he helped support the bookcase long enough for you to get out."

Bobby recalled how Ashley and her gang had been down in the archives as well. "That's all very convenient," said Bobby, "but you have no proof."

"You're a bright boy," said Cassandra. "Think about it. How many near-death encounters have you had since coming to the academy? Do you really think that if I had sent this man to kill you, with all those chances, he wouldn't have succeeded? What about when you went back to the bear cave? He could have let the mother bear kill you then."

"Except the bear didn't attack me," said Bobby triumphantly. "He woke the bear, and it attacked him!"

Cassandra rubbed the bridge of her nose. "Bobby, you woke the bear. He fought it off to keep it from getting to you. That's how important it is to both of us that you remain safe."

"That's a lie," said Bobby, shaking his head. "It's all lies."

"Bobby, how many times were you almost caught in a cave-in while fleeing the mines just now? How many times did something collapse right after you moved, or land mere inches away?"

"What are you saying?"

"That wasn't luck, Bobby; that was him. He has been sitting here, channeling anima into the mountain in an effort to keep it stable, to give you time to escape."

"If that's the case, then why is he still sitting there? Why doesn't he get up and answer for himself?"

"Because there are other people still inside. He radioed me and said he sensed an explosion in the mines. The mountain is collapsing. The Jade Academy is crumbling. He is trying to keep everything from falling apart long enough for everyone to get out safely."

Bobby ignored the sleet pelting his face as he turned back to the man on the ground. "I don't believe you. I don't know what kind of game you're playing, but it ends now." He raised the rock up high over his head.

"Bobby, stop," said a voice from out of the storm. "She is telling the truth."

Bobby turned to the speaker and almost dropped the rock. Even covered by a hood and after so many years, Bobby recognized that face instantly.

"Grandpa?"

—ᗯ—

The rock sank into the snow, forgotten as Bobby ran to his grandfather and gave him a giant hug.

"I can't believe you're really here," said Bobby. His grandfather had more gray hair than Bobby remembered and a stubbly beard that hadn't been there the last time they'd met. Despite the changes, his grandfather's eyes still twinkled with a mirth matched only by his smile.

"But what *are* you doing here?" said Bobby.

"You read my diary, right?" said Grandpa, taking a moment to catch his breath. "After my daughter was taken from me, I vowed to make sure that our family would always be safe."

"But why haven't I seen you? I mean, I saw him a bunch of times," said Bobby, gesturing to the man on the ground.

"Too risky," said Grandpa, trying unsuccessfully to shield them both from the storm. "Simpkins and Hayward know Cassandra and me too well."

"So it's true that Mom and Dad are alive?"

"Your parents contacted me shortly after the accident. Apparently two 'FBI agents' paid them a visit with some phony story about you being in witness protection," said Grandpa.

"FBI agents?" asked Bobby confused.

"From the descriptions, it sounded like Simpkins and Hayward," said Grandpa. "They must have used some type of hypnotic suggestion, because your parents bought the story and promptly gave up searching for you—something we both know they'd never do on their own. When they called me the next day to tell me the news, I knew exactly what had happened."

"Simpkins and Hayward," Bobby said slowly. "They were in the mines when the place started to collapse. Oh my gosh, the monks, too. They are all in the mines!"

"Then we have no time to waste," said Cassandra, who had been standing patiently off to the side. Kneeling beside the man in the snow, she whispered something in his ear. A moment later, the man opened his eyes and stood.

"How is it?" asked Cassandra.

"I have stabilized a few key areas to buy us some time," said the weathered man with a somber shake of his head. "It won't last long, but it is good that you disturbed me; I was waning and needed time to collect my strength. Which reminds me," he said, shifting his attention to Bobby. "Thank you for not bashing my brains in."

Bobby turned crimson. "You're welcome."

"I don't believe we've been properly introduced," he said. "My name is Chief Benson Eagleheart, but my friends call me Chief."

"You're the man who runs that facility in the forest," said Bobby. "The place Cassandra took me to. The Eagle's Nest, right?"

Chief bowed slightly.

"And that was you inside my head when Hayward was torturing me, wasn't it?"

Chief bowed again.

Bobby's mouth fell open. "Is it true you run a special team that protects the world against exso-terrorist threats?"

Chief gave Cassandra a piercing gaze.

"Don't look at me like that," snapped Cassandra. "You're the one who told me to take him to your secret hideout. What was I supposed to tell him after he saw the giant indoor forest filled with glowing plants—that it's an amusement park?"

Chief turned back to Bobby. "So, what did you think? Would you like to learn more about what you saw? Perhaps even train to become part of my team?"

"My team!" echoed Bobby, rushing over to the tunnel entrance. Grabbing Jinx by the hand, Bobby dragged him over to the others.

"Jinx, this is Cassandra, the woman I thought killed my parents and was trying to murder me," said Bobby. "Turns out she's actually a good guy."

"Pleasure to meet you," said Cassandra, offering a fox-fur-lined glove.

"And this is Chief, the man that I thought was an assassin sent by Cassandra. Apparently he's been helping us all along." Jinx's eyes went wide, clearly unsure what to make of the intimidating Native American.

"And this is our grandfather, Jeremiah."

Grandpa stiffened at these last words. "*Our* grandfather?" he said slowly.

"Jinx is the son of the headmistress," explained Bobby. "His sister, Ashley, is still inside the monastery somewhere."

"You mean to tell me that I have a granddaughter too, and that my daughter is the headmistress of the Jade Academy?"

Bobby nodded. "I figured you knew that already."

"You guys are family?" gasped Cassandra. "That is amazing." She seemed sincere, but her tone sounded bittersweet.

Grandpa shook his head as frosty tears swelled in his eyes. "I had no idea." Wrapping his arms around both boys, Grandpa pulled them into a fierce embrace.

"I hate to break up this touching family reunion," said Cassandra, "but we still have a job to do. You ready, Chief?"

Chief gave her a solemn nod. "I can proceed. But as I said before, I am going to need help."

"What do we need to do?" said Bobby.

"The first thing we need to do is get out of this storm," said Chief, already heading toward the tunnel entrance. "After that, we must combine all of our strength to try to stem the disaster currently underway."

CHAPTER 32

In the cramped hall of the Spine of the World, Bobby and his companions joined hands to form a circle.

"What you are about to experience is part of the spirit world," said Chief, "a realm between reality and dreams where anima exists in physical form. Everything you will see is part of my dreamscape: an interpretation of the spirit world which will provide a framework for your minds. Bobby, Jinx: since the two of you are untrained in how to reach the spirit realm, I will guide you."

Jinx swallowed hard. "Umm, maybe it isn't such a good idea for me to participate. My abilities can be *difficult* at times."

"Don't worry," said Grandpa. "I won't let anything happen to you."

A tremor shook the antechamber.

"We're out of time," said Chief. "Already, the work I've done begins to unravel. Please sit. Find your center. I will do the rest."

Following Chief's instructions, Bobby envisioned the Zen garden that housed his anima. Using strength from the others, he pushed through the invisible barrier and beyond the mist until he stood on the outskirts of the garden.

Not sure what else to do, Bobby walked to the pedestal with the lotus blossom. Setting a foot on the dais, he spun around to discover Chief standing behind him.

"I can see why you chose this place," said the old Indian. "It's very peaceful."

"I didn't choose this," said Bobby.

"Of course you did. Now gather your anima. We must hurry."

Bobby did as instructed, snatching the lotus blossom off the pedestal.

"Now eat it."

Surprised, Bobby put the lotus in his mouth and swallowed.

"Hold tight," said Chief, and he set two fingers in the middle of Bobby's forehead. "I am creating a feedback loop, magnifying the anima within you."

Warmth spread through Bobby, accompanied by a tingle that permeated his consciousness, all the way back to his real stomach. His skin began to glow, just as it had when he healed himself in the archives. Chief set a hand on top of Bobby's head, and light pooled under Chief's palm. Chief drew his hand outward and the light around Bobby's head expanded, shrouding his head like a halo.

With a nod of approval, Chief dropped his hands. Instantly, the scene around them shifted. The Zen garden disappeared, replaced by a spectral version of the antechamber. Still swathed in a spectral aura, Bobby stood behind his body on the ground. The spectral version of Grandpa appeared, followed moments later by Cassandra, but not Jinx.

"I will return in a moment," said Chief, who glowed like the others. He disappeared, reappearing moments later with Jinx's spirit at his side. "That was more challenging than I anticipated," Chief gasped.

"Told ya," said Jinx.

"Don't worry. Everything will be fine now that you're with us," said Grandpa.

"Come, we must hurry," said Chief. He headed toward the lobby, and the others followed.

Bobby gaped at the similar but subtly different spirit world. Their surroundings glowed, with certain objects, such as the earthen walls and the five of them, shining brighter than others. The rubble blocking their path was gone. Whether it was part of Chief's dreamscape or different physics, Bobby didn't know, but the stairwell in this reality remained intact.

Jinx waved a hand in front of his face, wriggling his luminous fingers in amazement.

Grandpa smiled and said, "The glow is caused by the anima within us—our soul or spirit, so to speak."

"The same is true for the stone," said Chief, pointing at the glowing walls. "The earth is a living, breathing entity, the creator of all life, all anima."

They reached the lobby and Bobby paused. An elevator door stood at the base of the spectral stairwell.

"Umm, I'm pretty sure that wasn't there before," said Bobby, pointing to the door.

"Remember," said Chief, pushing the call button, "what you see is an interpretation of the spirit world. Think of it as a mix between reality and the realm of pure anima."

The elevator door opened to reveal a familiar yet wholly unexpected sight.

"Is that the sphere tram from the Eagle's Nest?" asked Bobby, staring at the chrome sphere parked on the other side. This sphere appeared the same as the real one, except it wasn't on a track, and it glowed with an intense green hue similar to his own aura.

"Anything imbued with anima exists in both realities," said Chief. "As such, the sphere provides a conduit between realms." The hatch slid open and Chief led them into an interior much different than the cramped space Bobby remembered. Five seats were spread around a spacious room filled with screens and consoles.

Noting Bobby's look of surprise, Chief said, "Both the physical sphere and the anima sphere are capable of adapting to the required circumstances. Though, I must admit, the anima sphere does it with more style." As he spoke, the armrests of his chair morphed into a control pad, with a joystick below his right palm and buttons on the left.

Jinx's mouth fell open. "Whoa! How did you do that?"

Chief grinned. "I call it 'Instantaneous, Direct, Real-time Environmental Adaptation & Manipulation,' or 'I-DREAM' for short."

Cassandra coughed. "I call it showing off."

"All right, everyone, buckle up," said Grandpa. "The sooner we get this done, the sooner we can get you boys to safety."

The instant they strapped in, the sphere began its descent. Despite traveling much faster than the real version, Bobby felt neither nausea nor dizziness as they plunged straight down at incredible speeds. The monitor in front of him showed a spectral version of the earth's crust, with a vertical line plunging straight through it, surrounded by dozens of throbbing red spots.

"What is all of this?" asked Bobby.

"The vertical line is the Spine of the World," said Chief. "The physical shaft only descends to the base of the mountain, but the spirit version runs all the way to the core, where it draws its power."

"What about the red splotchy things all around it?" asked Jinx.

"Those are lava pools in real life, but in the dreamscape, they're anima clouds: living energy that has leaked from the spine over the centuries. The clouds send out tendrils, trying to reconnect with the source."

"That's what's destabilizing the mountain!" said Jinx. As he spoke, a bolt of lightning shot from one of the clouds. Chief flicked the control stick and the sphere veered to the side, narrowly avoiding the surge.

"What can we do to help?" asked Grandpa.

"Keep watching the monitors," said Chief. "Call it out if any of the pools look ready to spew another bolt."

"That's it?" said Cassandra. "You didn't need all of us for that."

"Don't worry, princess. There'll be much more to do on the return trip."

The sphere shook violently, rattling Bobby in his seat. He checked the screen, but there were no signs of lightning.

"What was that?" asked Grandpa.

"A tremor must have disturbed the antechamber," said Chief. "Remember: keep connected with your physical form and maintain contact with each other. I don't have time to go back and pick up anyone if you fall off the bus!"

Bobby let his consciousness drift toward the surface to check on his body. Satisfied he was safe, he returned to the monitor, calling out warnings whenever they passed too close to an anima cloud or one looked ready to erupt.

For several minutes, the crew bounced around as they traced a jagged path through the earth's crust and into the mantle. Gradually, the clouds decreased in size and intensity.

Bobby pushed back from his console and sighed. "Well, that wasn't fun!" His screen showed that they had passed beyond the mantle and were now entering the earth's outer core. Up ahead, a bright yellow ball grew larger and more intense until he had to turn away from the display.

Jinx leaned over and whispered, "I-Dream, remember? You can turn the brightness down with your mind."

Bobby stuck out a hand and twisted an invisible knob. The screen instantly faded to a tolerable hue.

"What is that thing?" he said, pointing to the glowing ball on his screen.

"The inner core," said Jinx.

"And our destination," said Chief. As they drew closer, a shaft of light came into view. Chief steered the sphere toward the beam.

"Where's that beam coming from?"

"Bobby, do you recall the Nexus, that strange glowing building on top of the plateau in the Eagle's Nest?" asked Cassandra. "That beam is the Nexus, sending us anima collected from the forest—"

"Which we are going to use to shore up the mountain," said Chief. Pulling the sphere alongside, he rose from his console. "I could use some help with this next part."

Beckoning the others, he waved and his control station disappeared, replaced by a giant screen displaying a long metal cable with a cap on one end and a massive hook on the other.

"Mimic my actions," said Chief. "I-Dream will do the rest."

Bobby grouped up with the others and, starting with a cupping motion, they hooked the cable to the ship. Next, they brought their hands together and slowly drew them apart. In response, the cable extended from the ship. The cap and cable floated through space like an astronaut on a tether until it reached the stream of light. Next, Chief thrust his hands forward, maneuvering the cap into position until it severed the Nexus's beam. Lastly, they all rotated their arms in a circle, screwing the lid onto the beam.

"This is now our supply line," said Chief, "providing the power we need to stabilize the mountain."

"So, we're going to use the power from the Nexus to calm the earthquakes?" asked Jinx.

Chief nodded. "Time to head back," he said, strapping himself into the newly reappeared pilot's chair.

The storm came into sight as they returned to the mantle. Chief steered them toward the darkest clouds.

"Use the power from the Nexus to shoot the clouds," said Chief.

Bobby searched the console in front of him but failed to locate a joystick or targeting device. Jinx leaned over and was about to say something when Bobby cut him off. "I-dream!"

Picturing the gunner's station inside the tank, Bobby thrust out his arms. Instantly, command controls appeared under his palms, along with a swiveling turret and bullseye targeting system on his screen. With a yip of glee, Bobby aimed and fired.

Dissolving his navigation controls, Chief took up a bow and arrow. Cassandra produced a sniper's rifle. Jinx materialized a suit of mechanized armor, equipped with a rocket launcher, while Grandpa manifested a pair of cowboy style six-shooter pistols.

"Take that, you yellow-bellied cowards!" yelled Grandpa, shooting at pop-up bandits on his display.

Bobby fired round after round, but the angry storm clouds continued to throw off bolts of lightning. Chief switched back to his pilot's chair and drew them in closer until they hovered directly over the thickest, darkest part of the storm. They continued firing, but the storm showed no signs of change.

"The anima from the Nexus isn't neutralizing the target," said Grandpa.

"Because the dreamscape isn't consistent with our objective," said Cassandra. As she spoke, a mighty bolt of lightning burst from the haze. Chief swerved the ship, but the bolt forked in pursuit. The impact tossed the sphere through the void like a pinball.

Chief flew from the pilot's chair, landing hard against the far wall. His eyes fluttered and then shut. Cassandra raced to his side and checked his pulse. "He's out cold." She grabbed his head, a panicked expression on her face. "What do we do?"

Grandpa knelt beside her and took her hand. "It's okay, Cass. The dreamscape is still intact. That means his physical body and subconscious are unharmed. As long as we get him back to the surface, he should wake up."

"But what if he doesn't?"

"Speaking of getting back to the surface," said Jinx, sliding into the pilot's chair, "we have a bigger problem: the controls are dead."

"How is that possible?" said Bobby. "I thought our minds controlled everything."

"Our minds control the interface," said Cassandra, "but remember: the sphere exists in both the physical and spiritual realms at the same time. The real ship must have taken damage."

Another bolt shattered the void. This one lanced up, toward the base of the mountain. The lights inside the sphere dimmed, plunging them into darkness for a moment before coming back on.

"That bolt didn't even hit us!" protested Bobby.

"No, but it hit the mountain," said Grandpa.

"It must have disturbed the passage where we're meditating," theorized Jinx. "We need to get out of here, now."

"That's a great idea," said Cassandra. "Any suggestions?"

"Before the accident, you said this dreamscape isn't working, right?" said Jinx. "So we try something else."

"What do you have in mind?" asked Grandpa.

When Jinx didn't reply, Bobby jumped in. "Those anima clouds are actually lava pools, right? So we shoot them with ice to cool them off."

"That might calm the storm," said Cassandra, "but it won't get the sphere moving again."

"Is there any way to tether the sphere to the spine?" asked Bobby.

Cassandra frowned. "If we drop our connection to the Nexus, we might be able to wrap the cable around the spine. Why?"

"Because I have an idea on how to get us out of here."

With Chief unconscious, altering the dreamscape proved to be a monumental task. It took all four of them focused on the same vision before the environment showed the tiniest sign of change. Slowly, the scene outside the sphere shifted from a raging storm to an active volcano, with pools of lava erupting all around them.

Manning his station, Bobby thrust out his arms and envisioned a giant ice cannon. The weapon took shape slowly, flickering several times before winking into existence. On his monitor, he checked the strength of the Nexus beam. It was little more than a pale glowing rope, half the thickness of the original beam.

"We're running out of power," Bobby yelled to the others.

"Then we'd better make this count!" said Grandpa.

Focusing on the outer rim of the volcano, Bobby bombarded one spot until a thin layer of ice appeared. Then he slowly worked his way in. The others followed suit, cooling the other edges of the lava pool as the energy streaming from the Nexus grew steadily weaker. Bobby brought two fingers together, tightening the cap to keep from losing the feed.

Meanwhile, the center of the lava pit still burned bright red. A great pool of magma swirled in the center, roiling and splashing as the cooling of the crater's outer rim closed around the molten liquid.

"It's gonna blow!" yelled Jinx.

"Hold on," warned Grandpa. "We need to time this perfectly."

Directly below them, the magma boiled and frothed, leaping from the surface to lick the void.

"We're almost out of power," said Cassandra.

"It's gonna blow!" repeated Jinx.

Bobby glanced back and forth between the withering Nexus beam and the pool of magma. Swiveling his ice cannon from the edge of the crater to the cap of the cable, Bobby shouted to his team, "Now! Do it now!"

The four companions fired at the cap connecting the sphere to the nearly depleted Nexus beam. Bobby spread his fingers, expanding the size of the cap until it dislodged. A split second later, the cannon blasts struck, sending the lid caroming off into space. Still attached to the sphere, the cap pulled the line tight before swinging in a wide arch. The cable hit the Spine of the World and wrapped around it three times before the cap twisted and caught.

The volcano erupted. Funneled by the layers of ice around the lip, the magma blew straight up through the middle of the maelstrom. The force from the blast would have tossed them into the void if not for the cable wrapped around the spine.

Bobby gripped the armrest, his knuckles white as the gravitational forces tore through him. Black spots crept into the corners of his vision. His breath turned heavy and labored. Then the g-forces slowly subsided and Bobby relaxed his grip. Having raced up the spine at breakneck speed, the sphere slammed to a halt, followed by a loud thud. The doors flew open, revealing the stairwell lobby.

Leaping from his seat, Bobby grabbed Chief by the wrists and dragged him toward the antechamber. Seconds later, Grandpa was there beside him, lifting Chief's legs while Cassandra and Jinx supported his torso. Together, they carried Chief down the hall to the meditation circle. Their physical bodies appeared to have been jostled quite a bit by the quakes; Grandpa and Jinx both slumped heavily to the side, about to fall, at which point the circle would break.

"It's okay," said Cassandra, spotting Bobby's worried look. "We're back now."

With the help of the others, Bobby positioned Chief's spirit beside his body.

"Nothing else we can do," said Grandpa. "It's up to him now."

Sitting beside himself, Bobby drew his spirit into body and opened his eyes.

—◊◊◊—

After being in the spirit world for so long, it took a moment for Bobby's eyes to adjust to the dim light of the atrium. Beside him, Jinx and Grandpa remained motionless for a long moment before stirring. Cassandra bolted upright with a gasp and dashed to Chief's side.

"Wake up!" she said, shaking him vigorously by the shoulders. "Wake up, damn you!"

She shook him so violently that Bobby thought the old Indian might topple over, and yet still he remained motionless. Cassandra pulled back a fist. For a second, Bobby thought she meant to punch Chief in the chest. Then she extended two fingers and touched them to the center of Chief's forehead, just as Chief had done to him inside his Zen garden.

Chief opened his eyes and the group let out a collective sigh of relief. Cassandra collapsed to the group as the deep wrinkles of Chief's face cracked into a faint smile. "I never knew you cared."

Cassandra glared at him. "I don't!" she said and punched him for real this time. "Just don't ever scare me like that again!"

"What is the status?" asked Chief. "Were we successful?"

"We did all we could to snuff the eruptions," said Grandpa, "but we weren't able to stop them completely."

"There's still one hot spot," said Cassandra. "I'm afraid it's only a matter of time before our efforts are undone."

"Then the academy is doomed," said Chief.

"We need to focus on locating the students and evacuating before the Core gets their hands on them," said Grandpa.

Bobby and Jinx both looked at their grandfather in confusion. "Isn't the Core destroyed now that the academy is gone?" asked Bobby.

"Do you boys remember from my diary how the Jade Academy has been testing and conducting DNA experiments on its students?"

Bobby nodded. "That's what convinced me that I needed to escape."

"But did you see any equipment at the monastery that could actually perform those kinds of procedures?"

"Now that you mention it," said Jinx, "the lab we found only had journals and a few computers."

"That's because they don't do any of the real experimentation at the academy—even the corrupt monks would have balked at that."

"What exactly are these experiments that I keep hearing about?" said Bobby.

Chief looked at Grandpa for approval. "It's okay," said Grandpa. "After what he's been through, he's earned the right to know the truth. They both have."

Chief nodded and turned back to Bobby. "We believe the Core is attempting to forcefully activate the gene sequences responsible for anima abilities in live subjects. The Jade Academy was just one piece of the puzzle—a place to test students' DNA for exso markers and activate dormant genes whenever possible."

"You're saying that students who graduated were taken someplace else for science experiments?" said Jinx.

Chief nodded sadly. "We haven't gained access to their other facilities. All we know is that the subjects that go in don't come out."

"But that's not all," said Cassandra. "We also know that Simpkins and Hayward are part of another project aimed at cloning exsos—something which they apparently believe represents the next stage of human evolution."

"Is that what the headmistress meant when she said that I would be sent off to help improve the program?" said Bobby.

"There can be little doubt that there is much more at play," said Chief. "The Jade Academy is merely the beginning."

"So, what now?" asked Jinx.

"We head back to the academy to rescue the others, but first we must wait out this storm and recover our strength," said Chief.

Bobby sprang to his feet. "I've got friends in there," he said. "We need to go now!"

"While I would normally agree," said Chief, "traveling in this storm without the proper provisions is quite impossible. We have no choice but to wait until it blows over."

—⁓—

In the dim light of the mines, Hayward set his back against the wall and rubbed the knot on his forehead. "What just happened?" he asked his partner lying beside him.

"What happened is we lost," said Simpkins, "and now the rebels are in control of the academy."

"It wasn't a fair fight. That old man had a stick!" said Hayward. "Ugh, I am going to have a headache for weeks."

"We need to regroup and find the headmistress," said Simpkins.

As the tide of battle turned against them, the partners had fled down a side tunnel to avoid being captured.

"Good thing those sissies quit chasing us to go rescue the children," said Hayward.

The passage rumbled as another tremor shook the mountain.

"We need to get out of here, now," said Simpkins.

Rising, they stumbled toward the main entrance, the ground heaving continuously.

"The tremors are getting stronger," said Simpkins, breaking into a jog.

Hayward grudgingly following suit, his body jiggling wildly with every step. A few yards ahead, a chunk of ceiling caved in, partially blocking the passage. Simpkins scrambled over it, but Hayward struggled to get his rotund torso over the debris.

Grabbing the back of his pants, Simpkins heaved Hayward to the other side. Their momentum sent both men sprawling as a mighty earthquake ruptured the tunnel.

Hayward rolled onto his back, staring up at a wooden support beam as it shattered into pieces.

"Oh crap," said Simpkins. Then the cave collapsed on top of them.

CHAPTER 33

It took nearly three hours for the storm to break. The instant the wind died down, Bobby raced to the entrance to the Spine of the World. Snow drifted by in fat, lazy flakes, like floating goose feathers.

"Come on!" he yelled to the others. "We need to get back up the mountain and rescue my friends!"

With barely a word, Jinx, Chief and the rest of Bobby's companions gathered their gear and drudged out into what was now little more than a light snowfall. Chief guided them out of the narrow canyon concealing the secret passage. Bobby and the others fell in behind him, with Grandpa bringing up the rear. For hours, they trekked along the base of the mountain until they reached the back of the hills that housed the bear's den. From there the slopes gradually gave way until they hit the dirt road leading to the forest.

By the time they reached the village at the neck of the woods, the sun had begun to set over the mountains they'd just traversed. Penetrating rays of twilight lit up the forest in splendid hues of russet and emerald. Chief looked back over his shoulder and called for a break. Instantly, the exhausted group fell to pieces.

Bobby sank onto a tree stump and rubbed his aching legs. Red faced and with inhaler already in hand, Jinx took several puffs before joining him. Grandpa had his hands on his knees. The old man was in great shape but clearly needed a break.

Cassandra stood with hands on her hips, doubled over, sucking in long, deep breaths. With a groan, she collapsed onto the muddy forest floor.

"You have no idea what I would give for a Burke Williams right now," she moaned.

Even Chief looked tired. "There's no way we can make it back up the mountain in the dark. We need to rest here for the night. Come, I know a place nearby."

A few minutes later, they broke off the main trail, following a dirt path to a tiny cottage set back among the trees. Even in the waning light, Bobby could tell the building was in ruins. Blackened by fire and riddled with holes, the structure looked ready to collapse.

"Whose house is this?" he asked as Chief led them up the front steps. Chief pushed open the door, hanging by a single hinge. The inside had been burnt as well, leaving nothing but a charred husk and a few pieces of furniture, most of which were smashed beyond recognition. It wasn't until the heap in the corner moved that Bobby noticed the old man with the long gray beard lying on the cot.

"Who's there?" said the old man, sitting up so that his beard dropped nearly to the floor. The man's milky white eyes took in nothing as he waited for a reply.

Chief approached the man slowly. "Are you Hatou, former groundskeeper of the Jade Academy?"

"You're too late," replied the blind man. "Anything you could possibly do to me has already been done."

"We mean you no harm," said Chief gently. "I am Chief, your correspondent from America."

Surprise registered on the old man's face. "What are you doing here? We thought you had abandoned us."

"Never," said Chief, kneeling by the man's side and taking his hand in his own. "Tell me, friend, what happened here?"

"The gaunt one with breath like onion grass came seeking the scrolls. When I wouldn't give them to him, the boy in the red robes gave me unspeakable visions. This is the result," said Hatou, gesturing to his eyes. "But I still wouldn't tell them anything. That's when they began to tear the cottage apart."

Bobby knew all too well that Hatou was referring to Simpkins. The presence of Willy the Creep, on the other hand, both shocked and disturbed him.

"Did they find the scrolls?" asked Chief.

"They found them, yes," said Hatou, "but never possessed them. After the boy took my sight, they paid me no mind while they ransacked the house. I made my way to the stove and lit a lantern. The man laughed and called me a fool, thinking that I was attempting to brighten the darkness so that I could see. I stood by the hearth with the lantern until I heard them open the cache. Then I threw the lantern, igniting the scrolls and setting the house on fire."

"You set your own home on fire?" asked Bobby.

"I knew what the man would do with me once he got what he wanted," said Hatou. "While they were busy trying to douse the fire, I escaped into the woods and made my way to a friend's house on the other side of the village. He kept me hidden for a while. After the monastery collapsed, I figured it was safe to return. Tell me; have you any word from my dear friend Jong?"

"We are heading up the mountain first thing tomorrow to see what remains," said Chief. "Hopefully we will find him among the living."

"In that case, you must stay the night," said Hatou. "I will give you what food and supplies I can spare to take to the survivors."

They set to work. Bobby and Jinx built a fire while Grandpa

prepared a meal of boiled potatoes with leeks and wild carrots. Meanwhile, Cassandra went with Hatou to the general store to gather supplies while Chief scouted the village in search of news and survivors.

It was late when Chief finally returned to report that the villagers hadn't seen so much as a single person come down off the mountain. The news hung heavy in the air as the companions picked out spots on the ruined floor to bed down for the night. Even Cassandra had nothing to say as she took a place by the hearth, balling her mink coat beneath her head to use as a pillow.

Bobby lay down nearby, closed his eyes, and tried to sleep. A few feet away, Jinx cried softly until exhaustion finally claimed him, transforming his sobs into gentle snores. Bobby was not so lucky. He remained wide awake as the others drifted off one by one, their breathing becoming slow and steady.

Restless, Bobby tiptoed to the door and slipped out into the chill night air. Picking a direction at random, he wandered down to the narrow creek that ran by the southern edge of the house. He stood on the banks, staring at the crystal-clear stream and thinking about how it reminded him of the one in his spirit garden. On the opposite shore, an enormous bear stepped out of the forest, its lustrous fur glistening like diamonds in the pale moonlight.

With its eyes locked on his, the bear extended its forepaws and lowered its head. Bobby stood there, barely able to breathe as he thought about Master Jong's comments about animal guides and how they supposedly looked after people on spiritual journeys. Purposefully, Bobby brought his palms together and bowed deeply at the waist. When he straightened up, the bear was gone.

A tear rolled down his cheek as Bobby turned and headed back to Hatou's cottage. When he finally fell asleep, he dreamed not of the accident, or of bears fighting, but of his parents, and of being with them once again.

—☇—

Bobby and his companions left before sunrise. As they walked, they ate a cold breakfast of flatbread and hard-boiled eggs washed down with goat's milk in sheepskin bladders. They reached the mountain pass just as the sun broke over the mountaintops to the east. They headed up the slope without pause and stood before the monastery's outer wall by early afternoon.

The thirty-foot iron gates stood wide open, a sight strange enough by itself, but it was the sight beyond that boggled Bobby's mind. The entire façade of the monastery was simply gone, sheered away by rockslides that had cascaded down from above, leaving nothing but rubble in their wake. All around the courtyard, chunks of roofs, balconies, and walls lay strewn about like a colossal dollhouse smashed to pieces.

Picking their way across the courtyard, the group quickly realized that entering through the main hall was out of the question. The entrance's thick stone pillars had collapsed inward, bringing down the massive archway above.

They split up and scouted the area. It was Jinx who finally found another way in—the doors to the monks' quarters were only partially blocked by a fallen terrace leaning against the doorframe. By combining their strength, Chief and Grandpa were able to pry the doors open just enough to allow everyone to slip through.

—☇—

They found the survivors huddled in the main dining hall, where the thick columns continued to support the roof despite tons of rubble from the mountain piled on top. The round tables had been moved off to the sides, allowing people to lie on the cold stone floor.

Monks tended to injured students, healing wounds and soothing the cries of the younger students. The mountain gave a sudden jolt that sent children screaming and cracks rippling across the stone ceiling. Then the room grew still once again and people returned to their business, almost as if earthquakes had become normal.

From across the room, Lily spotted Bobby. With a cry of delight, she raced over and threw herself into his arms.

"We were so worried!" she said. She crushed him so hard Bobby thought his lungs might explode.

She let go, hugging Jinx as Trevor and Jacob arrived and greeted them. Soon other people gathered around, asking about Chief, Cassandra, and Bobby's grandfather, Jeremiah. As quick as he could, Bobby explained all that had transpired after he and Jinx fled the academy.

"Wicked cool," said Trevor, as Bobby explained how they had escaped via the Spine of the World.

"That's great that your parents are still alive!" said Jacob. Trevor gave his buddy a sharp elbow to the ribs and Jacob winced. "Umm, right. Sorry about your mom," he said to Jinx. "And your aunt, too, Bobby."

Jinx dipped his head. "That reminds me, has anyone seen Ashley?"

Master Jong arrived, limping slightly but appearing otherwise unharmed as he wove through the crowd. "A lot of people are still missing," he said. "We have found no trace of Simpkins or Hayward, or any of the other academics, for that matter."

"That can't be a coincidence," said Chief.

"I am certain it is not," said Master Jong, "but we have neither the resources nor the energy to investigate at the moment."

Jeremiah stepped forth and greeted Master Jong. "We'd like to help, but this entire mountain is unstable. We need to evacuate right away."

"I'm afraid that's impossible," said Master Jong. "Even if everyone were accounted for, we have many who are too injured to travel. The stables are destroyed. We have no mules or carts to carry people down the mountain."

Another earthquake rattled the hall, causing a chunk of ceiling to break into pieces. Tons of stone smashed into the middle of the room, barely missing several injured students lying on the floor.

"We need to get out of here now before things get worse," said Cassandra.

"I can arrange for transportation," said Chief. "Once I get back to civilization, I can radio for helicopters to pick up everyone, and rescue teams to search for survivors."

"But where will we go?" asked one of the monks standing beside Master Jong. Bobby recognized Yemoni, from the garden.

"I have a large facility with a forest much like the one below this mountain," said Chief. "Any students without a home to return to are welcome to live there. Likewise, any monk who renounces the Core's agenda and wishes to study and help train these students is invited to join us."

Master Jong bowed to Chief. "On behalf of my brethren, I humbly accept your invitation."

"Great," said Chief. "I will head out right away to make arrangements. It may take a day or two, so gather all of the food and supplies you can and evacuate to the courtyard. The weather has broken, so you should be fine as long as you stay clear of the building. I'll send the copters back for you as soon as possible."

Master Jong bowed again and gave instructions to the other monks. As the monks gathered the students, Grandpa turned to Bobby.

"I'm guessing that you would like to stay with your friends."

"I do, but I also want to see my parents."

"I think it best that we depart with Mr. Chief," said Grandpa. "Your parents have been extremely worried about you ever since I lifted the hypnosis put on them by Hayward and Simpkins."

"I'm going, for sure," said Cassandra. "I don't care how far I have to walk, there is no way I am spending another night sleeping on the floor!"

"I know but I don't want to leave them," said Bobby. "We've been through so much together. What if I never see them again?"

"Might I offer a suggestion?" said Chief. "You can depart

with us now, and then come visit your friends at the Eagle's Nest once you've had a chance to spend time with your family."

Bobby turned to his friends. "You'll all be there, right?"

"Got no place else to be," said Trevor.

"Heck, I don't even remember my parents," said Jacob.

"I want to visit my parents," said Lily, "but I'm older now, I am sure they'll understand if I want to live with my friends." She gave Trevor and Jacob playful punches. "Besides, someone's gotta keep these two hooligans in line."

Bobby turned to Chief. "Is that okay?" Chief nodded and Bobby grinned. "That's perfect," he said and threw his arms around his friends. "I'll go see my parents now and then catch up with all of you at the Eagle's Nest in a few days."

Jinx coughed lightly. "Do you think it would be okay if I come with? My mom is gone. My sister is probably gone too. This place has nothing but bad memories for me and, to be honest, I would like to meet my aunt and uncle if that's okay."

Grandpa threw his arm around his grandsons and steered them toward the door. "Come on, boys. Let's go home."

Book Two
Prologue

From across the courtyard at the Jade Academy, the Core agent known as Sandman watched the weathered Indian and his companions head for the mountain trail leading to the forest below. Sandman ducked into the shadows, remaining there until long after the travelers were gone. Then he turned and went back down the trail that led to the garden by the cliffs.

Hidden back amid the rubble, the soldiers under his command stood at attention. "Are we moving out, sir?" asked one of his men. Some of the soldiers rose, checking their weapons and equipment.

"Mission review," said Sandman. "Neutralize the monks if necessary. The students are not to be harmed."

"Rules of engagement, sir?" asked one of his men.

"Wetworks only. Absolutely no explosives or live fire. Can't risk the noise."

The soldiers saluted as one. "Sir, yes sir."

"Radio silence. I will handle anyone who attempts to engage," commanded Sandman. "Not a peep. I want a bow on this before they even know we're here."

"Sir, yes sir."

Sandman nodded in approval and returned their salute. "Get some rest. We roll out at zero three hundred."

—ɯ—

Their execution was flawless. In the stillness found only in the dead of night, Sandman and his men crept into the courtyard occupied by the sleeping refugees. The mountain had continued to rumble and shake throughout the night, causing many of the students to have trouble sleeping, especially on the cold hard ground.

Sandman sensed those who were still awake as easily as he would a bonfire blazing in the dark. With a thin wisp of anima, he sent each person into a slumber so deep that even being lifted and carried wouldn't rouse them. The children were easy, their minds too poorly trained and undisciplined to shield themselves from his power. Some of the monks were tougher, requiring several attempts before they succumbed to his hypnotic suggestions.

One monk in particular kept resisting. Picking his way gingerly through the mass of sleeping bodies, Sandman maneuvered to the monk in question.

"You must be their leader," said Sandman. The diminutive monk at his feet twitched slightly, almost as if he were still awake and struggling to break free. He looked like an infant thrashing in a crib, restless with nightmares but unable to wake up.

One by one, Sandman's soldiers picked up the children and carried them down the path to the garden. There, the ropes he and his men had used to scale the steep cliff were strapped to each child to lower them down the mountain.

The process was slow, taking nearly every minute of darkness. *Once the sun comes up, the biological imperative to wake will be fighting against my control,* thought Sandman as he turned to the nearest soldier and signaled to pick up the pace.

They lowered the last student shortly before sunrise. Sandman remained standing in the crowd of sleeping bodies, now nothing but bald, middle-aged men. The baby-faced leader stirred once again, thrashing from side to side.

Sandman sent the monk a deep hypnotic suggestion for at least the tenth time, causing the monk to roll over and resume his slumber in silence. *No nightmares for you. At least, not yet,* thought Sandman. *But don't worry, the nightmare will be real enough when you wake up.*

With one final glance around the clearing, Sandman slipped out of the circle and down the path to the garden. There, he quickly affixed himself to the harness waiting at the edge of the cliff and began his descent.

Reader Discussion Guide

This quick guide will facilitate discussion in your local YA book club! *NOTE: If you would like to schedule a visit, in person or via Skype, with the author, please visit www.rscottboyer.com to contact the author.*

General

1. This book is pitched as a fast-paced adventure for young adults but suitable for readers of all ages. Do you feel that it lived up to this description? Why or why not?

2. Discuss how this book differs from other YA fantasy novels you've read.

3. What other titles by other authors is this book most similar to?

Characters

1. Among all of Bobby's friends, who would you like most to have as your friend? Why?

2. Did you identify with Bobby's motives and agenda throughout the book? If so, do you think he went about it the right way?

3. What, if anything, was compelling about the Headmistress and her situation? Did you find her actions plausible? What would you have done differently?

4. Jinx is a unique character in the book, both due to his intellect and abilities. How do you feel about his loyalties and decisions?

PLOT

1. The various conflicts in the book involve both kids and adults. Which sets of conflicts (kid or adult) were more interesting? Explain.

2. There are a lot of plots and subplots woven into the book, including the Headmistress' schemes, Master Jong's mission, and Grandpa and Cassandra's backstory. Which of these plots did you find most interesting, and why?

3. Bobby's journeys throughout the book are mental and spiritual, as well as physical. What, if anything, do you think he learned by the end of the book? How did he change?

THEMES

1. The theme of doing what is right regardless of the consequences recurs throughout the book. In what way, and with which characters, did you see this theme play out the most?

2. Do you believe that the special powers described in the book, such as elevated intuition/instinct, communion with nature and animals, telepathy, telekinesis, etc., are truly possible? If so, what is necessary to perform these feats?

ABOUT THE AUTHOR

R. Scott Boyer graduated from the Haas School of Business at UC Berkeley in 1996. In 2008, he became fascinated with the idea of blending young adult fantasy with new-age fiction and thus began his journey as a writer. While maintaining a full-time job, he couldn't help but envision the kind of book he wanted to read. This exploration led to the creation of the Bobby Ether YA fantasy series, which combines spiritual elements with ancient myths and legends to create fun, fast-paced stories tailored for young adults but suited for adventure lovers of all ages.

Through his writing, Scott likes to explore various spiritual and metaphysical themes, including karma, serendipity, communion with nature, and the interconnectedness of all living things. In his free time, Scott likes to play basketball and tennis, as well as bike with his rescue dog, Patch. Over the years, Scott has been involved with a number of volunteer youth organizations, including United In Harmony, YMCA summer and winter camps, various basketball programs, and C5LA.

Raised in Santa Monica, California, Scott still resides in the Los Angeles area close to his family.

CPSIA information can be obtained
at www.ICGtesting.com
Printed in the USA
BVHW032248280519
549345BV00003BA/197/P

9 781633 937451